ARKHAM HORROR™

T0061749

The DEADLY GRIMOIRE

ROSEMARY JONES

ACONYTE

First published by Aconyte Books in 2022

ISBN 978 1 83908 108 8

Ebook ISBN 978 1 83908 109 5

Cover art by Daniel Strange

Distributed in North America by Simon & Schuster Inc, New York, USA

Printed in the United States of America

9 8 7 6 5 4 3 2 1

ACONYTE BOOKS

An imprint of Asmodee Entertainment Ltd

Mercury House, Shipstones Business Centre

North Gate, Nottingham NG7 7FN, UK

aconytebooks.com // twitter.com/aconytebooks

ARKHAM HORROR

It is the height of the Roaring Twenties – a fresh enthusiasm for the arts, science, and exploration of the past have opened doors to a wider world, and beyond...

And yet, a dark shadow grows over the town of Arkham. Alien entities known as Ancient Ones lurk in the emptiness beyond space and time, writhing at the thresholds between worlds.

Occult rituals must be stopped and alien creatures destroyed before the Ancient Ones make our world their ruined dominion.

Only a handful of brave souls with inquisitive minds and the will to act stand against the horrors threatening to tear this world apart.

Will they prevail?

ALSO AVAILABLE

Dear Jeany,

Please don't fuss. I would never ask you to go back to Arkham. But I've had another note from the professor. Jim's started talking. So, hey ho, off I go. It's time I learned what happened to Max.

Mail me the keys. I promise to kiss Humbert for you. And that darling reporter. Do you know I'm probably the only woman in Hollywood with two subscriptions to the Arkham Advertiser? I bought one subscription and then all of a sudden another started arriving! Darrell sent the sweetest note, saying it was a gift to show his appreciation for posting him the publicity photos for The Flapper Detective and the Mysterious Sanctuary. Isn't that a whale of a title? I'm surprised they could fit it all on the poster.

And, if I say so myself, that Sanctuary idea was a bore. We needed some extra press. Far too many episodes of me standing around, waving my silver-

plated pistol at the shadows on a wall – that's not an action serial! No leaping off trains or bounding across roofs. I should have had Eleanor rewrite that script. She knows how to put in a good scare or two. The *Educational Screen* called it "pretty trite stuff." But they say that about everything. The *Arkham Advertiser* called it "sheer brilliance that will delight any audience." Maybe I should buy a third subscription.

I didn't even drive my new car in the picture. It's a snappy little roadster, and they painted it blue to match my eyes. At least that's what the publicity folks are saying. Actually, it was that blue when I bought it. So much for old Henry Ford and everything being boring black. Wait until you see it.

Still, dull as the movie was, I looked fabulous in your costumes. The beaded dress! I'm keeping it for the next time I go dancing.

This latest script is much better, more like the *Waves of Doom*. Except it's the *Wings of Dread*. We will finish up the big aerial scene tomorrow.

Are you going to *Don Juan*? I know somebody who will want to know how the synchronized sound works! Don't be surprised if he disappears during the screening. Bet you find him sitting up with the projector. Of course, that's if he can tear himself away from you. Honestly, you should put that man out of his misery and marry him. Now don't give me your objections. I know all the difficulties. But other people have found a way.

Not that anyone should take love advice from me.

Look what I'm doing. Searching for the one that got away in Arkham. Or did he? And is he the one I love?

Cross your fingers and wish me luck. Here's to not falling off the plane tomorrow.

With all my love,

Betsy

P.S. Did you hear about the rumrunners using a seaplane near Innsmouth? According to the Arkham Advertiser, they were smuggling a thousand cases a month from Canada. Someone squealed to the police. But they jumped bail and flew away. Now wouldn't that make a great story for the Flapper Detective?

CHAPTER ONE

My mother always said that men are like streetcars. If you miss one, just wait fifteen minutes and another comes along. But my granny said to be sure you catch the right streetcar. The wrong one could take you someplace you don't want to go.

I never knew if Max was the right one or not. Three years after he disappeared in Arkham, I still didn't know.

I went to Arkham with Sydney Fitzmaurice to film one of his terror pictures. Max was part of our crew. There were days when I thought he was the sweetie for me. There were days when his love of money drove me nuts. He made decisions that hurt people. I always suspected Max knew more about Paul's disappearance from the film set than he let on. Max wanted to be the next big cheese. Except when everything went horribly wrong, Max ended up toasted.

Or did he? They never found a body after the fire in the Fitzmaurice house. The officials blamed that disaster on us. Our fault for making a movie in an old house as dry as tinder and likely to burn, they said. I escaped, along with a few others, but when the smoke cleared, three men were gone.

They found one man dead, but they never found the remains of Max or another actor, my friend Jim. Despite the fact that there was no evidence, everyone from the Arkham police to the Hollywood studio suits were happy to pronounce Max missing, probably dead, and close the book on that story. And while Jim did reappear some time later, his poor health and length of his disappearance meant I had concealed his return from the suits because I knew they wouldn't have believed me. As for Paul, who disappeared before the fire, they just said it proved film people were flighty.

Which drove me nuts. I was a film person, and I was not flighty. I asked questions afterward because I liked happy endings, or at least an ending. I never liked puzzles without solutions. Max was an equation I could not solve, not without more information.

"Anything for the post today, Miss Baxter?"

I glanced up at my butler. I poached him two years ago from Valentino's wife. Farnsworth said he preferred a more tranquil household.

My mansion in Beverly Hills was quiet. Of course, people who knew me from the pictures would have been surprised. They probably thought Betsy Baxter danced all night and slept all day. They weren't trying to run a Hollywood studio and star in one of the most stunt-filled serials ever filmed at the same time. I was lucky if I found my bed before midnight, but it was paperwork that kept me sleepless, not kicking up my heels around the town.

I dropped my letters on the silver tray Farnsworth extended toward me.

"That's all for today."

"Very good. Will you be home for dinner, or do you intend to dine at the hospital in a cast?"

Farnsworth often thought he was a comedian. And, honestly, his deadpan expression was so perfect I was tempted to invite Buster Keaton to the house for a few lessons.

"I'm performing one wing-walking stunt and that wraps the picture. It's as safe as houses," I told my doubting butler.

"Yes, miss. I'll be sure that the crutches are near the door for your return," he intoned without a single twinkle in his melancholy eyes. His voice carried such a plummy undertone of doom that I almost expected to hear the tolling of funeral bells. But there was something about the cock of his head that said he knew that I knew that he was putting one over on me. If they ever perfected talking pictures in Hollywood, Farnsworth would have them rolling in the aisles.

"Farnsworth, one of these days, I will fire you," I said. A cheap shot and not truly worthy of our usual exchanges, but I was in a hurry to finish up the mail and go to the airfield. I couldn't wait to try my wing-walking stunt in the air.

"If you fire me," said Farnsworth, still in his most disapproving tone, "you would have to supervise the cook. And the maids. To say nothing of the gardener, who reports an aphid infestation in one of the rose beds."

Farnsworth had a point. Why I decided to buy a mansion after *The Flapper Detective* became a hit, I don't know. But when a gal checks her brokerage account and finds she has flashed past her first million dollars and is sprinting toward her second and her accountant is touting property investment, then suddenly twenty rooms or more all wrapped up in a Tudor-style estate on Sunset Boulevard seemed like a sensible idea. I admit that I paid little attention to the house when I was purchasing it. I even nodded when the interior designer started nattering about "accommodations for seven master bedrooms and baths with sitting rooms and a guest's gallery." I still have no idea what a guest's gallery is.

That year, I had too many stunts to learn and a business to run because I'd bought the studio lock, stock, and barrel at the same time. When, in June 1925, I moved into the mansion with a couple of trunks, I found myself a bed and went back to work.

Of course, after a few days, it became clear that living alone in a mansion wasn't possible. It needed people to keep the guest's gallery clean, to say nothing of the roses trimmed in the garden. I wanted to walk down the path to the swimming pool without bumping into thorns.

The mansion, at least the running of it, was a disaster before Farnsworth. That's why I offered him a fortune to come and work for me. Even before I had money, I hated housework. After I had money, I found out I hated supervising housework. When I dissolved one cook into tears by spending our time together trying to explain why she should invest in commodities, it was obvious I needed an intermediary. She wanted to talk about fricassee. I wanted to talk about finances and why women would never achieve independence without understanding investing.

Farnsworth made the cook, the maids, and even the gardener happy. He looked like a director's idea of a butler, all straight posture and silver-gray hair on top. The English accent also charmed them. They understood the orders he gave them. The house and the grounds looked gorgeous, and the meals arrived when I wanted to eat. Even my guilt about worker exploitation waned after Farnsworth came up with a savings account system where we quietly banked a legacy for each servant. When they retired or decided to leave for other reasons, such as the cook finally opening up her own bakery, the legacy would be paid out to them. Everyone became fully vested after a year of service and the amount grew the longer they stayed. Nobody could steal my maids or gardeners after that. I already paid the highest wages in Hollywood. The legacy sweetened the deal.

"In England, of course, longtime servants received such a sum after the master or the mistress died," Farnsworth explained.

"Let's not anticipate anything drastic," I said.

"One hopes not," Farnsworth said, "but the wild horses do make one wonder."

"It was not a wild horse," I reminded him. "It was a very well-trained rodeo horse. Yakima Canutt said I made the perfect jump from it to the buckboard. And I did not break my ankle. I just twisted it."

"Yes, miss," he said. Farnsworth had, at my estimation, about seven different ways of expressing disbelief or disapproval with a simple phrase. The "yes, miss" was absolutely devastating.

I tried it on the studio's board once or twice. Not the "yes, miss" because I was the only "miss" in those meetings with the misters. But I had my own tone of absolute disapproval. It's hard to impress a bunch of suits when you're five foot nothing and have a head of red-blonde curls. Men tend to want to pat your head or some other part of your anatomy.

I've had to break a few fingers, metaphorically and not so metaphorically, along the way. But I starred in the best-selling movie serial of all time, *The Flapper Detective*, with stunts that made Pauline's perils look pale, and therefore I was the woman who made them all a lot of money.

Also, the studio suits learned, to their regret, that I owned *The Flapper Detective*, trademark and all, and thus could take their lovely moneymaker anywhere I wanted. Before I even pitched the first script, I tied everything up nice and legal. When the studio agreed to the pitch, I plunged into production, making sure the fact I did my own stunts, from bareback horse riding through to piloting a submarine, was well publicized. The audiences loved it, and the money came rolling in.

When the series became an overnight hit, I used my profits to buy every share of stock I could find. It said BB Pictures on the stationery now and in big iron letters on the studio gates.

So here I was, a millionaire twice over, in a too big house with a swanky English butler and a pool outside that I never had time to swim in. Max thought being rich made you happy. It made me happier than being poor. But it didn't solve the problem of Max and what happened to him in Arkham. "What's the good of being rich if you cannot answer the question that makes you itch?" I once said to the others who survived that fire in Arkham. Except it sounded too much like an advertising jingle when it popped out of my mouth one evening. My friends told me to forget Max and enjoy life. I did enjoy my life. I loved my work. I just wanted to know what happened that day in Arkham. More importantly, I wanted to find Max. Because I was sure they had not died.

Something else had happened that day, something I saw, or thought I saw, out of the corner of my eye. A flicker of a memory that I could never quite catch, except when I woke in that very dead hour between midnight and dawn.

"The car is at the door," Farnsworth said as I wrapped up the last of the morning's instructions to various employees, both at the mansion and at the studio. "Do you want Henry to drive?"

"No, it's a gorgeous day," I said. "I'm going to let it out and make the run to the airfield in record time."

"The wind in your hair?" Farnsworth said in another tone that indicated complete approbation as I hurried out of my office.

"Somebody will fix my hair when I get there! I am a movie star! Besides, I have a hat," I said as I scooted across the hall, grabbing my favorite hat and scarf from the top of the Roman statue of Venus. Why have a marble Venus if she cannot hold your hat?

"Madam will drive herself," Farnsworth said to Henry as I ran down the steps and hopped into my lovely blue roadster. "As usual."

"Figured," said Henry, who started out as a mechanic, worked as a cameraman for a time, and then went back to cars because there was less chatter than what a man heard on a movie set. At least that's what he told me when I hired him. He kept all my cars running like kittens, engines purring, and was modifying a motorcycle for me. I had an idea for a stunt but needed a bit more speed to make it work.

"Thanks, Henry!" I shouted as I let out the clutch of my roadster. "See you for dinner, Farnsworth!"

The car roared down the driveway. I settled into the seat, loving the feel of the wind washing over me. As long as I kept moving fast, nothing could catch me. Not even my memories of Arkham's shadows.

The airfield was full of people. A crowd to watch our stunts always made for good publicity. I pulled my car as close to the planes as I could. Standing up on the car seat so I was above everyone's heads, I waved and greeted the reporters. The wind picked up and sent my scarf sailing over my shoulder. I twirled and smiled and threw my hands high in the air. I may even have kicked up a Charleston step or two. Some of my best performances took place before the press. This one was a doozy.

"Come on, Betsy, we won't have the light forever," said Marian. My director strolled in the direction of the planes. I hopped over the car door and followed her.

"Are you still sure about this?" she said as we walked across the field.

"They won't call us trite," I said.

"How about stupid and reckless?" she answered. Marian always worried before a stunt. In some ways, she was worse than Farnsworth. But she never said that I couldn't do it. Nor was she callous about any of the folks in the cast, right down to the smallest bit player. She was one of those women who asked, "How are you?" and then paused to listen to the answer. I worked with many directors, some crazier than others, and Sydney Fitzmaurice was perhaps the oddest of all. Not just because he liked to frighten people but also how he persuaded all of us to take part in the bizarre production filmed in his hometown of Arkham. Later, I wondered why we never left his strange old house on the day we arrived, except it was bred into the bones of all actors to never question the director. As I learned in the summer of 1923, never asking questions can lead to tragic mistakes. After that terrible final week in Arkham, I resolved never to blindly accept what others told me to do.

Working in Hollywood, I quickly observed that many directors couldn't even be bothered to say hello. And remembering favorite cookies and pet's names and the other small stuff that made up a life? Not a chance.

So I decided if I was going to break my neck on a set, I wanted a director who would at least think to call Farnsworth so he could give the servants a night off.

Marian was much more than that. She was a person who cared about others. After Sydney's callous disregard for our lives, and I must admit Max's loyalty to Sydney didn't help keep us safe either, I wanted a director who saw everyone on the crew as a person. Having Marian directing my pictures was important. At least if I was at risk of losing my life, it was only because of the stunts that I thought up, not the antics somebody else told me to do.

Marian had started out in small parts like many of us, so she understood the challenges we all faced. She happily abandoned acting for being behind the camera early in her career. Lois Weber liked her and recommended her to me. Having a mystery serial about a daredevil female detective directed by another woman helped sell a few newspapers by covering us. A few holy rollers insisted on banning us in their towns, but that never hurt ticket sales.

I couldn't pay Marian near what she was worth when

we started. However, I made sure her contracts gave her a share of the proceeds and then stock in the studio. She was a minority shareholder now, and her block and mine made us the majority by far. I voted and ran the business side for her, as she had no interest in it. When she wasn't directing me, she worked on a series of films intended to enlighten others about the pressing social problems of the day. Worthwhile but daunting to watch. I kept paying theaters to show her films.

"What do you think of the flyers?" I asked Marian, who was always a better judge of people than me. I tended to take people at their word, hence the problem of Max, and was wary of making the same mistake again.

"They have a good reputation. You'll like your pilot," she said. "They call her the Woman Without Fear."

"I thought that was my title," I said with a smile.

"No, Betsy," said Marian, absolutely serious, "you're the Fearless Flapper Detective."

We walked up to the biplane where the pilot was talking quietly to her mechanic. I had been practicing on a similar plane for a week, on the ground, along with a professional wing-walker as my partner for this stunt.

The regular wing-walker for the group, Charlie, was already there, all suited up and ready to go. He was a bit taller than the actor playing the villain, but nobody would be able to tell the difference in the long shots. We'd film a close-up with Roger later. Roger was terrified of heights, so we promised we'd do his bit on the studio floor and he didn't even have to watch my flight. Charlie was Mohawk and had worked around planes in the war, including a stint in Ireland. He seemed to regard standing on a wing in midflight the same as standing on the ground. He had been a terrific teacher, too, and his suggestions had helped craft the final scene.

We planned to recreate Gladys Roy's stunt of playing tennis with a partner on the top of the wing. Except instead of waving tennis rackets at each other, we'd brandish guns. Charlie would pretend to get shot and drop to the wing. Then I was set to slither down the wing and back to the front cockpit where my character was supposed to make a heroic landing. All the real flying would be done by the woman in the back cockpit. She made one last check of the landing gear before striding over to us.

"Betsy, this is Winifred Habbamock," said Marian.

"Wini," said the pilot with a calm nod. She was suited up in what I thought of as aviator's gear – leather hat with ear flaps, goggles, and heavy coat over trousers and boots, all to protect her from the wind and colder temperatures above the ground. On a warm sunny day, it must have been uncomfortable standing around in all that. Winifred Habbamock wore it with the panache typical of flyers. Well, the female pilots were the daredevils of the sky and the darlings of the press. That's why I'd wanted this picture to concentrate on a murder at an airfield. With reporters and adoring fans following the flying women around the country, I decided it was time for the Flapper Detective to have more adventures in the sky.

"It's a pleasure to meet you," I said to Winifred and meant it. I heard about this particular troupe of barnstormers from a couple of directors working on adding air stunts to their movies. Everyone said Habbamock was a spectacular pilot and that her crew had an admirable record for safety. Nobody had been killed on their tour, and that wasn't true of all aerial circuses crisscrossing the country. Of course, the possibility of seeing someone killed was what drew the crowds to the flying stunt shows and air derby races. Everyone knew that but just called it "the thrill" of watching planes buzzing above. The same good old bloodlust drew people to the pictures like mine or Sydney Fitzmaurice's horrid horror flicks.

Of course, my pictures had guaranteed happy endings. The Flapper Detective wins over all impossible physical perils... except the day that she doesn't. Underneath the squeals, the cheers, and the applause, there was that indrawn breath as my fans waited for me to fail.

"Charlie says you've been a good pupil," Wini said. "That you know all his signals and are smart about where you step. Are you ready to put on the harness and take to the air?"

"Absolutely! I can't wait. You sure about the tether?" I said. "I could do it without." Most of the wing-walkers didn't bother with ropes or parachutes. The more death-defying the better, but Charlie insisted on having safety lines and a harness with an "amateur" like me. The fact that I parachuted from a zeppelin in one of my earlier pictures hadn't impressed Charlie with my professional credentials as a risk-taker. Or maybe it had impressed him too much, hence the insistence on safety lines. People did call me "reckless", and I usually took such remarks as a compliment.

"Your choice on the tether," said Wini to me with a grin. "Your neck, too."

"Don't tease, Wini, or give me a heart attack," said Charlie. "It's a tether or a parachute."

"And wreck the line of my coat with one of your bulky parachutes? I cannot do that! Besides, we want to scare the audience," I said.

Wini gave me a wink. "Can't cheat the audience of their thrills. I keep telling Charlie the same thing."

He shook his head at the pair of us. "I walk the wing without any harness. Same as my brothers and cousins walk the steel in Manhattan. But Betsy has never done this in the air. First time, you always go with a tether."

Wini nodded. "I was just teasing. The rules are the rules. We may take risks, but we keep people safe."

Dottie, who acted as my dresser on set, came running up with the fur-lined velvet coat my friend Jeany had designed for the scene. The coat had clever splits in the back and the side, which concealed the harness. We'd already filmed the scene leading up to this where Roger took my supposedly unconscious self out of the trunk of a car, carried me across the airfield, and chucked me in the front cockpit. How we got from there to an aerial gunfight would not be shown. The audience would fill that out in their heads. Nobody ever said my movies made sense. Not even the *Arkham Advertiser*.

"Do you have your gun?" Marian said to me.

I reached into the pocket of the coat and pulled out the silver-plated pistol.

"It's unloaded?" asked Wini.

"Not even blanks," I said, pulling the trigger with the pistol pointed at the ground. It clicked but no bang. While walking out on the wing, which was waxed cloth wrapped around the lightest possible wood frame, the flyers insisted we shouldn't even discharge blanks. Any damage to the plane could be fatal if we were unlucky. Keeping my balance and avoiding a Betsy-sized hole in the wing was important, too, so I wore my lowest, softest slippers. In my head, I kept running through the sequence of steps I needed to make. Put a foot wrong and I might put a foot through the wing. Charlie had made that abundantly clear during our week of practice.

Wini nodded at my demonstration of the unloaded pistol. "Good. The only person allowed to carry a loaded pistol on one of my flights is me," she said.

I climbed up on the lower wing. Charlie mounted beside me and finished clipping the lines to the harness under my coat. One more wave to the press and I was ready to go. Very ready! I truly couldn't wait to get into the air that day. I'd flown before but never been allowed to climb out on the wing. Whenever I left the ground, I wanted to go a little higher, be airborne a little longer. Balloons were nice, and the zeppelin had been thrilling, especially the parachuting part. I kept thinking airship travel would replace trains fairly soon.

"Don't forget to relax," Charlie reminded me as he climbed into the front cockpit. It wasn't really built for two, but luckily I was small enough to slide into the seat. We were squashed, but we fit. "Keep your muscles loose," he added. "No good being tense on the wing."

Wini dropped into her seat. She waved to the red-haired woman mechanic as the prop started whirring, and the woman waved back. I gave one last thumbs-up to Marian, who ran back to the ground camera. Above us another airplane banked in a lazy turn over the field. In the second plane was our other cameraman, who would be filming the fight from above.

Wini's job was to keep the plane steady and low so we could get good shots from both cameras. If she took us too high, Marian wouldn't have much to film from the ground angle. That's why we paid for a barnstormer. They were used to low maneuvers so their audience could see all the action, especially when the wing-walkers did their stunts.

We rose into the air with that bump that said goodbye to the ground. "If you can do it on land, you can do it in the air, Betsy, my girl," I said to myself. The wind hit us full in the face and it felt wonderful. The racket of the plane's engine and the wind made it unlikely Charlie could hear me muttering my usual litany of "up and at them" to steady my nerves. For me, as I explained later to Wini, it was never fear, not exactly, that made me almost quiver at the start of a stunt. It was something headier than that, an anticipation of the excitement to come.

Charlie tapped my shoulder, our prearranged signal, and I stretched my arms over my head to grab one of the struts. He gave me a bit of a boost that got me out of the seat. And then it was step, grab, turn, and step again, and reach for the next handhold. Just like we practiced, only now we were nearly a thousand feet up in the air. Not that I looked at the ground. My focus was all on the plane and the marks that told me where it was safe to place my feet. The wind hit me with a force like I'd never felt before. The plane's vibrations ran into my bones.

But I was in place, and Charlie was in place. I pulled the

silver-plated pistol from my pocket. The sun sparkled off it as I mimed shooting at Charlie.

Charlie shot back with his prop gun. I shot again with lots of arm waving to make it evident to the audience that something had happened. Charlie then dropped flat. All went exactly as we rehearsed.

Until the wind turned and buffeted the plane. I felt the shudder as Wini tried to correct, but the plane tilted. All of a sudden, my footing was no longer secure. I bounced a bit on my toes, trying to adjust. It happened so fast I didn't have time to worry, not then. The worry would come just a few moments later.

Charlie's still prone body started to slide toward me. Then Wini adjusted, and the wings went level again, and he slid away. I huffed a little breath of relief. So far, so good. We had the stunt done. I trusted Marian to have captured the footage needed, even if the wind had thrown us off a little. So I started the sequence to return down the wing toward the cockpit.

Only now my lines were entangled with Charlie. His weight was pulling me off my feet. I fought to keep my balance as I slipped nearer to the edge of the wing. Even at that moment, I wasn't nervous. When I was in the middle of a stunt, I always felt this peaceful calm. Maybe that was why I kept challenging myself with harder and harder tricks. To prolong that moment of peace. People always asked me afterward, "Aren't you afraid?" But the fear came later, much later, when I thought about all the others who depended on me and what would happen to them if I fell.

The ground was a blur a long way down. Too far a fall to

walk away alive. I remembered Charlie's lectures about not falling completely off the plane. Even if the tether held, I could strangle myself in the ropes before he could haul me back. Best case scenario was that I'd break a few bones.

Farnsworth, I thought, would not be pleased.

Then I fell.

CHAPTER TWO

My stomach hit the edge of the wing hard enough to knock the breath out of me. Charlie struggled with the lines, trying to untangle us and get himself back into the cockpit. He had to go in first for me to be able to slide in after him. Given our difference in sizes, me landing on the bottom would have meant a flattened Betsy for sure.

I kicked with my feet and clawed with my hands to stop my slide off the wing. The lines bit into my ribs. I wondered if they'd break. I had cracked a couple jumping off a speeding train last year. And the doctor had warned me about not breaking my collarbone again after doing a dive off some rocks onto more rocks concealed by the ocean in the first Flapper Detective adventure.

My legs kicked in a grotesque can-can over empty air as I slithered down the wing. I just couldn't reach the bottom wing or propel myself toward the center and the safety of the cockpit. Instead, I slipped closer and closer to the tip of the wing. And after that, well, it was nothing but nothing. If I got out of this, I vowed never to refuse a parachute. Well, maybe I would refuse a parachute if it looked better to the audience to be without one. Then I firmly told myself to stop arguing with myself. Now was not the time for nerves. The time to be afraid was after I managed to save myself, I said very firmly to the inner Betsy who wondered why she hadn't thought up a movie plot with less death and defying in the same scene.

I glanced over my shoulder to gauge the difficulty of dropping down to the lower wing and crawling my way back to the cockpit from there. Or I could just hold onto a strut and ride the wing all the way down to the ground. Some wing-walkers did that. Of course, if the bump of landing knocked me off the wing, there was a chance of being run over by the plane itself. That, and several other warnings sounded by Charlie during our training, echoed through my head.

Far too far away, the people watching us were tiny figures, just little dolls in the distance.

The ropes jerked as Charlie thumped off the wing and back into the seat. He angled forward, extending his arms toward me, trying to catch hold of a leg or other bit that I had waving wildly in the wind.

Unfortunately, I had skidded a bit too far along the wing. I realized I needed to shove myself back toward the center. Then I could descend, or at least fall in a controlled way, into Charlie's arms and back into the cockpit.

I kicked again with my legs. Nothing but the air beneath me and the wind up my skirts. "This is a ridiculous position," I told myself through gritted teeth. I eased the death grip of my right hand on the lines and felt along the edge of the wing. Clawing for something, anything, that I could use to pull myself where I wanted to go, I felt my hand slide along the rough canvas. My lower half also shifted. I was now much more off the wing than on it. I said a word that would have made Farnsworth blush.

Then the plane tilted. I yelled another profanity. One set of wings, the one that I was on, went up toward the sun and the other set waved at the earth. I slid toward the center like a kid going down a banister. Charlie's big hands grabbed my ankles and yanked me toward him. Then he used the lines and my coat to haul me into place like a fisherman reeling in a particularly ungainly trout.

So I completed the most ungraceful return to the cockpit ever done by a wing-walker. Well, Marian could edit that out, I decided. Or film a close-up on the ground. Definitely on the ground, I thought, as I wiggled into place.

If I ever did this again – and why wouldn't I do this again? – I could drop into the cockpit and then pretend to have a battle with another plane. Why hadn't I added that to the script? I wondered. My heart was pounding, my hair was a wind-tossed mess, and I had lost my hat. But it didn't matter. I smiled as we descended.

Looking over Charlie's shoulder, I saw the pilot, Wini, give me a big thumbs-up. I returned the gesture. If she hadn't banked the plane and slid me back to the center, I might have ended my career right there and then.

The plane touched down on the field and rolled without incident to a stop. A crowd of excited reporters waved notebooks and cameras to catch our attention as they swarmed onto the field.

"Give me a boost," I yelled at Charlie.

He lifted me out of the cockpit. I staggered a little but managed a credible little dance along the wing with a neat jump onto the grass. I resisted the urge to sink down and hug the dirt.

"What do you think?" I yelled at the reporters shouting at me. "Is it going to be the most exciting thing ever seen in a theater?"

"Weren't you terrified?" one woman with a notebook asked me. "When you fell?"

"It's all part of the stunt," I claimed. Now was the time when the bumps and bruises started to make themselves felt. Now I knew that cold fear, the one that always ran like a shiver through me at the end of a stunt, when I thought about how I might not come up with anything better ever again. What if the next stunt isn't as terrifying as I think it will be? What if the audience just yawn and turn away? But I quieted those nerves. I had an audience of journalists in front of me, all clamoring for me to be the brave Betsy Baxter, the unflappable Flapper Detective, and I gave the reporters exactly what they wanted.

I said, "I knew my pilot had her plane under control. And my partner here, Charlie, is the best wing-walker in the business. These fine performers wouldn't let anything happen to me. Now, go on, ask them your questions! They have a show tomorrow night. Everyone should come out to see some real tricks."

The reporters turned from me to mob Wini and Charlie as they climbed out of the plane. I walked a few feet away and tried not to collapse. I would be black and blue tomorrow, I knew from the ache along my ribs, but I was sure that I had managed to avoid breaking anything. Being back on the ground in one piece counted as a victory of sorts.

Marian came running down the field to give me a hard hug that made me wince and groan.

"Your own fault," she said over my protests about bruised ribs. "And don't ever, ever do that again. The entire crew nearly died of fright."

"No shoot-outs in midair," I agreed. "But I have an idea about an air battle. Maybe after the Flapper Detective jumps from a motorcycle into an airplane."

"Oh, Betsy," said Marian, shaking her head at me.

Wini walked up to us. "I've seen that done," she said. "Leaping from a cycle to a plane."

"How did it go?" I asked.

"Fool broke both his arms and a leg," she said. "And I tore up my plane crashing through a fence to avoid running over him." She spoke with an accent I couldn't quite place. A bit New England, a bit something else. There was a crackle of humor under her words as Wini pulled her pilot's helmet off her head and shook out her long black hair. "You have courage," she said. "Maybe not much in the way of brains, but definitely courage."

"I thought you were the Woman Without Fear," I said. "Seems like you've done some death-defying stunts, too. And had a few accidents."

"Never said that I was smart," she said. Again, the words were soft spoken, but I could see a smile at the corner of her dark eyes. "I just like to fly. And it takes money to fly. So, we loop the loop or go upside down under a bridge or let somebody jump on our plane from a moving vehicle. That makes the folks come out to see us. But only the first time. Enough pilots do the same trick, the audience loses interest. Then we make the stunts bigger and bigger!"

"It's the same in the movies," I said. "Do the same stunt too often, or too many others copy you, and there goes the box office."

"Well, at least we can put on the posters that we flew with the Fearless Flapper Detective," said Wini. "That should net us some good press in New England. I hear you're popular there."

"You're going to New England? Whereabouts?" I asked.

"A number of smaller towns and cities all the way up the coast, then ending up in Boston for a big show with several different pilots. We are starting with three days in Arkham. Not happy about that, but I want to be back east this fall," she said.

"Why?" I was surprised to hear her mention of Arkham. And I was genuinely curious to know why Arkham made her unhappy.

"On the East Coast? They're talking about launching a transcontinental air derby for women pilots. Taking off in New York and landing in Los Angeles with a prize of ten thousand dollars for the winner. The closer we are to the start, the easier it is to get the plane onto the field in one piece."

"No, I meant why aren't you happy about flying near Arkham?" I asked. I had my own fears about that place, but it was the first time I'd heard somebody outside Sydney Fitzmaurice's small company of actors and crew voice similar thoughts.

Wini stared at me, a long measuring look. The kind of look I'd seen cowboys and sailors who spent time outdoors give to a cloudy sky. The look that said there's a storm on the horizon.

"You've been there," she said. "Arkham." The smile and the humor disappeared from her voice. Instead, she sounded serious and not too sure about continuing the conversation. Talking about Arkham tended to do that to people, at least those I knew who had been there.

No questions, just that statement about knowing Arkham firsthand, but I felt compelled to answer. "Three years ago. I was there. Something happened."

"Something bad," said Wini. It was not a question.

"I think so," I admitted. "Except the memories are vague. I know there was a fire, and some friends were lost. Except one of them turned up unharmed this year. Jim is in a sanitarium. I'm planning to visit him after this picture wraps."

Wini nodded. The crowd around us had moved away to inspect the planes as well as to pepper Charlie and the red-haired mechanic with questions. "Arkham's like that," she said. "The further you get away from it, the more unlikely the memories seem. Once you leave, the more it seems like a dream."

"What happened to you?" I said.

She shrugged. "I flew into an oncoming storm. My instruments were spinning like mad, so I dropped down, trying to find a train track or something to guide me. Except," she said, "nothing looked right. Then something hit my plane."

"A bird?"

"If it was a bird, it was the ugliest one in all creation," Wini said. "No feathers. Never seen anything like it. It had legs like a squid, but it was flapping through the air like a bird."

"A flying squid," I said. It sounded unlikely, but I had once seen another world reflected in a mirror. A world where a flying squid might well be a creature of its skies. A world that had looked so wrong and so terrible.

At least, that's what I think I saw in the mirror on the final day of shooting in Arkham. Like my last memory of Max, it was so frustratingly vague, almost dreamlike when I tried to recall what exactly I had seen and heard.

"Whatever it was, it was big, it was slimy, and it rolled its one eyeball at me like it was considering lunch," Wini remarked.

I shuddered. It sounded like one of Sydney's nightmare movie scenarios or the professor's pulp stories. Come to think of it, both wrote stories inspired by their lives in Arkham. "What did you do?" I said.

"Pointed the plane toward the sun and flew straight through that electrical storm. I don't know if it was the thunder or the lightning that scared it away, but that creature dropped off my wing and disappeared. Still, that wasn't the strangest thing that happened that day."

"What next?"

"When I leveled out above the clouds, everything changed. No storm at all. Just some nice peaceful white puffs rolling by and the ocean below that, very calm and blue, and nothing to be seen but the shadow of my plane dancing across the waves."

"But you were flying over Arkham?" That's how the story had started.

"That's what I thought. Except all of a sudden I wasn't. I was miles off course and cruising above the Atlantic Ocean. Luckily, I had a nearly full fuel tank and all my instruments returned to good working order. I made it to land. At least as far as Innsmouth. They didn't have much of an airfield then, but I found it."

"And now you're going back there. You are the Woman Without Fear," I said, and I meant it as a compliment.

Wini smiled this time, the cautious type of smile you give someone who believed your crazy stories. The type I felt myself giving once or twice discussing my experiences with Jeany and the others who had worked with Sydney Fitzmaurice that summer in Arkham. All of them said they would never go back. I was the only one who wanted to return to Arkham, but then my friend Jeany said I was the only person in our group of friends who was willing to drive a car across a flaming bridge or jump out of a zeppelin wearing a parachute. In many ways, Jeany was one of the bravest people I knew, but she was not and never would be reckless. Wini, on the other hand, might well be an ally that I needed. From everything that she had said, it was clear she understood Arkham. At least the Arkham that haunted my dreams.

"I'm going back and telling myself that nothing strange will happen this time. I don't know if that counts as courage or wishful thinking," Wini said. "I'll earn my money and enter the derby. Why are you going?"

"I lost a man," I said. "And it's driving me wild. But another friend, Jim, is now in Arkham, and I think it's time to return.

There's a professor and a reporter who have been sending me stories about a variety of strange happenings in the area. But not enough answers. I plan to investigate."

"Then you really are the Fearless Flapper Detective," said Wini with a laugh.

"Yeah," I said. "Isn't it terrible when you start believing your own press?"

"Can get a woman into trouble," Wini agreed.

"That's exactly what my butler says. You should come to dinner and meet Farnsworth. He'd like you. And you can tell him I was in no danger at all today."

"Well," Wini drawled.

"Or you can say nothing at all and let me lie to him," I said.

Three days later, one gramophone was cranked up in the first-floor ballroom for those who wanted to Charleston or Toddle. A second one was blaring jazz by the pool, my film crew and Wini's flying circus gang having a grand time.

"More drinks, Farnsworth," I said as I moved between the rooms, checking on the overall state of the festivities. "And we are not talking about tea."

Farnsworth sighed at this attempt at a witticism. "Certainly. There are letters for you."

He handed over the post. I scooped the stack off the silver tray and shook out the envelope with a promising bulge. It was the keys to the Fitzmaurice house from my friend Jeany. That's where my mystery had started, and the burned-out house would be one of my stops when I reached Arkham. I dropped the keys into the pocket of my lounging pants and frowned at the note. Jeany wrote her usual warnings.

My friend truly suffered in Arkham and I would never force her to return. But I wasn't Jeany. If risking Arkham's horrors meant finding Max, I would go.

"And your two copies of the *Arkham Advertiser* arrived," said Farnsworth. "I placed one in your office and another in the library."

"Oh, good," I said. "Please add another subscription for the staff or some other spot in this house. We need to encourage them."

"Certainly," said Farnsworth. "We could always acquire a parrot. The extra papers could be placed under its pole."

"Farnsworth, you're a genius," I said as I sped off to my office on the second floor. Hanging over the railing, I added, "Buy two parrots and all the newspapers you need. Parrots would be splendid in the greenhouse."

"It is called a conservatory," Farnsworth replied as he moved toward the back of the hall.

"Put them where you want!" I yelled.

In my office, I transferred Jeany's keys to my traveling handbag. I picked up a briefcase and stuffed in the accounts, contracts, and other business papers strewn across the desk. The train trip took nearly a week and with nobody able to reach me, except by telegram, I planned to complete a fair amount of work. Not as much fun as playing poker with the boys back when I was just an extra traveling with the crew, but I had booked a car all for myself and looked forward to some time away from Hollywood.

Then I spread out the latest *Arkham Advertiser* that was sitting on my desk and read the headlines. "Professor Christine Krosnowski Disappears! Foul Play Suspected!"

I dropped everything else to grab up the newspaper. I corresponded with Christine regularly. She'd helped Jeany in Arkham and answered all my questions as best she could. Which was often in grim detail. Although a professor of poetry, Christine had a definite interest in the strange history of the town. She also possessed a nearly photographic memory when it came to the odder occult volumes stored in the Miskatonic University's library. She used that knowledge to write the most marvelous thriller stories for the pulps, all published under a fictional name so her colleagues in the English Department didn't know and couldn't criticize her more torrid writing. I'd optioned one or two of her humdingers for the studio.

All in all, she was a good egg, and I wanted to know if she was safe. I scanned the article, which was brief and lacking the type of detail that my fan Darrell would have given it. The professor had failed to appear at a dinner where she was expected to present a paper on a new addition to the Miskatonic University's library, some rare volume she'd discovered in a Boston bookseller's catalog. Some more boring bits about how the book was so valuable that it was being transported by hand to the university and the professor was the only one who knew when it was arriving. Then the writer described the crime scene. Or the lack of one. No blood, no body. How had they managed to stick "foul play" in the headline? All the writer said was that friends went to the professor's house, found the door unlocked, and the professor missing. The article concluded with the usual admonishment for the police to take disappearances like this more seriously.

The Arkham police were useless when it came to disappearances. I'd been trying for years to stir them up over three men vanishing from one film set and their response had been, "They probably went back to Hollywood, Miss Baxter." Even when Jim reappeared, unable to speak about what happened, the Irish desk sergeant simply sighed and said on the phone, "Looks like the lad landed himself in a spot of trouble. They'll take good care of him at the hospital."

From all I had learned, it was clear waiting around for the Arkham police to save Christine was a terrible idea. I could add pressure through phone calls or even hiring a private detective, but that might not be enough to help a woman who had become a good friend. I was done waiting for others to find answers to the questions that so plagued me. I wanted to be in Arkham as soon as possible. The idea of sitting for days on a train now made me fidgety. I needed to cross the country more quickly, I decided, and I knew just how to do that.

I ran back down the stairs with my bags clutched in one hand and the *Arkham Advertiser* in the other. Wini was sitting by the pool chatting with Marian. The two had struck up a friendship.

"Wini, Wini," I said, cutting ruthlessly into their conversation, "how fast can you fly to Arkham?"

"Three days if nothing breaks along the way," she answered. "Maybe faster if the wind cooperates."

"Let's go!" I said. "I need to get there as swiftly as possible."

"Wait a minute," said Wini, rising from her seat. She had that look that many of my crew and Marian always adopted when I proposed a stunt, as if they weren't sure whether I quite understood the dangers. I did, of course. And I wanted to succeed much more than I feared to fail.

"Are you serious?" Wini asked. "You want me to fly you to Arkham?"

"Absolutely!"

"Do you know how many airmail pilots and others have gone down on transcontinental flights? Almost twenty percent. I don't mind risking myself, but I don't carry passengers."

"I thought you wanted to win an air derby. You're heading to the East Coast just in case the women's air derby is financed," I said. There had been a great deal of outcry in the press over the past week about encouraging women to participate in the reckless speed flying of the air derbies. Early backers of the race were starting to drop away, and I knew that worried Wini. Like me, she wanted to win. And it was impossible to win if you couldn't even play the game.

Wini nodded slowly, but there was a new look of interest on her face. "I want to fly in that derby. So do many women."

"But if the backers don't come through, the women cannot race." I'd found that out during our chats. Flyers like Wini might be the darlings of the press and a big draw for the air shows. They all wanted to compete but lacked the backing that the male pilots had for the big prize air derbies. For the safety of the women, or so the moneybags said, and for all the talk about organizing a "ladies only" air derby, every attempt to do so had stalled so far. "If this derby falls through again, you won't race this year," I pointed out.

"There's still a chance they will pull it off," Wini said, "and

I'll be in a good position to join if we are on the East Coast."

"I know, I know," I said. "Here's the deal. Fly me to Arkham as fast as you can. I'll finance an air derby. One that lets any woman enter. Ten thousand dollar prize, did you say? I'll double that amount. Think about it. Twenty thousand for the winner and serious stakes for those who finish second or third." I stuck out my hand. "Go on. Shake on it."

Wini grinned and grasped my hand to give it a light shake. "You are one crazy lady, Betsy Baxter, but you have got a deal."

"Oh, good," I said, as I raced away to organize this change in plans. Of course, if Wini had said no, I would have still financed the derby. The check was already written and sitting on my desk upstairs. The women deserved to fly as fast as they wanted. So did I.

"Farnsworth," I shouted as we went back into the mansion.

"You bellowed?" Farnsworth said, coming into the entry with my coat over his arm.

I took my coat. "You're a treasure, Farnsworth," I said. "Have my things shipped to Arkham."

"Already done," Farnsworth reminded me. "The large luggage left last Friday. Including the trunk with your hats."

"Excellent! And cancel my train tickets. I'm going to fly," I said.

Farnsworth removed a few of my calling cards from a tray on a nearby table and tucked them into my coat pocket.

"I'm not making social calls," I told him. "I meant that I'm flying to Arkham."

"Yes, Miss Baxter, I heard your discussion by the pool while I was refreshing the beverages," said Farnsworth. "If you have your cards, it will make it much easier for the authorities to identify the body."

"Well, with luck, we'll make it in one piece," I said. "After all, if twenty percent of the planes crash on the way, that means eighty percent make it to their destinations. That's pretty good odds."

CHAPTER THREE

Black smoke trailed us as we made an emergency landing just outside Kansas City. All because a small fire had broken out in the luggage compartment.

I looked at the scorch marks on the single carpet bag that I'd allowed myself. I was thankful my hats were safe on the train. "Farnsworth won't believe me when I tell him we were in no danger. Perhaps I'll lose this bag before I return to Hollywood," I said, brushing some ash off the side of the bag. "At least my stockings didn't go up in flames."

Wini had her head stuck inside the plane. I heard her grunt and then swear.

"Here's the cause," she said, backing out and tossing a still smoldering cigar on the ground.

"Where did we pick that up?" I said.

"Probably that guy who fueled the plane at the last stop," she said.

I remembered him, the man chewing a cigar and muttering, "Dang me if it isn't a couple of dames."

Every stop we made, the ground crews rushed up to us at various airfields, only to gape when two women climbed out of the plane – even though more and more women received their pilots' licenses each year. Wini had said some of the manufacturers hired women pilots to show that anyone could learn to fly a plane. I recalled telling her that I wasn't sure that was a compliment.

"Compliment or not," she said, "it means those women are paid to get their license. And the more of us there are flying, the harder it is for others to say that it isn't a woman's place to be in the air."

"My mother always thought when we won the vote, all the arguments about equality would end," I said.

Wini didn't even bother to comment about such a foolish statement. She just shook her head and told me I had ten minutes to eat and then we needed to be airborne again.

Other than the fire, and that was more smoke than flame, we didn't have another serious mishap until a wing strut wire snapped. But, despite several dire predictions that we were sure to meet our doom, none nearly as awesome as what Farnsworth would have made, we were able to get repairs done very quickly in an airfield outside some town further east of Kansas City. By that time, I'd lost track of what state we were flying over.

Wini grumbled about leaving her favorite mechanic behind, but Lonnie and the rest had needed to wrap up some business in Los Angeles. They were following by a slower route.

Still, Wini flew us safely through every mishap. By the time we landed, without smoke or a wobbly wing, in an airfield near Cleveland, the press had gotten wind that the Woman Without Fear was flying across the country with the Fearless

Flapper Detective. The airfield was mobbed by reporters and spectators when we arrived. One intrepid reporter and photographer drove their car after us, trying to catch a picture of us as we taxied down the bumpy runway. Wini barely missed crashing into the car as I shouted at the men to get out of the way.

"Is this a stunt for one of your films, Miss Baxter?" asked one reporter as Wini gulped down sandwiches and coffee, eyeballing the road map that she used to navigate from city to city. She chatted up the airmail pilots as well since they often knew the best routes.

"After my last picture," I said to the reporter, "I'm thinking about more aerial stunts. Or maybe something dangerous like driving a car after a moving airplane." The photographer had the grace to blush. "But this is only a little vacation trip for me. I wanted to see New England again."

"But are you going to keep flying with Miss Habbamock?" he asked.

"If she lets me. I've never had so much fun," I said. I meant it, too. There was something about being up above the ground, the air rushing around you, that made all the everyday worries fall away. I talked to Wini about taking flying lessons, and she said that if I could handle a car and a motorcycle, I could definitely learn to fly.

"I did it backward," Wini told me on one of our stops. "I learned to drive a car long after I could pilot a plane."

"So how did you become a pilot?" I asked.

"Met a man."

"Oh!" I'd landed in a few briars for the same reason.

She shook her head. "Not like that. He was old. Seemed

ancient, although he probably wasn't all that much older than me. Nobody in flying is. Ancient means you're turning thirty."

I laughed. "Hollywood is a bit like that. We're getting some gray hairs, but many folks started in the business after the war. I acted in my first picture in 1920."

She looked at me. "How old were you?"

"I told the director I was eighteen," I said. "Really I was sixteen, but I'd been hoofing it on the vaudeville stage in Chicago for nearly a year. Nobody asked too many questions. How old were you when you started flying with your pilot?"

"An ancient seventeen," Wini admitted with a chuckle. "And, like I said, I called my first teacher the old man. He acted like it. All quiet and beat down. He'd flown in the war, and it did something to him. Made him want to stay far away from everyone. So he moved to my corner of nowhere in particular. The only place that he was happy was in the sky. At least that's what he told me. First time I saw his Jenny, I wanted to take it flying. Of course, I had to steal the plane to persuade the old man to give me lessons, but I didn't damage it."

"I like that about you," I said, chewing on my sandwich. You wouldn't think sitting in a plane, watching the clouds racing under you, would stir up an appetite. But I was always ravenous when we landed. "You dare to take what you want."

"I haven't noticed that you're shy about pursuing what you want," said Wini.

"I'm good with math," I said, "and nobody wanted to hire me for those skills, like counting cards or balancing books. And I'm athletic. Love to dance. Love thrills even more. Then I found I could use all my talents in the pictures."

"So you bought a studio?" Wini said.

"Mary Pickford had the right idea. Control your contracts and you make more money," I said. "And I knew the Fearless Flapper Detective was a winner. It's the best of Pearl White's stunts and more but with a woman in charge, not in peril. It's what modern women want to see." Wini blinked and rocked back in her seat as I leaned across the table to make my point. "Sorry, I didn't mean to give you the whole pitch. That's how I sold the studio on taking the serial seriously."

"And your films sell tickets?"

"Of course, same as they come out to see you perform your stunts and buy newspaper accounts of all the fly girls. You ladies receive more press than the men. Same for me and my stunts."

Wini winced. "Fly girls. I hate that nickname the most. I'm fine with aviatrix. But why can't they just call us pilots?"

"Because then they'd have to call us equal," I said.

We both laughed at the truth of that statement.

Wini pulled a silver cigarette case out of her pocket. Balancing it on one corner, she began to spin it on the table. I never saw her smoke or even open the case, but she often fidgeted with it when we were on the ground.

"What is the record?" I said, with a nod to the silver case that she twirled like a top.

"Three," said Wini. She lifted her hand away from it. It spun once, twice, and, on the third spin, it fell over with a clatter.

Wini scooped it up and tucked the case back into her pocket. "Except in Innsmouth," she said. "Whenever I was there, it spun seven times."

"Lucky!" I exclaimed.

Wini blew out a breath that was a bit too gusty to be called a sigh. More a sound of exasperation. "Guess so. Except Innsmouth never felt lucky to me. It's stranger than Arkham, at least according to some of the pilots who fly near there."

"No place is odder than Arkham," I said with the great conviction of sheer ignorance.

"You should visit before you say that. I wasn't the first plane to go off course near Arkham and land outside Innsmouth. Gossip gets around the airfields. Most pilots don't like flying that route. Including the mail pilots, and they will make any run."

I had noticed in our discussions with the airmail aviators that they took the "neither rain, nor snow, nor sleet, nor hail" saying seriously. In part because when the Aerial Mail Service started contracting out bids, it was good steady money for the companies who won those bids, Wini had said. But her biggest praise was for the lighted fields and runways built to help the mail service.

"They've set up hundreds of beacons for night flyers," she said. "And dozens of emergency landing fields for planes." Despite those lighted fields and my desire for all the speed possible, Wini wasn't so reckless as to fly through the night. Sundown always found us safely on the ground, often staying with the family of a local pilot. It made for a few hours of sleep and many hours of stories about flights. One thing I discovered during that trip was that probably the only thing pilots loved as much as flying was talking about flying.

The more I heard, the more I thought Hollywood needed to be making movies about pilots. I must have jotted dozens of notes in those evenings. Everyone agreed the greatest daredevils were the barnstormers, those pilots who made their living entertaining the crowds, and a movie about those men and women would be marvelous indeed.

During those stops, I picked up what newspapers were available, but nothing was written about Arkham or Christine's disappearance. I tried phone calls and telegrams from the airfields. Farnsworth sent what information he could. However, my frustration mounted. Even moving so much faster across the country than a train, travel seemed infuriatingly slow. I wished for a way to walk out the door and simply be where I wanted to be.

Wini watched me paging through a newspaper at one stop. "Anything helpful?" she asked.

I had told her a little about what drove me back to Arkham, but it was hard to explain why Jim's reappearance had spurred such desperation in me to finally solve the riddle of Max. I was never good at examining my own motives. I preferred to act and think about why I acted much later, if ever. My friend Jeany, a much more introspective person, would often shake her head at me and say, "Betsy, one day, you will race right past what you are looking for."

To Wini that day, I said, "Nothing new about Arkham. I guess that's too small a place to make the national news."

"It always seemed too large a place to me," said Wini. "Too big to fit it all in one neat little article. Innsmouth is much the same. Some of the families in that area have been there a long time. There were always odd stories swirling around that section of the coast."

"Odder than fiction," I said, remembering a phrase that Darrell put into one of his newspaper stories.

"Odder indeed," said Wini.

At that point, one of the mechanics came into the canteen to inform us that Wini's plane was ready to take off. I promptly forgot about Innsmouth, except for a niggling memory of some newspaper story about seaplanes and rumrunners. I meant to ask Wini about it but forgot in the rush of getting airborne again. We still had a few hours of daylight left.

The rest of the journey was smooth, with no mishaps at all, and we reached Arkham's airfield in record time. As I was informed by the *Arkham Advertiser* reporter who met our plane.

"Darrell Ethan Simmons!" I squealed as I hopped off the wing. "Look at you!"

It had been three years since I'd seen him, and the reporter had filled out some. I'd slung the most horrible baloney at him, all sorts of fairy tales about the film business, when we'd first met. But he'd been good-natured about it and a regular pen pal since. There wasn't much that happened in Arkham that Darrell didn't hear about. He was a terrific photographer, too, and I kept telling him that he had the talent to come to Hollywood. I'd have hired him in a heartbeat to be the studio's publicity photographer. But he kept writing back that there were things he still needed to document in Arkham.

"Miss Baxter," he said and produced a small bouquet of roses from behind his back. "Welcome back to Arkham."

I smelled the flowers and then grinned at him. "You want some photos," I said.

"If you could stand by the front of the plane and wave," said Darrell, producing his camera. "An *Arkham Advertiser* exclusive! I can sell reprints to the New York papers."

"Hey," Wini said as she climbed out of the plane. "Don't back her into the prop. It's still moving."

"Sorry," said Darrell. "If I could get a picture of both of you. A famous flyer and a glamorous Hollywood star land in Arkham!"

"You're talking in headlines," I said to Darrell as I posed. Wini shook her head at the pair of us joking back and forth, but she also posed with good grace. We made our money off being public figures. Newspaper photographers were just part of it.

When we were done, I begged a ride into town with Darrell. "Are you coming?" I asked Wini as Darrell good-naturedly transferred my carpet bag and documents case from the plane to his car.

Wini shook her head. "I need to stay with my plane until the rest of the crew gets here," she said. "I'm used to sleeping rough." We had heard that morning that the remainder of her aerial circus had nearly caught up with us. Once they reached Arkham, Wini was planning a few days of overhauling the planes before starting up her first round of performances.

"And our advance man quit," she grumbled to me as I handed over the check to cover her expenses for our flight. That had been part of the morning's phone call with her friend Lonnie Ritter, and she was obviously still vexed by the news. "I guess I'll have to figure out the ads and posters and whatever else he did."

"We'll give you an excellent rate for printing whatever you need," said Darrell.

"Thanks," said Wini.

"So now you're the sales rep, too," I said to Darrell.

"Les sells the ads," said Darrell, "but we all need the money to pay our salaries. Even with your new subscriptions, Miss Baxter."

"Oh, good, Farnsworth remembered," I said.

"His telegram said something about the latest being for Polly and Jacks."

"Probably," I said, looking forward to visiting the new parrots in the conservatory when I returned home.

As we started toward town, I waved out the window one last time at Wini, then settled back into my seat for a good gossip with one of the smartest guys I knew. Darrell might look like a regular newspaper joe, but he had a nose for a very special kind of trouble. The sort that Arkham brewed up.

"So, tell me about the professor. What happened? Has anyone found her yet?"

"She reappeared yesterday," said Darrell.

"And what did she say?"

"I couldn't get into the hospital to see her," Darrell said with some frustration. "I tried a couple of friends, but her room was off-limits to everyone except her doctor and the nurses."

I needed to talk to Christine. In her last letter, she'd spoken about understanding more about how Jim might have reappeared in Arkham. But she hadn't said much beyond that. "But is she all right?" I asked. "She can talk?"

Jim couldn't when he reappeared. Not a word for weeks.

Darrell nodded. "I bribed one of the nurses. A nice girl named Hilda. She said the professor was chatting with the doctor when she went into the room. Very animated, Hilda said, but they both clammed up when they saw her."

"I could disguise myself as a nurse and sneak in," I pondered out loud on the feasibility of that plan.

"Or you could wait and see if she's discharged tomorrow. Or go talk to her doctor," said Darrell.

"That seems too easy," I said. "Next you're going to give me solid advice like my butler."

"Oh," said Darrell as he pulled to a stop in front of the grandest hotel in Arkham, "what does your butler say?"

"Life, Miss Baxter, is not an adventure serial."

We both laughed because we knew that wasn't true in Arkham. And that very night, I got caught in a shoot-out with a couple of gangsters over a handsome bookseller with the improbable name of Tom Sweets.

CHAPTER FOUR

The confrontation happened after dinner. I decided the hotel dining room was too fancy for my mood. I needed to walk off my fidgets. With my luggage not due until the next day, I couldn't do much with my appearance but dressed as nicely as possible from the carpet bag. My brown velvet cloche had survived the trip, but I sighed when I put it on. It was the very plainest of my hats. I longed for the others making their way from California, as I was heartily sick of the plain cloche.

Within a short walk of the hotel, I found myself a diner. The food was not nearly as good as Velma's, a place I'd visited before in Arkham, but I needed to think. Nobody recognized me at the restaurant as I chewed my way through a plate of steak and potatoes. And I had to chuckle at my own surprise at not being approached for an autograph. While I might be recognized regularly in Hollywood, they obviously weren't quite as picture mad in Arkham. I blamed my very dull hat. Who would expect the Fearless Flapper Detective, the jazz baby who had "it" appeal, in brown velvet?

The waitress didn't even make any wisecracks to me as she refilled my coffee cup. Everyone was concentrated on their food and no gossip was to be heard. Unusual, really, for Arkham, not at all like my memories of the place or Darrell's articles or Christine's letters, but the anonymity suited my disposition.

Twilight settled over the streets. Shadows pooled in doorways. The whole town felt deserted. Too late for anyone heading home from work, too early for anyone seeking mischief. Just that in between time when the sky turned from blue to violet and the earliest stars began to appear above the streetlights. A quiet hour, so quiet that the sound of a fist smacking into someone's stomach and the soft *oof* of somebody losing their breath sounded exceptionally loud. I paused at the entrance of an alley. It came again, a grunt and a thump, and then the distinctive rattle of a body hitting a garbage can. So of course I had to investigate.

Peering down the alley, I saw two roughs cornering a third man. A big man dressed in a canvas jacket and sailor's cap backed a tall gentleman in a summer tweed suit and Homburg hat against the dirty brick wall of the adjacent building. A smaller guy danced around the pair, jabbing like a fighter warming up in the ring but not actually hitting anything.

"Come on, mister, one last time, Miss Nova wants her package. Give it up," said the larger of the two gents to his captive. The man in the Homburg shook his head and received a punch to the belly that knocked him to the ground.

"Not so smart now, are you?" jeered the little man. He aimed a few kicks at their victim.

The man on the ground groaned and curled his knees up to his chest in that universal move of protection. "I don't have it anymore," he said. "I told you. It disappeared."

"We want the book," grunted the big mucker. The little one aimed another kick at the downed man's head. The man on the ground had good instincts. He rolled away at just the right moment to catch the kick on his shoulder rather than his skull. But it was obvious who was going to lose this fight without a little help.

Never say that a Baxter ran away from trouble.

"Hey," I yelled into the alley. "Leave him alone!"

The larger man turned. Judging by the rough clothes and the broken nose, to say nothing of the meaty fists swinging at the end of his arms, he would have fit right in with the dock workers who fought on the weekends for the entertainment of the swells. The muckers, my grandmother used to call such men. The little guy's shiny suit and flashy tie looked more like the garb worn by some of the Chicago mobsters who used to hang around the stage doors when I was hoofing in the Windy City.

"Leave him alone," I repeated a bit louder. My experience of such mugs taught me you needed to speak loudly and firmly. No matter how afraid you were. And this pair didn't intimidate me. I faced down much worse in Chicago, including one of Torrio's men. Of course, Torrio's takeover of the mob after Colosimo's murder was one of the reasons I hotfooted it to Hollywood. But this was Arkham, and I stood my ground and yelled.

"Stay out of this, ma'am," the big man said. "None of your business."

The "ma'am" suggested I'd overdone the schoolmarm talk. Or maybe it was my hat. No matter. The pair weren't budging.

I planted my feet in the stance suggested by my shooting

instructor. Bringing up the pistol that I'd pulled from my purse, I said, "Beat it, boys, before I start shooting. At this range, I can hit both of you with one shot."

The smaller one ducked behind his larger companion, making the probability of me hitting them both with one shot that much greater. Not the brightest criminal, but then this type of brawn was rarely hired for their brains. Little plug ugly pulled out his own pistol and waved it about.

"Hop it," he warned, "or it will be the worse for you!"

"Hey now, don't do something daffy," said the larger one, turning away from the man on the ground to eyeball his partner. "You can't start popping off downtown. Miss Nova won't like that."

The little one growled at the big sailor.

"Well," I said, continuing to talk tough, "you don't want to shoot or to be shot. Myself, I'm not afraid of the first or the second." Well, I didn't want to be shot, but watching how the smaller man handled his gun, I thought I had a fair chance of ducking out of the way.

I shifted a little in the mouth of the alley to line up on the big one. I figured if I could wing him, a little blood would discourage them both. At least that's what I hoped. If the one with a gun took offense, then I'd be diving for cover and saying goodbye to my silk stockings. More than that I refused to contemplate.

"Why, she is only a little doll," said the one with the gun, and he probably didn't top me by an inch. "She will never shoot."

To prove him wrong, I pinged one off the garbage can's lid. All three men yelped. The lanky one on the ground curled up even tighter. The other two goons backed away. The flashy dresser was so startled that he dropped his gun. Luckily, it didn't go off.

"Hey, lady," said the big man, sounding very aggrieved, "that's not nice."

"It will be worse if you don't leave," I said.

His friend dropped down on his hands and knees, trying to retrieve his pistol from where it had skidded under some boxes stacked against the grimy brick wall. He practically had to go flat on his stomach to reach it, which didn't do the suit and tie much good. The boxes teetered above his head, threatening to avalanche down on him.

The little man popped up with a cry. "Got it!" he said in triumph, drawing his hand back with the pistol in it.

The sailor looked at his companion. He shook his head. "Come on, Albie, let's go. If you keep waving that thing around, Miss Nova will do something harmful to our health."

Little Albie ignored his friend and growled at me. "Don't make me get rough… or I will make you sorry." He waved his gun at me. I tightened my grip on my pistol, lining up my shot.

But his companion grabbed his arm and pulled him further down the alley. "Don't talk to the lady like that. Do you want to get us into trouble with Miss Nova?"

As he pushed his companion away from the fight, he looked back at the man on the ground. "Miss Nova will be all churned up if she doesn't get her book. Best you find it for her."

From his position on the ground, their victim moaned and said, "I don't have the grimoire. It disappeared with the professor."

"Scram!" I yelled. Never back down, never let them see you're afraid. That's what another instructor told me. Seemed it worked, as both lugs slunk off. Which was why I kept taking all those lessons. Because if there was one thing I hated more than anything in the world, it was feeling afraid. As long as I was in control, I could not be scared. Not like that day when I lost Max and Jim to the flames and mirrors.

Now all that was left from the confrontation was a groaning knot of humanity lying in the dirt of the alley.

"Miss Baxter?" I heard a voice behind me. "Are you all right?"

I swung around, pushing the pistol into my purse as I turned to confront the hotel's bellboy. Judging from the cigarette stowed behind his ear, he'd been heading to this alley for a quiet break.

"I'm fine," I said, "but my friend needs some help."

Between the two of us, we managed to pull the thugs' victim to his feet. He swayed there, looking like he'd been Jack Dempsey's sparring partner. Although he probably wouldn't have been up to even one round with the heavyweight champion of the world. Tall and gangly, he reminded me a bit of the stunt rider Frank Cooper, who'd been doing bit parts on several Zane Grey pictures.

Under the dirt and bruises, he wasn't a bad looking man. But I had sworn off tall and handsome after Max.

"What should we do with him, Miss Baxter?" asked the bellboy, who introduced himself as Irving.

"Well, if we let him go, he's dropping back onto the dirt," I said. "And that suit cannot take much more."

"I'm fine," said the gentleman, swaying so heavily against my shoulder that he nearly took me down.

"Sure you are, slugger," I said, shoving his weight more firmly onto Irving. "But let's get you cleaned up before we turn you loose on Arkham. What's your name?"

"I thought you said he was a friend," said Irving, looking perplexed as he helped me walk the man into the hotel lobby. The night manager bore down on us, heading across the lobby with a disapproving stare that even Farnsworth would have admired.

"Absolutely he is a friend. I'm a friend to man and beast, especially the ones that I rescue. You should meet my parrots," I said to Irving. To the other one, doing his best to lie down and take a nap on the carpet, I added, "Now, sweet, tell Betsy your name and where she can send you."

He blinked down at me. "That's it. That's my name. Tom Sweets. But who are you?"

"Betsy Baxter," I said, giving the hand draped over my shoulder something between a shake and a pat. I also pulled the brim of his Homburg a little lower to shade his face and hopefully obscure the dirt and bruises. "And this here is Irving. Please straighten up and pretend you are sober."

"I am sober. Sober as a judge," said Tom Sweets. "But, oh, how I wish I wasn't."

He spoke with the tones of a college man, a Harvard type, to judge from the accent and the wide cut of his pant legs. Both matched the style of the Ivy League gentlemen I'd met in Hollywood. We managed to march the staggering Tom halfway across the lobby before the night manager intercepted us.

The night manager's face was stuck between a sneer and frown, which did not improve his looks. I smiled my best winsome young lady smile at him. The smile that Pickford copied from me to play Little Annie Rooney. "Tom had an accident on our way back from dinner. Please send bandages to my room."

"Is this Mr Baxter?" the disagreeable night manager asked. There had already been some unpleasantness about me taking the honeymoon suite without having a bridegroom in tow. But it was the only suite that had a sitting room, a bedroom, and a private bath. I maintained that honeymooners didn't need nearly so much space.

"If he is Mr Baxter, will you let me put him on the elevator without a fuss?" I asked.

"Madam," said the night manager in a disapproving tone. When had I devolved from a miss to a madam? I wondered. It had to be the hat. "Madam," he repeated himself. "Surely you know whether or not this is Mr Baxter."

"You would think that, wouldn't you?" I answered as I maneuvered my tall rescue into the elevator. Irving remained stalwartly glued to the man's side, probably in hopes of a generous tip. I aimed not to disappoint and whispered promises of a reward to the bellboy. Besides, I needed Irving to operate the elevator.

With the grace of long practice, Irving managed to clang the door shut, push the buttons, and keep our rescue from sliding to the floor by propping him in one corner.

"Are we moving?" asked Tom Sweets. His eyes were still closed. At least, one eye was closed. The other was swollen shut as far as I could tell, peering under the brim of his hat.

"Yes," I said. "Next stop, hot water and bandages."

"Oh, good," he said and slumped a bit more.

With a bit of shoving and pulling, Irving managed to drag the man down the hall, retrieve my hotel key from me, open the door, deposit his burden in the nearest chair, and pocket the tip. Buster Keaton couldn't have done it better. I watched the whole sequence with the idea that we might try something similar in my next picture. Or I could sell the idea to Buster.

Sacrificing a couple of towels from the bathroom, we managed to clean the worst of the dirt and blood off the man in the chair, despite his occasional squawk of protest. He muttered the loudest at the removal of his hat and jacket, but I assured him his virtue was safe with me.

"Madam," he said, without opening his eyes, "a Harvard man never fears for his virtue. But he also hangs onto his hat." Then he slid further down in the chair. He looked so beat that I let the "madam" go. Apparently, that was my role tonight, elderly lady detective. Tomorrow, I swore I would go buy myself a new hat in the brightest red possible. Obviously the brown velvet cloche that I wore to dinner was too somber.

"I don't know," I said to Irving. "If he faints again, we should probably call a doctor. Or send him to a hospital."

"No hospital," mumbled the man in the chair. "I did not faint. I am keeping my eyes closed. I simply refuse to accept that I have been beaten in an alley and now am in some stranger's hotel room. Such things do not happen to men like me."

"And what sort of man are you, sport?" I said as I wiped the last of the mud from his face. He certainly looked like Frank Cooper. But he didn't talk like a cowboy.

"I am a bookseller," he said, straightening up and taking the towel away from me. "From Boston. A dealer in rare books and manuscripts. A purveyor of antique volumes. A man who knows an incunable edition when he sees it. In short, a staff member of Sweets and Nephew, provider to gentlemen's libraries since 1778. I am the current nephew, Thomas Alfred Sweets the Fourth."

"That's quite the moniker," I responded.

He nodded gingerly, then opened both eyes with a wince. "My name was the bane of my school days. And the butt of jokes throughout my time at Harvard. But if you call me Tom and ignore the rest, I will be content."

I pulled off my cloche and fluffed out my hair. Tom Sweets narrowed his eyes and gave me a long look from top to bottom. I handed my coat to Irving to hang in the closet, having been spoiled with servants for a few years. Tom's next long look started at my shoes, paused only momentarily at my silk-stocking clad ankles, noted the handkerchief hem of my skirt was barely past my knees, and managed to finish on my face without noticeably stopping anywhere else. I flashed him a smile for being a gentleman.

He straightened even further, and said, "You can definitely call me Tom, Miss Baxter."

I was impressed that he remembered my name from that small altercation in the lobby. "Please, call me Betsy, and how about I call for a Tom Collins? Irving can fetch us the soda water and lemon."

Tom Sweets sat up all the way. "And the gin?"

I sent Irving out of the room with another tip and a few whispered instructions. I held up the flask I'd taken from Tom's pocket while I was brushing the mud off his suit jacket. "Homebrew or imported?" I had already sniffed it and discerned the sharp tang of juniper.

"Imported from Canada as far as I know," Tom said. "It was part of the payment my uncle took from Miss Nova Malone."

"The two mugs in the alley mentioned her name more than once."

"Yes, she is not the most patient of customers. We have had a little trouble with her delivery."

"I noticed the trouble. They didn't act like book collectors. Or even the type that reads anything past the betting pages. What's their boss lady like?"

"I have not had the pleasure of meeting her yet. We have only corresponded since my uncle's error came to light." After hearing the rounded tones of this pronouncement, I believed Tom's claim to be a Harvard man.

"And what was your uncle's mistake?" I asked him.

"My dear but scatterbrained uncle sold the same book twice."

I took the bloody towels and chucked them out the door into the hallway. Irving could take them down to the laundry after he returned with the glasses and soda water.

"How can you sell the same book twice?" I said. "And why would that be a problem? Couldn't you just send them a different copy of the same book?"

"Not this one," said Tom. "It's our grimoire." He said it like the book was an unruly pet or undisciplined relative. The emphasis on the "our" as in "our problem" but with that underlying, grudging affection that one gives to a misbehaving child or a dog that tends to snap at the neighbors.

"What's a grimoire when it is at home in the Sweets and

Sons bookstore?" I asked. I never could resist a mystery, and this one sounded like a lulu. Besides, now that I had twitted the night manager by bringing Tom up to my room, I might as well hear the full story.

"Sweets and Nephew," corrected Tom. "The owner of the grimoire doesn't have sons. That's part of the curse."

"Curse?" Welcome back to Arkham, I thought. Of course there was a curse.

"The grimoire," said Tom with the exhausted air of someone telling the same story for the umpteenth time, "has been in the possession of a Sweets since 1789. The book was rebound a few times, and the current binding was gorgeously ornamented in 1909 in an attempt to compete with Henry Sotheran's *Rubaiyat*. But after each sale, it always comes back to us. Each time the grimoire returns to our shop, the book brings about a certain amount of calamity. Thus the family leaves the grimoire and the store in the possession of a bachelor uncle. That way the owner has less to lose when it returns. And the grimoire always returns, trailing disaster in its wake."

"But why do you keep selling your grimoire, then?" I said, because the flaw to me in every story like this – and I had been pitched something similar for one of my movies – was the curious reluctance people had to destroy cursed items. "Seriously, why hang onto a book that brings calamity?" Of course, somebody might ask the same of me about returning to Arkham.

"Because we make an enormous profit every time a Sweets sells the grimoire. The antiquarian book trade is an expensive enterprise," said Tom without even a moment's reflection. "Very few of my ancestors could resist a sure sale, even when you must keep it locked in a lead-lined box in the basement."

A knock at the door announced Irving with an ice bag for Tom as well as a pair of glasses, soda water, and the other ingredients needed for cocktails except the gin. I tipped Irving appropriately and shooed him out the door. Tom applied the ice bag to his black eye while keeping the other eye wide open to track my progress on the drinks. After mixing, stirring, and spiking from Tom's flask, I handed him one glass and took the other back to my chair.

"If you have a concussion, a doctor would tell you not to drink," I said.

"Thank all the angels in heaven that there are no doctors here," said Tom. He tipped back the glass and drained it half dry with a couple of swallows. "Nothing like some liquid courage to heal a man."

"Who bought your grimoire this time?" I said, because obviously there was more to his tale, and I never liked to leave a story unfinished.

Tom swallowed again and then set down the glass with a clink on the tabletop. "I'm not sure I should tell you. Family business. For all I know, you are a rival bookseller looking to seduce my best clients from me."

"Does that happen often in the antiquarian book trade?" I said with a chuckle. Nobody ever took me for a femme fatale before. I was never cast as the vamp, not even when I worked for Sydney Fitzmaurice, who loved a wicked lady in his films. As the Flapper Detective, my persona was wholesome gamine with the courage to tackle evildoers.

"I haven't been distracted by a Mata Hari so far," admitted Tom. "Most of the dealers and the customers look like my uncle. Short, bald, and so on. Dressed in tobacco-stained tweeds with leather patches at the elbows. But a man can dream."

"Well, I'm not a bookseller. I'm an actress," I said. If he knew who I was, he gave no indication of that. It was rather restful to just be "an actress" again rather than the head of a studio or the star of a popular movie serial. "And I have a friend who disappeared recently in Arkham. Professor Christine Krosnowski."

Tom gave a start. "That's the professor who bought the grimoire."

I nodded. When he'd been attacked in the alley, I had heard Tom say more than once that a professor had the book the goons were seeking. Christine disappeared after acquiring a rare book for the Miskatonic University. It didn't take the Flapper Detective to see those clues scattered about.

"What happened?" I asked Tom.

"The grimoire did what it always does. It made people disappear," said Tom, adjusting the ice bag and settling back into his chair.

"But the professor is back again," I said. "I heard from my friend Darrell that Christine was found."

Tom nodded. "That may be the grimoire, too. It certainly makes people disappear and sometimes lost people appear. Just not where you expect them. Or when."

"But who has the grimoire now?" I asked, thinking about the implications of a book that could make people appear, lost people like Max.

"That's what I need to know," said Tom, "before Nova Malone's goons put some more holes in me. The gin is good, but my uncle should never have sold the grimoire to a bootlegger."

CHAPTER FIVE

The mix-up was partially his fault, Tom had said with a shrug and grimace at how that movement pulled his ribs. "Uncle left the bookstore to attend an estate sale in Providence. While he was gone, I wrote a description of the grimoire for our cabalistic catalog. All the usual about its condition – very good with no markings save one or two faint stains on second signature, foxing on the end leaf, one corner bumped, binding as done in 1909 in ornamented shagreen, and so on. I added a few comments on its provenance, all in my signature style, far livelier than most book catalogs if I say so myself. Then I mailed the catalog to our usual buyers of occult volumes."

"Sell many of those?" I said. The handsome bookseller was definitely perking up as he explained the marketing of grimoires. "Occult books?"

"We send that particular catalog to an exclusive list, mostly academic librarians and a few select collectors," Tom said. "I usually have less than fifty catalogs printed. But it does seem like half the buyers are here in Arkham, including several professors at the university."

"Not surprising." I considered my own correspondence with Christine and her frequent discussions of particular titles that she was hunting to use in her research.

"When the professor called about buying it, I wrapped the grimoire up and brought it to Arkham," he said. "It wasn't until I returned home and Uncle Alfred arrived back from his expedition that we discovered we'd both sold the book. That was an awkward moment. Especially since one of Miss Nova Malone's Boston friends came into the shop to collect the grimoire."

"Do gangsters often buy rare books?" I asked, wanting to get the story straight in my head. This Tom was a bit of a charmer, and that might mean that he was spinning me a whopper. The whole tale seemed unlikely, but I had encountered some strange characters ever since I'd left home. I learned of even more after I started inquiring about disappearances in Arkham.

At my raised eyebrow, Tom chuckled and said, "Most of our buyers are no more gangsters than your average book collector, who will try to wheedle down a price until it is practically highway robbery. But there's a fellow in West Egg who keeps buying volumes to fill the shelves of his mansion's library, and we don't ask how he made his money. Buys books by the yard if the colors of the bindings match the colors of his shirts! Half bound, three quarter bound, quarter bound, he doesn't care what's in between the covers just so long as the book looks expensive. We put all the unsaleable stuff in his boxes. As long as the part showing is bound in dyed leather and trimmed in gilt, he's happy. That's not uncommon for many of our richer clients. They just want a library that amazes the people viewing it," concluded Tom.

"I know what you mean about folks wanting to impress people with objects they don't need," I said. When people suddenly became rich in Hollywood, they tended to throw their money around buying the strangest things. Like a marble Venus for their hallway. So other people then had to act like them just to keep up appearances.

"That kind of competition to have the best of everything could lead a girl to owning a mansion with an English butler and two parrots in the conservatory," I said out loud. "But it sounds like the person who bought the grimoire didn't want just any fancy book. Nova Malone wanted that specific book enough to send a couple of thugs to fetch it for her."

"Both buyers wanted the grimoire for the contents and paid handsomely for it," Tom agreed. "The fact that the book is fully bound in shagreen, ornamented in gold, and inlaid with jewels added to the price, too. Neither buyer would want to lose it so soon after paying so much. Which is why Uncle sent me back to Arkham. He thought I would do a better job of negotiating a settlement. We'll refund whoever gives up the grimoire. Except now neither buyer has it. And both are very cross about it. I assume the professor is vexed, but she disappeared before I could talk to her. I know another party who helped with the university's purchase is angry. I ran into him at the library looking for the professor. You saw Nova Malone's reaction."

"Jewels? Why jewels?" I asked, distracted by his description. I liked my diamonds for movie premieres, but I couldn't see myself pasting any gem on the cover of a book, no matter how occult the interior text. The whole thing sounded a bit ridiculous to me, but the mention of disappearances and reappearances did intrigue me.

"Sangorski and Sutcliffe started it. Jeweled bindings for rich clients. Very rich. And we had to copy them…" Tom sighed and took another swig. "Nobody ever said anyone in the rare book trade had any financial sense. Commissioning that cover meant my great-uncle used up almost all of his reserves and barely recouped the expense."

"Guess I'm glad that I'm in the movie business and not in the book business," I said. "Most people come to Hollywood to make money and build bigger mansions to astound the neighbors." Which sounded like a joke but was a fair description of Pickfair, Falcon's Lair, and the new "beach house" that Hearst was building for Marion Davies.

Tom chuckled. "At least we don't have those problems in Boston. Uncle and I live in an apartment above the store. The money all goes to the books, their care and proper handling as it were. As well as our constant search for more books to expand the stock and perhaps even sell someday. Although nobody in our family ever seems to be too keen on the selling part. Uncle practically breaks down in tears every time I list a volume in a catalog."

"So when did your bootleggers become bookleggers?" I asked. "You never said how Nova Malone bought the grimoire."

"The usual way." Tom tipped his glass up and drained the last drops from it. "A request through the mail for a certain type of book that matched our grimoire's description exactly. When Uncle called the number in the letter, he talked to Miss

Malone, who said she did not wish to haggle nor did she wish for the book to be posted to her. A messenger arrived with a suitcase full of cash and a bottle of gin as a thank you, along with a request to hold the book until another messenger arrived to collect it. Uncle put the gin in the cupboard and the cash in the safe and went off to Providence without telling me about the sale. He was in search of Gould's *A Monograph of the Ramphastidae, or Family of Toucans*. Anyone can see how that would drive thoughts of everything else out of his head."

I leaned forward to pluck the now empty glass from Tom's hand. "I know nothing about toucans and their power of distraction. But what happened next?"

"As I said, I already handed the grimoire to the professor, along with the usual warnings about not reading it aloud and so on. Not that the warning ever works, but we do have a list we give to every buyer. Also a contract saying Sweets and Nephew is not responsible for anything that happens between when we deliver the grimoire and when it may again become available for sale."

I blinked. I doubted bookselling normally involved all that! I glanced at Tom's empty glass and wondered if the booze could be blamed for his story. The whole thing sounded improbable. But still, that summer with Sydney in Arkham there had been warnings from many people, and we had all ignored them. We hadn't believed. Not believing could be as dangerous as believing. As my friends found out.

"And all your buyers are happy to take the grimoire with a warning?" I asked out loud.

"Collectors," said Tom in a grim tone of voice. "They will do almost anything to add a certain book to their collection.

Especially the type who purchase the grimoire. The professor seemed savvier than most and she was purchasing it for the university. I told her it was unlikely to stay in their library for more than a decade or so, but she was content with that. After we learned of the mix-up, I returned to take the grimoire to the rightful owner and refund the university's money, as much as the loss of this quarter's profits pained us, Uncle and me. Except the professor was gone along with the book. And Miss Malone's goons found me."

To judge by the two mugs roughing up Tom in the alley, Miss Malone was not a woman to wait patiently for her book delivery.

I set our empty glasses on the tray. At the click of glass on metal, Tom raised his head hopefully, but I shook mine. "That's enough for tonight," I said. "Have you some place to go?"

He looked much better than an hour ago, but his one eye was still puffed nearly shut. From the hesitant way that he straightened in his chair, I wondered if a rib or two were cracked. I knew the feeling.

"If they took your wallet," I said, "I'll pay for the cab to your hotel or to the hospital."

Tom snagged his suit jacket from where I had left it folded across the chair's arm. He groped in one pocket and, with a satisfied grunt, fished out a hotel key from an inner pocket that I had missed.

"That's this hotel," I exclaimed, looking at the oval brass tag.

"I thought I recognized the lobby," said Tom.

"But why didn't the night manager know you?" I said. The

small interrogation that we'd received earlier that evening argued that Tom was unknown to the staff.

"I never met him," said Tom. "I checked in during the day and kept to my room last night. Never met Irving either until tonight." He dangled the key's tag in front of his nose and squinted at the number. "What floor are we on?"

"The top one," I said.

"Ah, well," he said, rising to his feet and carefully pulling on his jacket. He even straightened his tie. With the buttons done up, his suit jacket hid his crumpled shirt. "I am considerably further down. I will find the elevator and descend to my more humble bed."

"But what are you going to do about your two buyers for the grimoire?" I said, because now I truly wanted to know how his story would resolve. I hated questions without answers and stories without ends. That was probably my curse. It certainly landed me in trouble more than once.

"Worry about it tomorrow," said Tom, with a second shrug that made him groan.

I never wanted to be responsible for other people. Good time Betsy, that was my plan when I first left home for Chicago, devoting my life to being footloose and fancy-free. Somewhere along the way, I took a great number of people under my wing in the form of a studio and a household. But I definitely wasn't going to add another to the list. Especially another tall and handsome man. All my trouble with Max was enough for a lifetime. I intended to solve the mystery of Max and return to being fancy-free.

"Are you sure you don't want me to call for a doctor?" I asked Tom, ignoring all my resolutions.

Tom limped to the door. "No," he said. "I'll be fine. Tomorrow I'll be at the hospital anyway. I need to talk to Professor Christine Krosnowski."

"So do I. Talk to the professor, I mean. Meet me in the hotel restaurant for lunch, and we can go together."

Tom cocked his head so he could examine me with his uninjured eye. "Why do you need to talk to her? Are you actually after the grimoire? You are the Mata Hari of the book trade!"

"No," I said. "I need to talk to Christine about a man I lost."

Tom grunted at that. "Why wait until after lunch? Why not do it in the morning?"

"Because I never rise before ten, always eat my breakfast in bed, and have other errands in the morning," I said lightly, shoving Tom toward the door. In truth, I usually worked on contracts and other legal rigamarole in the mornings, but who would ever believe that of a gamine ingenue?

"Also, with luck, my luggage will arrive from Hollywood tomorrow," I said to Tom. "I need to see it off the train as well as make some other visits." Jeany's keys were a hard lump buried in my bag. I wanted to check on the Fitzmaurice house and send my reassurances to her before I did anything else.

Tom departed. I locked the door as soon as he was gone. Then I pulled out all my notes about Arkham and added what I had learned: "Jeweled grimoire, makes people disappear and appear." Then I wrote down the question that I wanted to answer the most: "Is this the way to find Max?"

I wondered if I could persuade Tom to sell the book a third time to me. The professor wouldn't mind too much,

I knew, not if I bought one or two of her stories for script development and promised a large gift to the university. I thought the gangster, Miss Nova Malone, might be more of a problem.

As I pondered how I could buy off a bootlegger, or at least stay out of shoot-outs, someone knocked very quietly on the door. Just a couple of quick raps as if they didn't want to be heard by anyone else.

While I respected the discretion, I wasn't in the mood for visitors. Besides, as I glanced at the clock, it was nearly eleven. Far too late for a lady, or even an actress who played a lady, to be entertaining. Then I spotted the Homburg sitting on the side table. Tom had obviously forgotten his hat.

Picking up the hat, I went to the door, unlocked it, and opened it. "Here you go," I started to say. But the person who hurried into the room was not Tom.

Wini dodged inside. She clutched a knife, practically a dagger, in her hand. As soon as she was in the room, she clicked a button on the knife and the blade slid into the handle.

"Thank goodness you are here," she said. "Lock that door." The knife disappeared into a pocket of her leather coat.

Full of questions, I clicked the door shut and turned back to Wini. "What's happened? And what's with the knife?" Over the past few days, I had never seen Wini shaken by anything, even a lit cigar rolling about in her plane, but she definitely looked worried now. "Is everything all right at the airfield?" When I had left her, she'd been planning an evening with a friend, a moment of rest before her crew arrived and they began preparations for their air show.

"Somebody has been hijacking mail runs," Wini said. "And I think they are after my plane, too."

CHAPTER SIX

"I met my friend Stella for dinner," Wini said. "She works for the Post Office. The airmail deliveries for the Innsmouth airfield disappeared twice last month. And there's rumors of more planes disappearing earlier this year."

"Didn't you say a lot of flyers go down on these runs. Especially if it's late at night?" I asked. I'd offered to ring down to the desk for coffee or tea, as the flask had left with Tom, but Wini just asked for a glass of water. I filled a glass from what was left of our jug.

"Yes," said Wini, "but these pilots didn't disappear. Just their planes. The pilots were found but nowhere near the airfield." She'd settled into the chair that Tom had occupied. She picked up the glass of water, started to sip, then put it back down again, clearly distracted. Her hands thrust deep into the pockets of her leather coat, and I heard the distinct sound of jingling as she fidgeted with the objects inside – keys, coins, that silver cigarette case, and presumably her switchblade.

"Where were the pilots found?" I asked, wondering if these incidents were similar to Jim's reappearance a few months ago. He'd simply been found wandering down a road with no indication of how he had gotten there. "Did the pilots all turn up in the same place?"

"Not really," said Wini. "All were found near Innsmouth but in different spots. Down along the shore. Near the old sea caves. Along the cliff road. Always near the ocean. One pilot was found on the beach, sleeping away."

"Odd place to take a nap," I said.

"Very odd!" Wini agreed. "Everyone claimed they had no memory of how they got there or what happened to their planes. Which have not been found yet."

"But why do you think that someone is after your plane?" I asked.

"Stella drove me back to the airfield after dinner," Wini said. "We were sitting in her truck, just gossiping, when we spotted a man coming out of the barn where I stored the Jenny. He didn't notice us, or if he did, he must have assumed we were fetching the mail."

I must have looked puzzled because Wini explained, "We were sitting in Stella's postal truck. The Post Office workers come and go from the airfield at all hours, says Stella, dropping off the sacks and picking up the mail for the area. Farmers want their Sears catalogs and packages!"

I nodded. Sears sold everything from dresses to plows, and everyone needed something that could be found in those catalog pages. I had moved to Chicago to get away from small town life and ordering the Sunday hat from Sears, but I still remembered the thrill of turning the catalog pages and dreaming about all the things shown there.

"So what did the man do?" I asked, watching Wini fidget,

sure she wasn't telling me everything. Something about the incident truly rattled her, but I suspected it would take a little coaxing to get the whole story. "Why do you think he was after your plane?"

Wini sprang out of her chair and began pacing back and forth. "There were three planes on the ground at that airfield. The only one that he spent any time around was my Jenny. Then the man got in a Tin Lizzie and drove away. We followed him back to Arkham."

"Where is he now?" I asked.

Wini shrugged and wandered back to the chair. She sat down, dangling her hands between her knees. "I lost him somewhere around this hotel. Stella had to head home. She starts work early. But I wanted to see you."

"Why? What can I do?" I said.

"You're the Flapper Detective," Wini replied, but I had a feeling she wanted to say more.

"I play a detective," I said. "I am an actress. I pretend to be a detective."

"But you're here to investigate a disappearance. You said so."

Now it was my turn to fidget in my chair. "I'm looking for someone as I told you," I admitted, "but I'm not prepared to stop all the crime in Arkham."

"Well, after I left Stella, I kept looking around for the big guy. I finally spotted him heading into the alley behind the hotel," Wini said. I knew she was talking about the alley where I'd saved Tom from Nova Malone's men. "He met with a smaller man and argued with him."

"I know those two," I said. Arkham was hopping these

days, it seemed, but what was everyone looking for? Tom? The grimoire? Something else? And why had Wini sought me out?

Wini did not look surprised at my statement. "I hid at the end of the alley, trying to hear what they were saying, but this man in a Homburg came sliding out the back door of the hotel. The big man grabbed him and started yelling about a book."

"The man in the Homburg was Tom," I said. "I'll tell you about him in a minute. But what happened next?"

"Then I heard gunshots and you shouting," said Wini, glancing at the Homburg that I'd put back on a side table. "What are you mixed up in?"

"I truly don't know," I confessed to Wini. "I am here to find out what happened to my friend Jim." I wasn't quite ready to explain all my theories about Max. Because how could I tell Wini I saw a man fall through a mirror and disappear? Even for Arkham, that sounded crazy.

Except Wini understood Arkham, maybe better than I did. All I had to go on was what I had learned over the past three years, from a distance. Darrell's photographs and stories in the newspaper, Christine's letters, and Jeany's reluctant retellings of what she had seen during the final days of filming.

Wini sighed. "I trust you," she said. "But my plane is my livelihood. It's hard enough scrabbling from town to town. If anything goes wrong, we could lose everything. I want the women's air derby to be on the up-and-up. All the pilots deserve that."

"I'm no villain," I told her. "I promise you I'm not mixed up with anything criminal. I want to find out how my friend

Max disappeared. Jim was with him. They were both in the Fitzmaurice house on the final day of our filming. A fire broke out and one man died. But nobody ever found any other bodies. Then Jim came back to Arkham. So maybe Max is out there, too."

"So maybe you are a detective," said Wini.

"Stranger things have happened to me," I responded. "And tomorrow looks to be a busy day."

I explained to Wini that I planned to check the Fitzmaurice house where the fire had happened, visit my friend Christine at the hospital, and try to find out more about the grimoire from Tom. Thinking about all that, I giggled. It was late. Perhaps I'd mixed my earlier cocktail a little too strong, I decided, startled by my own laughter.

Wini looked up at me. "Now what?"

"I suppose I will need a vacation to recover from my vacation in Arkham," I said.

Wini grinned. "It will be late tomorrow before my crew needs me," she said. "I'll help you. And you can help me figure out what happened to those pilots who disappeared and then reappeared without their planes. I don't want to suffer the same fate."

"Very well," I said. "Do you want me to arrange a taxi back to the airfield or are you willing to sleep in a real bed? I could call down to the desk and arrange for another room."

Wini shook her head. "I'd better return to my plane. I'd rather stay there tonight."

I nodded. "Can you come back here by lunch tomorrow? I'd like you to meet Tom Sweets, the man with the Homburg hat and a strange story."

"Tom Sweets? Is that a real name?"

"He says it is Thomas Alfred Sweets the Fourth."

She snorted. "That's too horrible to be a false name."

"I thought the same."

With assurances that she would be safe enough at the airfield and that she didn't need any help finding a taxi, Wini left.

I puttered about the room, unpacking my scorched carpet bag and sighing a bit over its condition. That bag had been on many adventures with me, but this might be its last, I thought. An honorable retirement to the attic after this trip, I decided. I was fairly sure my house had an attic. I would have to ask Farnsworth.

The next morning, I was awake and working on some contracts that I'd brought with me when there was a sharp rap on the door. This time I did not fling it open, rather I called through it. "Who is there?"

"Your breakfast, Miss Baxter," said a familiar voice.

"Irving," I said, opening the door with some pleasure. "Shouldn't you be off work by now?"

"Last duty of my shift," he said, wheeling in the cart laden with breakfast elegantly hidden under a silver dome, a pot of coffee smelling delicious, and even a small red rose in a crystal vase.

"Very nice," I said, waving my hand at the chair near the window. "And delightful to see you, too. Can you do me a favor?"

"Certainly, Miss Baxter," said Irving, unrolling the napkin swaddling the silverware and then snapping out the same napkin to lay across my lap. The young man served with a definite panache. "What can I do?"

I nodded at the Homburg hat still sitting on the side table next to me. "Can you return that to Mr Sweets without anyone knowing where you found it?"

"Absolutely," said Irving. "He's on the second floor. I'll stop on my way back to the kitchens."

"Thank you," I said, slipping a tip with the Homburg to the efficient Irving. "Oh, Irving, do you have any copies of the *Arkham Advertiser*?"

"We have all the local newspapers and a selection of the New York and Boston newspapers in the lounge downstairs," said Irving. "Several days' worth."

"Excellent," I said, pouring myself a cup of coffee and thinking about bootleggers and books. "I'll take a look when I come down."

Nearly a month's worth of newspapers were stacked in a room the hotel grandly labeled "The Library" with a small polished brass sign. They had that wilted look of most hotel newspapers. Too many people had idly flipped the pages while waiting for something else. Most of the stories I vaguely remembered from my readings of the newspaper at home. But then I had been mostly focused on unexplained disappearances and the occasional reappearance of someone, like what had happened with Jim. This time I looked more closely for mentions of rumrunning and airplanes. The earlier story that I had seen about a captured seaplane loaded with illicit cargo was there. And it was written by Darrell! But in the days that followed the story vanished from the front pages when no one had been arrested or charged.

The problem with the airmail pilots and their planes dis-appearing was not mentioned. It seemed nobody wanted to talk about missing planes. Or perhaps only a few people knew. There was a brief mention of the airfield near Innsmouth being expanded as well as night lights being installed by the mail service. In one issue, I found a letter to the editor from a farmer, asking if anyone had seen some lost sheep, blaming this on increased flights over his fields. The noisy contraptions, as he put it, were scaring all his animals and keeping his hardworking family from a decent night's sleep. Then one night a pilot had landed in the middle of his fields, claiming to have lost his way to Innsmouth, and made "an almighty fuss" until the farmer had driven him "a considerable way" to the nearest phone.

I shook my head at this intrusion of modern life. But a nighttime landing of an airplane, the lost pilot struggling across a field of fierce animals (probably not sheep!), and then having her pound on the door of a seemingly abandoned farmhouse was a fetching scenario. It would certainly make a good opening for one of the Flapper Detective's adventures, I thought. I pulled out a small notebook from my handbag and jotted a line or two. The question, of course, was the role of the pilot. Would it be the Detective herself, off to save another lost soul? Or would this be our introduction to the eventual murder victim or even the villain? This was why creating fictional mysteries was so intriguing.

But as to clues for solving my personal mysteries, I found very little of help and left the hotel to complete my other errands before lunch.

The train station was my first stop. With delight, I watched them roll my largest delivery from California down the ramp from the boxcar and onto the ground.

"Oh, baby, how I've missed you," I crooned to my brilliant blue roadster, patting the hood. Farnsworth had arranged the car to be shipped before I had even left California.

"That's a nice machine," said a red-headed woman supervising the unloading of some crates. She looked vaguely familiar.

"Hello," I said. "Do I know you?"

"Lonnie," she said, holding out her hand to shake mine. "We met at your mansion. During that swell party you threw for our crew."

"Of course," I said, pumping her hand with enthusiasm. "You're Wini's mechanic."

"That's me," she said. "The rest of the crew is heading to the airfield. But I needed to pick up these tools and a couple of spare parts."

"Wini's there and waiting for you," I said.

"Oh, I know," replied Lonnie. "I spoke to her this morning on the phone. Sounds like you had some adventures on your trip. Set fire to my darling even."

"Just a little smoke, almost no flames," I assured her. "The Jenny flew like a dream."

Lonnie grinned. "Wini is the best. When we race in your air derby, we're going to take the grand prize."

"You sound certain of that," I said.

"There's many great pilots," said Lonnie. "But Wini can outfly them all!"

"It will be exciting," I said as I hopped into the roadster. Farnsworth had already made arrangements with the railroad for the rest of my luggage to be taken directly to the hotel. "Sure you don't need a ride?"

"No," said Lonnie, pointing at a battered old truck. "I must make some more stops on the way to the airfield for supplies. We have a performance on Saturday. Hope to see you there, Miss Baxter."

"You will," I promised. "I wouldn't miss it for the world. I wish I could try that wing-walking again." I meant it, too. I loved going up in the plane, and the stunt had been grand. I started to ponder how I could persuade Wini to add me to the show. I needed a holiday, and stunt flying would be an amazing vacation.

The next stop was the Fitzmaurice house. The place looked as grim as I remembered, a blackened shell of a place where Sydney's last film had gone so disastrously wrong. The last place where I had seen Max. I drove past the house itself, having no wish to explore its fire-damaged remains. I still recalled the heat of the flames, the searing sting of the smoke in my lungs, and Max pushing me out the door before I collapsed.

I guided the roadster past the house and to the barn where Humbert, the caretaker, was waiting for me. The tallest man in Massachusetts, Jeany once called him. He was a giant, closer to seven feet than six, and rail thin as well. A kind man, he had been tolerant of the ruckus we'd caused during the filming.

"Those trunks are safe," Humbert said to me, pointing to the pile casually stacked behind bales of hay kept for gardening and feeding the mule he still used to pull his old-fashioned lawn-mowing machine.

The pile looked like it had been there forever rather than just three years. A barn cat showed her kitten how to hunt mice over the tops of the trunks, leaving behind a trail of little cat footprints in the dust. Hiding in plain sight, I doubted any of the Hollywood suits still hunting for Sydney's last script would bother to push aside hay bales or pry open locks that were already starting to rust with the exposure to New England's winters.

Humbert pulled a scythe off the wall and began to sharpen it on a whetstone wheel that he kept near the entrance of the barn. Listening to it make that awful screech of steel against stone, I thought that would also discourage any prowler.

"What are you cutting down with that?" I asked.

"Weeds," said Humbert, never one to waste words. "Spreading out back. Coming from the woods. Been a bad summer for weeds."

He stood up and tested the edge of the scythe with a gnarled thumb. "Something has been bothering the crows, too."

Humbert believed the crows were not altogether normal birds. So did my friend Jeany, who claimed I should keep a close eye on any that I saw flying around Arkham. But I saw none in the sky or nearby trees as I walked around the house with Humbert. We went across the lawn, kept trim by Humbert's mowing machine, toward the fence that separated the house from the wooden copse beyond.

The woods were the last remnants of a primeval forest, according to Christine, fenced in and contained by the first families of French Hill. Despite the green canopy shading the path leading past the locked gate, this was a place where people didn't picnic or let their children play amid the shadows of the trees. It was not a nice place.

After we reached the fence, Humbert began to swing his

scythe to cut back long olive-green vines growing through the slats. I moved further away, closer to the gate that once allowed the family access to their wood. Turning back toward the house, I could see that the fire had not burned this side as devastatingly as the front. From where I stood, looking back into the sun at the kitchen door and the path leading across the lawn, I almost expected to see the door swing open and a member of our film crew start down the steps. Would it be Jim slouching toward the pair of broken wicker chairs that still sat in the center of the lawn to steal a smoke and a nap while he waited to learn what part he would play? Or Paul packing his pipe as he came out to join Jim? Or even Max, who actually never relaxed enough to slouch in a broken chair and watch the sunset? Not when sitting would have wrinkled the perfect line of his suit. No, if it was Max marching out the back door, he would have been jotting lists in his monogrammed notebook, a place to go, a thing to do, or a person to impress. Max had wanted to be a big man in Hollywood. He saw himself as the next mogul, dwelling in a mansion, and running a studio.

Odd that I ended up living Max's dream.

Something curled around my ankles. Something damp and cold, clutching me with a painful pinch. Like a dead man's hands reaching out of a grave to grasp my legs.

I shrieked and jumped away from the fence. Long tendrils of slimy green vine were wound around my leg, causing me to stumble. The vine pulled me back toward the woods. From the other side of the fence rose an insistent and awful buzzing, a chittering of insects, and suddenly I felt like dinner being dragged into a lion's den.

Humbert loomed in front of me, swinging his scythe in a wide arc behind his shoulder, and then chopping down with the blade.

CHAPTER SEVEN

"Yep," said Humbert. "Those weeds have been awful bad this summer." The one that had entrapped me was now neatly cut in two.

Humbert's expertly swung scythe cut the vine so the protrusion through the slats of the fence was not more than an inch in length. How large it was in the woods, I had no desire to find out.

I reached down and unwound the damp, clinging mess from around my leg. It felt horrible. Sticky and slimy at the same time. I dropped each piece as quickly as possible, relieved to step away from the strange vine. As the last bit squelched through my fingers, a sharp briny scent, overlaid with hints of decomposition, rose from the rapidly disintegrating mess on the lawn.

"That's not a weed," I said, recognizing that peculiar smell. "That's seaweed." The brownish green blades resembled the giant kelp that swept ashore on the beaches of Northern California. The smell also brought to my mind the scent created by rotting piles of seaweed thrown by a high tide so far up the beach that the ocean could not drag it back. But seaweed doesn't grow in backyards, I told myself. We were miles from the coast. Perhaps some bird had flown inland and dropped it, I thought, while knowing that explanation wasn't likely. The woods beyond the fence were more than peculiar. The first of our crew to disappear in 1923, Paul, had vanished in that tiny patch of wild ground. Nobody ever knew what had really happened. Except, later, we were all sure Sydney had lied to us about the dangers and Max had helped him.

"Weeds," Humbert nodded, walking carefully along the fence line, scouting for any other intruders. One or two smaller vines were efficiently severed in two by the scythe. As soon as they were cut, the leaves began to curl up on themselves, drying to an ashy powder in only a few minutes.

"I don't remember anything like that when we were here before," I said to Humbert.

He shook his head. "New this summer, these weeds. Started a few weeks ago. Got worse this week. The mule doesn't like them."

"No, I suppose not." I stirred one small pile of ash with the toe of my shoe and then grimaced at the stain. My stockings were ruined, too. Arkham was proving hard on my clothes. The nearness of the Fitzmaurice house wasn't doing much for my nerves either. I wasn't afraid. Not in daylight, walking along the fence with Humbert, but I didn't like the feeling of those weeds winding around my ankles. Or the prickles going up and down my spine. As if something in the woods was watching me. I thought of Jeany's warnings, but when had I ever turned back from anything? I stared hard at the house. It was just a house. A burned-out old place that deserved to fall into ruin, just as Sydney deserved to become a footnote in some film history. There were better films to be made, ones with happy endings created by smart women who saved themselves. I planned to make those films.

"Thank you for your help, all your help," I said to Humbert. "I wanted to make sure those trunks were still locked."

"I never answer when any of those men come around asking about Mr Fitzmaurice's things," said Humbert.

"About that," I said, pulling a photo out of my purse. "Did any of the men look like this man?"

Humbert stared at the photo of Max and shook his head. "I remember him," he said. "He came with Mr Fitzmaurice that last time. Same as you and the rest."

"But you're sure that you haven't seen him anywhere in Arkham since then?" I asked, although I'd been asking this question through phone calls, telegrams, and letters for nearly three years.

"No, miss," said Humbert. "I would have remembered."

Looking at his long sorrowful face, I believed him. If Max had returned, if Max ever returned, it would not be to the Fitzmaurice house.

I thanked Humbert again and drove away. The answers I was seeking weren't there. If Max was out there, he was somewhere else. How entirely elsewhere I would not learn until later.

At the hotel, I changed my shoes and stockings. Then I realized my trunks were artfully stacked about the room and that I could change even more. Arriving at lunch in a pleated skirt scandalously skimming my knees, a sailor blouse with a red tie, and a bright blue cloche that simply shouted frivolous miss, I was a flapper in all her glory. Unfortunately, Tom and

Wini, both arriving in the dining room shortly after I was seated, seemed intent on discussing serious crimes and how we might solve them. So much for renouncing responsibilities with a ritzy hat.

"First, introductions," I said to the pair as they each launched simultaneously into suggestions on what to do next to solve their problems. "Winifred Habbamock, Tom Sweets, bookseller of grim grimoires. Tom Sweets, meet the daredevil of the air, Winifred Habbamock."

"Habbamock," said Tom, after shaking Wini's hand. "That's a New England name, isn't it? I have heard it before, somewhere near here."

"Probably," said Wini.

"My ancestors got off the boat from Scotland in 1772," said Tom, "with a delivery of books for Thomas Jefferson."

"How nice," said Wini. "My ancestors watched the pilgrims splash ashore in the 1600s. And some say we met the Vikings even earlier."

"Ah," said Tom. "My apologies. I remember where I've seen that name before. Habbamock. It's connected to the Praying Indians."

Now Wini frowned. "If there's any name I hate more than fly girl," she said, "it's Praying Indian. Call us by our real names. Call us Wampanoag, Patuxet, Pokanoket, Mashpee, and all the names that your ancestors failed to record but mine never forgot. Don't erase us from history with some fool's map marked with Praying Indians."

Tom had the grace to look abashed. "I am sorry," he said. "I've been cataloging libraries of early American history. I tend to read while I'm cataloging and remember exactly what

I read. But I know as well as anyone that history is only one step away from fiction."

"You are not the first to get it wrong, but you're the first to admit it to me," Wini said with a nod at Tom. Seeing my confusion, she added, "Many of the tribes in New England who converted to Christianity were listed on the early maps and histories as Praying Indians. As in, here's a town of Praying Indians."

"Not too flattering," I said.

Wini shrugged. "You could read it as here is a town that's more like us than some of the other ones. Except we weren't. At least not to most of the folks around here. Still aren't. Heck, I didn't officially become an American until 1924 when the Indian Citizenship Act passed. And I'm still not sure if I can vote."

"But I thought we had the vote," I said. "It's why I took off to Chicago. Women are equal now and all the rest." Except I knew that wasn't true for so many people, hence buying my own studio so I could make those rules for myself. As I learned long ago from my older siblings, if you can't win a game by their rules, then make up your own. Betsy Baxter's croquet might not be played the way other people played, but it was a game I could win.

"Maybe yes, maybe no, when it comes to voting," continued Wini. "It's better than it was. Still there are a lot of towns that manage to keep their ballot boxes locked away from the people who live there. Not that I ever stay in one place long enough to figure it out."

The waiter came with our plates. Wini grinned down at her steak and potatoes. She grabbed a roll from the basket in the center of the table and spread butter on it with reckless abandon. She took a big bite, swallowed, and then looked at us. "We can't change the past," Wini said, "but we can change the future. When I win your race, Betsy, there will be no place I can't go. There will be nothing out of my reach. I just need my wings and a good tailwind to lift me there."

I nodded and tucked into my own lunch. The right play of the diamonds and hearts, even if I had to count all the cards in my head, once led to a fat stake and a chance to change my future. I was happy to give Wini a shot at her own big win.

"But before I can even get off the ground for your race," Wini said, "I need to find another wing-walker. The show doesn't pull them in without that stunt. And we need big audiences this trip to make the planes top notch for racing."

"What happened to Charlie?" I said. "He's all right, isn't he?"

"Charlie's fine," said Wini, "but he had to go home. Brooklyn. One of his brothers was injured on a construction project and a cousin died. They work the high steel." She sighed. "Charlie was the best I ever had. But his family needs him. So now I'm down a wing-walker and an advance man."

"That's rough," I said. Charlie leaving would be hard on the act, I knew. I started to consider ways I could help Wini.

Now it was Tom's turn to look confused. "I know what a wing-walker is," he said. "And no thank you. I'm afraid of heights. You'll never see me go up in an airplane. But what's an advance man?"

"It comes from the circus folks, and we're a flying circus. In the old days, the advance man rode into town a few days ahead of the show to put up posters, take out ads, and stir up publicity. Anything to encourage people to buy tickets," Wini explained. "These days it's more a case of working the phones, but we still need someone to take our posters around the route, too."

"Like what I do," said Tom.

We both stared at him.

"What? You think booksellers just sit in the back of their stores and read until some customer arrives to buy a book?" he said. "Essentially, my uncle does think that, but that method doesn't work. As the rising tide of red ink in our account books proved. But a few well-written catalogs and advertisements placed in the proper journals, and sales will come."

"I can see you are a revolutionary in the antiquarian book trade," I said.

"I personally battled through our bookstore filled with the volumes purchased by my dead ancestors far too many times," said Tom. "It became clear that something had to be done before we drowned in literature. Thus I wrote a catalog, mailed it out, and sold some of the books. I wrote an advertisement and sold more books. I unearthed the names and addresses of past customers and sent out personal letters and sold even more books. I then used the money to pay for something other than books, like the water bill."

"Shocking!" I laughed.

"Yes, when my uncle realized his desk was cleared of overdue bills but there was exactly six inches of shelf space empty in the store, he nearly swooned. He feels empty shelf space affronts the booksellers' creed and should be filled as quickly as possible, so he immediately doubled the number of auctions he attended," said Tom. "Hence our need to sell the grimoire this summer. Although sometimes I fear the reinvention of Sweets and Nephew is coming a little too late in this modern era. They say that the book trade is doomed by the movies. Why would people buy a book when they can spend a dime to see a picture show?"

"The picture people need books," I said. "After all, books and magazine stories account for most of our script ideas. We're even poaching writers from New York to script our shows."

The talk then turned to Wini's performances and how she could make up for the loss of Charlie's stunts.

"I'll call Mabel Cody to see if she knows of anyone to take over the wing-walking. She's the woman I was telling you about," Wini said to me. "The one that jumps from cars to planes. She's working on a stunt with a speedboat."

I liked the sound of that. Such a jump from a boat to a plane would look fantastic on film. I asked Wini for Mabel Cody's phone number, while Tom finished off his ice cream dessert, and began to think about ways I could persuade Wini to let me take Charlie's place.

After listening to us chat about Mabel, Tom said to us, "You know many dangerous women. I think I prefer the bookseller's life."

"You're the one with a gangster named Nova Malone trailing him," I said.

"Ah, true," said Tom. "Apparently our two friends from last night were making inquiries at the front desk this morning. Irving slipped me a warning along with my hat. Thank you for returning the Homburg."

"Two friends?" queried Wini. "The ones I saw in the alley?"

I nodded. "The ones who gave him the shiner."

Tom tapped his black eye and then groaned.

"Don't poke it," I said automatically. Then chided myself internally for fussing. Start fussing over a man and he'll think he has a claim, as I'd found out a time or two.

"Anyway," Tom said, "they wanted both my name and room number. I'm thinking of moving out of the hotel. At least until I can find the grimoire and return it to Miss Malone."

"That might be wise," I said. "Wini, do you have room in your barn at the airfield for an advance man?"

"Sure," she said. "Ours usually sleeps in his car between stops."

"But I don't have a car," said Tom.

"I do," I said, "and I'd be happy to help you with the advance work. You could even sleep in the car. Although, it is a roadster, and the backseat is small." I looked at Tom's lanky frame. "Well, bend your knees and you'll be fine. And I won't have to worry about someone stealing my car if I have a twenty-four-hour-a-day occupant. Just don't scratch the paint."

"The advance work does sound intriguing. I don't want to go back to Boston until we find the grimoire. Besides," Tom said with a smile, "I am beginning to see the appeal of knowing dangerous women. However, I cannot accept the loan of a car. I don't drive."

Wini and I now stared at him. He shrugged. "I live in Boston in an apartment above the store where I work. I am an antiquarian bookseller. I have neither the money nor the inclination to own a car. When I want to go someplace far, I take a train. Close by, I walk."

"Not a problem," I decided. "I will drive us from town to town. You can search for the grimoire as well as promote Wini's show." I decided I could use our trips to investigate mysterious disappearances and reappearances of people. To see if anyone had seen Max. Also, this meant that I would be on hand when the grimoire was found, which might answer all my problems.

"That's a solution!" said Wini, looking relieved. "I hate advance work, so it's kind of you to take it on."

"What do we do first?" said Tom.

"Talk to the professor," I said, checking my watch. "Let's see how our combined charm does at gaining us entrance to that hospital." I waved the waiter over and signed the lunch to my room.

Tom looked a little disturbed. "I know you're a Hollywood actress and all that," he said, "but can you afford this?" He gestured at the meal we had demolished while making our plans.

"It will be fine," I told him as we waited in the lobby for the hotel's garageman to bring my car. "The studio pays my bills." Perhaps I should have said that I owned the studio, but some men acted strangely when they found out I was a boss lady. It was nice being just Betsy Baxter again for this trip. Just Betsy with a larger trunk of hats.

"The studio pays?" said Tom, sounding astonished. "I'd heard that people were getting rich in the movies, but I didn't know it included free lunches."

"Mr Sweets, you would be surprised," I said as we piled into the roadster. Wini took the front seat next to me while Tom folded himself sideways into the backseat.

"I may have to sleep sitting up," he said with a smile.

Wini glanced over her shoulder at him. "We've got cots and bedding at the barn. We'll find you a spot where you can lie flat."

"Now, how do I get to the hospital?" I said.

Tom shouted directions from the backseat. For a man who didn't drive, he had a good, almost perfect memory of the instructions given by the doorman at the hotel. We arrived quickly and without ever having to stop and ask the way.

"I'm handing you the map and letting you navigate on all further journeys," I told Tom.

At the hospital, we were told Professor Christine Krosnowski was well enough for visitors. I nipped across the street to purchase some candy and a few pulps from the five-and-dime.

Wini eyed my offerings as we were conducted down the corridor by a stiffly starched nurse, whose skirts practically crackled with efficiency. "Didn't you say your friend was a poetry professor? Are you really going to offer her some of those magazines?" she said, looking at the pulps in my hand.

"Trust me," I said. "She'll love them."

When we were ushered into the room, we found a doctor standing by the professor's bed.

"Doctor Ezra Hughes," he said, stepping forward to introduce himself to us. He was one of those men whose hair had receded enough to give him a high, domed forehead. I suspected he was younger than the hairline indicated but still guessed him to be in his late thirties. The hand that shook mine was firm. The shoulders beneath his neat suit jacket indicated some athletic tendencies. Further, he had a certain wind-chapped look around the cheekbones and prominent nose to indicate he was an outdoorsman or a sailor.

"Betsy Baxter, Wini Habbamock," I said to him. "And this is Tom…"

"You!" shouted the doctor. "You scoundrel! Where is my grimoire?"

Tom took one wild-eyed look at Ezra Hughes and bolted from the room.

CHAPTER EIGHT

"Now, Ezra," said the professor from her hospital bed. "It is not your grimoire. It belongs to the university."

The doctor turned back to Christine with a frown. "But I need it for my research. Our agreement was that I would have the grimoire in hand as soon as that villainous young man returned it to you," he said.

I thought his description of Tom was a bit harsh. As far as I knew from Tom's story, he was as much a victim of the book thieves as anyone else. On the other hand, perhaps this Ezra Hughes had good reason to be angry at Tom. Out of the corner of my eye, I watched him fuss. There was something odd about the man, but I couldn't say exactly what. Perhaps I preferred booksellers to doctors. Also, I'd never liked hospitals. The way hospitals smelled made me uneasy.

This hospital smelled like hot water and plenty of soap. All hospitals did. But there was always a note under that antiseptic odor. One that reminded me that illness and death lurked around the corner. When I considered all the ways to escape the farm where I had been raised, becoming a nurse had never been an option. The sight of my own blood never scared me, but I hated to see someone else suffer.

However, Christine looked as cheerful as any woman confined to a hospital bed could be. She wore a crown of bandages but still appeared remarkably well. When Tom fled the room, his hasty departure sparked a definite twinkle in her eye. I knew her best from letters and one short visit she made to California the previous year. She'd been on the hunt for some reference book and also gave a few lectures at the University of California's Southern Branch. We had gone to lunch, and I had been charmed by her humor as well as her rather pointed remarks about academic life. She seemed to find my tales of stunts and Hollywood executives equally entertaining.

As I bustled up to the hospital bed to kiss Christine on the cheek and fill her hands with good candy and bad fiction, I calculated the best ways to encourage the doctor to spill more information about the grimoire and his conflict with Tom.

"Dear professor, how are you?" I cooed in as silly a voice as I could manage. Christine raised an eyebrow at my antics, but the doctor looked diverted, much as I intended. Wini stayed by the door of the room, content to watch.

"Miss Baxter," said Christine in a slightly bemused tone, "I did not expect a visit." She leaned into my kiss and whispered in my ear, "How did you get here so soon?" I had written her that I intended to visit Arkham to check on Jim as soon as my current movie finished filming.

"I read of your disappearance in the newspaper," I said

loud enough for the doctor to hear, "and simply had to come to make sure that you were well." Then I whispered back to her, "I flew! Tell you all about it later."

"How very kind of you," said Christine, transferring the candy and the magazines to the small table beside her bed. She couldn't resist taking a quick peek at the table of contents in one magazine. Her eyes smiled, but she kept her mouth prim. I winked at her.

Plopping down on the chair next to the bed, I batted my eyelashes in the direction of the doctor and said, "Now tell me all about this grimoire that makes people disappear."

The doctor made a sound like a kettle attempting to boil, but Christine chuckled. "I wonder how you found out about that," she said. "Are you now in the hunt for the book?"

"She found out from the horrible bookseller who just fled the room. As he should," said Ezra Hughes. "And you should not say another word, Christine."

At that point, Christine became very much the professor and gave Hughes a look that would have sent her students scurrying out of her way. Then she turned to me and said very clearly, "Several books in the university's library mention the Deadly Grimoire might open a doorway or path, especially when its spells are invoked in a weaker spot. Of course, like all mystic writings, it's hard to be sure if the authors are talking about a philosophical pathway to enlightenment or something else entirely."

Well, that wasn't what I expected. "Weaker spots?" I said.

"Cold places, shadowed spots, mirrors and windows that do not reflect truth," she said. "Or those that show a truth we don't understand." I gave a start, remembering the fire and my glimpse of Max falling through a mirror, a mirror that didn't break but became a doorway to someplace else.

But I didn't mention Max, not then, although perhaps if I had, I could have saved us all considerable trouble later. Instead, I said, "It's sounds very *Through the Looking-Glass*." I adored reading about Alice's adventures as a child. One of my earliest acting attempts had been playing out Lewis Carroll's many topsy-turvy scenes for my grandmother in our kitchen. The poems always made her laugh.

By the door, Wini looked troubled. "We had a window like that, one that showed something that wasn't there," she said. "At the schoolhouse. When I was a little girl." There was a tension in her voice and face that suggested it was not a happy memory. I noticed particularly because Wini usually projected such an air of reckless nonchalance, especially around strangers.

Christine gave her a keen look. "You're from this area, then?" she said.

"Further up the coast," said Wini. "When I was very small, before I was sent out west, we went to a one-room schoolhouse. It had been built from parts scrounged from other buildings. The window had this old glass, the kind with bubbles and rings in it."

"Colonial glass, I expect," said Christine.

"I don't know," said Wini. "It was all warped. The other kids said you could see into the past through it. They used to dare each other to look. People said that you'd see terrible things, horrible crimes that had happened long ago, if you looked out that window."

"And did you look?" I asked, but I already guessed the

answer. Wini was so like me. She'd march up to such a window as soon as she heard about it.

Wini gave her a fierce smile. "Of course! All it took was one dare and I marched right up to that window," she said.

"And what did you see?" I said, pleased I had guessed her reaction correctly.

"I saw people like me," said Wini. "Mending fishing nets, cooking over open fires, and laughing with their children. I had never seen so many people like me in one place."

"And then what happened?" asked Christine, and there was a sadness in her voice as if she already knew the ending to this story.

"A man walked into their camp," said Wini. She waved a hand at the doctor. "A man who looked like him, except dressed in those funny old pilgrim clothes. All dark and flapping around him. Except it wasn't his coattails waving in the wind. There were dozens of shadows all bunched around him, shadows like snakes, striking out at the people. Then all the people were gone except for the stranger ensnared in shadows."

"That's terrible," I said, remembering fire and smoke and Max disappearing into shadows that stretched like hands or tentacles to engulf him. I noticed Christine did not seem surprised by Wini's tale. Nor did the doctor react to her descriptions with more than a slight bemused shake of his head. Arkham, I thought, makes people believe in ghost stories.

"I was so angry," said Wini. "So angry that the people were gone. I ran out of the schoolhouse and searched all over for them. But, of course, there was nothing there. It was just a reflection in the glass. Such a mad, sad little girl I was that day. Searching for ghosts of a people long gone. I picked up a stone and threw it straight through the schoolhouse window so it wouldn't frighten any more children. Broke it all to bits."

"Good for you!" I exclaimed. "That's the way to handle your ghosts." I meant it, too. It was exactly what I would have done. If I had to break windows or mirrors to find Max, I intended to do just that. After all, I'd never been a patient person. Why start now?

"It's the best way," said Wini, looking straight at me. "Never look back. Keep flying forward."

The doctor's reaction to Wini's story was completely different from mine. "Such a loss," said Ezra Hughes. "There are so few of those items left. Far too many have been broken by ignorant souls afraid of the secrets they reveal."

"So you know of windows like that?" I asked, quite intrigued. Perhaps this doctor could give me a clue or two about what happened to Max.

"Of course," said Hughes. "I used to search for such glass on the beach. Just fragments left from the windows and mirrors thrown into the sea. Ignorant fools would do that to rid a house from a haunting. But if you held those shards to your eye, you would see wonders. As a boy, I had a collection of such sea glass. I still do." He had one hand in his jacket pocket and was fiddling with something, much like Wini tended to jingle the items in her pockets.

"It seems like you had a slightly different childhood than Miss Habbamock," said Christine. Her tone was not complimentary, but the doctor didn't seem to notice.

"I was raised in Innsmouth," he said. "Our house overlooked the town and the sea. It was built by my ancestor, Captain Bulkington Hughes. A great man."

"A whaler," explained Christine to Wini and me. "Call me Ishmael, and all that."

Hughes looked pleased. "Melville may have modeled his Bulkington on my ancestor. After all, Melville is the one writer who realized the genius and glory of the sea and the tribute that must be paid to the waves if men are to prosper."

"Do you know," Christine said to me, "I cannot remember a single female character in that book."

"There was a romance in the movie," I said. "Dolores Costello played the lady. She's why the brothers fight and Ahab loses a leg to the white whale." I'd read the book, too, but why ruin the effect of a spoiled jazz baby? Especially when I could practically see the doctor's face turning purple. In my experience, angry men grew careless with secrets and their cards. Of course, provoking that anger was a dangerous game to play. After a certain poker game went very much my way and very much against a guy named Alphonse Capone, I skipped out of Chicago and headed to Hollywood to try my luck there.

"That travesty of a film," groaned the doctor. "They ripped Melville's meditations apart and made it a melodrama. There is no romance in the novel! There is no place for women in such a story."

"That leaves me wondering where all those men came from," interjected Christine. "Did Ahab spring from the head of some old sea god like Athena from Zeus, and was that why he was so intent on killing that white whale? Freud would have had a field day with all those references to sleeping partners and cannibalism."

Wini tried to smother a laugh while I refrained from giggling at the doctor's expression.

"You will have your little jokes, Christine," said Hughes. "But there is a spiritual truth to be discovered within Melville's work. As you well know." Then, as if he was a preacher on Sunday, he proclaimed, "Consider the subtleness of the sea; how its most dreaded gods glide under water, unapparent for the most part, and treacherously hidden beneath the loveliest tints of azure. Consider also the devilish brilliance and beauty of many of its most remorseless deities, as the dainty embellished shape of many species of spirits. Consider, once more, the universal cannibalism of the sea; all whose divinities prey upon each other, carrying on eternal war since the world began."

Again, I had to almost physically restrain myself from responding to such pompous nonsense. Hughes had misquoted Melville quite badly, in my estimation, and there was something about his general tone that I didn't like.

"Yes, yes, Melville was a decent writer," said Christine in such a placating tone that I was sure she had simply shut her ears to Hughes or had heard him spout off too often. "But I dread teaching that book. After so many years of freshman literature, I find it so…"

"Fishy?" I said, unable to resist.

Wini gave a muffled shout of laughter and, looking at the doctor's reddening face, ducked out the door, saying she would wait for me outside.

The doctor ignored us both, addressing himself solely

to Christine. "I know you do not appreciate the majesty of Melville, but I found the inspiration for my oceanic therapies within the pages of his great work."

"I know you mean well," said Christine. "And there's no doubting the number of people you've helped."

"But I could do so much more with the grimoire," stated Hughes. "If that vile young man hadn't lost it. Or stolen it back. All this talk of selling it twice by mistake. I cannot like it, Christine. I'm sure he is lying."

Now that last statement interested me far more than an argument about the merits of Herman Melville and the movie based on his whale book. I liked Barrymore in *The Sea Beast*, and the scene where his leg was cauterized caused half the audience to shriek and squirm when I went to see it. But the entire movie was far too much men on ships for me. I did remember that one reviewer called the story "quite preposterous". But then again, that reviewer found my films preposterous, too.

"Ezra, we will find the grimoire," Christine said. "Have a little patience. You know its history. It is sure to reappear in Boston if not in Arkham."

If, as Tom said, the grimoire did make people appear, I might find the answers I needed within its pages, especially with Christine's help. And, if Ezra Hughes understood the book as well as his conversation indicated, perhaps he would make a better ally than a butt of fish jokes. If the grimoire ended up being only a load of philosophical nonsense, as Christine suggested earlier, I could give it to the university. Perhaps with a note of apology to Ezra Hughes for teasing him so this day.

The doctor made a dissatisfied noise, more of a snort of disbelief than anything else, and bid Christine a formal goodbye. At the last moment, he recovered his manners enough to thank me for visiting my friend.

"I am sure she will find comfort in a woman's company," he said.

Christine and I refrained from rolling our eyes at each other until he left.

"Does he always quote snatches of old fiction and talk like a character from a hundred years ago?" I asked.

"Only when he's on his high horse," responded Christine. "I have seen him be quite modern at a few faculty parties. His foxtrot is exceptional."

"Hmm," I said, not convinced. "But why does he want to read your grimoire?"

"It's not my grimoire," said Christine again. "It belongs to the university. Ezra teaches on the medical faculty. He was instrumental in procuring the funds to finance its purchase. An anonymous donor, or so he said."

"You don't believe in the unknown benefactor?" I asked, curious to find out why Christine would look such a gift horse in the mouth.

"I think he may have contributed the money himself. Although why he didn't want to take credit for it, I cannot say," the professor replied. "He's the one who brought it to my attention. There's considerable Hughes family history tied to that book."

"I thought it belonged to the Sweets family. In between other owners," I said, remembering the strange tale that Tom had told in my hotel room.

"Yes, but the grimoire appears in Innsmouth more than once in its complicated history. It's said that the sharkskin that forms the cover was from a beast netted out of the waters near the coast. A great green shark."

"I've never heard of a green shark," I said.

"It's possible it is simply arsenic-dyed sharkskin," said Christine. "Which would explain both the color of the shagreen cover and the number of fatalities among the owners. Although the current binding was done in this century, and thus wouldn't account for all the fatalities. I wore gloves when I was examining it to determine if it was the Deadly Grimoire."

"Do you know why it's called the Deadly Grimoire?" I asked, thinking Tom had left a great deal out of his story. He hadn't mentioned arsenic.

"That's one name for the book. Other histories called it the Grimoire of the Sweets, which led to numerous misunderstandings. At least one source listed it as an alchemical cookbook of desserts." Christine chuckled over this error. I wondered exactly what mayhem that had caused. "Then there's the False Grimoire. Which caused considerable trouble for the Hughes family."

"Tell me more," I said. Christine pulled herself even straighter in the hospital bed. I plumped the pillows behind her, then settled back into my chair.

In language as precise and erudite as her letters to me, she explained that a Sweets, back at the start of the last century, had printed up a second grimoire. "The story goes that the Sweets family was unwilling to give up their most valuable book but still needed money to purchase more stock for their store, so they made the False Grimoire to have something safe to sell. Others say that this particular Sweets was paid to create a counterfeit so an unscrupulous sea captain could steal the Deadly Grimoire from a rival."

"Name me names," I said, enthralled. This was better than one of my movies. "I never knew the book trade was so full of crooks."

"You'd be surprised what collectors will do around truly rare volumes," said Christine, in an echo of what Tom had told me earlier. "And the captain who paid for the counterfeit was supposed to be the upright Bulkington Hughes."

"Oh," I said, "this sounds like one of your stories. Why haven't you pitched this to the pulps or to me?"

"Because I'd need an ending and the history of the two books is so murky," said Christine. "All that's actually known is that Sweets did create a nearly perfect forgery, but there was a deliberate error in the final signature."

"Somebody signed the book wrong?" I asked, puzzled by her description.

"No, a signature is the collection of pages within a book, all the pages printed on a single piece of paper, then folded and cut apart to form the pages of the work. Everything printed has signatures, from the oldest books to this magazine," she said, ruffling the pages of the pulp to show me what she meant. "On the final signature of the False Grimoire, the printer inserted his colophon. It may have been from habit, that was a common way to mark a book's end, or perhaps Sweets wanted a way to prove the book false at a later date. According to one bibliography that I found, the colophon is quite small, a fish biting its tail, and printed so close to the interior edge of the page that the fish is almost lost in the spine of the book."

All very interesting for someone who was a student of the book trade, but I focused on the important piece of news in the story. "Then there's a fake grimoire that can be told from the true grimoire by the fish picture on the last page." I jotted that information into the small notebook I kept in my purse. A habit that I acquired from Max. However, I didn't bother to have my notebooks engraved with my name. Rather I used plain brown pads from the five-and-dime. My pencil, however, was chained to the interior of my bag by a sterling silver chain and holder. I so disliked losing pencils that I'd had the silver device crafted for me by Tiffany.

"That's what I said," Christine agreed. "Two grimoires, one Deadly and one now known as the Fake or, to more precise bibliographers like myself, the False Fish Grimoire. That's why Hughes wanted me to purchase the grimoire for the university's collection. So I would examine it and verify it was the true grimoire."

"But if his family has the False Grimoire, wouldn't Hughes know that the other one was the Deadly Grimoire?" I said.

"Both books were lost at sea," said Christine. "At least that's what everyone thought until 1910, when another Sweets revealed he had the Deadly Grimoire. He's the one who ordered the book bound in green shagreen and ornamented."

"Tom told me about that. Jeweled and gold decorations. Quite elaborate and unnecessary," I said. "Although he didn't mention any false grimoire. I wonder why."

Christine shrugged. "It was an embarrassment to the family. They are very proud of their reputation as purveyors of rare books with excellent provenance. After their previous handling of the book, the next generation of Sweets removed the original binding to prove that the Deadly Grimoire being sold was the true grimoire, no fish mark. After being certified as free from the fish colophon, the Sweets replaced the binding with jeweled ornamentation, which was popular with a certain type of collector before the war."

"What happened to that owner?" I asked. "The one who bought the fancy version."

"Drowned when the *Titanic* went down," replied the professor. "It was thought the Deadly Grimoire went into the sea with the ship. But apparently it never left Boston. Sweets sold it again to another owner."

"What happened to him?" I said.

"Killed in the war," the professor said. "His estate went to auction and the Sweets bought the entire library."

Killed in the war was the fate of too many men, and it didn't take a curse to make that happen, I thought, but I still realized owning the grimoire didn't sound terribly lucky.

"What happened to the fake grimoire?" I said.

"No one knows for sure," Christine said. "But I've heard some speculation that it also fell into the hands of the Sweets a few years ago. If that's true, it's almost as valuable as the Deadly Grimoire. I would love to see it."

A nurse rapped on the door. "Almost time for rounds," she said. "You'll need to leave, miss, so the doctor can examine her patient."

"Wasn't that what Hughes was doing here?" I asked the professor.

Christine shook her head. Even the nurse gave me a

wintery smile of disbelief. "Now, miss," added the nurse, "no more questions. It's time for visitors to leave."

Christine waved the woman away. "I'd much rather chat with Miss Baxter," she said to the nurse, "than sit in bed staring at the wall. I'm quite tired of the wall's company."

"Very well," said the nurse with a sympathetic smile. "But only ten more minutes." She bustled out the door, obviously intent on sweeping all strays out of the ward before the doctor's rounds.

"Ezra Hughes isn't my doctor. He's wild to see the Deadly Grimoire and wanted to hear about the robbery. He's questioned me almost as many times as the police," Christine said in answer to my earlier question. "But he does treat patients on the mental ward and at his sanitarium. You'll see it soon enough."

"What do you mean?"

"The sanitarium, Bluff Mansion. That's where your friend Jim is staying. Didn't you know?" Christine looked slightly bemused.

As soon as she said the name, I did remember it. I had arranged to have Jim transferred out of the hospital and to private treatment as soon as it was safe to do so. Christine had recommended the place to me.

"I do remember your letter about a doctor who specializes in the treatment of lost memories or amnesia," I told her. "I didn't realize Hughes was the man."

"Yes, he's become quite well known in this area," said Christine. "Rather a local boy made good. He's fascinated by memory loss. Especially among those who claim they have experienced a gap in time."

"A what?"

"I guess you could call it a period of time that can't be accounted for."

"You mean people who have disappeared and then reappeared later some place completely different."

"Well, yes," the professor admitted.

"Isn't that what happened to you?" I finally asked. "Did the grimoire make you disappear?"

CHAPTER NINE

Christine chuckled at my question about the cause of her disappearance and touched the bandage that wrapped around her head. "Oh, no, nothing so unearthly as a cursed book," she said. "Somebody knocked me over the head, dropped me into the back of a car, and drove me a considerable distance out of town before leaving me propped up against a road sign. Considerate of them. They could have rolled me into a ditch instead of leaving me where I was found by the next passing milk truck. However, they also stole the grimoire, so I'm less happy about that. Ezra wanted to question me about my memory loss and offer me treatment at his sanitarium if I felt so inclined. Which I don't. Cold seawater baths and tea made from kelp! Thank you, but I'd rather recover here."

"His treatment sounds horrid," I agreed. I wondered now if sending Jim there had been the right decision. What had poor Jim experienced over the past few months? "Does anyone recover at Hughes's sanitarium?"

"The doctor's treatments have been unusually successful,"

Christine said with conviction. "It's one of the reasons I was not surprised your friend has recovered some of his memories and begun to talk again. Ezra calls his treatments oceanic therapy. He says he uses the sea to restore memory and well-being."

Her words were reassuring, although I still wasn't certain about cold seawater baths or drinking seaweed tea. I took Christine's view of such treatments – Hughes's ideas sounded unpleasant. I resolved to visit Jim as soon as possible. If he seemed well, then I would allow the treatment to continue. If not, I intended to move him back to California as quickly as possible.

"But who stole the grimoire?" I asked Christine. "Do you have any idea?"

"I do not remember much," she sighed. "I was finishing my examination of the book at home and working on my speaking notes for the evening. It was an honor to present the Deadly Grimoire to the library, and I wanted to make an occasion of it. I was sitting quite comfortably at my desk when somebody struck me on the back of my head."

"I read in the newspaper that your friends found your door open and you gone," I said. "That's why I flew out here."

"Did you really fly?" asked Christine. "I've always wanted to go up in an airplane."

"It's marvelous," I told her. "You have to try it. But how did they get into your house, and who would have stolen the grimoire from you?"

"As for getting in, that was easy. The door was unlocked as I was expecting friends. As for who stole it, Ezra thinks it was your handsome bookseller, Tom Sweets," she said.

"He's not mine," I answered very quickly. I simply did not need another responsibility. "I found him being beaten up by some muckers who work for Nova Malone."

"Ah, the Deadly Grimoire's other claimant," Christine exclaimed. "It was the Malone family who bought the Deadly Grimoire once before and wreaked havoc on the fortunes of the Hughes family and others in Innsmouth. Or at least that's Ezra's story. The other side is the False Grimoire was created to cheat the Malones out of their book. Again, nobody is sure what is true. This all happened in the last century."

"So what a tangled web these sea captains and booksellers did weave?" I said.

"*Marmion*," replied the poetry professor, "Sir Walter Scott, 1808. Betsy, I'm always impressed with your knowledge."

"I run with a smart crowd," I said. I did, too. Folks from all backgrounds landed in Hollywood. "I keep telling you that you'd love teaching out west. They're planning big things for the California universities. I expect Berkeley and Stanford to rival Harvard soon."

Christine just smiled and shook her head. "I am happy enough here," she said. "Arkham can be a strange place, but it is my home."

The nurse popped her head back into the room. "Now, I must insist that you leave," she said to me. "The doctor is almost here."

"They will let me out in a day or so," Christine said. "Let's plan on dinner. Bring your friends. I want to hear about your adventures."

"We will take you flying," I promised.

As I walked out of the hospital lobby, I spotted Dr

Hughes talking with two large, roughly dressed men. One of them looked familiar, and I was pretty sure he was Little Albie's friend from the night before. An orderly was doing something with a mop and pail. Despite being hit by a cloud of that horrible hospital soap smell, I ducked behind the orderly to eavesdrop.

The two men seemed to be in something of an argument with each other with quick interjections from the doctor. I wondered if they were patients or friends of patients. Their attitude seemed to indicate the latter. I heard one say to the doctor, "So how long until he can tell us where the boxes are?"

"I cannot rush treatments. As Miss Malone very well understands," said Hughes. "However, if you would only tell me more about the route that he took and where he was found?"

"We've told you all we can," said the larger man, and I was certain that he was Albie's friend. "But Miss Malone repeats, she doesn't have the book. However, she is not giving up her claim on it either."

Following that intriguing statement, the two men talking to the doctor took off. Restraining my natural impulse to follow and question the roughs directly, I lingered in the lobby for a few moments. Then I ran after the doctor. When I caught up to him, I stuck out my hand. "Thank you so much for taking care of my friend," I said. "And chasing off that lout of a bookseller. That young man pestered me for a ride to the hospital and, I'm sure, will want me to take him back to the hotel again. I had no idea that he was such a goof."

Burbling like the most witless of flappers, I shook the doctor's hand heartily.

Ezra Hughes looked a bit befuddled by my statements – perhaps he didn't know what a goof was – and said with a paternal air, "Now, you must be careful of such men." I glanced out the door at his recent companions and thought he should take his own advice. "A young lady alone can be prey to the most terrible of villains."

Not since the Brontës wrote their gothic novels, I wanted to say but replied, "How kind. I have a friend with me, a regular fire extinguisher, to protect me from Lothario booksellers," I said, although I'm sure describing Wini as a chaperone would have amused her to no end. "Now, you take good care of the professor, and I'll be back to see her quite soon."

"Ah," said the doctor, apparently placing me and my flapper slang in his mental filing cabinet. "You are one of the professor's students."

As if a student could afford such a hat as I wore! But really, one couldn't expect a New England doctor from a small town to recognize Paris fashion. "Ah, I've learned a great deal from the professor," I said, and that was nothing but the truth. "However, I hear from her that you're the true expert on missing men."

Ezra Hughes looked surprised at my statement. "Missing men?"

"People who have been lost and don't remember where they were, even after they've been found," I said, which was Jim's case in a nutshell.

"I am considered one of the foremost experts on the recovery of memory," Hughes said. Obviously, he didn't think modesty was a virtue. Well, I didn't either, so why judge him for that?

"Have you ever treated a man named Max Taelsman?" I said.

"Max Taelsman?" said Hughes. "No, I don't think so." And before he could ask any questions of me, a nurse came to remind the doctor that he was wanted for a consultation on an upper floor.

With another wave of my hands, I dashed out the door. I'd learned a great deal in this visit, but now I had a number of questions for Tom Sweets.

Outside the hospital, I spotted Tom and Wini waiting for me by the roadster. As soon as I reached them, I said to Tom, "The ancestors of Nova Malone and Ezra Hughes seem to have a history with your family. What's this about a false grimoire?"

"Ah, that," said Tom, rubbing the back of his neck with one hand. He gave me a shy smile, tilting up his head in a way that must have made the hearts flutter among the college girls. "Ancient family history?"

"Not good enough," I said, having a heart of stone and being impervious to the wiles of college boys, no matter how they shyly peered through their absurdly long lashes. Such a waste for a bookworm to have such pretty eyes when he wasn't in the pictures. "Spill the beans, mister," I said, in as stern a tone as I could manage on a sunny day in the summer with a breeze fluttering the hem of my dress and wearing a Paris hat. "The doctor claims you're a no-good character and a danger to the ladies to boot."

"As for being dangerous, I'm not the one who carries a

pistol in my purse," said Tom. "Nor am I wearing a skirt that would shock my grandmother and delight my grandfather and a hat that would please them both."

"Thank you for the lovely compliment," I responded, "but tell me about your multiple grimoires."

The pair of men who had been arguing with the doctor had carried on their conversation outside. Having obviously settled something between them, they strolled across the street.

Tom eyeballed the pair. "Let's cover my family's convoluted past in another place," he answered. "I don't like the look of those characters."

Wini, who had been watching the two of us with mild amusement, looked over Tom's shoulder at the men heading toward a parked Model T a little way away from us. "I know the one man," she said. "That's the guy who was snooping around the airfield. The one I followed into town." She pointed at the biggest guy, the one I thought was Albie's friend.

"Those two were jawing with the doctor on my way out. He's definitely the one who roughed you up, Tom," I said. The two men climbed into the Tin Lizzie with a dented fender. Neither glanced at us. Apparently, their discussion was more interesting than idle bystanders.

"I agree, which is why I suggest leaving the vicinity," said Tom. "At least his little friend doesn't appear to be with him. Albie was vicious. But I'd rather not tangle with any of that particular fraternity again."

"At least this time you're close to the hospital," I said.

"But will you be my nurse a second time?" Tom replied

with another flutter of those lashes. I frowned at him. Tall, handsome, and trouble was not a combination I needed, I reminded myself, no matter how much he might make me want to laugh.

"That's certainly the car I followed," said Wini as the pair started their vehicle.

"Shall we see where they go?" I asked as I hopped into the driver's seat.

"I'm game," said Wini with a grin. She grabbed the passenger seat beside me. "Let them go down the road before you start after them. That way they might not notice us."

"I know how to trail a car," I said. "I took lessons from a writer who used to work for the Pinkertons." I started the roadster and heard the reassuring roar of its engine. I loved learning a former Pinkerton detective's tricks one winter in San Francisco and was delighted to try a few of the techniques that Dash taught me.

"Are you sure you want to do this?" said Tom as he settled himself sideways in the backseat.

"We can leave you here," I said.

Hughes emerged from the entrance of the hospital. Seeing Tom, he pointed at him and began to shout. There was definitely a shaking of fists, but I couldn't make out the words, except "crook" and "fraud".

"Let's follow that car," said Tom, essaying his own cheerful wave at the doctor as we drove by Ezra Hughes.

I laughed then and shifted into another gear, setting a good pace but not moving too close to the car ahead of us. Of course, in a bright blue roadster, we were not exactly inconspicuous. However, the car in front of us headed down toward the river along one of the main streets. There was enough traffic, including a boy madly ringing his bicycle bell and a cranky horse kicking up the traces in a farm delivery wagon, to keep their eyes on the road in front of them.

"Where do you think they are going?" I said to Wini as we made another turn down a street that looked far more industrial than residential. Small factories and the types of businesses that catered to other businesses rolled by.

"Warehouses?" said Wini. "Look, you can see the river now."

The river glinted green and greasy in this section of the town, and there was a definite odor rising in the warm August afternoon.

"Slow down," said Tom. "Looks like they are turning in there."

The Tin Lizzie pulled through the open double doors of a warehouse and stopped. I drove past without even glancing at them, just as the detective once showed me. "Never let them catch you looking," he'd muttered out of the corner of his mouth when we were trailing a pair of crooks through San Francisco's meaner streets. "If you stop behind them, they'll check you out. Go down the street and park around the corner. Always give them time to go about their business. It also gives you time to find a place to watch them."

Sliding the roadster down an alley, I parked in the shadow of another tarred warehouse. The smell of creosote, hemp, and river waste was strong enough to taste in this Arkham neighborhood. I could hear the hooting of tugs as the barges moved up and down the Miskatonic River in the afternoon heat.

"Now, wait a moment," said Tom as Wini and I began to sidle back toward the warehouse where the two men had parked. "Is this safe?"

"Probably not," said Wini to Tom. "But that's more fun."

"Hush," I said to the pair of them. "Let's see what they're doing." I went first, eager to follow the two men and check what they were up to. Their earlier conversation with the doctor about a lost man had certainly sparked my curiosity about their business.

But when we got to the warehouse, a cautious peep through the windows on the side showed the car parked near some crates and no sign of the men who had ridden in it.

"Let's go inside," I said.

"Let's not," said Tom.

"Where's your sense of adventure?" asked Wini.

"I'm a bookseller," Tom said. "An antiquarian bookseller, which means I don't even have to talk to authors, as all the volumes I sell were written by dead people. The most exciting thing I do is search attics for possibly valuable volumes to auction."

"Ever find any?" I said, still balancing on my tiptoes to see through the window, but I couldn't spy anything unusual.

"Not as many as my uncle would like," Tom said. "Boston attics tend to be stuffed full of old clothes, far too many mothballs, sleds with rusty runners, and portraits of dead husbands. An amazing number of portraits of dead husbands. You'd think their widows would want to keep them downstairs."

"Well," I said, "I suppose that depends on the marriage. No portraits of dead wives?"

"Only if there is a new wife downstairs," said Tom.

"This is fascinating," said Wini in a tone that indicated she wasn't too intrigued. "But are we breaking into this warehouse or not?"

"I don't think it's breaking in," I said, dropping back on my heels. I strolled around the corner to the pair of open doors I'd spotted through the windows. "Not if the doors are wide open. We can always say we are lost and looking for directions back to the hotel."

"But I know where the hotel is…" Tom started to say but then blinked. "Oh, right, we could say that, I suppose."

I hooked my arm through Tom's. "Come on," I said with a chuckle, "this will be more fun than a Boston attic."

Inside the warehouse, we found no one, certainly not our suspicious pair of men, and almost nothing else of interest. The crates stacked around the walls held nothing but the straw lining their insides.

"What do you think they held?" I asked Wini and Tom.

He shrugged, but Wini plunged her hands in and stirred up the straw. I waited for mice or bugs to appear, but the packing was clean. Wini noticed that, too.

"This is pretty fresh," she said. "My guess is that the cargo was something breakable. Like glass. That's odd." From the interior of the box, she pulled a long strand of withered seaweed. The briny smell overwhelmed almost everything else and brought back memories of Humbert's weeds.

"That's ugly," said Tom, pointing at a bony little fish that dropped from the seaweed strand. The specimen had bulging eyes and needlelike teeth that jutted out of its mouth. "Looks like a piranha."

"I wonder how that got in there," I said. I was tempted to poke it with my foot but remembered the demise of my last pair of shoes when I kicked the seaweed at the Fitzmaurice house. Instead, I bent as close as possible without touching the thing. The smell was rank and familiar. Those horrible weeds I'd encountered that morning smelled exactly the same, like seaweed rotting in the sun. Then I noticed something else. "Tom, do piranhas have three eyes?"

"I don't think so," he said.

I looked at the third eye, centered in the creature's forehead, and shuddered a little. It was a singularly ugly fish.

"Do we take it with us?" Wini asked.

"No," said Tom and I in a harmonious chorus.

"It might be a clue," Wini said.

"It's dead, it smells, and I don't want it in my car," I replied. "Let's leave it here and see if there's anything more helpful in their flivver."

The men's car looked exactly like the rest of its Ford's Model T brethren, but one front fender had a slight dent, which would distinguish it if we encountered it again. I did a quick rummage around the driver's seat, finding only a matchbook printed with the insignia of the Strike True Match Company of Ontario.

"Somebody's been in Canada," said Wini, tossing the empty matchbook from hand to hand in the same way she jiggled her silver cigarette case.

I moved around to the passenger side of the car and ran my hands along the seat, then peered under the bench on that side as well. There I found half of a burnt cigarette and a business card with a footprint on it, indicating that someone had dropped it on the floor of the car and other people had stepped on it getting in and out. That much of a detective's explanation I could give to my companions.

"In the detective magazines," said Tom, "that footprint would indicate a short man with a limp who previously worked for a banker in Cleveland."

"I'm not even sure if this is a man's footprint," I said, looking at the dirty mark on the card. "But at least we know it came from a place named the Purple Cat in Innsmouth." The name and address were printed under a very stylish cat. All the art and type were done in purple ink. When I showed it to Wini, she frowned. "I don't know it but we can ask around," she said.

"My guess is that they don't serve just tea," I said, flipping over the card. "This is a membership card." The number five hundred and eighty-seven was written on the back in a distinctive flowing script. Like the front, the number was done in purple ink but definitely in a person's handwriting and not printed. The seven was underlined twice.

"Membership card?" said Tom. "For what?"

Wini shook her head at his ignorance. "Blind pig," she said.

"What?" said Tom.

"Juice joint," I said. "Don't they swill the hooch in Boston? Please don't expect me to believe Harvard men are teetotalers who would never enter a drinking establishment."

"House parties," said Tom with a smile. "And certain places of entertainment, which may have included beverages. There is the Bibliophile Club. But I never had to show a card."

"Probably because you were with people who knew people," I said. With booze being banned, I'd seen all sorts of creative ways to keep the wines flowing but the cops unknowing. As I told Wini and Tom. "Cards like these are common enough. Lets the bouncer at the door know you're legit, not a cellar smeller, out to turn them over to the bull."

"Your butchery of the English language is amazing," said Tom in a complimentary tone. He gave a little bow in my direction.

"If you play a flapper detective, you need to know how the jazz babies talk," I said with a curtsey back at him. I didn't need tall and handsome in my life, but it was fun to flirt.

"But there's no dialogue in the movies. The films are silent," Tom rebutted.

"My lips still move in the scenes where I am supposed to be talking," I said, "so the writers create dialogue for me. Or I give them lines."

"She's right," said Wini, who had kept rummaging around the car and largely ignored us. As was probably wise. "About that being a membership card. I've seen such before. There are probably two levels to the place. The first would look legit, but there's a door in the back or a flight of stairs…"

"To where the drinks and the entertainment are!" I said. "We'll have to find out!"

"Why?" said Tom.

"Why wouldn't we?" I said. "Don't you like to dance? I love to dance. I bet this place has a band." I wasn't altogether kidding. I did love to dance, and such joints usually had wonderful bands. Besides, there was that strange seaweed and other aquatic creatures showing up at the warehouse. Something about the scent of decay and ocean lingering around the boxes made me uneasy. A prickle went down my spine. I thought of fire and smoke, even though it smelled nothing like fire or smoke. But every time I caught a whiff of brine, it made me think of Max. I wasn't sure why.

As we left the warehouse, a roaring sound came from the river. Wini's head snapped up. "That's a plane," she said. "A seaplane."

"More a river plane," said Tom. "Look! There it goes."

Peering between the warehouses, we saw a small plane skimming along the water. Wini practically purred when it skipped up into the air, streams of river water trailing off its floats. Several boats tooted as the plane flew overhead, including a long, grumbling blast from one barge.

"Tricky takeoff with all the boats out there," said Wini, "but a good pilot."

I glanced at the plane, though I was more concerned with the memories stirred by the oddities I'd seen that day. But I was never good at introspection, and I shook off my preoccupation. "Where to next?" I said out loud.

As we walked back toward my car, we argued about where to go. Or rather, Wini and I proposed a visit to the Purple Cat, and Tom wondered out loud if it was a place for ladies and booksellers. We assured him that ladies would be fine in any hooch joint on the coast, even if Boston booksellers needed a little protection.

"I'll take my pistol," I said.

"I have a Mauser stored in my plane," Wini offered. "We could fetch that. Oh, and Lonnie, too, she swings a mean wrench in a bar fight."

"I think going armed makes it more dangerous, not less," objected Tom. "And who said anything about bar fights?"

We rounded the corner of the warehouse to spot a man rummaging in the front seat of my roadster, much as I had searched the Model T just a few minutes earlier. All I could see was his back as he bent over my open car, peering inside.

"Stop, thief!" I shouted.

CHAPTER TEN

The man popped up at my shout.

"Hello, Miss Baxter," said Darrell. "I guess I should have known this swell car would belong to you."

"Darrell," I squealed. "What is my favorite reporter doing here?"

"Following a lead, of course," he said. "And you?"

"Working on some things." I liked Darrell very much, but I was well aware anything I said to him might end up in the newspaper. And I wasn't quite ready to explain about not breaking but definitely entering the warehouse down the road.

"Any particular reason you are here?" said Darrell, who wasn't a fool and also knew to follow up on a question.

"Did you see that plane take off from the river?" I said to stall while I tried to think up a plausible explanation for what we were doing.

"Of course," Darrell said. Then he looked more closely at the three of us, especially Wini, and jumped ahead of me by asking, "Are you planning on a water stunt in the air show? Boat to plane, plane to boat? Will you be performing with Miss Habbamock?"

I knew Wini lacked a wing-walker after our discussion at lunch. Perhaps that could be my excuse for poking around where I shouldn't be. I was famous for learning new tricks for the movies.

Because there's nothing that will convince a reporter faster that he has a story than a denial, I shook my finger in Darrell's face. "Now, I cannot tell you all our secrets. But I will say that anyone who comes to Saturday's show will be in for a surprise!"

Wini rolled her eyes at me, not sure what I'd just promised. But still, I had thought performing as a barnstormer might be the way to shake the blues out of my head. I had an idea already for a trick with a motorcycle, having practiced with one for my last picture.

Darrell spotted Tom, standing close behind us, and waved in a friendly manner. "Are you with Miss Habbamock's circus, too?"

"Oh, yes, he is," I said, since we already discussed Tom's place in the show at lunch. "He's our advance man. Darrell, please give Tom your card so he knows where to call in the stories."

Tom shook hands with Darrell. I kept talking, asking about the possibility of printing posters with the newspaper's press.

"We could probably do the printing," said Darrell, "or I can give you the name of a couple of others in town who do such work."

Both Wini and Tom were whispering behind me, possibly wondering what I was playing at. I tipped my hat to a more rakish angle and settled into turning the questions back on Darrell.

"What are you investigating?" I asked Darrell.

"Disappearances," he said. "Several from this neighborhood."

"Like the professor?" I said.

"No." Darrell shook his head. "That's just a plain kidnapping and robbery." He looked a bit disappointed in the ordinariness of the crime but perked up as he described how he secured an interview with the professor. "I managed to talk to her last night. Dressed as an orderly and delivered her a cup of tea."

"I took candy and magazines this afternoon," I said.

He shrugged at my tame foray into hospital visits. "From everything she said, it's clear they stole that old book for the jewels," Darrell said.

"Well," said Tom, "I'm not so…" But Wini trod on his foot before I could, and he had the sense to shut his mouth before Darrell noticed.

"Guess that's what happens when you dress up an old book with gold and jewels," said Darrell.

"Shagreen cover, gilded not gold," muttered Tom in my ear. "And semiprecious stones."

"I figure that they heard about it and broke into the professor's house to steal it," said Darrell, too busy explaining his theory to listen to Tom's objections. "They probably weren't expecting to see the professor there but were afraid that she'd raise the alarm too soon if they left her. Hence the ride out into the country."

"Perhaps," I said. I thought that it seemed like a lot of trouble for a book, no matter how pretty the cover. "But what about these disappearances you're investigating?"

"Those are very odd," said Darrell. "There's been some planes gone off course. Then the pilots reappeared miles from where they were supposed to be."

"I heard about the airmail planes," said Wini.

Darrell nodded. "And then there were the boats."

"Boats?" I asked.

"A couple of fishing boats out of Innsmouth vanished near Devil Reef."

"Sank?" I asked.

"No sign of that," said Darrell. "Just gone. The crews were found later, asleep in a cave. With stalks of seaweed draped all over them. They are still searching for the boats."

"A storm?" ventured Wini. "Something that blew them off course and off the boat? Perhaps they had to swim for it?"

"If they did, they have no memory of it. None of them could explain what had happened. Then there were the delivery trucks," added Darrell. "At least three have disappeared in the countryside near Innsmouth. Same as all the rest. The drivers are found days later near the shore. No memory of how they got there or where they had been. And the trucks are still missing."

"Hijackings," I speculated, remembering some of the stories I'd read about Chicago and New York. Bootlegging wars weren't unknown, and there'd been some sensational tales in the news recently. I kept a box of clippings, just for script ideas to give to the writers of the Flapper Detective. Still, I'd never heard of bootleggers' victims just turning up with no memory of where they had been. That sounded eerily like what had happened with Jim.

Darrell shook his head. "I don't think it is hijackings.

There's something strange happening, and it seems to occur near Innsmouth. It's just a feeling that I have, but my feelings are rarely wrong."

Given some of the stories Darrell had written over the past few years, I also had faith in his feelings. The more I thought about my lost Max, Tom's missing grimoire, and Wini's discovery of vanished airplanes, the more I wondered what was happening in this place called Innsmouth.

As the others climbed into the car, I showed the Purple Cat card to Darrell. "Know the joint?" I asked.

"Oh, sure," he said. "It's on the cliff road near Innsmouth. Just outside the village where the road forks. Follow the left branch to the Purple Cat. It belongs to Miss Nova Malone."

Ah, the bootlegger with the interest in grimoires! I glanced over my shoulder at Tom. He gave a frown and shook his head. Tom also circled around the car, heading for the passenger side, obviously wanting to keep out of the conversation. He climbed into the back, and Wini hopped into the passenger seat. I kept chatting.

"Honest place, this Purple Cat?" I turned back to Darrell.

"What I've seen," replied Darrell. "But there's a purple door inside, just behind the stage, with a big man stationed in front of it. I haven't been able to talk my way past him. Or Miss Malone. You don't want to upset her."

Definitely not on the complete up-and-up, I thought, patting my purse with the membership card inside. That made the Purple Cat even more interesting.

"Ever heard of a sanitarium named Bluff Mansion?" I said.

"Of course," said Darrell. "The sanitarium belongs to Dr Hughes. He's gaining quite the reputation for his work as a specialist and soother of society's nerves. We did a little feature on the sanitarium a few months ago. You can find it on the same cliff road as the Purple Cat. Just take the right-hand lane and drive a little further north. If you go too far and miss it, you'll be at the lighthouse."

Wini leaned over the wheel and lightly tooted the horn. "Are we going now?" asked my impatient friend.

"When does the Purple Cat open?" I asked as I climbed into the driver's seat. I thought it might be easier to go there first. I needed to visit Jim, too, but I didn't want to take Wini and Tom along. That was a conversation best held privately at a later date.

"The Purple Cat never closes. Well, almost never. Maybe for a few hours after midnight." Darrell leaned over the door to answer me. The advantage of the convertible was that I could still hold a conversation and start my car. "It's a nice little place with a small dance floor and a band on Friday and Saturday nights. In the early mornings, Miss Malone serves hash and eggs to the fishing crews. In the afternoon, it's coffee for the ladies coming off the cannery shifts. Everyone in Innsmouth knows Miss Malone's place. Miss Malone even started broadcasting the Purple Cat's dance band on the radio. We did a story about her investment in radio fairly recently."

"Well, I'll be sure to stop there," I said. "And meet the famous Miss Nova Malone."

"Be careful," said Darrell. "Strange things happen to people who upset the Malones." I thought I heard Tom gulp from the backseat, but I didn't want to call attention to his fears of Malone reprisals.

"I'm not rude," I said as I gunned the motor.

"She's not one for sauce," Darrell said firmly. "Of any kind. And Innsmouth can be unfriendly to day-trippers. Folks from Innsmouth stick together, and Miss Nova Malone is one of theirs."

"Point taken," I said. "I'll be on my best behavior."

As we drove away, Wini said to me, "Do we go by the airfield and pick up my Mauser?" Tom choked a bit more in the backseat. Wini grinned over her shoulder at him. "Or maybe just Lonnie and her wrench?"

"No," I said. "Let's make this a friendly visit. If there's coffee and gossip in the afternoon, that's when we should visit the Purple Cat. I'd like to know more about those disappearing trucks, boats, and planes."

As we went down the road, I asked Tom, "Has Miss Malone ever met you?"

"No," he yelled back over the noise of the wind and the engine. "Just her gentlemen friends called on me in that alley."

"Still, they know you are in Arkham," I said. Showing up with Tom at the Purple Cat might lead to more explanations and book discussions than I wanted. "We should drop you at the hotel first."

We left Tom at the hotel to gather his belongings and move out to the airfield. Wini scribbled a note on the hotel stationery to introduce him to her crew. "I mentioned that we had a new advance man coming," she said. "They'll show you where to bunk and what materials we have."

Tom nodded and pulled Darrell's card out of his pocket. "I'll call the local newspapers to set up some publicity," he said. "This should be fun. As long as I don't have to go up in an airplane."

"I promise you can keep your feet on the ground," I said.

Tom rubbed the back of his neck in a gesture I was beginning to anticipate. "I'm not so sure my feet have touched the ground since sometime last night." But he smiled as he climbed out of the car.

"Darrell already has photos of Wini and me when we arrived in town," I told him. "Remind him I'm performing in the show. That will help sell a few papers."

"And tickets," said Wini. "We need a good turnout. And then you and I need to talk about this performance idea, Betsy. One week of training in wing-walking…"

"Is plenty," I said. "Besides, I have an idea. It will be marvelous."

Wini looked slightly skeptical but reminded Tom that she needed advertisements to go out as soon as possible.

Tom scribbled some notes on the back of Darrell's card. "I'll see about some posters," he said.

"We've got a cache that shows the plane with a wing-walker on top," said Wini. "You just need to have the printer overprint with the dates and times of the performances. Lonnie or Bill, my other pilot, will have the list. Bill can run you through the sequence of the show, too. It helps if you know the names of the tricks when calling on the newspapers."

Tom nodded and patted his pockets for more paper to write on when he ran out of room on Darrell's card. I tore a page out of my notebook and handed it to him.

"Be careful at that speakeasy," said Tom as we left him.

"We will," I promised, patting my purse with the silver-plated pistol inside.

The left-hand road was hard-packed dirt and the countryside desolate with trees twisted by the wind blowing steadily off the ocean. The smell of salt was strong in the air, and certain twists of the road brought us close enough to the cliff's edge to spot the white-capped waves. Not a road I'd want to drive in the dark but easy enough on a bright summer afternoon.

Despite Tom's doubts and Darrell's cautions, Wini and I found the Purple Cat as threatening as a grandmother's house with cheerful geraniums in window pots, pale dimity curtains hung café style in the windows, and a purple china cat on the doorstep. A neatly painted sign proclaimed that we had found "The Purple Cat: Open Breakfast, Lunch, and Dinner. Midnight Suppers Our Specialty."

"I wonder what they serve at midnight," muttered Wini as we pushed the door open. A bell merrily tinkled to announce our entrance.

"Probably not just water to drink," I guessed.

We found the interior of the Purple Cat matched the exterior for homey warmth with neat round tables covered in gingham checked cloths, sturdy wooden chairs, and a number of women seated in what were obviously their favorite spots. Most had a cup of coffee clutched in one reddened hand. A buzz of gossip filled the room. A buzz that didn't stop when strangers entered.

"Shuckers," said Wini, looking at the other women there. "And scalers."

I raised an eyebrow in inquiry.

"They work in the processing plants," Wini explained with a nod at the women gossiping at the end of their workday. "Shucking shellfish or scaling fish. I remember helping my grandmother with shucking when I was barely high enough to see over the table. Plunging your hands into buckets of cold saltwater leaves them red and chapped and aching for hours. I could never handle it as a factory job, but there's not that much work available in places like this, especially for women. It's one of the reasons I wanted to be a pilot."

"Corn," I said. "Stripping the leaves. That was the shucking we did as kids. That job motivated me onto a train bound for Chicago. Corn shucking was hot and prickly. The cuts and blisters on your hands stung all night long."

"Chickens," added Wini with emphasis. "There is another chore I don't miss. Pecking and scratching and pooping all over when you're hunting for eggs."

"Chickens, wringing their necks and plucking out feathers, just to fry up a Sunday supper," I agreed with a shudder. "Another reason to leave home."

"My people were good people," said Wini. "Everyone worked hard to make it a little better for everyone else. But the work…"

"Stank, and hurt, and was mind-numbingly dull," I said.

Wini laughed. "Guess neither of us would make good farm wives."

"I can safely say being domestic was never my ambition," I said. Which was true. Even when I was entertaining ideas of marrying Max, I never pictured a country cottage and a picket fence. I'd had to paint too many picket fences growing up as well as wash the stairs every Saturday afternoon and polish the silver before Sunday dinners. Rather, I'd imagined a couple living in a nice city apartment, drinking champagne with breakfast, and dancing at the nightclubs after a day of working in the studio.

"I miss the clambakes, though," said Wini as we found a table and sat ourselves down. "The clambakes at home were the best, especially when all the families would come together. We'd build a big bonfire on the beach. The elders would tell stories until dawn. I always tried to stay awake until the very end, but I'd be so full and warm and curled down into the sand. Then I'd wake up the next day in my bed with my grannie scolding me for sleeping the day away but in a grandmother's cheerful way, which meant she was only teasing and not very mad."

"I went to a clambake in California," I said. "It was at the end of a movie shoot. All the extras and the crew in one spot, and the stars off around their own bonfire, but someone brought a Victrola and a bunch of good jazz records. Then everyone ended up together on the sand, eating, and dancing, and waiting for the dawn."

"Sounds like fun," Wini said.

"It was nice," I said, remembering how cold the wet sand had been on my bare feet with the Pacific lapping little waves over my toes in time to the jazz. It was the first time I had danced with Max. He'd been stiff, and awkward, and so sweet.

"What can I get you ladies?" asked the waitress as she arrived toting a notepad and pencil. She wore a white apron tied around her middle that was embroidered with a small purple cat in one corner.

"How's the pie?" I said.

"Best in the state," the waitress answered. "I've got a tomato tart if you want something to fill you up."

"And for a sweet?"

"Deep dish apple," she replied. "With ice cream, of course. Or cheese if you prefer."

"I'll take mine with cheddar," I said.

"Tomato tart for me," said Wini. "And coffee for both of us."

"Be right up," said the waitress. The food came out as quickly as promised. The summer tomato tart was almost as sweet as the apple pie, I exclaimed upon sampling Wini's dish. She announced herself equally impressed with the apple pie after trying a bite from my plate.

"There's nothing like New England apples," she said. "These taste like Cortlands."

The waitress watched us trade bites with a smile, and she absolutely beamed when Wini named her favorite apple. "Those are Cortlands," the waitress said. "From my grandpa's farm. Miss Nova buys several barrels every fall. That's about the last of the 1925 apples. The new crop will be coming soon." She poured us our coffee and set down a pitcher filled with real cream. "But you gals aren't from Innsmouth. I know all the locals by sight."

"We're with the circus," I said.

"The flying circus," added Wini. "Winifred Habbamock's Flying Circus."

"No!" the waitress exclaimed. "We heard that the show was coming to the airfield. It's exciting watching those airmail boys land and take off. My Willard loves to watch the planes flying overhead. But you do tricks?"

"Oh, yes, ma'am," said Wini. "All the best. Loop the loop, low flying, high flying, barrel rolls, and other feats to astound."

"Wing-walking," I added. "Death-defying stunts. Wini is the pilot, and I'm the wing-walker."

"I never!" exclaimed the waitress. "Wait until I tell Miss Nova that we have celebrities from the flying circus at the Purple Cat."

"Tell me what, Mildred?" said a deep voice behind us. We turned to see the largest woman I have ever beheld. A giantess, well over six feet tall in her stockinged feet and nearly as wide as she was long. This mountain of a woman was dressed all in lavender, very stylishly cut. On her broad bosom she wore a large, jeweled pin, a purple cat made from amethysts and diamonds, that twinkled in the afternoon sunshine.

"Why, Miss Nova," said Mildred the waitress. "These gals are from the flying circus."

"This gal owns the flying circus," said Wini, standing to shake Nova Malone's outstretched hand. Wini's own slender hand disappeared inside the other's mammoth paw, but when I also rose to shake hands, I noticed that Nova Malone didn't squeeze hard like a man. She had no need to demonstrate her obvious strength.

"Flyers, are you?" Nova said. "That's an interesting profession."

"I like it," said Wini.

Nova grabbed a chair at another table with one hand and lifted it easily to a place at our table. She settled herself down with considerable grace, rather like the opera singer I saw portraying Turandot in Buenos Aires.

The chatter at the other tables muted just a little, not exactly silence but more a respectful lowering of voices now that the queen of the establishment had entered.

"Tell me about your show," Nova said. "I have questions about airplanes."

Turandot, I remembered, asked questions, too. And those who gave her the wrong answers lost their heads.

CHAPTER ELEVEN

"It's the most daring air circus you'll ever see," said Wini. "Unless you come twice. Then you'll see just as terrifying a show the second time as the first."

Nova Malone smiled at this. "I have never been afraid," she said. "It might be worth watching to see if I could be terrified."

"Well, they call me the Woman Without Fear," said Wini, "but it doesn't mean that I've never known fear. There's been times in my life when I've been very scared indeed. But I went forward despite feeling afraid. Every flyer must do that."

"People call me fearless," I added. "Fear never stopped me from being in charge of my own life, but I know what it is like to be afraid." Sometimes I ran harder toward trouble just to quiet the fear inside me.

"Oh, I understand the emotion exists," Nova answered, "but I have no such memory of ever feeling fear. There's never been a man nor beast that could knock me down or even set me back. After all my siblings died in infancy, my father took me aboard his ship when I was still a baby. Papa thought a sea-raised baby would thrive. And thrive I did. I grew up with no creed except a healthy respect for the gods of the ocean. But even those I do not fear."

"It seems a lack of fear has done you no harm," I said, noting the jewels on her breast and the diamond rings she wore.

Nova tilted her hands to let the sunlight twinkle on her diamonds. She also wore jeweled bracelets, more likely platinum than silver by the style, that caught the light and reflected it back on us. "I have done well for myself," said Nova Malone, "and every jewel that I wear I bought for myself. I do take some pride in building my own businesses."

"As you should," I said. Nova Malone might be a crook, but I admired her attitude. Also, I had to admit, if BB Pictures failed in its early days, who knows what I might have done to keep my fortune. The lure of easy cash drew many a soul into bootlegging. I knew a few Hollywood women who were now running "clubs" for the elite and anyone else willing to pay well for a stiff drink. I'd even danced at the 300 Club when Wilda Bennett married her Argentinian dancer. Which was how I ended up in Buenos Aires earlier this year at the South American premiere of *Turandot*.

"This is a fine place that you have here," said Wini to Nova, "and a very fine tomato pie."

"My cook is the best in Innsmouth," agreed Nova. "I lured her away from Bluff Mansion, which vexed Hughes no end, but the woman was glad to get away from his seaweed recipes."

"I've heard the doctor has some strange ideas," I said.

Nova narrowed her eyes and looked more closely at me. "Unusual for a woman traveling with a circus to know our local nerves doctor," she said.

I nearly bit my tongue, so annoyed at my slip, but Wini saved me from stammering some excuse. "We met him at the hospital, visiting a friend," she said.

"Yes," I said. "Our friend mentioned that Hughes had a sanitarium near here, but I don't understand about the seaweed." Which was nothing but the truth.

Nova snorted. "The fool thinks that any seaweed has healing properties. Cooks it into a broth or boils it into a tea. Then tips it down his patients' throats. Only Ezra Hughes could be that ridiculous."

"So seaweed has no benefit?" I asked. It sounded awful to me, but people were always touting all sorts of cures. Some even worked, like cod liver oil for rickets. Maybe seaweed was a cure for lost memories.

Nova shrugged. "It's a stretch to see it as a cure-all," she said. "My papa fed me on seaweed mash when I was very young, barely past suckling, and washed me with saltwater every day in an empty codfish keg. My size or health may owe something to Papa's practice."

The talk then turned to flying with the big woman asking several pointed questions about the type of planes in Wini's show, their range, and, without directly saying it, their capacity to carry cargo.

Wini neatly sidestepped certain questions while frankly answering others. It was an interesting tango between the two, but neither admitted defeat.

"It's Byrd's flights that fascinated me the most this

summer," said Nova. "Do you think it is true that commercial polar flight will become possible?"

"That's certainly the theory," said Wini. "It would considerably cut the time from the West Coast to Europe."

"Yes, it would," agreed Nova in a speculative tone. "Imagine the possibilities. One of my ancestors spent all his life seeking the Northwest Passage. The ice defeated him every time. But he could not fly."

"Someday," said Wini with conviction, "we'll fly to places we cannot even imagine now. We haven't even begun to hit the limits of what powered flight can do."

"I am convinced science will provide us with many new opportunities," said Nova. "Many trips would be far more successful if the journey was accomplished through the air than by land or sea. Certain recent incidents have persuaded me that air routes could be far superior to other ways."

I wondered what air routes Nova was trying to navigate. Could the missing planes be flying her cargo? Again, I remembered the story of the feds busting up a bootlegging run made by plane. Was Nova trying to fly liquor from Canada to this part of the country? But what use would she have for the grimoire that Christine described, except to use the "routes" in it.

At the end of our discussion, Nova offered us a second slice of pie on the house.

"I would truly like to take a slice," said Wini, "but I fear that I'll explode like a firework if I eat one more bite."

Nova chuckled at Wini's statement and motioned away my purse when I started to pull out the payment for our meal. "You have entertained me very well," she said. "The least I can do is feed you." She waved over the waitress. "Mildred, let's box a few more slices of pie for these ladies." To us, she said, "Please take the pie for a later dessert, when your hunger comes back to you, or to share with others."

"That's very kind," I said.

"Indeed, it is," Wini said. "You must come to see our show. You and all your staff. I'll leave tickets at the gate for you."

"All of them?" Nova challenged her as the cook came out of the kitchen. The Black woman had placed our pies in a neat paper box all tied up with a purple string.

"Everyone," said Wini firmly. "No one is ever barred from one of my shows. I owe too much to Bessie Coleman to do anything else. She taught me the barrel roll and how to parachute."

Looking pleased by this answer, Nova escorted us outside. Glancing at my roadster, she said, "There's a storm coming up. Do you have chains?"

"I do," I said, "in the trunk." I carried chains as a precaution, but I certainly saw no need for them that day. The horizon was clear as far as I could see, and the dirt road was perfectly dry. There was no reason to suspect bad weather was coming.

"You might make it back to the airfield before the storm breaks," said Nova, looking at a few fluffy white clouds racing across the bright summer sky. "But turn off into Innsmouth if it starts to hail."

Once we drove away, Wini let out a whistle. "That's an interesting woman," she said. "I have no patience for rumrunners, but I like her."

"I had much the same impression," I answered. "But never tell me that you marched for temperance."

"Some communities might be better dry. A man or woman who drinks away their money and lets their children go hungry, that's hard on everyone. It is still hard to lose someone that you love to the bottle," Wini said. "But I'm not sure making alcohol illegal solves the problem. The Eighteenth Amendment seems to have made no difference except to jail a few more people for doing what they've always done."

"Smuggling alcohol has made some folks rich, to judge by Miss Nova's diamonds," I said.

"And some end up full of bullet holes," said Wini, "if all the stories that you hear about Chicago and New York are true."

The road turned into a dense wood where the overhanging branches formed a tunnel of dark green shadows. When we drove out the other side, the bright afternoon sunshine was gone. Apparently, Nova Malone was a better weather prognosticator than I gave her credit for.

"That's quite the storm cloud!" said Wini, pointing to the east.

I glanced up to see the sky filling with a great dark cloud. The rising wind buffeted the side of the roadster, yet the road was still smooth and dry. It was a dirt road, though, and if the rains came, I could see it quickly becoming mud soup. Still, the storm clouds building on the horizon were far enough away that I hoped we could outrun the rain.

"Let's avoid that storm," I said to Wini and shifted gears again.

Despite my speed, the storm was faster still. The wind howled and raindrops began to splash on the windshield. The overcast sky made it almost as dark as night. I switched on the headlights, but the beams barely cut through the gloom.

I swore and gunned the motor, trying to outrace the storm. Wini went diving over the seat into the back and wrestled up the roadster's top to protect us from the increasing rain. A flash of lightning lit up the underside of the cloud. A rumble of thunder followed.

The road began weaving in and out of the wooded area. Branches creaked overhead as the wind caught the treetops and sent them swaying. "Keep going!" yelled Wini. "We don't want to stop under these trees." The world turned white as another bolt of lightning forked above us.

I took the curves as fast as I dared. The world narrowed in my vision until it was just the road in front of me, the thunder of the engine in my ears, and the vibration of the wheel clutched in my hands. I felt the addictive sense of being balanced between success and disaster. I forced myself to relax into each swoop of the road.

The final turn brought us back out to the cliff road and the edge was far too close to the wheels. I wrenched the steering wheel around as Wini popped into the front seat again. She dragged the top over us just as the hail hit.

The hailstones pinged like bullets off the hood of the roadster as the road turned into a river of mud under the wheels. Glancing over the cliff's edge, I could see a froth of white waves curling around large rocks far below us.

"Don't slow down," Wini shouted over the storm. "Or we'll be stuck fast."

"Keep an eye out for shelter," I yelled back. The next clap of thunder sounded more out to sea than directly overhead. Slowing slightly, I wondered if I should stop to put on the chains, but I decided Wini was right. Once we stopped, the wheels would sink even further. The road was too far out of town to expect any help to come along. I hadn't seen another car all afternoon. The best we could hope for was a wet hike back to the Purple Cat.

The hail changed back into rain. The sheets of water pouring down on us made the visibility even worse.

Wini practically had her nose on the windshield as she peered ahead. "Take the next turn," she said. "That looks like a gravel road."

With a popping of sticky mud and the squeal of the roadster's engine, I forced the car off the muddy road and onto the better surface. Large drops of rain continued to splash against the windshield, but the wind seemed to be dying down. My relief did not last for long.

"Look out!" Wini yelled.

A rowboat suddenly dropped out of the air and crashed directly in front of us. Shards of wood flew up as the boat exploded on impact. I hit the brakes and fought to hold the wheel steady as I swerved to avoid the unexpected wreck.

CHAPTER TWELVE

"Missed it!" I cried with satisfaction as my lovely roadster ran to a shuddering stop on the grassy edge of the road. Luckily, there was no ditch. But Henry was going to be upset when he saw the state of my poor darling. I decided to find a garage in Arkham and make sure the roadster had a good cleaning before I put it back on the train for Hollywood.

Then, all of a sudden, it hit me. I had just driven around a boat that had dropped from the sky. I had never heard of a storm spitting out rowboats! And where was the storm? Once again, the sky above us was a brilliant blue with no sign of clouds. The whole thing had happened so quickly, I would have thought it an illusion or a dream, except for the scattered wreckage now blocking the road. "Where did the storm go? And where did that boat come from?" I exclaimed.

"I have no idea," said Wini. "Waterspout? They can act like tornadoes, picking things up and dropping them elsewhere." But she sounded as puzzled as I felt.

I got out of the car and walked up to the shattered boat. It looked like a dinghy or small rowboat. A ship's name was painted on the side. *Gulliver*, it said, although that name was now scattered across three pieces of shattered board. I picked up one piece.

"There's too much here to clear away easily," I called back to Wini, who climbed out of the car and scanned the sky for signs of the storm that had overtaken us.

I walked around the wreck. The ground was soft from the hail and rain. I could even see some hailstones still scattered among the grass at the edge of the road. As I squelched around the pile of lumber littering the road, I sighed over another pair of wrecked shoes and stockings. Arkham was turning out to be hard on the wardrobe.

"What do you think?" said Wini when I got back to the car. I tossed the board I had salvaged into the trunk.

"That I need to invest in a good pair of boots like yours," I said as I climbed into my seat.

Wini smirked a little at the mud sticking to my shoes and stockings. "You could have stayed in the car," she said.

"No, I couldn't," I replied. "I'm driving. I need to know what the road is like."

"And?" Wini asked.

"Too much debris to get around or even turn around," I decided as I threw the gears into reverse and backed along the narrow road. I hugged the side furthest from the cliff edge because there was no knowing how that strange storm had softened the ground. Driving in reverse was slow, finnicky work, just the thing to keep me from worrying about vanishing storms and boats appearing from nowhere. "Let's find another road. Ah, I thought I saw a turnoff."

We came even with a smaller track, luckily also graveled and running straight uphill away from the sea.

"What do you think?" I asked Wini.

"I was thinking this is easier when I'm in the air," she replied, squinting at a map we had bought at the hotel earlier. "But if this squiggly line is that road," she gestured up the hill, "then it should loop back around and land us in Innsmouth, I guess. And no telling how long it is going to take. How's your gas?"

"We should have enough," I said, peering over her shoulder at the map. "Especially if we can refill the car in Innsmouth."

"If not, we're sure to pass a farm," said Wini. "Someone will have spare petrol."

"Maybe," I said as I carefully turned the roadster and pointed its nose up the hill. "Let's hope we find something before dark."

"Odd," said Wini as we climbed the hill over the protests of the roadster's engine. Poor thing had taken quite a beating since rolling off the train only this morning, I thought.

"What's odd?" I asked Wini as I worried about the engine lacking Henry's tender care.

"How Nova Malone predicted that storm," said Wini. "I would never have guessed hail or winds like that. I'm pretty good at reading the sky, too."

"I wouldn't have guessed there was a storm coming at all. Or even that one passed through. Nova lives out here," I said. "Guess she knows when storms are expected."

"Maybe," said Wini. "But the way she spoke, she was so certain. Perhaps she's like my grandmother. Granny always said she had a certain feeling when bad weather was coming."

"My grandfather used to say the same thing," I said. "Except with him, it was the first big freeze of the year. He said he could feel it coming in his bones. But it was odd. Maybe Nova's weather predictions come from eating seaweed mash as a baby."

Wini chuckled at my joke. "If that's what it takes to know when a storm is going to blow up, every pilot in the sky would be eating seaweed."

The track continued up and over the hill. As we crested the top, Wini shouted at the sight of a house. "What do you think?" she said. "Do we stop there?"

I glanced at the gauges. The fuel was low, not enough to worry us yet, but we didn't know how far we still needed to go to reach Innsmouth. "Perhaps we should stop and get directions," I said.

Unlike Nova Malone's Purple Cat, this was as unfriendly a house as I'd ever seen. The paint had been peeled off long ago by weather and age, leaving behind a bleak gray house with a sagging roof. The porch that ran around two sides looked ready to collapse into the dirt. Shutters with missing slats were half-closed across the windows. The only door had a conspicuously large and new lock beneath its knob. There was no knocker or doorbell visible.

"Are you sure anyone is living here?" I said as we walked to the door. The place seemed deserted, but I couldn't shake the feeling that someone was watching us. I heard a harsh caw and, glancing up, saw a trio of crows looking down at us.

Wini gestured at the yard and surrounding outbuildings. "Somebody is keeping the place up. At least as much as they can. There's a lot of poor folks in this part of New England," she said. "But there's fresh tire tracks in the yard and not a lot of weeds."

We walked up the creaking steps and across the wobbly porch to knock on the door. There was no answer from inside.

Wini pounded the door a couple more times, but the house remained silent. I cracked open one shutter and glanced through a window. The glass was so dirty that the interior was murky, but it was clear there wasn't much in the way of furnishings. I could make out a bare table and a few plain chairs scattered about. If somebody was keeping the place up, their attention was focused on the outer buildings and the yard, not on the house itself. Despite what Wini had said, I doubted anyone was living there.

"Let's look around the barn," Wini said. "Maybe they're working in the back and cannot hear us."

As we stepped off the porch, the trio of crows took flight. With one long mocking caw, they flew away.

"Think that's an omen?" I said, and I was only half joking. This place was wrong. I could feel it in my bones but, at the same time, I felt that familiar urge to figure out why rather than run. I never could stand to be afraid.

"I don't believe in omens," said Wini. "Crows are just crows." And the way she said it, I caught the echoes of a long-standing argument with somebody. "No matter what they say in Arkham," she concluded.

We walked around the barn. As we got to the far side, we started to hear noises – a steady banging like somebody hammering away at something. Wini walked up to one big shed with a closed wooden shutter. She rapped on it with her knuckles but received no response, so she grabbed the edge and lifted it up to peer inside.

"Oh, damn," Wini said as she looked inside the shed.

"What do you see?" I asked as a man's shout rang out.

Wini grabbed my arm and began to drag me toward the

shed's doorway. "We'll have to brazen it out," she said, "but he'll be upset we're sneaking by his workshop. Leave the talking to me."

"What are you jabbering about?" I said. "Who's there?" It wasn't like the woman who'd just told me crows were only crows to suddenly take fright. Except she didn't seem frightened. More resigned and a little wary when a shadow crossed the doorway.

A heavyset man with a thick black beard stepped in front of us. Despite working in a farm shed, he was neatly dressed in a three-piece suit. His maroon tie looked like silk to me. In one meaty hand, he carried a hammer. He smacked the hammer against his other hand when he saw us. It was not a friendly gesture.

"Chuck Fergus," said Wini. "Been a long time."

"Winifred Habbamock," said Chuck, "what are you doing out here? Snooping again?"

"The storm caught us on the road," said Wini, without a blink at the hammer and belligerent tone of Chuck's voice, "and we had to turn off. We're just looking for a way back to Innsmouth."

Chuck looked skeptical at Wini's response but then he spotted me. "Who's your friend?"

"Betsy Baxter," I spoke up. "I'm the driver who succeeded in making us lost. And ruining my shoes in all your lovely New England mud." I waggled one wet foot at him. I figured a man who dressed so nicely on a farm might appreciate the heartbreak of trekking good shoe leather through the muck.

Distracted by my antics, Chuck almost grunted something sympathetic. At least he seemed less inclined to put the hammer to immediate use. "You need galoshes," he said to me, and pulled up his pant leg slightly to show how he protected his good shoes.

"An excellent idea," I said.

As if realizing the hammer didn't send a friendly signal, he turned and tossed it back into the shed. Then he walked us around the shed and back to our car. A better description might have been that he herded us away from whatever he had been working on.

Since Wini made no objection, I followed her lead and went meekly enough. I had questions but sensed this wasn't the time to ask them. Although I couldn't resist a peek through the shed door as we passed it. I spied several crates, much like those we'd seen at the warehouse near the river, only these were all nailed tightly shut.

"Still flying in your circus show?" Chuck said to Wini as we reached the roadster.

"Always and forever," said Wini. "I'm never giving up the sky."

"Lonnie with you these days?" he asked almost shyly.

"She's making the engines purr like kittens every day," said Wini. "She's always up to her elbows with adjustments on my darling or another of our planes."

Chuck huffed at that, almost a chuckle. "Lonnie does love to get her hands dirty," he said. "Give that woman a wrench and she's as happy as some dolls are to get flowers."

When we got back to the roadster, he also looked at the fuel gauge. "You probably have enough gas to make it to Innsmouth," he said to me, "but I've stashed some extra cans in the barn. I'll top you off so you won't have to worry."

As he walked away, I said to Wini, "Who is our gentleman farmer?"

"No farmer and no gentleman," said Wini. "Chuck drives for the O'Bannions. I wonder what he's doing so far out of town."

"Are you going to ask him?" I said, wondering who or what an O'Bannion was.

"Oh, no," said Wini. "You don't ask about O'Bannion business." The way she emphasized "don't ask" told me that an O'Bannion wasn't a local farmer. "But Chuck is a bit sweet on Lonnie, so he's always been friendly with me. As long as he thinks I'm not interfering with the O'Bannions' affairs."

"How does Lonnie feel about him?" I asked as I watched Chuck return with a can of gas.

Wini tugged her ear. "Don't know," she finally admitted. "Lonnie likes the cars he drives."

"Flashy?" I asked.

"Fast," said Wini. "All the better to outrun the law."

"Ah," I said. "That kind of business."

Wini nodded. "Always that kind."

Chuck made quick work of filling up my gas tank, then he gave us some pointers on how to get to Innsmouth, shaking his head over the map Wini showed him and penciling in a lane that wasn't clearly marked.

"These maps," he said. "Out of date as soon as they are printed. It's almost as if the roads move to fool the mapmakers. Better avoid this stretch if you ever come back out here." He ran a thick finger along the cliff road that curved toward the Purple Cat.

"Why that bit?" said Wini, not mentioning that we'd already driven it in a storm.

"The road crosses Malone territory along the cliff," said Chuck. "And funny things happen on Malone's bit of the coast."

"Really?" I exclaimed. "What type of things?" We also hadn't told Chuck about the boat that had dropped out of the sky.

Chuck screwed the cap tight on his gas can. "There's men who have been driving these back roads for years who get lost when they cross Malone land. Same for those who sail along the coast near here," he said. "They say it's the curse of the *Bolide*."

"What's a *Bolide*?" I asked, itching to know more about this particular curse. Curses seemed as common as crows in this part of New England.

Chuck backed away, obviously reluctant to talk, but Wini piped up, "Thanks for your help. Be sure you come to the show later this week. Lonnie will be performing her motorcycle tricks."

His eyes smiled at her invitation, even if the rest of his expression was hidden by his beard. "I'd like to see that," Chuck admitted. To me, he added, "The *Bolide* sailed out of Innsmouth and disappeared when it was returning loaded with enough whale oil and ambergris to make everyone rich. Some folks think Gulliver Malone conjured a devil to destroy that ship and ruin his rival, Captain Bulkington Hughes."

At the mention of Gulliver Malone, I asked, "Any relation to Nova Malone?"

Chuck grimaced at my question but nodded. "An ancestor of Nova's. Gulliver was about the only person in Innsmouth who hadn't invested in the *Bolide*'s shares, so folks suspected him first when the *Bolide* disappeared. Certainly the Hughes family accused him of sabotage."

"Ships go down all the time," I said. "Even the unsinkable *Titanic* sank."

"The *Bolide* disappeared as it was entering the harbor," said Chuck. "It didn't run into an iceberg or a storm. It vanished. Now boats, cars, and even planes have started to disappear when they cross Malone land or sail near their portion of the coast."

"Bad weather," guessed Wini. "Storms blow up suddenly along this coast."

"Or Nova Malone has found Gulliver's book," said Chuck.

"His what?" I said, but I was sure I knew the answer. Chuck was talking about the Deadly Grimoire.

"Everyone knows Gulliver Malone used a book to conjure up some new ways to sail from place to place," said Chuck. "He went searching for a way to corner the trade from east to west and back again. He challenged a number of captains to beat his sailing times, and they never could. Some said Gulliver always won, even when the wind and tide turned against him, because he had other ways of completing his race."

"So he was a good captain or good at cheating," I said. "Winning a race or two doesn't mean magic books were used." Although I had my doubts about the last statement.

"Maybe not," said Chuck, "but then Gulliver Malone turned against the Innsmouth investors when they picked Bulkington Hughes's *Bolide* over Gulliver's ship. That's when they say he spoke the deadly spells in his book and made his rival vanish."

"What happened to Malone?" I asked, but if Chuck's story was anything like Christine's, I knew what had happened to the sea captain. And that his spell book, or whatever it was, ended up back with a Boston bookseller named Sweets.

"His words rebounded against him," said Chuck. The big man looked deadly serious for a man telling ghost stories. With the sun now shining on all of us and no sign of storm clouds on the horizon, Wini unlatched the car top and folded it down behind the backseat. Chuck helped her fasten it back into place.

"They called it the *Bolide*'s revenge," Chuck continued, "as Malone's own ship vanished the next time it sailed out of the harbor."

"There's nothing to fear from dead men. That was all long ago," said Wini to Chuck.

"Except his spells keep working," said Chuck as he opened my car door like a gentleman. Wini shook her head and opened her own door. "At least, that's what they say in Innsmouth. That Gulliver Malone woke the old sea gods, and those gods are still angry about it. Hungry and angry."

I considered the smashed boat tossed onto the cliff road like a child's abandoned toy. How far did those sea gods roam, I wondered.

As we pulled away from the farm, I asked the more obvious and immediate question of my companion.

"So how mixed up are you in the O'Bannions' criminal business?" I said to Wini. "And does that business have anything to do with the fact that you fly with a Mauser in your plane?"

CHAPTER THIRTEEN

Wini grimaced. "I'm not involved in anything criminal," she said. "At least, not now. I run an honest show."

"But?" I said, because I could guess some of the shortcuts Wini might have made.

"Betsy Baxter, you look so sweet that someone might think the rain would melt you away like sugar," said Wini. "Will you refuse to finance the air derby if I tell you that I once worked with the O'Bannions?"

"Heaven knows I've made some interesting choices," I said to Wini, shifting gears as we headed down the road that Chuck had suggested. "You might say playing poker with a bunch of drunken executives when they didn't know you could count cards was... perhaps... slightly dishonest. On the other hand, you might also say telling a gal she could bet her garters if she wanted to was just inviting the lady to cheat those executives blind."

Other than the occasional puddle, there was no sign on the road that a storm had blown through. The further we went from Malone land, the drier the terrain became, and I wondered if the storm had blown out before it reached this section of the coast.

Wini laughed at my last statement and explained her relationship with Chuck as we drove along under the now calm blue skies. "I never played cards with the O'Bannions, but I flew a few messages for them back when I first started my own air business. Messages that the O'Bannions wouldn't trust to the telegraph or the mail. I never asked what was in those envelopes. That's one of the reasons I took the show west as soon as I'd raised enough cash. I didn't want to be anyone's errand girl."

"I thought you didn't like rumrunners," I said.

"I don't," said Wini promptly. Then she turned more thoughtful. "Though I like some of the people fine, like Chuck. Many end up in the business because there's not much opportunity to do anything else."

"Signs might not say 'No Irish Need Apply' anymore," I guessed, "but there's plenty willing to tell you that the Irish or the Swedes or the Mexicans cannot work in their business." I'd run into a fair number of barricades myself and had a great deal of sympathy for anyone who faced similar opposition in trying to do what they wanted to do. That's why I hired Marian and a number of other people on my crew. They deserved a chance.

Out of the corner of my eye, I saw Wini give a thoughtful nod. "Bootlegging is a way to get around that. Although I won't say they don't have their own peculiar prejudices, but I never was an actual member of any gang. I also never saw smugglers as heroes or villains. Most come to a sad end. According to stories that kids used to tell, there was a hanging judge in the area who used to order pirates and smugglers staked out. He said let the high tide drown them and save the expense of a hangman. Only, one time, when the tide went out, the smuggler's body was gone. Only chewed ropes and deep gouges on the stake were left. The story scared me silly as a kid. The idea of being tied down and having something chewing on you while the water filled your lungs."

"Gruesome," I agreed. "But I think the feds just send people to prison these days."

"I have no desire to spend any time behind bars. Not being able to fly, that would be the worst punishment ever," Wini said. "But it's so hard finding honest work. I couldn't get a regular contract with one of the larger flying outfits, not being a woman and with brown skin, too."

"But you're a daredevil," I said. "The Woman Without Fear. I thought you flew those stunts because such flying paid better than contracts." Yet I understood the lack of choices Wini faced. Success came at a price, but some people weren't even allowed to pay that price because of who they were.

"I fly stunts because, like Bessie Coleman, people will buy tickets to see me despite my ancestry," said Wini. "But when Bessie died earlier this year in that stupid accident, it started me thinking. I don't want to end up in a grave, forgotten in a year. I want to make history, make it so nobody can ever forget that a woman dared to fly higher, faster, and better than anyone before her. Eventually I want to beat the men in their own race."

"I'll still back your derby," I said. "And I'll back you against any man in the air. But only if you stay honest with me."

"That's a fair deal," said Wini. "I'd shake your hand, but you're driving."

I chuckled and switched gears so we could go faster. "What do you think your friend Chuck Fergus was doing on an old farm in the middle of nowhere in particular?" I said.

"Not growing potatoes, that's for sure," Wini answered promptly. "My guess is that it's a convenient stop for the distribution of booze."

"You saw the crates in the shed," I said.

"Of course," said Wini. "I'm not blind. Chuck wouldn't hustle us away so fast if there wasn't someone coming to pick those up. My guess is whoever owns the place turns a blind eye once or twice a month when the O'Bannion shipment comes through. Or the O'Bannions own that farm. There's plenty who would sell out for the kind of cash they can flash around."

"Truck, boat, or plane?" I mused on the possible conveyances for smuggled liquor.

"Could be any of the three. Could be all of the three," Wini speculated. "There's a flat enough field out back of the barn for landing. There's plenty of spots along the coast close to the road where a ship could offload. And there's all manner of backroads if you want to run a truck from Canada to here."

"Is it all coming from Canada?" I asked.

"From what I hear, that's true in these parts," said Wini. "The best comes from Europe, of course. Nobody has outlawed whiskey in Scotland."

"Or champagne in France," I said. "Or beer in Germany."

"Which is why we will never be dry in America," said Wini. "Even if we board up all our own breweries."

"Some of the breweries make decent ice cream these days," I said.

"Yes, but those pints will never outsell pints of suds," said Wini. "Hey, there's the sign for Innsmouth."

Chuck's directions had saved us some winding through the back roads and led us straight to the main road running through Innsmouth. As we drove through the outer edges of the town, the impression was of a place far less prosperous than Arkham. I saw many boarded-up houses, some looking as if the building was ready to collapse.

"Is it just me or does the town feel unfriendly?" I asked Wini as we drove down a quiet street leading to a slightly better neighborhood. At least there were storefronts without boarded-up windows or doors. But even those signs of commercial life seemed peculiarly lifeless. "Do you think anyone is out and about?"

"It's not lively," Wini answered as we passed one closed shop after another. No one was on the sidewalks either. "Perhaps it's nearly suppertime for most folks?"

"Seems early for that," I said. "The sun's still high."

"This town is mostly fishing folk," said Wini. "Up before dawn and down before dark."

We took another turn and suddenly overlooked the harbor. Below us, crowds of people were hurrying toward the weathered and dilapidated wharf. I immediately turned the car in their direction, but as the streets narrowed, it became increasingly difficult to navigate around the people suddenly appearing from everywhere. The crowd swelled around and past our car, and I caught shouts about help needed down at the pier. Of course, that made me want to see what was happening. Luckily, my companion was just as curious.

"Guess we found everyone," I said, parking the roadster.

"Follow the crowd?" said Wini as she got out. She looked as eager as I felt.

"Don't you love it when you can hear trouble brewing?" I said as I brushed the dried mud from my stockings and straightened my hat.

"Betsy Baxter, some people head in the opposite direction when they see a crowd forming," laughed Wini. "Will you pass up any opportunity to get into trouble?"

"Absolutely not," I said. "A Baxter is always an opportunist."

"I suspect that I am, too," said Wini. "Let's see what's going on."

We followed the crowd down to the shore. While I could not swear the whole town was there, it seemed likely. On the edge of the crowd, I spotted someone I did not expect.

"Look, there's Ezra Hughes," I said.

Wini turned away from me and pointed in the opposite direction. "And there's Nova Malone, riding in like the Queen of England."

She was quite right about the ride. Nova Malone stepped out of a stately Rolls-Royce Phantom, the 1925 model Henry had kept casually mentioning to me as a possible car. He was dying to look under the hood of the new replacement for the Silver Ghost. Nova Malone's chauffeur looked familiar, too.

"That's one of the men I almost shot in the alley last night," I said to Wini. "The excitable shortie. Albie."

The little man was now dressed in a neat suit and very circumspect dark tie. Albie barely came up to Nova Malone's shoulder, I noticed, but he held the door for her with much more grace than he'd used to wave his gun earlier. After she got out and had a few words with him, he retreated around the Rolls to watch the crowd.

"This is becoming interesting," I said.

Ezra Hughes and Nova Malone exchanged a pair of glares, which should have sizzled everyone in the crowd between them. Then they both turned away from each other.

"All we are missing is your reporter friend Darrell," said Wini.

"Nope, he's here, too," I said, pointing to a motorcycle with a sidecar rolling down the street. The man riding on top of the motorcycle was Darrell. After he parked, a tall figure unfolded himself from the sidecar. I swore when I saw Darrell's passenger. "What's Tom doing here? This will cause trouble." Luckily, neither Ezra nor Nova spotted Tom, and I moved to intercept the men before anyone saw them.

I ran around the edge of the crowd to the pair standing by the motorcycle. "You idiot," I said, smacking Tom on the arm.

"Ow! What did I do?" said Tom.

"Came to a town gathering with at least one person willing to shoot you for your grimoire," I said, tugging him around to point out Nova Malone and her chauffeur. "And one who wants to tar and feather you," I added, pointing out Ezra Hughes. "What are you doing here?"

"I caught a ride into town and took Wini's posters to the printer," said Tom. "Your friend offered to give me a lift back to the airfield after I placed a few ads with his newspaper. But there was a phone call just as we were leaving, and Darrell needed to make a detour for a story. I said I was happy to ride along as we didn't know when you or Wini would return from your riotous outing."

"My perfectly proper trip to the Purple Cat involved apple pie, a muddy road, and a slight detour through the local farmlands," I said, leaving out a few details about local bootlegging that I'd learned along the way. As for the boat that fell out of the sky onto the road, I wasn't going to mention that anywhere near Darrell's sharp ears. Not yet, as it was exactly the type of story he'd insist on investigating immediately, and he would possibly want to take my photo next to the boat. I wanted to answer a few questions of my own before I turned Darrell loose on that particular mystery.

Tom ducked his head and rubbed the back of his neck. "Where's your roadster parked?" he said, shifting his hand to shield his face from any possible watchers.

"Over there," I said, pointing to my car.

He reached into the sidecar and pulled out a leather helmet along with a pair of goggles. "Mind if I borrow these for the ride back with Miss Baxter?" Tom asked Darrell.

Craning his head to see what was happening at the other end of the wharf, Darrell waved a hand in consent as he adjusted the camera strapped around his neck. So intent was he on the possibility of a story, Darrell barely acknowledged me, other than a "Hello, Miss Baxter. Could you please move a bit? I need to get down there."

I stepped smartly aside so the reporter could weave his way through the crowd. Luckily, both Nova Malone and Ezra Hughes also seemed intent on whatever was happening out on the water. Neither glanced toward us.

Tom pulled the leather helmet over his head and adjusted the goggles across his eyes. The gear covered his face as effectively as a mask.

"Slump a bit," I said, worrying his height would make him more visible.

Tom hunched his shoulders forward and practically bent double as we slipped away through the crowd. When we got back to the roadster, he slid into the backseat.

"Better put the top up again," I said to Wini, who gave me an incredulous look. But she obliged and wrestled it back into place for the second time that day. At least we weren't moving while she did the maneuver this time.

"Now, stay put," I ordered Tom. "I want to see what's happening." Wini latched the roof into place, shook her head at both of us, and headed toward the pier.

"I don't suppose you have something to read," sighed the man in the goggles.

I slapped our road map into his hands. "Figure out the fastest way back to the airfield," I said.

Wini was already ahead of me, working her way through the crowd to the edge of the water. When I caught up with her, I saw what had so fascinated the entire town.

A tugboat was coming into the harbor. Rather than towing a ship behind it, the tug pulled a familiar seaplane in its wake. One wing was half gone, and the plane listed terribly to starboard, but the floats still held it above the water.

"More storm damage?" I said to Wini. I didn't know much about airplanes, but there was something not quite right about this one. It wasn't just the damage to the plane. Something about the broken wing made me uneasy. Also, the smell of rotting seaweed as we approached the pier was nearly overwhelming. I wondered how the rest of the crowd could stand it. Perhaps they were used to the briny smell of decay.

"Maybe it was the storm," said Wini, peering intently at the damaged plane, but she sounded unsure. "Look at that wing, though. Does that look like it just snapped off to you?"

"No," I said, taking a closer look as the plane was pulled level with the dock. The curved indentations in the skin of the wing seemed so very familiar, although I'd never seen any such marks so large before. Then I remembered the time a big German Shepherd grabbed a sandwich off an extra. The pair ended up in a tug-of-war over it. The tooth marks the dog left on the disputed lunch looked much like the indentations on the fragile wing of the airplane. "It appears something chewed on that wing."

"And bit it clean off," said Wini with a nod of agreement.

CHAPTER FOURTEEN

"So what would chew on an airplane?" I said as we drove away from Innsmouth.

"And take a bite that large?" said Wini.

"A whale?" speculated Tom.

"Whales are in the ocean. Planes are in the air," I responded. The road from Innsmouth to the airfield was smooth and without any of the challenges of our earlier route along the cliffs. I shifted the gears and picked up speed, enjoying once again the feeling of zooming to a destination. Innsmouth bothered me. Not the accident to the plane, although that was odd enough, but something about the entire place felt wrong. It wasn't that it was poor. I'd grown up poor. Boarded-up windows or unpainted front doors weren't uncommon in the small town where I was from. But Innsmouth felt different. Perhaps it had been the overwhelming smell of ocean debris that blew through the town – there was a depressed air about the place.

"But it was a seaplane," Tom yelled over the engine's roar from his place in the backseat, still arguing for his whale theory, "so presumably it was in the sea at some point."

"I still think it was the wind," Wini finally said after a few more miles of pointless speculation. "Something like a waterspout that tore the wing and hurled the plane off course."

We'd learned earlier that the plane ran a regular route, taking supplies to several isolated island communities before landing each evening in the Innsmouth harbor. A chief investor in the project appeared to be Nova Malone. Several of the townspeople referred to it as Miss Nova's plane.

The plane carried no passengers, but the two-man crew was missing.

"Did you see the name of the plane?" I asked Wini and Tom. When they shook their heads, I said, "It had *Gulliver* painted on the tail." The boat that had fallen from the air to land in front of us was named *Gulliver*, too. I salvaged a board with the letters "Gulliv" and put it in the trunk of my car, I told Tom.

"What? A boat fell out of the air?" he asked.

"Makes more sense now," I said. "The dinghy must have fallen from the plane before they crashed."

Wini shook her head. "I don't think they'd be carrying anything that heavy. If they had any type of lifeboat with them, it was probably canvas or rubber. Besides, didn't people say the seaplane disappeared earlier today? From what I heard, their flight plans went further east."

"Perhaps they were lost nearer to the cliffs," I speculated.

"Well, if that's true, then we should start our search along that stretch." As soon as a call went out for volunteers, Wini asked to join the search parties for the missing pilots. She intended to take up her own plane to see if she could spot the two men. Boats had been launched from the Innsmouth docks before we'd left. Chief among the organizers had been

Nova Malone, who promised to set up a round-the-clock meal service for the searchers as well as a reward for any information about the missing men.

"But didn't Chuck Fergus say that area was dangerous to fly over?" I said, remembering his warnings earlier that day.

"Wait!" said Tom from the backseat. "Who is Chuck Fergus?"

"A bootlegger friend of Wini's," I explained.

"Of course! I assume he's one of Nova Malone's men," Tom said.

"No," said Wini. "He's an O'Bannion man. Which makes it interesting that they are operating out here. If this is Malone's territory, I wonder if that's the issue with the missing planes."

"What do you mean?" I asked.

"Sabotage," said Wini. "If there's a battle over who is moving liquor through this area, then they might be sabotaging each other's transportation."

"Cars, ships, and planes?" I asked.

"It's possible," said Wini, with a rare frown. "I wouldn't have thought that the O'Bannions would stoop to such tricks."

"Where there's money," I said, "there's mischief." Look at all the trouble Max caused, running after the riches he decided he deserved, I thought. As I told Darrell earlier, missing vehicles could be as simple as a snatch and grab of each other's cargo. Such tactics in Chicago tended to leave a lot more dead bodies on the ground, rather than just men with missing memories, but perhaps New England bootleggers were politer.

"I hope that's all it is," said Wini. "Mischief and not malice or something more deadly."

"I was just thinking the same thing," I said. "I knew a few of the boys in the trade in Chicago. They wouldn't just hit someone politely over the head and leave them in a ditch somewhere."

"This," said Tom, "is why I much prefer reading about adventure and not living it. Will you go to the police?"

"With what?" I asked. "A boat that fell from the air? I've been calling the Arkham cops for nearly three years. Even three men disappearing couldn't move them to do much. Darrell might be more helpful if he's not off pursuing some other story."

"I'd rather not involve your reporter friend," said Wini.

I could understand her reluctance. If she had past dealings with one of the bootlegging gangs in the area, the resulting press would do her reputation no good and might impact the circus. Knowing the type of muck the press was often inclined to rake and the harm they had done to friends of mine, I decided Wini was right and it was best to stay quiet for now. If, or when, we needed Darrell, I was certain of his sense of fair play. The trick would be to give the story to Darrell before anyone else started writing about Arkham's latest peculiarities.

"So what next?" asked Tom.

"I will take my plane along the cliff and a few miles out to sea," Wini said. "We might spot more wreckage or even the crew. Although why they would have left the plane when it was still floating, I can't figure out. It would have been safer to stay with the seaplane. They would have been found quickly then." She planned to take her own plane aloft when we reached the airfield to search as long as daylight held. Night searches were nearly impossible, she said, but luckily it was late summer. Sunset was still hours away.

"Perhaps the whale chased them off?" said Tom. He'd pulled off the goggles and helmet as soon as we'd left Innsmouth, but the headgear had left his hair standing up every which way. As he leaned over the seat to join our debate, I couldn't repress a smile at his wildly crumpled hair.

"I still doubt it was a whale," I said. "I've never even heard of them attacking ships. Except in the movies or books."

"Oh, a whale will turn on a whaler," said Wini. "There's more than one story of that happening."

"The *Essex*," said Tom, "was sunk by a giant whale in 1820. That was what inspired Melville to write *Moby Dick* according to some."

"How do you know these things?" I asked him.

"Abandoned in a bookstore as a baby," replied Tom. "I teethed on the *Encyclopedia Britannica*, according to my uncle."

"What did your mother think of that?" I said.

Tom shrugged. "She washed her hands of the family by the time I reached school age. She wanted a career in art and left for Europe. She currently enjoys running a gallery in Lucerne. She once said it was much more serene to deal with cubists than booksellers."

"And your father?" I asked.

"Oh, he's still in Boston," said Tom, "and drops into the bookstore on a regular basis. He's been a book scout for years and prefers that to a settled life."

"A book scout? Anything like a Boy Scout?" I said.

"Not nearly so prepared," said Tom. "He travels around New England, visiting estate sales and auctions and so on.

Book scouts sort through the bins of other bookstores looking for treasures."

"So you survive by selling books to each other? Bookseller to book scout to bookseller?" I said.

"Correct," said Tom.

"But how can you make any money doing that?" I said.

"Very astute," replied Tom. "You see the basic flaw."

"You are just passing the money back and forth," I said.

"Exactly, but we always have something to read." Tom sounded very much like a Harvard professor pleased with a bright pupil. "However, that's why the grimoire was so valuable. It helped us acquire cash from new buyers once every decade or so."

"About that peculiar book of yours," I said. "We need to talk. It seems the Deadly Grimoire has quite the reputation all along this coast. And I'm not sure that dealing in curses is the best way to make a living."

"We do not sell curses," said Tom emphatically. "We sell books. What the buyers do with those books is none of our business."

"I am not sure it works that way," I said, but Tom was right. What people did was up to them. Hollywood had been accused of corrupting the morals of the country for years, but I wasn't convinced someone switched from upright virtue to jazz and gin overnight just because they watched Clara Bow. The owners of the Deadly Grimoire could put their purchase on a shelf and admire it as a work of art.

"It is complicated," I reluctantly admitted.

Tom straightened up in his seat. "Oh, look, we're here. There's the airfield."

Wini snorted as I gave him a hard look over my shoulder. Obviously, this wasn't a debate he was prepared to have. And, since I wasn't sure of the answer I wanted, at least not then, I let him off the hook.

Once we parked, Wini jumped out of the car and raced across the field to organize her search flight.

"Won't you go with her?" Tom asked.

I shook my head. "She'll take up one of her crew who is experienced at spotting. I'd be dead weight."

Tom unfolded himself from the backseat. "Well, I have a cot here," he said. "And a few more calls to make. If someone did steal the grimoire to sell it, there's only a few dealers who would take it. I need to let them know the grimoire is on the loose again."

"Would they buy it from a thief?" I said.

"If I ask them to. They will try to grab it back, but if they can't do that, they'll pay for it and call us," said Tom. "It's not the first time we've recovered the grimoire from another bookseller."

"You don't think they'd try to sell it to one of their other customers?" I said.

Tom shook his head. "Most of the dealers who know the grimoire also know about the curse."

"And those who don't?"

"Wake up to the smoking ruins of their store," Tom said nonchalantly. "Sometimes it's not as drastic as that," he added upon seeing my expression. "But whatever happens, it generally persuades the bookseller that it is better to send the grimoire back to Sweets and Nephew. There's a bookplate with instructions on what to do inside the front cover."

"So, you do acknowledge there is some danger in handling the grimoire," I said.

Tom sighed. "We're not completely heartless. Over the generations, we've mollified our doubts with the knowledge that good people are rarely harmed by the grimoire. The types who want it, let's just say they are not the most virtuous of souls."

Which did leave me wondering about Ezra Hughes and his fascination with the book. Nova Malone, I understood. Like her ancestor, she thought it might lead to more riches and, judging by her jewelry, she was a lady who believed in getting rich. But why would the good doctor want it? And was he indeed a good doctor? My worries about Jim being in his care surfaced again. I resolved to go see my friend as soon as possible.

I walked over to the airfield's offices with Tom. We watched Wini's crew push her plane into position. She jumped into the cockpit with her regular co-pilot, Bill, in the second seat. With a wave and a roar, they were airborne and headed to the coast to search for the missing pilots.

After they left, Tom and I followed Lonnie back into the barn to watch her work on Bill's plane. I told her how I wanted to learn how to fly.

"Anyone can learn to fly an airplane in a month or two. It takes real talent to learn how to fix an engine so the plane flies," Lonnie said, grabbing a wrench from the ground. "At least that's what I tell Wini."

"Is it really so hard?" Tom asked.

"Not if you understand the theory of the internal-combustion engine, carburetion, compression, ignition, and explosion," she chuckled at our expressions. "I trot out all the big words when I want to impress someone." Then she shrugged. "Just know absolutely nothing is easier when the engine works and nothing is more of a devil when it breaks," she said. "I've worked on lots of engines. They all have their quirks, but once you get into the guts of one, you'll probably understand the others." She looked a little doubtfully at Tom. "If you understand engines, I mean. It helps if you've worked on automobiles."

He cheerfully acknowledged that he did not even drive.

Lonnie shook her head at that. "Not a career for you," she said.

"Probably not," said Tom, looking at her greasy hands.

"It is more than just keeping the engine tuned," Lonnie said. "There's the rigging checks and truing up the wires and struts. I overhaul every plane after a show to tighten sagging wires as well as looking for any other problems."

She ran her hands along the wing to demonstrate. "A rip in the stitching or any tear in the fabric could be a disaster. Not long ago, a wing's cover ripped off when the pilot went past one hundred and fifty feet. The fall killed him."

She patted the wing with satisfaction. "My planes won't wash out. I keep Wini and the rest of the pilots safe. If you are a mechanic, you need pride in your work. You're responsible for people's lives."

It was fascinating to hear her views, and the more she talked, the more I began to think about a new film, one that featured a woman mechanic who saved the day. Lonnie laughed when I ventured the idea. "People will never believe that mechanics are heroes," she said. "Not the way that the pilots are!"

"Then we will need to show them that," I said. Marian would love to make a movie about female mechanics, and it was time people like Lonnie had their stories told.

"Well, I should make my calls," said Tom.

I left Tom with promises to return the next day to drive him around the countryside and help him place Wini's posters in the nearby towns. I also needed to speak to Wini about the tricks I wanted to do for the show. Despite my earlier fall, I was sure I could climb out on the wing and wave to the crowd without Charlie's harness. I also had ideas about borrowing Lonnie's motorcycle and making a jump to the plane. Or perhaps Lonnie could drive the motorcycle and I could ride behind her. That might work, I thought, as I walked back to the roadster. It was sure to be a crowd pleaser. All I had to do was convince Lonnie and Wini to let me try it. There was nothing like devising a few death-defying stunts to take a gal's mind off her other worries. By the time I started the car to head back to Arkham, I felt much better.

I might not have the answers yet about Max's disappearance, but I had some ideas now on where to look for those answers.

After an unusually quiet night for Arkham, I breakfasted early and requested my car from the hotel's garage. I checked our much folded and refolded map to locate Bluff Mansion.

Once again, I was on the twisting cliff road near Innsmouth, although the turns took me further north than the previous day's journey to the Purple Cat. But like the countryside near Nova Malone's restaurant, the sea winds had twisted the trees and hollowed the hills. Even in the late summer sunshine, the land felt bleak. Or perhaps that was my own emotions as I raced toward a rendezvous I both wanted and dreaded.

Jim had disappeared more than three years ago at the same time Max was lost, and his return was nothing short of a miracle. But why Jim? Why not Max? Those were the questions buzzing in my mind as I followed the road away from the sea and along a high stone wall. The way people kept disappearing around this area and then reappearing in other spots was all part of a larger pattern, I was convinced. I was also certain Hughes and possibly Nova Malone knew more than I'd learned so far. Their entangled family histories suggested that.

Eventually, I came to a pair of handsome wrought iron gates, propped open for the day with a discreet brass plaque that proclaimed I had found Bluff Mansion.

The driveway leading to the sanitarium was smooth and white, made from crushed seashells. With a perfectly centered door flanked by white pillars that stretched past the second-floor windows to the roof, the sanitarium looked like a Hollywood version of a Roman temple. I could see how this place would impress its potential patients with its sense of importance.

I circled a bubbling fountain before drawing up to the grand entrance of the Palladian style house. Opening my handbag, I took a quick check of the contents. My silver-plated pistol was snugly secured in the special pocket designed for it. Unusually nervous, I drew out my compact and checked myself in its tiny mirror. While the prohibitions against ladies painting their faces had faded over the years, this was New England. I didn't want to look too much like a Hollywood actress. Not for this visit. I had represented myself as a close relation of the patient, rather than the studio mogul who was paying for his care.

Satisfied my powder was subtle enough to pass for natural and my dark green hat was somber enough for a visiting relative, I walked up the steps of the mansion and rang the bell.

The door was answered by a neatly dressed woman with dark hair secured in an old-fashioned chignon.

"How can I help you?" she asked.

"My name is Betsy Baxter," I said. "I am here to see my cousin Jim Janson."

"Ah, yes," the woman said, clicking away from me in heels that made a distinct rat-a-tat on the polished marble floor. I followed her inside. "I have you down in the book as visiting today." She settled herself behind a desk set neatly to the side of the door. The whole arrangement, while something like a hotel's desk for checking guests in and out – complete with a wall of cubby holes for mail and keys – was positioned in such a way as to not be clearly visible from the door. Instead, the first impression, most certainly deliberate, was that I had stepped into a mansion of the Gilded Age, complete with grand staircase, impressive paintings in heavy gold frames lining that staircase, and, I glanced up to check, a crystal chandelier that would rival any found in New York or Hollywood. Not exactly a New England saltbox, that was for sure.

At some point, the Hughes family possessed considerable wealth to judge by the marble stairs and mahogany banisters twisting away to higher floors. Looking around the place, it was obvious that an older, more palatial mansion had been converted into a facility that met the needs and aesthetic expectations of a wealthy clientele. I wondered how the family money had been lost and when the need to turn the place from a home to a sanitarium had occurred.

I turned away from the center and followed the woman to the reception desk.

"If you could just sign here," she said, extending a fountain pen toward me and pointing to a leather-bound ledger with cream-colored pages. Like the desk, it bore a resemblance to the type of guestbook you would find in the fancier hotels. I signed my name, the date, and the time as indicated by the signatures above mine.

"Thank you," she said, closing the book on her desk. "I'll call for one of the nurses to escort you to the patient. Would you like to speak to Dr Hughes today? He's available in an hour for a brief consultation."

I pondered the wisdom of another encounter with Dr Hughes so soon after meeting him at the hospital. Oh well, why not, I thought. "In for a penny, in for a pound," I said out loud to the puzzlement of the woman waiting for my answer.

"I'd be delighted to speak to Dr Hughes about poor dear Cousin Jim," I continued. "But can I see Jim now? His mother worries so, and I'd like to give her as complete a description as possible."

"Yes, of course," said the woman at the desk, picking up a phone and speaking a few words into it. In the distance I heard the clank of an elevator door and then the light footsteps of someone wearing rubber-soled shoes. "Ah, Nurse Roberts, can you escort our guest?" said the woman at the desk to the nurse that entered through a side door.

"Certainly," said Nurse Roberts, waving me toward the door she had just come through. "Your cousin is in the conservatory today. We have all the windows open. It's such lovely weather, and our guests so enjoy the view."

"Our guests" seemed to be the name for both visitors and patients, perhaps to give the place a more refined air, I decided as I followed Nurse Roberts down the corridor. Certainly, there was no hospital smell nor the sterile feeling of an institution as we walked along a hallway carpeted in a fine blue wool runner. Other than her uniform, Nurse Roberts might be taken for a superior sort of maid or even a maiden aunt, directing guests to where they could take a light refreshment and a little entertainment before venturing home again.

The size of the sanitarium's bills made much more sense after seeing all this. Hughes obviously catered to the expectations of very rich clientele. I was glad for Jim's sake, for it was as civilized and comfortable as possible.

"Ah, here he is," said Nurse Roberts, after we had entered a very pretty glass room filled with potted palm trees and delightfully vivid flowers spilling out of porcelain urns. All the windows along one side were cranked open, and a light breeze carrying the scent of recently cut grass played through the room. Glancing out those windows, I realized the gardens were surrounded by high hedges that blocked any view of the sea. Instead, we could have been gazing upon a tranquil garden set anywhere in the world. The flowers outside were a mix of roses with the blowsy open flowers of late summer.

"Wake up, Mr Janson. Your cousin is here," Nurse Roberts said.

Jim was seated in a white wicker chair with his feet up on a stool. In keeping with the rest of the "guests" I saw lounging in similar chairs, he was neatly dressed in what appeared to be casual clothes. No patient's pajamas and robes here. Rather, he wore simple flannel trousers, a blue shirt, and a cotton sweater draped over his shoulders. Only his footwear betrayed him as a patient rather than a visitor, as he wore soft leather slippers on his feet. All of which I'm sure had been billed to the studio, as he'd been found in rags earlier that year.

But I didn't care about the cost. I wanted Jim to recover, and the money was well spent if that was the result. Of all the things that frightened me, and I was no Nova Malone immune to fear, the idea of losing years of memories scared me the most. I wanted to remember every minute of every adventure. I wanted that for Jim, too.

The luxury of the place reassured me. At least Jim looked as if he was being well cared for. Watching Nurse Roberts, I decided she had kind eyes.

Nurse Roberts shook Jim's shoulder very gently. He stirred under her hand and blinked sleepy eyes at me. "Oh," he said, sitting a little straighter in his chair, "is it time for lunch?"

"No, Mr Janson," said Nurse Roberts. "You have a visitor. Your cousin Betsy."

"Hello, Jim," I said to the man I'd last seen being engulfed by smoke in a burning house three years ago. I drew a breath to calm myself. I was finally there. I could finally ask about Max. But first I said, "How are you?"

CHAPTER FIFTEEN

It took Jim a minute or so to come fully awake. Or as awake as he appeared to be capable of. Throughout our conversation that day, I felt that Jim was looking beyond me into some dream that never quite finished for him.

"Hello, Betsy," he said after I repeated my name again for him. "How's tricks?"

"Life's good," I told him. "Living in a big house these days with parrots and an English butler to look after everything. I even have a conservatory but not as pretty as this one."

Jim nodded at me with another fleeting smile, but his eyes slid to the open windows, looking at something I could not see. After disappearing on the day of the fire, he stayed lost for years until someone found him wandering the road near a town called Kingsport. According to the hospital reports I had read over and over again, he'd been completely incapable of speech during his short hospital stay. Also of sleeping without the aid of considerable narcotics. Several doctors expressed worry about the amount of sleeping drugs it took to stop Jim from climbing out of his bed and wandering the hallways, always in search of a mirror or reflective surface.

When Jim found a mirror during his nighttime stroll, he would stand in front of it, silently regarding his reflection until fetched back to bed.

Ghost catchers, that's what my mother called mirrors, and she always veiled them when there had been a death in the family. Dangerous was what my friend Jeany believed, and she had banned all mirrors from her home after a stay in Arkham.

But what actress can live without mirrors? I spent far too much of my life looking at myself, first as a dancer and then as an actress in the movies. Mirrors were a necessary part of the trade. A mirror in the studio showed you how your body moved or how your face looked to the audience. I needed mirrors, but I never feared the reflections I saw.

Jim's distraction that day was a frustration. I wanted to pelt him with questions, but at the same time I didn't want to frighten him. From every report I had read, he became most agitated when pressed about the missing years and where he had been. I needed a way to lead the conversation around to the topic without too much fuss.

"How about a stroll?" I asked Jim, glancing at the nearby Nurse Roberts. She nodded encouragingly at me.

"I suppose," replied Jim with no great enthusiasm. He'd been a bit player when we'd first started at the studio. He was also a man without any ambition as far as I could remember. Jim's greatest talent, said one director in my hearing, was his ability to stand or sit perfectly still for hours. Apparently that predilection had not vanished, no matter what had happened to him in the past few years.

With some gentle nudging by Nurse Roberts and

myself, Jim stood and wandered toward the door of the conservatory. He even offered me his arm as we walked into the rose garden.

"He's been quite the gentleman during his stay with us," remarked Nurse Roberts as she followed us through the garden.

"His mother will be so glad to hear that," I said over my shoulder. As far as I knew, Jim had no relations. At least, the detective I hired never found any after Jim made his reappearance. Still, it would have been awkward to tell Nurse Roberts that and more awkward still would be to explain why I was murmuring questions to Jim about his friend Max.

Not that Jim had much to say. He'd never been a talker, not like Max, who could talk for hours about his plans and dreams for the future. But I didn't remember Jim as being this silent. Jim responded, although very slowly, to any direct question I asked, but the answers he gave were vague in the extreme.

"So, Jim," I said, deciding at last to force the issue, "where exactly have you been?"

Jim looked down at me with a puzzled frown. "Not here," he said as we paced slowly on the gravel path that wove round and round the rosebushes. The crunching of the stones under our feet was almost louder than Jim's reply.

"No, not here," I agreed. "You only came here a few months ago. But where have you been?"

Jim heaved a great sigh as we passed a fishpond set in the center of the rose garden. He paused to peer down into the murky water, seemingly fascinated by our wavering reflections. Overhung with rose bushes, a few petals and dead leaves floated on top of the water. If there were any fish in this artificial pond, they were in hiding.

"I don't think it is very nice," Jim said to me after several minutes of silent contemplation.

"The pool?" I said, gesturing at it. The brackish water reflected the clouds chasing across the sky. Peering into it, the ornamental pool seemed fathoms deep with twists of seaweed impossibly long and entangled filling its depths. I blinked again and it was only a small fishpond in the center of an overgrown garden, desperately in need of a good gardener with a rake.

Jim sighed again, perhaps at the futility of trying to explain his thoughts, and shook his head. "Where I was," he said. "It always smelled wet. Like the ocean."

We were not far from the sea. In fact, the cliff was on the other side of a tall and neatly trimmed evergreen hedge. Even in this sheltered rose garden, I could smell a faint whiff of brine and seaweed. Very faint but clear, I could hear the boom of the surf as the ocean met the rocks at the base of the cliff hidden by the hedges. But how had Jim gotten himself from a burning house on French Hill to someplace near the ocean?

"Do you remember the fire?" I said. Jim screwed up his face as if he'd bit into something sour but remained silent. "How did you escape the fire?" I pleaded, hoping Jim's answer would give me a clue to Max's own possible route to safety. But that apparently was the wrong question.

Rather than answering me, Jim took off in long strides, startling both Nurse Roberts and myself with his sudden quick action. We followed him as he headed back into the conservatory. Jim continued without pause through the room and up a narrow staircase. This one lacked ornate steps or mahogany banisters, probably once built for the servants needed to keep such a large house running smoothly.

"Where is he going?" I said to the nurse, annoyed with myself for setting Jim off. I knew he didn't like being questioned, and I scolded myself as we loped after him. With his long legs, Jim took a considerable lead.

"I think," the nurse panted a little as we crested another flight of stairs, "he's returning to his room. He will do that sometimes when he's agitated."

Sure enough, Jim turned into a room near the top of the stairs. He walked across the room to yank the curtains closed and then lay down on the bed. Nurse Roberts fussed forward and removed his slippers before he could get any marks on the clean white coverlet. She pulled a light blanket from the cedar chest at the end of the bed and spread it across his legs.

"I'll fetch his tea," she said to me. "He will feel much better after a cup and short nap. Won't you, Mr Janson?" she said to Jim.

Jim nodded into his pillow.

"Can I stay with him?" I asked her. "Until you come back? Then I'll talk to Dr Hughes."

Nurse Roberts looked a little uncertain but apparently came to the conclusion that since we were in the twentieth century, perhaps I could sit with my cousin in what amounted to his bedroom. "But keep the door wide open," she said to me as she bustled out.

"Of course," I said. I pulled a straight-backed wooden chair closer to the bed and repeated the question I had asked earlier in the rose garden. I knew it bothered him, and I pledged silently to make it up to him in the future. But I had to know. "How did you escape the fire, Jim?"

He kept his eyes closed and his face turned into the pillow away from me. But after a few minutes, he whispered an answer.

"Please, Jim," I said as gently as I could. "I cannot hear you."

I hated pestering Jim so. What if my questions undid all the good the doctor had accomplished over the past few months, I worried. But what if Max was lost somewhere "not nice" and needed to be rescued? How else could I find him?

Then Jim raised himself up on one elbow and looked directly at me. "I walked through the mirror," he said with absolute conviction and clarity. I was so astonished by this statement I couldn't form another question.

No sooner had Jim spoken, Nurse Roberts returned. She carried a tray with a steaming cup of tea that appeared distinctly green and smelled quite unlike any tea I had ever encountered. I would have called it a sulfuric odor, not unlike rotten eggs or, more probably, boiled seaweed. It also unpleasantly reminded me of the way Innsmouth had smelled. And the scent rising from the boxes at the warehouse by the river.

With professional efficiency, the nurse swung a small table next to the bed and placed the tray on it. She then helped Jim to sit up in bed and supported his trembling hand as he sipped the tea. Neither of them seemed bothered by the smell, so I held my breath and didn't say anything.

"There now," said Nurse Roberts quite kindly as Jim slid back down in the bed. "Have a nice nap. We'll see you downstairs for supper this evening. Maybe we can even listen to the radio for a bit."

Jim murmured some agreement.

"We have a new radio," Nurse Roberts said to me with a bright smile. She also nearly pushed me from the room. I guessed visiting relations were not supposed to see the patients slide backward on their climb to socially acceptable behavior. "We hear lectures broadcast almost nightly from the university. There's dance music on Saturday nights sponsored by the Purple Cat. Our guests enjoy the entertainment."

I resisted her efforts to remove me from the room. I needed to know Jim was all right. As he drifted off to sleep, I asked Nurse Roberts if he was still being dosed with sleeping drugs.

"Oh, no," she said, sounding a little shocked. "Dr Hughes tries to avoid such medications whenever possible. Mr Janson has been sleeping quite naturally for several weeks."

"Well, that's good," I said. I reached over to touch Jim's hand, giving it a light squeeze in the way that I used to wake my grandmother when she dozed off in the evening.

"I have to go," I said to Jim. "But don't worry. Everything will be fine. I'll take you home to California as soon as I can."

Jim stirred and turned his head toward me. "Oh, Betsy," he said without fully opening his eyes. "Are you going to help Max? Some nights his shouting is so loud in the mirror."

CHAPTER SIXTEEN

Of course, with Nurse Roberts standing over me and Jim snoring quite contentedly into his pillow, I could not do what I most wanted to do upon hearing Jim's extraordinary statement about Max shouting in the mirror. I refrained from shaking Jim awake and peppering him with more questions. Instead, I followed Nurse Roberts out of the room and down the main staircase, this time to the entry hall.

"We do have an elevator," Nurse Roberts informed me. "The doctor made that improvement recently for our frailer guests. It's a blessing when we need to take trays up to the patients, but I thought you might prefer this way." By that pronouncement on my preferences, I took her to mean she wanted to show off the fine paintings and other small luxuries I had glimpsed when I first arrived. Again, I was reminded that a private sanitarium like this relied on the contentment of the paying relatives, if not the patients, to make ends meet.

As we came to the bottom of the stairs, I saw Dr Hughes standing at the reception desk, chatting with the woman there. He wore a very fine suit and looked quite the dapper doctor in it. He turned toward me with a smile that dimmed as I thrust out my hand.

"Betsy Baxter," I said with no explanation, shaking the doctor's hand with as much enthusiasm as I could manage.

His eyes narrowed. Ezra Hughes said in an almost accusatory tone of voice, "Didn't we meet at the hospital yesterday?"

Oh, bother, I thought, he does remember me. But I flashed my largest smile and pumped his hand up and down like a Fuller Brush salesman, or rather saleswoman, and said, "Why, yes, we did meet yesterday when I was visiting my friend the professor. Today I'm visiting my cousin Jim at your lovely institution."

"You seem to make a great many patient visits," said Hughes with a perplexed look. He gave a definite tug to retrieve his hand. I smiled like a cherub, radiating innocent goodwill with all my acting skills.

"I do try to make the rounds," I said. "At least in terms of spreading a little comfort and cheer to my friends and relations. By the way, I am impressed with the improvement in Cousin Jim." No need to mention that I agitated him into hiding under his pillow not ten minutes past, I decided. "He seems like a new man."

Hughes preened a little at the praise. "I find the patients respond most satisfactorily to rest, well-ordered days, and a diet of my own devising," he said. "We try to rebalance the sentient humors while honoring the connectivity of the human psyche to the primordial substance that grants us all life."

Call me a Scopes monkey, but I couldn't decide if the

doctor was advocating for evolution or arguing against it as he lectured me about his theories. But his lecture seemed to contain many references to returning to the ocean that spawned us.

"Of course," he said to me, "not everything is visible to the naked eye. At times we must look beyond what we normally see."

"I am certain you are right," I said, resisting the urge to look about for the nearest exit. Hughes might be a bore, at least when it came to discussing seaweed, but he knew something about disappearances and their peculiar effects on people's minds. I was convinced of that.

The doctor fished a piece of cloudy glass out of his pocket. "The evidence of the transcendent supremacy of the ocean can clearly be seen when examined through such relics," he said. "As a boy, I scoured the shore for these fragments of greater windows and mirrors that revealed the psychic currents. Observe it yourself."

I had no wish to handle the beach glass he thrust into my hand. It felt unnaturally icy to the touch but also slimy as if covered with some mucus. There was something about the feel that reminded me of oysters and how they felt unpleasantly cold as they slid down the throat. Max had adored eating raw oysters. I found them foul.

Still, I raised the piece of glass to my eye as Hughes instructed. Through it, I saw a blurred and distorted version of the room. "I don't see," I started to say, but then the view shifted as I moved away from the window and into the shadows cast by the long drapes. Suddenly the room seemed infused with a purple light, and the shadows became extended tentacles or strands of seaweed, swaying as if observed underwater. It was a repellent view of the world.

I didn't want to look, but like a horrible dream, it seemed to draw me into its distorted realm. I was reminded of the terrible movie we were making that summer in Arkham when Sydney and Max whispered in corners of the house as the rest of us suffered from nightmares. Nightmares like this, of places we should never see.

"Uh, fascinating," I said as I thrust the piece of glass back at Hughes. I stopped myself from pulling a handkerchief from my purse and wiping my hands. But just barely.

Hughes beamed as he took the peculiar piece of glass from me and dropped it into his suit pocket. "Once," he said, "I believe the world was covered in water. This echoes through all the flood myths from Deucalion and Pyrrha in Greek mythology, Bergelmir in Norse mythology, and, of course, the tale of Noah. All of these speak to the power that comes from the ocean to change the world."

As he continued to explain his reasoning to me, despite my obvious backward walk away from him and toward the door, phrases like "divine oceanic currents" and "wisdom of the deeps" threaded through his discussion of his practice. As much as I wanted to learn more about the grimoire, I wanted to be as far away from that piece of glass as possible. My urge to run nearly overwhelmed my manners. However, the doctor seemed used to people edging away from him when in full explanation mode, as he paced along with me.

I smiled and nodded, seemingly the only contribution

Hughes wanted, until I reached the door. With the handle firmly grasped in my hand and a quick exit assured, I took advantage of a pause, as Hughes drew breath, to squeeze in a question of my own.

"So, does Jim still sleepwalk looking for mirrors?" I said.

Hughes almost continued his speech over my question, but the word "mirror" caused him to hesitate.

"Mirrors," he began. Then he stopped and frowned at me. "Mirrors have nothing to do with my treatment," he said with an emphasis on the nothing. "Reflections deceive and often mislead the viewer. Windows, certain windows, can increase our understanding of past events and even give us a view into the world under water."

I remembered Hughes discussing this at the hospital in response to a story Wini told. But as I had already received a bucketful of his views, I refrained from inquiring more about windows. Instead, I asked again about mirrors and more specifically: "Do you think Jim hears people in the mirror?"

"My dear young lady," said Hughes, in that amused tone of voice certain men use to deflect the questions of persistent women, "mirrors cannot convey sound."

That, of course, was a scientific fact. But if Hughes thought such a tone or retort could stop me, then he didn't know Betsy Baxter.

"Still, we worry about Jim," I said, leaving vague how many people were inquiring about Jim's health. "Is he talking about Max being trapped in a mirror to anyone?"

Perhaps Hughes inferred that Jim had plenty of protectors, or at least family members, who might stop paying the bills if "Cousin Betsy" didn't have her questions answered. At least this time, he directly responded to the question I was asking about Max.

"The patient spoke once or twice about a nightmare. Perhaps there was some mention of mirrors, and while some counsel removing mirrors to avoid encouraging dysmorphic tendencies, we find that such a practice might create greater harm," said Hughes, now very much the polite and civilized man of medicine responding in ten-dollar words to a worried relative. "Those dreams seem to have faded as his sleep patterns returned to normal. I am certain a few more weeks in our care will find him fully restored."

That didn't answer my question, not completely, but I wasn't exactly sure what I needed to know. As for leaving Jim in care somewhere, I had no disagreement there. I was happy to pay anyone's large bills if it meant Jim was restored to health. And, from everything I had seen, Jim was indeed much better. If he continued to improve, then this was the best place for him, despite my continued uneasiness about the strange shard of glass in the doctor's pocket.

As I dithered, the doorknob was wrenched from my hand and a short man pushed his way inside. I recognized the new guest instantly as Albie, Nova Malone's driver and the gentleman who menaced Tom and me in the alley. Anxious to avoid exclamations and explanations of our past encounter, I twisted away from the door and wished my modest green hat had a veil. Turning my back to the doctor, I pretended a sudden and intense interest in one of the family portraits decorating the entry.

"Could this possibly be a Whistler?" I said, while facing

a painting portraying a grim-faced lady dressed all in dismal brown. I found myself talking to the air.

The doctor and his receptionist were intent on the story being gasped out by their most recent visitor.

"Slow down, Albie," said the doctor. "Tell me exactly what happened."

"We found the pilot and his partner," said Albie. "They are just like the others. Sleepwalking down the cliff road. One of them even tried to take a nap right there on the road. Draped in seaweed like all the rest."

I wondered what the seaweed smelled like. Unpleasantly dead like all the other aquatic vegetation encountered in the past two days? Remembering the scene glimpsed through the shard of glass and the cold slimy feel of the piece in my hand, I was beginning to suspect that this seaweed was not entirely natural.

"Have they been taken to the hospital?" Hughes asked.

"Not more than an hour ago," said Albie. "I knew you'd be grateful to hear the news as soon as possible."

"We do have a phone," said Hughes.

Albie had a hand held out, and I realized why he had come in person with his story. Hughes obviously caught the hint, too. With a grumble, the doctor pulled his wallet from his breast pocket and passed a few dollars to Albie.

Albie nodded his thanks as the bucks disappeared into his coat pocket. "I better be going," he said. "Miss Nova will expect me to drive her to the hospital later this evening."

The little man left as quickly as he had come without a single glance in my direction. He did not seem to make the connection with the gal who had waved a pistol at him a few days earlier. There was something to be said for owning multiple ensembles when roaming the countryside investigating mysteries. At least I was wearing a different coat and hat for this encounter.

As soon as Albie's car could be heard speeding away, I made my own goodbyes to Hughes and his receptionist, assuring them I would tell the "family" that Jim was well cared for. At the same time, I resolved to cable Farnsworth and set in motion our plans to move Jim to California for his final recovery. The nurses seemed kind and the place well run, but Hughes disturbed me in a way I could not quite fathom.

As I drove toward the airfield to collect Tom, I mulled over all I had learned. Nothing Jim said truly gave me a clue to where Max was. But as Jim improved, perhaps he could tell me more. As for the reappearance of the crew of the missing airplane, I wondered how Nova Malone would react to the knowledge that Ezra Hughes had a spy in her camp. Poorly, I suspected, which argued that the doctor at least had courage. I wouldn't have wanted to make the lady cross, and even Darrell had warned against angering Nova Malone.

But why was Hughes spying on Nova Malone? What was his interest in the missing pilots? Simply more patients for his sanitarium? Or something more? That I couldn't answer. "Arkham," I muttered to myself. "It's as frustrating as always. And Innsmouth is no better."

When I arrived at the airfield, I parked the roadster next to a mail truck. Glancing around, I spotted Wini sitting on a bench outside the small hut that served as the field's office. Seated next to Wini was a good-looking Black woman dressed in a postwoman's uniform.

"Betsy," yelled Wini when she spotted me. "Come meet my friend Stella."

I walked over to the pair. After shaking hands with Stella, I said to Wini, "I heard they found the missing crew of the seaplane."

Wini nodded. "Stella and I were talking about it," she said. "She's the one who found them."

"I was out on the cliff road," said Stella. "The regular postman was sick and the Innsmouth office called us asking for help. Most unusual for them, they generally keep to themselves, but apparently something made several people ill."

"Bad fish for lunch?" I guessed, and Stella gave me a slightly disapproving look for my flippancy.

"The mail has to go out," she said. "So I drove to Innsmouth, picked up the deliveries and started out. I was taking the mail to the Purple Cat and the sanitarium. I just rounded the corner, right near the cliff edge, when the wind caught the truck."

"I've been on the cliff road," I said. "In a storm. It's frightening."

"I know what you mean," said Stella. "Everyone warns about driving across Malone land. I've never driven to the Purple Cat before, and I wouldn't want to go back unless I absolutely had to. For a moment, I thought the road had disappeared under my wheels. I hit the brakes, and it's a good thing I did because those two men walked right in front of me. I was lucky not to hit them."

"Sounds like luck was with them all right," said Wini. "They might have gone over the cliff if you hadn't found them."

"They definitely acted strange," said Stella. "Like they were sleepwalking. It took some pushing and pulling just to get them into the truck. Then I drove them to Miss Malone's place. Sure wasn't the mail that she was expecting."

"I expect she was grateful to have them found," I said. And I meant just that. Everything I'd seen of Nova Malone indicated that she cared about her employees.

"Oh, yes," said Stella. "She bundled those two men into her Rolls and had her driver take them to the hospital."

"I was visiting a friend who is staying at Bluff Mansion," I said, "when I heard the pilots were found."

"I bet Ezra Hughes was interested," said Stella. "A friend told me that he's been going around the hospital here in Arkham interviewing everyone who disappeared and then reappeared. Then he's been moving them to his sanitarium for treatments."

That answered my earlier speculations about his motives. At least in part.

"You don't say," I said to the pair. "The friend I was visiting had an episode like that. A period of lost memory."

"Then Dr Hughes is the man to cure him," said Stella with considerable conviction. "He started in the war, working with the shell-shocked. Some people consider him quite the hero, according to what I've read in the newspaper."

But there was something about Stella's tone that conveyed a few doubts, too. I wondered if he had ever handed her that peculiar bit of glass he carried with him.

As we chatted, Stella related a story that matched what others had said. That Hughes came from an old Innsmouth family who lost their riches in the last century with the sinking of their ship and had a long feud with the Malones because of it.

"Not that there are many Malones left to carry it on," said Stella. "Nova Malone had a couple of older siblings, but one was lost at sea, and the sister married a man who went out west. There's a niece or two, I've heard."

"And Hughes?" I said. "Any family there?"

"None as far as I know," said Stella, "but he's an Innsmouth man. He may work at the hospital and teach at the university, but he's from there."

Which, her tone implied, meant beyond the reach of the Arkham Post Office. Still, I had learned a great deal from Stella.

"Obviously, every detective story should begin with a trip to the post office," I said, thinking I'd learned more the past few minutes than my entire time racing around the countryside. Of course, there had been other distractions.

Stella nodded. "I'm always surprised folks don't ever wonder more about how their mail appears at their house. Sometimes I think they assume it is magic. And all they have to do to send a package or a letter to a friend is scribble their first name in illegible handwriting on the label, along with a town name... and sometimes not even that! Some of the things that our last postmaster let pile up in the dead letters box. Heavens, you could see why the poor man gave up."

"But you didn't," said Wini. "Stella cleared nearly ten years of lost mail out of the local post office in her first six months."

Stella looked a little embarrassed by Wini's praise. "It's a talent I have," she said to me. "My granny could douse water with a willow stick. Seems like all I need to do is hold a letter to know where it should go. No matter how poorly it is addressed."

"That is a talent," I said. "We could use someone like you at the studio to sort out all the mail that comes in. Half of my mail comes addressed to the Flapper Detective instead of Betsy Baxter."

Stella blinked. "Did you say your last name was Baxter?" she said to me.

"Yes, it is," I replied.

"Oh," said Stella, digging into the satchel sitting beside her on the bench, "then I have a letter for you. It was addressed to a Miss Baxter and the airfield. I meant to ask Wini about it."

I recognized the writing on the outside of the envelope as Farnsworth's neat script. By the postmark date on the letter, he must have sent it just after I left for Arkham with Wini. I tore it open to find another envelope and letter inside the first one. This one had been addressed to me but mailed from Arkham. On a note written on my own stationery, Farnsworth said he was sending it after me to my "last known destination with hopes that madam will still be in one piece to read it." I snorted at this sally, as it clearly brought his voice to me. I did miss Farnsworth's pessimistic attitude toward adventure and thought Tom might enjoy meeting him. They would both withdraw into the library to shake their heads over me.

"How odd," I said to the others. "This letter has been following me around the country. Or at least crisscrossing back and forth."

Once I opened the smaller envelope, I found two more sheets of paper. One looked as if it had been torn from a child's notebook. The other was penned upon a blank recipe card. The writing on the smaller card was odder still. Wini, who openly peered over my shoulder when Stella stepped back to give me some privacy, whistled at the strange little note. "Is it some kind of code?" she said.

"No," I said, after staring at it for a moment longer and then realizing what it was. We'd used a similar device in an early episode of *The Flapper Detective*. "It's mirror writing. Like Da Vinci. You can read it if you hold it up to a mirror." I pulled my compact out of my purse to show her.

The card said, "Help me. Max."

CHAPTER SEVENTEEN

I was so startled by the message that I nearly dropped the letter penned on the second sheet of paper. In a different handwriting, this letter stated:

"Dear Miss Baxter, my wife told me to send this to you as you are the Flapper Detective and certain to know the answer. Ever since my Minerva disappeared and returned, she's been having funny dreams. We talked to Dr Hughes more than once, and he prescribed some mighty peculiar seaweed tea, but it has done nothing to settle my Minerva's nerves. Then we went to the picture show in Arkham and saw you there. You were clever in how you found the villain and helped the poor family who had lost all their money to him. On the way back to our farm, Minerva opined that you would know what to do with these messages that she keeps writing out in her sleep. So please find one enclosed. Should you wish to speak to us, we would be happy to answer your questions. But we don't own a telephone, so please send a letter. Most sincerely yours, Jared Knowles."

I puzzled through the letter, for Knowles's handwriting was

almost as hard to read as the note by Minerva, even though it wasn't written backward. Then I read it out loud to Wini and Stella. My voice sounded completely calm, but my mind was in a whirl. First Jim and now this. Where was Max?

"Fancy Farmer Jared writing to a Hollywood actress," said Stella with a laugh. "I wouldn't have thought the old fellow had that much gumption."

"Do you know this couple?" I asked.

"Certainly," said Stella. "They have a farm not far from Bluff Mansion. They don't raise much anymore, the children being gone, but get by with just enough for themselves and what they can sell to the neighbors. I understand both Bluff Mansion and the Purple Cat buy produce from them. I had forgotten about Minerva's disappearance."

"Was she gone for long?" Wini said.

Stella shook her head. "Not more than a day. She went fishing and never came home for supper. It's the first time that had happened in forty years, according to Jared, so he drove into Innsmouth and organized a search. The next day, some kids spotted her in one of the caves near the town. As I recall the story, she couldn't say how she came to be there."

"I would like to talk to her," I said, turning the letters over in my hands. Like to talk to her? I absolutely needed to question her. Here was a clue I couldn't afford to ignore, no matter how strange. "If they don't have a phone, it might be easier to drive out there."

"This time of day, they are bound to be home," Stella said. "I can give you directions. The roads around here are confusing."

"I have a map," I said, running back to the roadster to fetch it. When I returned to the hut, I found Tom had joined the others.

"Are you ready to take some posters around?" Tom asked me, waving the rolled-up paper at me.

"Oh, I did promise to help," I exclaimed. "But I want to talk to Jared and Minerva today."

"Who?" said Tom.

"You can do both," said Wini. "Take Tom and the posters with you and come back through Innsmouth. And maybe decide what we are going to do to replace Chuck's act."

"Oh," I said, suddenly conscience stricken. Wini's livelihood depended on a good show, and I knew she needed a quality act to succeed. "I had some ideas for Saturday's performance. I haven't forgotten."

"Go," said Wini. She obviously took pity on my quivering eagerness to run off. "Go and do what you have to. Later we can decide what stunts are best for the show."

"Here, let me help. I know some of the rural roads outside Arkham," said Stella. She took my map from me and, between us, we puzzled out a route so I could run all our errands from the airfield to the farm to Innsmouth and back again.

Tom listened intently to Stella's suggestions, asking one or two questions, and then nodded. "I can navigate, Betsy," he said.

Remembering how quickly he directed us through Arkham when we visited the hospital, I happily agreed. "I'm sorry to drag you off on my quest," I said as we climbed into the car. "I don't know what we'll find at this farm."

Tom shrugged. "I've made all the calls about the grimoire that I can. Other book dealers know it is possibly back on the market. If the grimoire doesn't show up that way, I'm fresh out of ideas. I might as well enjoy the scenery for now. And we can help Wini with the posters on the way back here."

With a wave at Wini and Stella, we pulled away from the airfield. Tom was an easy passenger full of entertaining stories about the book trade and quick to spot the signs marking turns in the road. If I hadn't been so preoccupied with the strange messages about Max, he might have turned my head. As it was, I sincerely appreciated his calm good humor.

We followed the route laid out by Stella through pleasantly rolling hills and small woods composed mostly of maple and oak. While only a few miles from the sea, at least as a gull flies, the countryside felt vastly different from the area nearer to Innsmouth. The air smelled of late summer flowers and newly cut grass. The wind in my face felt fresh and held no touch of brine in it.

Ever since I had peered through that warped shard of glass, I felt as if I was drowning in a sea of worry and fear. Now the feeling eased, and some of my worries seemed nonsensical. My old confidence bubbled up. I was certain I was on the right road to finding Max, and Tom was the perfect fellow traveler for my journey.

Perhaps it was the late summer sunshine or perhaps it was my handsome companion, but for the first time since coming back to Arkham, I began to sing as we drove along. Tom joined my rendition of "Yes! We Have No Bananas" followed by a spirited version of "California, Here I Come!" that would have put Jolson to shame.

Giggling, I said to Tom, "If you ever visit Hollywood, I can promise you bananas and oranges."

"And how about a sun-kissed miss?" he asked, quoting the lyrics of our last song.

I winked at him. "I may know one or two," I said, thinking that the ladies at the studio would like this man.

"It certainly sounds more fun than sitting in a bookstore waiting for my uncle to uncrate a new shipment of books," said Tom.

"That song has brought many a romantic soul to my state," I said, "and the others are drawn to fame and possible fortune in Hollywood."

"And do all their sunny dreams come true?" Tom asked.

"Mine did," I said. As I said it, I realized it was true. While I worked hard for every penny, I couldn't deny the happiness that I found with my friends. Over the past few years, I had helped many friends achieve their own dreams, and that felt good, too. If only I hadn't let go of Max and lost him in the fire. If I could find him safe and sound, then I could look back at my whole life without any regrets. I could plan my future without any shadows hanging over me. I almost told that to Tom when he looked up from the map and spoke first.

"I think that's the farm," he said, pointing at a neat little house surrounded by a white picket fence. A big old oak spread its branches in the front, shading a porch complete with two rocking chairs and a wicker table.

As we pulled up in front of the house, a gray-haired woman came backing out the screen door. She was carrying a tray laden with a lemonade pitcher, a tall glass, and a plate of cookies.

"Oh my," she said when she turned around and spotted us getting out of the roadster. "I wasn't expecting guests."

"I'm sorry to disturb you," I said, "but I had a letter from Jared Knowles."

"That's my husband," she said. "I'm Minerva Knowles. Wait! I know who you are. You're the Flapper Detective girl, the one who solves all the movie mysteries. Oh my, oh my, you came, and here's me with nothing but a few cookies and lemonade. Come up to the porch and sit down! Sit down. I'll go find a couple more glasses. Jared! Jared! You'll never guess who is out here."

Minerva plunked the tray on the wicker table and rushed back into the house.

"Heavens," I said, blinking a little at the enthusiastic reception, "she seems very well."

"Were you expecting something else?" Tom said.

"Maybe," I said, walking up the porch steps. "Most of the people who disappear seem, well, quieter." I thought of Jim, dreaming away on his bed, and wondered if he might do better with lemonade and cookies than tea made out of seaweed.

The screen door crashed open again as Minerva pushed her pudgy husband out the door in front of her.

"Woman, woman," he moaned, "I'm in my overalls. Oh, dear, I'm sorry. I just finished cleaning out the barn." He looked every inch the farmer from the worn overalls pulled tight over a round belly to his well-worn work shirt open at the collar. A tattered straw hat protected his very pink scalp from the sun. He lifted the hat off his head in greeting and then pulled a red bandanna out of his back pocket to wipe the sweat off the top of his shiny bald head.

"I should apologize for visiting without any warning," I

said. "But your letter mentioned you had no phone. I thought it would be easier to drive out here than to go back and forth with letters."

"We're delighted," said Minerva very firmly. Then she poked her husband in the side with an elbow. "Where are your manners? Find these folks some chairs."

"Here," said Tom, bounding up the stairs and fetching a couple of ladderback chairs from the far end of the porch. We settled around the wicker table while Minerva went running off for more glasses and another plate of cookies.

Jared stood awkwardly, shuffling big feet encased in scuffed boots, as Minerva bustled about.

"Please sit," I said, dropping down onto a ladderback chair.

The farmer nodded and gingerly lowered himself into his rocking chair. "You got my letter?" he asked after a long pause.

"Yes, but just a few hours ago. I'm very interested in hearing about what happened," I said.

Minerva was persuaded into the other rocking chair by Tom. She gave it a few brisk rocks, and then said, "I have never been a fanciful woman, so it's been the most peculiar thing."

"Disappearing?" I said.

"No. That happens around here. It's the sleepwalking," Minerva said. "And the spirit writing. My goodness, I haven't been so plagued for a good many years. I think the last time I was this haunted was when I was a little thing of eleven or twelve years old."

CHAPTER EIGHTEEN

Tom leaned forward, obviously intrigued, and asked Minerva, "So you're a medium?"

"Not anymore," the farmer's wife said. "When I was young, my mother was quite the believer in spiritualism. Oh my, that was another century."

"Minerva was famous," said Jared Knowles with shy pride. "We have a scrapbook of articles about her."

"Pshaw," said Minerva. "My mother made that scrapbook more than fifty years ago. She wanted me to have it for my children. Not that I ever wanted to give them any ideas. More recently, I haul it out to shock the grandchildren. None of them ever believe that I was once twelve."

"How about the spirit writing?" asked Tom.

"Oh, I think they find that much easier to believe than their old granny being a child like them," Minerva chuckled.

But I was more interested in her talk of disappearances. It sounded like Minerva had much greater insight than anyone else I had questioned.

"You said that people disappear around here," I said,

interrupting their conversation. "Can you explain what you mean?"

Minerva gave a few brisk rocks and then cocked her head at me. She reminded me of the birds around Arkham, the crows with their wise old eyes looking sideways at a person. "You have to be careful where you walk. Don't go into the woods alone."

"Don't cross Malone land," I said, remembering the warnings uttered by Chuck Fergus.

Minerva nodded. "I was foolish when I went fishing. I forgot to watch the tides. Any grandchild of mine would have done better."

"Now, Minerva," said her husband. "The fish were biting. You said so. Not unusual to be distracted by that."

"Fish were biting too well," Minerva retorted. "That should have warned me that I'd drifted into another current. But then that darn old motor wouldn't start, and I needed to use the oars. I was caught contrariwise when the tide came in."

"The fish were biting too well?" said Tom.

"Practically jumping into the boat," said Minerva. "Rising up to the surface and making a feast for the gulls. I had birds diving all around the boat, which is why I wasn't paying as much attention as I should have. When the fish are in a hurry to get out of the ocean, you should ask yourself what's hunting underneath them."

There was a late summer breeze ruffling the edges of our cloth napkins. It carried a bite in it, a chill that was the first warning of autumn. Or maybe it was just Minerva's story with an echo of greedy gulls on the hunt and fish desperate enough to swim into oblivion.

I put a hand to my hat to make sure it was pinned tight in place. I had no time for fancy tales and stray breezes. Ever since I unfolded that note in Minerva's mirror writing, there had been a buzz in my stomach. A feeling that I was finally coming close to the place that I needed to be.

"These notes that you write, the ones that are backward, do you do that while you are asleep?" I said.

"Oh, yes," said Minerva. "My spirit writing only comes out of my dreams."

"I've seen her do it," said Jared. "She just climbs out of bed and marches to the kitchen table. Writes down whatever she's dreaming and then goes back to bed. Most times, it's just reminders to one or the other of us. Things we need to remember."

"Birthdays, shopping lists, chores for the coming season," said Minerva. "I went and talked to that mind doctor Ezra Hughes. Not that he was much help. And the tea he prescribes is simply awful."

"I understand he is quite famous," I said.

"It's hard to take a man seriously when you've known him as a baby and a boy," admitted Minerva. "Ezra used to play with my children back when that big house of his was still a family home. Not that there was much Hughes family left to rattle around in all those rooms. Unlucky, they were."

"And the Malones?" I said, for it seemed that whenever a Hughes entered the tale, a Malone wasn't far behind.

"Unlucky, too. There's only Nova left close by," said Minerva. "She's a bit older than Ezra, but they are much of a generation. She has a sister and a niece or two out west. Ezra has nobody left. Not family, at least. Makes him more than a bit peculiar, I think. Not that he liked me telling him so when I went to see him."

"The analyst was analyzed by the patient?" asked Tom with a smile.

Jared chuckled at the question. "I was waiting for her in the hallway of that fancy sanitarium. Both of them came stomping out of the doctor's office buzzing like angry hornets after her last visit."

"Now, Jared, it wasn't nearly as bad as you tell it," said Minerva, with a swat at her husband.

"Did you tell him to stop poking through other people's dreams and pay attention to his own?" said Jared, ducking out of the way of her friendly swipe with the ease of long practice. "Also, didn't you tell him to try drinking his own tea?"

Minerva winked at her husband and gave a giggle that sounded decades younger than her actual age. In her youth, Minerva must have been a charmer. She obviously still held that charm for her husband. "I may have made some suggestions to Ezra. I'm a mite prone to giving advice, and that's never welcome for some folks."

"She poked him right in the chest," said Jared. "Poked him and told him to stop messing around with seaweed and steer clear of the ocean because he wouldn't like what he dredged up."

"Ezra was always messing down on the beach," said Minerva. "Dragging home all sorts of unhealthy flotsam and jetsam when he was a boy. What the tide brings in should be left for the tide to take out. At least when you're crossing Malone land."

I remembered the greasy bit of beach glass that so

fascinated Hughes. I had to agree with Minerva's assessment and told her so. I described the shard Hughes asked me to look through and how unwholesome it had felt.

"There's a reason why people threw those windows in the ocean," said Minerva. "Those bits rolling back on the beach can be dangerous. The things you see through such glass! You never know what's looking back at you while you're spying on it. I told Ezra to be careful. It could be much worse than squinting down a clam hole and having the clam spit saltwater in your eye."

She passed around the plate of sugar cookies and took a large one for herself. After a couple of happy bites, Minerva said, "It was obvious to me that Ezra was going to be no help with the messages I was receiving. But after I saw your movie, I just knew I needed to send the next note to you."

"The next note?" I exclaimed, very surprised at that statement. How many messages had Minerva received?

"I wrote several after I was found down on the beach," said Minerva. "Ezra took them. That's one of the things that made me so mad. He said he wanted to analyze my handwriting for possible personality quirks. As if I don't know all the bumps and tangles of my own self at my age! But after I got home, I went sleepwalking again. It was obvious to me that a message needed to be sent. I rarely write the same thing twice. Not after the right person reads the note. It's only when a delivery goes astray that it happens again. Mother and I figured that out long ago."

"Back then Minerva used to give messages to all sorts of folks," said Jared. "That's why they wrote her up in the newspapers when she was young."

"Who do you think is sending these messages? Is it the dead?" I said. If that were true, how was I to help Max's ghost? "And why did you think that the messages were for me?"

"I told you," said Minerva, shaking her head at my foolishness. "The minute I saw you in the movie, I knew you were the one who needed to hear what that spirit was saying to me. Happens like that. I see someone's picture or hear their name and I immediately know a message is for them."

"And who do you think is sending those messages to me? Do you think it is a ghost?" I said, and I almost dreaded the reply. For what could I do to help the dead?

"Perhaps," said Minerva. "That's what my mother thought. That my messages came from the dead."

Some doubt in her voice caused my next question. "Who do you think is talking to you in your dreams?" I asked.

Minerva heaved a giant sigh. "It's so difficult to explain," she said. She fussed with the plates and the cookies until Jared reached behind her rocking chair and pulled out her bag of knitting. "Show them," he said, placing the bag on her lap. "Like you do for the kiddies."

Minerva clucked. "Oh, my tricks are only for the little ones because it's hard to explain," she said.

"Works a treat for me," said her husband with a twinkle.

She smiled and patted his hand. "That's because you're still a child at heart," she said fondly to her husband. To us, she said, "You should see him at Christmas when he gets to play Santa at the school, handing out presents all around. Spends all autumn growing out his scratchy white beard."

They both chortled at that. Minerva fished her knitting

needles out of her bag and began to cast the wool on one.
She was fast and had a few rows knitted in a twinkling as she
pulled a second yarn into the pattern, making diamonds and
stars appear in her work.

"You know why fishermen's wives knit patterns into their
men's clothing?" she asked us.

"So they can identify the drowned," said Tom, proving
once again that growing up in a bookstore left a person with
a head stuffed full of strange knowledge.

Minerva nodded at him. "The women of Innsmouth added
something else to their patterns," she told us. "They added
maps of stars that we never see. Not when we are awake and
wondering. The women knitted the stars and roads needed
to guide a man out of the night that never ends." She pulled
more yarn out of her bag and added more colors, colors that
formed swirls and patterns that did not so much as jar the eye
as unsettle it altogether.

"Do you understand tension in knitting?" she said,
sweeping both of us with a stern look which suggested she
doubted our understanding of the term.

Digging into my memory of knitting lessons from my
grandmother, I responded, "Does this have anything to do
with purl one, knit two?"

"A bit," said Minerva, shifting to a second pair of needles.
It was clear now that what she was knitting would eventually
become a mitten. "You have to keep the tension steady or
the pattern won't turn out true. If you rush, you end up with
a mess you need to unpick and start again. I think," she said
as she clicked her way through a few more rows, "too many
people rush through the pattern. Innsmouth is a dangerous

place to make such an error. To drop a stitch, to create a hole." She deliberately skipped a stitch and a hole appeared in her work. Minerva yanked the yarn, just slightly, and the whole pattern rippled in a way that made Tom and me flinch.

"You feel it, too," Minerva said. "How the world drops away, just for a second, and you land yourself someplace else. Just for a second, just for a breath, just enough to unnerve you."

She gave a vicious twist to her needles and the whole pattern fell apart in a knotted, tangled mess. "Sometimes, though, you can be unraveled into someplace else."

I gave an involuntary cry of dismay at the destruction of her work.

Minerva smiled and picked the yarns out of her lap. "It is nothing," she said soothingly to me, the way that you would comfort a child frightened by a nightmare. "I can always wind it into a ball and start over. Hold your hands up."

I did as I was told, much to my surprise, and Minerva cast her yarn back and forth between my two hands. How many times had I sat just so in the late summer sunlight or close by the kitchen stove in winter while my grandmother did the same, looping me into her skeins and stories.

"If you know where you are, if you know where you are going, if you have a pattern, you can find your way home," Minerva almost whispered. "You can carry it all in your head as easily as you can wear a mitten or a scarf. Remember that. Then you can never be lost. That's what the women know and the men forget."

"Except the ones who learned how to knit," said Jared a

little smugly. He'd retrieved another pair of needles from Minerva's bag. In his hands, a sock was growing, covered in the same stars and swirls of Minerva's pattern.

"Ezra's problem," said Minerva, "is the lack of patience in the boy. He thought windows would be a quicker way to where he wanted to go and what he wanted to gain. And Nova Malone is no better, for all that she knows the patterns as well as anyone. She knows her glittering book is just a cheat, a way to shortcut across the old ways."

At this statement, Tom leaned in, obviously planning to ask about his grimoire because what besides a jeweled cover could be described as a glittering book. I shook my head at him just a tiny bit. Tom, bless his heart, leaned back and let Minerva continue at her own pace. I didn't want to distract Minerva, not now, not when I was so close to finding the answer to my own mystery. Later, I told myself, later we can ask about her reference to a glittering book. Except the next few minutes drove it out of my mind.

Minerva unwound the yarn from my hands and into a neat ball on her lap. Another loop of yarn, and another winding and unwinding, and a second ball joined the first. As she cast her third strand across my hands, my patience broke and I blurted out, "But how do you find somebody who is already lost?"

"By looking, of course," said Minerva as the third ball grew into a neat round shape to match the other two. "Nobody can find anything if they don't look first."

"I'm not sure that is exactly true, ma'am," said Tom. "I've found a great many things I didn't intend to find. Stumbled over them, you might say."

"Are you sure?" said Minerva. "Perhaps you didn't know what you were looking for until you found it."

The last of the yarn slithered away from my fingers. I almost clutched at it if only to tether Minerva to her chair and her story. There was an answer here, I was certain of it, an answer to the questions that had haunted me for three years.

"So how do you bring back someone who is lost, someone who doesn't know your pattern?" I asked.

Minerva nodded briskly at me, the way a schoolteacher might nod at a pupil who finally stumbled upon the point of a lesson. "That's the right question. What do you do if the men won't wear the pattern that you've made? What do you do if they are foolish enough to sail without it? There are words to say, there are songs to sing, but you have to be careful. Drop a stitch, sing the wrong note, make a mistake, and you've opened a hole for a good many things, not just the person who you're looking for. You cannot be reckless."

Minerva and Jared rocked in time with each piece of advice. The creak of the rockers blended with the chittering of the insects stirring at the end of a long hot afternoon. Far away, I heard a crow's harsh cry.

"Who holds your hand and writes words when you are sleeping?" I asked again. "Is it the dead?"

"I think not," said Minerva. "I never believed the dead would try so desperately to speak to us. I think it is the lost souls. The ones still alive who cannot find their way home."

There were shadows under the oak tree. Black shadows, and the shapes made by the branches shifting in the wind looked like tendrils of seaweed floating beneath the water, clutching at a drowning swimmer.

"Ever since I saw you at the picture show," said Minerva, reaching out and patting my knee, "I knew why I dreamed about Max, night after night. The message is for you. Max is trying to reach you."

CHAPTER NINETEEN

When we drove away from the farm, we did not sing. We did not laugh. We did not even talk. For mile after mile, I sat silent. Tom respected that silence. Until we reached the first town where we had promised to display Wini's posters. Even then, I spoke first.

"Where do you want to start?" I asked. It was a tiny town, not more than a few stores clustered on one straight main street called, of course, Main Street. If the town had a name, I forgot it as soon as we left its boundaries. Most of my thoughts were about Max and the terrible weight of the words Minerva had placed upon me.

"General store, dentist's office, and the diner," said Tom. "That's all there is."

"There's the church," I said, pointing to the plain white wooden building.

"Would a church allow a circus poster?" Tom asked.

"They might," I said. I slid out of the roadster and straightened my hat. I unknotted the scarf around my neck and looped it in a more conservative style. "Give me a poster for the church. I'll ask nicely. Where are the free tickets?"

Wini had given us a handful of tickets to spread around with the posters. We were supposed to persuade the most influential people in town to come to the show. Once they came, Wini predicted the rest would follow for the second or third day. In the theater, we called such tactics "papering the house". It was always a good way to open something new and lure in a crowd.

"I'll give a couple to the reverend," I said to Tom. Stepping across the road, I found the church door closed but unlocked. Inside, the pews and pulpit were as plain as possible. Near the door, a woman was dusting a table or perhaps just rearranging something on it. For when she turned to face me, I saw a paper bag in her hand and not a dust rag.

She was dressed in a long skirt and conservative jacket, very much in the style popular before the war, and the whole ensemble looked like it might be ten years old or more.

"Can I help you?" she asked, and her tone suggested she thought I needed more help than I was going to ask for.

"Yes, ma'am," I said, ignoring her pointed stare at my much shorter skirt and darling cloche hat. Apparently my more traditionally tied scarf did not impress her. "I am with the air show and wondered if we could leave a poster on your community board."

I offered the poster to her. She looked as if I had tried to hand her a serpent.

"I am certainly not…" she started to say, but a man's voice interrupted her.

"Now, Mother," said the minister, walking through a door set in the back of the church, "let's see what the lady has to offer."

Like his mother, the minister's suit was old with the black beginning to turn to dark gray along the seams. But his collar and cuffs were shining white and immaculate. Whoever did his laundry did an excellent job. Judging by her red knuckles, I guessed it was his mother, and I smiled at her more sympathetically.

"I am performing with the aerial circus," I told the minister. "A clean and wholesome show, intending to introduce children and their parents to the marvels of flight. It includes a homage to our brave pilots who served so gallantly in the war."

From conversations with Wini, I knew that Saturday's entertainment would include plane rides for a dollar as well as a mock air battle to mimic the dogfights of the last war. Both were popular bits of business to perform between the bigger stunts.

"Of course, we would love to have you attend," I said, turning and handing the free tickets to the minister's mother. "You would enjoy it."

"I don't know," said the woman, turning the tickets over in her hands. It was obvious that very few gifts came her way. Minister's mothers, like minister's wives, were usually expected to do the giving. At least in the small town where I grew up, that was true. "I have never been to a circus. Just a revival tent show once when I was young."

"You will love it," I assured them both.

"A day out, Mother, would be a pleasure," said the minister with a pat to his mother's hand. "I cannot think of a woman who deserves a holiday more." His last statement considerably raised my opinion of the reverend gentleman.

His mother gave us both a tentative smile. "I could wear my new hat," she said, moving away from the table. Rather than covered with church literature or hymnals, I saw that shells were spread across the tabletop. Seashells of all types were arranged in swirls and patterns that reminded me of Minerva's knitting. These unsettling patterns seemed to whirl in front of my eyes.

"That's unusual," I said, turning away from the table before it made me seasick. "I would expect flowers for decorations."

The woman looked distressed, but the minister answered smoothly enough. "It's a tradition of the area. Something that the fishermen's families have done for a long time."

"Since the *Gulliver* disappeared," the woman almost whispered.

"The *Gulliver*!" I said. "Do you mean the plane that was lost earlier this week?"

"Oh, no," she said. "Gulliver Malone's ship, the one that vanished from Innsmouth's harbor."

"And not the Hughes's ship, the *Bolide*," I said, recalling the story Chuck Fergus had told.

"The Hughes!" she said with real scorn. "As if they ever cared for the people hereabouts, not the way the Malones did. Not the way Miss Nova does."

"Now, Mother," said the minister with a long-suffering sigh, "we must be charitable toward all."

"Name one basket of food that Hughes has given to a poor family," his mother flashed back. "I can name ten families this week who received help from Nova Malone. The Hughes family only wanted their fancy house and to order around all the rest. The Malones always cared for their neighbors." She was quite the warrior, the minister's mother, when she got started. "What was true in the past is still true today."

"Old feuds, all in the last century," the minister said to me as he walked us to the door. "Ezra Hughes is an educated man, a doctor, and I am sure he has helped many sufferers to heal."

"Good is as good does," sniffed his mother as she waved me goodbye from the church's front door. I did like her attitude. And I couldn't disagree with her assessment of humanity.

Back at the roadster, I found Tom had successfully persuaded the general store, the diner, and the dentist's office to display Wini's poster in their windows. "I even talked the woman at the store into taking a stack of tickets to sell. She'll bring the cash to me on Saturday when she comes to see the show," Tom said.

We drove through several small towns, convincing most of the businesses we found to take a poster, a few to take tickets to sell, and many willing to accept the offer of a free ticket for themselves. Airplanes were still not common in this area, and everyone seemed excited by the chance to see an aerial show.

"Have you decided what trick you will do?" Tom asked as we drove toward Innsmouth. The farther we went from Minerva and her story, the easier it was to bury all she had said underneath light chatter about the possible stunts, the people we met in each town, and the good weather. In short, everything except what Minerva had told us. After all, how do you discuss that the world can fall away as quickly as a knitter can drop a stitch? It didn't fit into a normal day, a day like this, full of sunshine and birdsong.

Rather than trying to wrap my head around the impossible, I proposed a few stunts.

"A jump from a motorcycle or car," I said. "I've done that often enough. I could jump onto the wing if the plane is still moving on the ground. Or onto a ladder. I once did something like that from a little boat to a ship's ladder. Both were moving at the time. It was a tough shot to get, as my cameraman was in a boat, too, bobbing up and down. It took three tries, and I landed in the water twice."

"You're lucky you didn't drown," exclaimed Tom in astonishment.

"I'm a very strong swimmer," I said. "That's why I have a pool. But it is different when you fall into the ocean. Colder. And there are currents, too." I remembered the waves breaking over my head and some screams from Marian that day. Perhaps even a few oaths from Farnsworth when I finally squelched my way home. But it had been an exciting stunt and the pictures of me dangling off the ship's ladder sold tickets galore.

"It sounds like the life of an actress is much more dangerous than I knew," said Tom.

"You have no idea," I said as we turned down a hill. Innsmouth lay below us, the harbor and the town visible in the distance. Driving through Innsmouth revealed another place than the one we had seen the day before. Today the shops were open, and people strolled along like any small town. But there were still sidelong looks at Tom and me after we parked the roadster and started to visit businesses that might display the posters.

"Not exactly friendly," I said to Tom as we exited from a drugstore where the owner had agreed to take both the poster and tickets with as few words as possible. No excited questions about the show like other places.

"Perhaps they are just shy," said Tom, but he also sounded baffled by our reception. "Oh, look, there's a bookstore. Let's see what they have."

"Where?" I said, glancing up and down the street. "I don't see any bookstore."

"Just around that corner." Tom waved a poster at the far end of the street where it curved into another road. The corner of a shop, at least it was probably a shop with a painted name on its door, was barely visible from where we stood.

"How do you know that it is a bookstore?" I said. From the way the sun reflected off the glass, the name painted on the door was mostly obscured.

"I am sure that there is a *B* and a *K* on that sign. And there is enough space for an *OO* between them," said Tom. "See that crate by the door? That's the sort of crate dealers drop five-cent books into. You never know what treasures can be found in such places."

"Serves you right if it is a barber's shop," I said, trying to think of other businesses with a *B* in their names. "Or a baker! Baker's shops have a *B* and a *K*." Then I spotted Nova Malone's driver, Albie, coming toward us. As he was not somebody I wanted to meet again, I pushed Tom into the bookshop. The store apparently specialized in very old and dusty books to judge by the dim interior after we entered. Tom tried not to look smug but failed.

"Go on," I said. "Say that you told me so." Glancing out the window, I saw Albie continue down the street. With any luck, he hadn't noticed us.

"I would never be so rude to a lady as to say I told you so," Tom answered. "Oh, isn't it wonderful." He took off down the aisle like a hound puppy chasing rabbits.

"It looks like this store hasn't seen a customer since the *Bolide* went down," I said.

"Exactly," said Tom. "It appears many of these books were acquired years ago. It's always a battle to accumulate prime stock."

"I'd say this is a shop where the books won the war, and whoever bought these books is probably barricaded in the back," I said, maneuvering around stacks on the floor. The shelves were stuffed so tight nobody could even pull out a volume without risking an avalanche. "How many shop owners end up crushed under their own inventory?"

"Well, as long as they are not in earthquake territory," started Tom. Then he stopped and dropped back on his heels to paw through one of the piles. "I thought I saw... Yes, indeed! Betsy, look at this. It's Melville's *White-Jacket*. This must be a first." Tom shook the book free from the pile.

"That's a treasure?" I asked, nearly tumbling over another stack of books.

"Oh, definitely," said Tom. "For seafaring readers. Quite famous for its influence, even if Melville didn't much care for the job. He called it a book written for money."

"Oh, aye," said a rumbling voice from behind the shelves. "Melville's story saved many an American sailor's back from a flogging. And I have an affection for the character of Guinea, for I had an ancestor who shipped on a similar voyage, but he successfully used it in his bid for freedom."

Stumping around the shelves came a heavyset old man.

Although his tightly curled hair was barely touched with gray, his beard was a white cascade down his chest. He dropped the books he had been carrying onto a pile and shook Tom's hand. "Do I see a fellow bibliophile before me?" he said.

"Tom Sweets," replied my friend. "This is a wonderful store."

The Black man nodded with pride at Tom's praise. "This store has been my great pleasure since I came ashore," he said. "Captain Leonard Pease, at your service. Welcome to Captain Leo's Books." Then he looked at Tom more closely. "Wait, did you say you were a Sweets? Any chance you're from Sweets and Nephew, the Boston booksellers?"

"Yes," said Tom. "I'm the nephew."

"Poor man, it's a hard burden to bear if all the tales are true," said Pease with real feeling. "But I've seen your grimoire quite recently. Being loaded onto a plane."

CHAPTER TWENTY

"The Deadly Grimoire?" exclaimed Tom. "How did you know about that?"

"Who doesn't know about the grimoire in the trade?" said Pease, gesturing to us to follow him down a crowded aisle overflowing with books. "Not the sort of thing I stock, being much more inclined to maritime tales, but I've been keeping an eye out for it since I heard it was stolen. Especially given its history with the *Bolide* and the *Gulliver*."

"Ha!" I said to Tom. "I knew the Deadly Grimoire was to blame for the original disappearances."

The bookseller smiled at me. "Are you a Sweets as well?"

"No, I'm a Baxter," I said. "Betsy Baxter. I'm not in the business of books, cursed or otherwise." Although I was beginning to feel that was slightly untrue. At times, I thought the whole story of the Deadly Grimoire a terrible distraction from my own quest. At others, like now, it seemed the grimoire might be the key to unraveling the whole mystery. After all, it was hard to believe more than one thing could cause people to disappear in this quaint corner of New England. "What was the grimoire's history in Innsmouth, Mr Pease?"

"Call me Captain Leo as the rest of the town does," said the genial bookseller. "What I know is both the Hughes and the Malones once sailed the coast, and further still, into currents and oceans best avoided. Eventually their rivalry grew so fierce that Gulliver Malone went all the way to Boston to acquire the Deadly Grimoire just to outdo Hughes on the trading runs. And it led to bad luck for both families."

"We've heard much the same from several people," I said. "Including Minerva and Jared Knowles today."

"Never argue with Minerva Knowles," said Captain Leo with a twinkle. "The woman knows the whole history of every family in this region. Has it all knotted up in her knitting. She's a terrible force for good, she is, selling her scarves and mittens every winter at the church holiday bazaar."

"Do you own some of her patterns?" I asked.

"I never sailed without one of Minerva's scarves," he replied. "And I never lost my way, no matter how strange the currents ran. Come along, come along, Tom, let me show you what else I have that might interest a Sweets."

As Tom promptly followed Captain Leo further into the store, I glanced back toward the windows and grimaced when I saw Albie's large friend of a few nights ago walking by with a sailor's rolling gait. Best we stay in the shop for a little time, I decided. I didn't feel like another confrontation with either man.

Although my largest problem looked to be liberating Tom from the store, given how he stopped every few feet with a cry of "Now look at this," and Captain Leo would pluck another book from a pile or shelf, saying, "Well, if you are interested in those books, you should see this as well.

A second edition but in as good a condition as I've ever found." Soon Tom's arms were full of books. I predicted a crate needing to be strapped onto the back of the roadster in the near future.

The pair finally found "a snug berth" as Captain Leo called his cozy backroom. This den was piled high from floor to ceiling with books, but there was a small fireplace in one corner, and the books gave it just enough space to be safe. A pair of men's boots sat drying on one corner of the hearth. A battered old kettle swung over the flames through a clever arrangement of a hinged iron rod stuck in the side of the chimney.

"One of these days," said Captain Leo, "I will have to electrify back here as well as the front of the store. But I like this old fireplace. The man who sold me the building claimed one of Paul Revere's sons forged the kettle and hook."

"Quite possibly," said Tom. "It always seems to me that you cannot walk ten steps in Boston without seeing some evidence of his industry."

"Did you know the Reveres once held the commission to forge nails for the early navy ships?" asked Captain Leo as he swung the kettle away from the flames with the help of a poker. "Clear off the chairs. Don't let the books stop you from sitting down."

I cleared with a will, wanting to sit down and question Captain Leo about the grimoire. Tom, predictably, became distracted by one stack of books as he lifted it from a straight-backed chair and stood thumbing through a volume.

Using a towel to protect his hands, Captain Leo lifted the kettle off the hook and poured the boiling water into a waiting teapot. "There are some cups," he said. He looked vaguely around the piles of books. "Perhaps by the Conrad?"

I spotted Joseph Conrad's *The Rover* on the table that obviously served as the captain's desk. Beside the novel sat several stout mugs. I plucked three out of the welter of books and papers, holding them aloft. "Here are the cups," I said, handing them to the men.

Tom started to wave off the tea, pleading too much lemonade and cookies only a short time before, but then he saw the hip flask the captain pulled out of his jacket pocket. "Just a drop of rum to sweeten it," said the captain, dropping a generous dollop into each cup. "Better than sugar or cream, I reckon."

Tom finally sat down. He took a sip and sighed with pleasure. "Much better than sugar and cream," he said. "So how did a sea captain become a bookseller?"

"In my early days," said Captain Leo, "I was a poor sailor, but I took the jobs others didn't want, including whaling, although that was a terrible experience. Eventually I worked my way up to owning a boat. At first, I used it for fishing, but as my ambitions grew, so did my ship. I added to it, upgraded the engines, and redid the rigging. It was as ugly a ship as ever sailed the seas, a patchwork of sails and steam, but I loved my *Molly Gee* dearly. I went south to the Caribbean in the winter and north to Nova Scotia in the summer. Wherever the ports were friendliest to me. Carrying a little of this, trading a little of that. But such sailing was a lonely business. Books became my comrades. I found myself haunting whatever stores or market stalls I could find. Being a seafaring man, I tended to purchase books about the sea."

"I'm surprised your ship didn't sink between ports," I said, looking around at the piles. "There's quite a bit of ballast here."

"A bit of ballast," Captain Leo roared. "A bit of ballast! Why, if I'd put all these on the *Molly Gee*, she'd have disappeared beneath the waves. No, no, every time I came home, I left my purchases with my friend Cuffe. When I finally retired, he told me I could live with him only if the books found a new home. Eventually I sold my ship and bought this shop." He pointed at the ceiling above us. "I've added a few more books since then. The attic is practically full now. But don't tell Cuffe. Oh, don't tell Cuffe!"

His shoulders shook with silent laughter. "A bit of ballast." He wiped his eyes with one hand. "What an idea!"

"Still, this doesn't seem like much of a town for a bookstore," I said, remembering the general air of a place past its prime we had seen in Innsmouth.

Captain Leo shrugged. "Property is cheap here, and we need businesses other than shipping and fishing. Devil Reef is a problem for ships, but the world's changing. Miss Malone has some ideas for reclaiming the harbor. She's even been talking about dredging, but that's a good many years away. Sometimes, a little rot can be a help, too. I doubt I'd have bought a building so easily in Boston or even Arkham."

After taking a few fortifying sips of tea, I asked, "When did you see the grimoire?"

"A day or two ago," said Captain Leo. "I was down at the water's edge, fishing off the dock in the early morning, and watching the two young men loading the *Gulliver II.*"

"The seaplane?" I asked.

"Yes. Fascinating contraption. Nova Malone named it after her ancestor's lost sailing ship, but her latest vessel sails through the air, right over Devil Reef. If I were younger, I'd be tempted to learn how to fly such a thing. Imagine how quickly and easily you could go up and down the coast," said Captain Leo. "No fear of storms or rough seas. You could fly above the waves and the clouds."

"Well, it can still be pretty rough," I said, thinking about my cross-country trip with Wini. "If you hit a rising or falling column of air, it bumps the plane. Some flights can be very bumpy indeed, just like being tossed around by the waves."

"Oh, have you flown?" said Captain Leo with great interest. "I would dearly like to ride in an airplane."

"Then come to the air show," I said, handing him a pair of Wini's tickets as well as a poster for the show. "Bring your friend, too. There's considerable entertainment, including a daredevil female pilot and an even more daring wing-walker."

"I will," declared Captain Leo. Looking at the line "All are welcome!" printed across the bottom of the poster, he nodded again. "I will indeed."

"But the grimoire?" said Tom, finally looking up from the book he was reading.

"Ah, yes," said Captain Leo. "The cover of the book glittered in the sun so naturally it caught my eye. Albie gave the book to the pilot as they were preparing to take off. I heard him say something about using it for their navigation."

"Albie? Nova Malone's driver?" I exclaimed. That man kept popping up like a bad penny. I wondered why he was wandering the streets of Innsmouth today. I glanced toward the windows, but the bookshelves completely obscured the front of the store. Just as well, I thought. If we cannot see out, Albie cannot see in.

"You know Albie?" Captain Leo asked.

"We have not been formally introduced," I said, "but we've certainly had encounters."

"Yes, when Albie gave the pilot his instructions, I clearly saw the book had a most unusual cover, green shagreen with gilt and jeweled decorations. When you said your name, Tom, that's when I remembered where I'd heard of such a cover. On the Deadly Grimoire."

"It certainly sounds like our grimoire," Tom said.

We thanked Captain Leo for the tea. Tom made a significant purchase of books from the bookseller, and I helped him carry his haul back to the roadster. Quickly checking up and down the street, I saw no sign of Albie or his partner.

"Captain Leo saw the Deadly Grimoire," said Tom. "I'm sure of it. Why, that little… uh…" Glancing at me, he modified whatever he'd meant to say. "That plug-ugly Albie kept saying he didn't have it. He kicked me, too, when I told him I didn't have it."

"Do you think Albie and his partner stole the grimoire from the professor?" I said. "Why would they do that?"

"To retrieve it for Nova Malone," said Tom. "She was furious we had sold the grimoire twice and delivered the book to the professor."

"But you told her you would honor the sale and recover it from Christine," I said, loading Tom's books onto the backseat of the roadster. I was trying to figure out what had happened in the last week. "Why steal the grimoire before you had a chance to make good on your promise?"

"Perhaps she didn't want anyone to know she had the grimoire," speculated Tom.

"Nova Malone arranged to have the grimoire stolen from Christine," I said, "but pretended she was still hunting for it. Perhaps so Hughes wouldn't know she had it. After all, most people would assume if you were looking for something, you didn't know where it was."

Tom nodded. "That makes a devious sort of sense."

"Oh, I suspect Nova Malone is a very devious woman," I said. "And clever, too. Then Albie gives the grimoire to the pilots. The seaplane goes… where?"

"To judge by its condition when it was towed back to the harbor," said Tom, "the flight was somewhere very unsafe."

"And the pilots reappear on the cliff road like others who have flown for Nova Malone," I said. "I bet all the planes that have disappeared recently were flying the same route. Except only the seaplane returned. For the rest, the planes and the pilots are separated, and only the pilots make it back." Perhaps Nova, like Captain Leo, purchased scarves and mittens from the church bazaar designed to lead lost sailors or lost pilots home, I thought.

"But where is the grimoire now?" I said as we climbed back into the roadster. "Still on the seaplane? Then Nova has it. She would have searched the plane for the grimoire as soon as possible."

"Could the book be with the pilots?" said Tom. "If one of them was carrying it in their clothing?"

"Oh, dear," I said, remembering Albie's visit to the doctor. "If it's with one of the pilots, then it's probably at the hospital. Hughes was heading there this afternoon."

I turned the car around as quickly as possible and started out on the road to Arkham.

"Where are we going?" Tom shouted over the engine's roar.

"Back to Arkham," I yelled. "Back to the hospital. To steal the grimoire before Hughes finds it." I told Tom how Albie had visited the doctor and Hughes had been anxious to return to the hospital to see the pilots. "I'm sure Hughes is after the book, too."

"Why?" said Tom, gripping the door handle as tightly as he could. "And do we need to go so fast?"

"Yes," I said. "Hughes is searching for the same thing as Nova Malone."

"And what's that?" yelled Tom as we soared down the road.

"Gulliver Malone's secret way," I said. "His Northwest Passage." Gulliver Malone had found a way to do more than fall through the mirror, I thought. Gulliver Malone found a way to sail a whole ship to wherever it was that lay behind the windows that so fascinated Hughes. If Nova Malone could navigate a similar route, it gave her a superb way to smuggle liquor from Canada or Europe to the United States and avoid the other gangs. If I could follow the same route, could I finally find Max and bring him home?

We may have hit a bump or two, and the books were rattling around in the backseat, but I was still maintaining a safe speed as we hurtled toward Arkham. Certainly nothing I couldn't handle in the roadster.

But then a battered old delivery van came barreling out of nowhere. It raced alongside the roadster. When I glanced up, I looked into the face of Albie staring down at me with a most terrific frown. His hands were clenched around the wheel as he swerved his vehicle toward my car. Obviously, Albie had seen us in Innsmouth.

"Watch out," I yelled to Tom and sped up my darling car, trying to outrace Albie in his van.

Tom yelled something, but I couldn't hear what as we zoomed along the road.

Albie swung the van at me again. I went up and off the road onto the grass verge, hoping the heavier van would bog itself down in the softer ground.

Albie followed, racing toward us, intent on ramming the back of my roadster. I hit the gas, willing every last ounce of speed out of the engine as I roared back onto the road. Albie's van followed, sounding like some monstrous beast as it labored behind us. But it wasn't built for speed.

"Hold on," I cried to Tom as we came to a turn. I made as sharp a right as I had ever done, yanking the wheel hard and zipping along this new track. Albie tried the same maneuver, but the van was having none of that. It rocked and swayed and tipped over behind us.

Tom looked back and gave a shout of triumph. "You did it!" he yelled.

I geared down and risked a glance over my shoulder. Albie came climbing out of the van with a rifle in his hands.

"No!" I cried as I swerved to avoid being hit.

Albie shot twice. The first shot missed us. The second caught my rear tire. With a tremendous bang, the tire blew and sent us into a long sliding skid.

CHAPTER TWENTY-ONE

"What are you doing?" said Tom as I pulled the car straight and continued on.

"Driving on a flat tire," I said, wincing at the sounds coming from under my car. "At least until we make it behind those trees." I skated around another corner, more on three wheels than four, and brought the roadster to a halt. I reached for my handbag and pulled out my pistol. Enough was enough, and I had had it with that little bully Albie.

"You cannot start a shooting match against a rifle," said Tom, eyeing my gun with some trepidation.

"No," I said. "But I doubt he expects me. This should surprise him." I climbed out of the roadster and stalked back down the road. "Shoot my car! Wait until I catch him."

But Albie was gone. The van was still lying there on its side, but the man was nowhere to be seen. I heard the roar of an engine and spotted the Model T with a dented fender driving down the road. The driver looked like Albie's big friend. Albie was in the passenger seat beside him.

I walked back to my car in an absolute steam. Albie was

sure to reach Nova Malone or the doctor long before we could reach the hospital.

"Now what?" asked Tom.

"There's a jack and a spare in the back," I said. "I'm going to teach you how to change a tire. It's something everyone should know."

Tom looked over his pile of jumbled books in the backseat. He straightened them up as I pulled out the tools to change the tire. "I used to have time to read," he mourned, but he accepted the lug wrench from me and began to loosen the wheel as directed. Together we managed to pull off the wheel and roll it out of the way. The spare took just a little tugging and pushing to get it into place. All in all, with Tom's help, it was the fastest I had ever changed a tire.

"You have some amazing talents, Betsy Baxter," Tom said to me after we secured the flat tire on the back.

"Thank you," I said. "Henry insisted I learn how to change a tire. He said I couldn't go driving all over Hollywood without knowing at least that much about cars."

"Who's Henry?" said Tom as we climbed back into the roadster.

"The man who takes care of my cars," I said. "And how I'm going to face him, given the state of this car, I don't know. Maybe Lonnie can do some repairs at the airfield."

Driving on the spare, I kept our speed down as I wasn't too sure of the tire.

By the time we reached the hospital, no visitors were allowed. Tom and I did our best, but the nurse at the front desk was firm that we had to wait until morning. We could not go into any patient's room, no matter how urgent.

"But what will I tell my mother?" I finally wailed in desperation. "He's quite her favorite son."

"Who, dear?" asked the nurse.

"The pilot…" I burbled on Tom's shoulder as he tried to look concerned and not puzzled by my antics.

"Who is she talking about?" asked the nurse again.

"The pilot, the one found on the cliff road," Tom muttered. Of course, neither of us knew the names of the pilots, which made our inquiries quite suspicious. Even I wasn't sure if this latest attempt at sliding by the nurse's guard would work.

"Oh, why didn't you say so immediately?" said the nurse. "Neither of those men are here. Nova Malone had them checked out hours ago."

"Really?" I said, lifting my head off Tom's shoulder and making as big a play as possible with the white handkerchief Tom stuffed into my hand. "Did she take them home? Mother will be so delighted."

"Oh, no," said the nurse. "They went to Bluff Mansion. The men were sent in an ambulance with all the proper attendants. Miss Malone took Dr Hughes in her fancy car. Everyone knows her car."

I'm sure they did, I thought. The Rolls was hard to miss. Still, I was baffled by this seeming cooperation between Hughes and Malone. Who had the grimoire? Or were they sharing it?

"Was Albie driving?" asked Tom in a casual way.

"Oh, you know Albie," said the nurse, revealing herself to be a local woman. "Yes, he was driving. He'd had an accident earlier, just some bruises and scrapes, but we patched Albie up here while Miss Malone made her arrangements with Dr Hughes. Then they all left together."

Outside the hospital, Tom watched me pace back and forth by the roadster. "Where to next?" he said.

At that point, I was convinced the Deadly Grimoire was exactly what I needed to find Max. Which was foolish, as I had absolutely no idea how to use the thing. Still, I was tired of everyone stealing it and shooting at my car and causing general misery all around. I felt it was time to take the glittering book away from Nova Malone and the doctor. Eventually, when I cooled off, I might give it to Christine. Then I decided Christine would know exactly what to do with the grimoire.

With everything solved in my head, I still needed a plan of action as I told Tom. "I would go back to Bluff Mansion," I said, "but I've already been to the sanitarium today, and Ezra Hughes might well question my sudden interest in the pilots. Besides, by now, either Nova or Ezra has the grimoire. If it's Nova, she will keep it close. Perhaps a return trip to the Purple Cat would be wise."

"Or perhaps we should find a garage," said Tom. "Is the car supposed to be leaking like that?"

I looked down to see a spattering of oil drops on the ground. Bending further to look right under the car, I could see that my forays over rocks and other debris had done my poor roadster no good at all. "You are right," I said. "I'm not even sure I should drive as far as a garage. Let's find a phone and call for a tow."

We arrived back at the airfield riding in the front seat of a tow truck with my roadster being dragged behind. Lonnie was the first to come running out.

"What have you done to your beautiful machine?" she cried to me.

"A few minor mishaps," I said.

"We ran off the road after being shot," Tom added.

Wini came strolling out onto the field with a grin. "Sounds like fun," she said. "I should have gone with you."

"If you had been driving," Lonnie said as she directed the tow driver where to park my car, "there wouldn't even have been a chassis left!"

"Can you repair it?" I asked Lonnie. "I am sorry to put you to this work so close to the show."

"The planes are fine," said Lonnie as she dived under my car to assess the vehicle's condition. "Betsy Baxter! You cannot drive through fields in a lovely machine like this. Stick to the roads!" Her voice was a bit muffled from being halfway under the car, but her scolding was clear enough.

Tom pulled his stack of books out of the backseat. "I will add these to my luggage," he said. "It will be nice to have something to read on the train trip back to Boston. Although Boston is going to seem very tame after all our adventures."

More clanging and Lonnie's annoyed shout could be heard from under the car. "Honestly, you shouldn't be allowed to drive anywhere, not if you're going to do this to a car!"

"Are you a menace on the roads now?" Wini asked with a grin.

"I'll leave you to explain," said Tom, walking off.

"Coward," I muttered after him. But when I related our adventures to Wini, I gave him full credit for his help. "I'm not sure the nurse at the hospital would have even told us where the pilots were, except he kept batting those eyelashes at her and waving handkerchiefs at me. She asked me if he was married when we went back to call for the tow truck," I said.

"And then complimented me on having such a gentleman for a brother."

"He's a nice man," said Wini. "The crew agrees. He's also a whiz on the phones with the press." She pulled a newspaper clipping from her pocket and displayed her smiling photo along with a large paragraph of text on the upcoming show. In bold headlines, it proclaimed "Read All About the Woman Without Fear Who Flirts with Death in Her Airplane." The following story gave Wini's height and weight and mentioned twice she had recently appeared in Hollywood, lending her talents to the movie studios and immortalizing her stunts on film.

Reading the article, I was struck by an idea. "You should show films of your flying along with the show. I can send you reels of our movie."

Wini cocked her head at me. "How could we do that?"

"Set up a projector and a screen," I said. "Lots of small towns just drape a sheet against a wall and set the chairs outside."

"I think people come to see the actual flying," said Wini. "Or to go up in a plane. That's popular and why Bill does the short hops between my stunts. We were going to take people up, circle around Arkham, and then land back down here. On Sunday, we might even fly between Arkham and Innsmouth. There's a little landing strip there used by the mail flyers."

"Movies would be popular while people wait to go up in a plane or for the stunts to start," I said. "We could even cut a special reel from the footage we took in Hollywood. Insert a few cards to explain what is happening."

"Wouldn't we need music?" Wini said. "To accompany it?"

"A wind-up phonograph works," I said. "Or hire a local musician. If you have a talker in your group, have somebody narrate the stunts as they are shown on the screen."

"Who needs a talker?" asked Tom, who returned without any books in his hands.

"Apparently I do," said Wini, outlining my idea to him.

"Five cents for the movie," said Tom, "and sell a pamphlet about your life to the crowd afterward. It's a clever idea, Betsy, and sure to make money for the show."

Wini looked at the pair of us. "I would have to hire somebody to run the projector as well as give the talk. Bill and I need to fly the planes."

"Local crew," I said. "Didn't you tell me you hired a few in every town? This would be only a couple more."

"Sounds interesting," said Lonnie, coming out from under the car. "I wouldn't mind having some cameras to tinker with as well. I had a thought about mounting them in the undercarriage of the plane."

"Aerial footage of your stunts," Tom said. "There'd be a market for that."

Wini nodded. "Perhaps. I'll have to think about it. You and Betsy do have good ideas."

"Fantastic at publicity ideas," said Lonnie, rummaging in her toolbox. "But useless around machines."

"Tom helped me change a tire," I said, feeling the need to defend our mechanical prowess.

"Anyone can change a tire," said Lonnie, unimpressed. She pulled up the hood of the car and sighed. "This is a mess. Betsy, you're a worse menace than Wini to cars."

"Ah, you did make menace status with Lonnie," said Wini with satisfaction. "I'm a bona fide menace to planes and automobiles, according to her. I think it is a compliment."

"It is not!" retorted Lonnie's muffled voice as she practically went upside down under the hood.

"I am not a reckless driver," I muttered to Wini as we left Lonnie to her work. "It's simply been an unusual day."

"Those seem to happen around you," Wini responded. "A car chase and a shoot-out. I'm sorry I missed the action!"

As I told her the story of our day, Wini agreed with me that it was too soon to return to Bluff Mansion. "Hughes may be in love with the sound of his own voice," I finally concluded, "but he's not completely unobservant. I've been a visitor to so many patients in the past few days they should fit me for a nurse's uniform."

Tom then made a sensible suggestion. "Visit the place when Hughes isn't around. He seems to spend a good deal of time at the hospital, and doesn't he teach at the university, too? Go when he's not there."

"I could," I said, "but what if the grimoire isn't at Bluff Mansion? What if Nova already has it at the Purple Cat?"

Wini nodded her head. "I think it is most likely that she has the grimoire now. I cannot see her moving her pilots to Hughes's place and letting the book slip through her fingers. Didn't your reporter friend say something about dance evenings at the Purple Cat? They must have a band on Friday nights. There will be a lot of people there, so we could slip in and look about for the grimoire."

"Oh, I still have the membership card," I said, digging into my purse for the numbered card we had found in the warehouse. "Do we use it to try for the other door that Darrell told us about?"

Wini grinned. "I'm game if you are."

Tom groaned but said, "I have a dinner jacket and some decent shoes."

"Shoes!" Wini said. "I have a pair of dancing shoes. Actually, they belong to Lonnie, but she always lets me borrow them. But I don't have much in the way of party gear."

"When do you think Lonnie will have the roadster repaired?" I asked.

Tilting her head at the clangs and bangs coming from my car, Wini shrugged. "It won't take her long, knowing Lonnie."

"I'll take a taxi back to the hotel. Bring the roadster this evening, say nine or ten? We don't want to get to the Purple Cat too early." Then thinking about how far it was from Arkham. "Maybe you better come by eight."

"It's a full moon night," noted Wini. "Good for flying or driving."

"Or dancing at a bootlegger's club," I said. "You're a bit taller than me, but if you don't mind a scandalously short skirt, I can lend you a sparkly dress and some pearls."

"Trying to turn me into a jazz baby?" laughed Wini.

"You'll be stepping out with one," I said.

"Whatever you can do, I can do better," Wini said. "Bring on your pearls and fancy clothes, Betsy Baxter, and let's go catch some bootleggers in action."

CHAPTER TWENTY-TWO

In my red dress with the crystal beading and a triple loop of pearls around her neck, Wini looked stunning.

"What should we do with my hair?" she asked me as we both peered into my hotel room's mirror to finish our makeup. Since her hair was longer than was fashionable, none of my bandeaus or clips, styled for my bobbed hair, appeared quite right. I looked her over and sighed. "This is so easy when my friend Jeany does it. She always knows the right piece to complete an outfit." Then an idea struck me. "Oh, we could roll it in the back and finish it off with my jeweled comb." I went digging through my jewelry box. The enameled piece I'd purchased in Argentina was probably meant to secure a mantilla, but it looked lovely affixed in Wini's coiled braid. I sprayed some perfume on her hair to help keep everything in place.

"I'm not sure I recognize myself," Wini said with a dubious glance at the mirror. "And I don't know that I could stand to do this much powder and perfume every day."

"Oh, you get used to it," I said, driving a couple more

hairpins into Wini's arrangement to be sure it held through a Charleston or similar energetic dance.

"Ow, enough with the hairpins," protested Wini. "I could build an entire fuselage out of the hardware you've stuffed into my hair."

"Never doubt the power of a good hairpin," I said. "You'll be thankful for them by the time the evening is done."

In the lobby, Tom was chatting with Irving, the friendly bellboy, but sprang to attention when we emerged from the elevator. Like us, he was very polished, so much so that I suspected he'd talked Irving into giving his coat a brush and his shoes an extra shine while he waited.

"Don't we all look fine?" I said, looking at my friends.

Tom gallantly offered an arm to Wini and me. We managed to make it out the door without collapsing into giggles at the stunned expression of the night manager when we swept past him.

Between the moonlight and my headlamps, the drive to the Purple Cat was easily accomplished. The place was lit up, with cars parked up and down the road, and the sound of the band very clear as we approached the open door. I always loved a good band, and my toes were tapping on the walk to the door.

Inside, the tables and chairs had been swept to one side. The small dance floor was filled. The quartet on the stage sounded as if they were playing twice the number of instruments as they had. The crowd responded by stepping out with enthusiasm.

"Shall we?" Tom said, offering me an arm as Wini laughingly waved off the advances of the men who had descended on us as soon as we came through the door.

"Don't mind if I do," I said as we took to the floor in a Toddle. As we bounced about the room, I looked for Darrell's mystery door. As the door was painted in purple and had a certain large sailor planted in front of it, it took no great detective skills to spot.

"Isn't that one of our friends from the alley?" I asked Tom.

He maneuvered a turn and even sallied a little cheek-to-cheek to eye the mug by the door. "That's him," he said. "But he seemed a more even-tempered gentleman than our friend Albie."

"I recall that the big man counseled against shooting us," I said with a heel kick and a shimmy.

"Nothing ventured," said Tom.

"Nothing gained," I replied.

We swept in the direction of the door, collecting Wini on the way, much to the dismay of her partner. A little breathless, our trio trotted off the dance floor right in front of the purple door.

The man in charge glared down at me. "Get back to the dance," he muttered.

I pulled the Purple Cat's card from my bag and flashed it in his face. "I have an invitation," I said. "Miss Nova Malone is expecting us."

He blinked at that. "Miss Nova never said…" he began.

Wini turned to me and said, quite clearly, "If Miss Nova isn't interested, we could also discuss our ideas with the O'Bannions."

At this, the big sailor looked astonished. "You'd never give Miss Nova's business to the O'Bannions," he said.

"Why not?" Wini bluffed. "I've flown for them before."

He pulled the door open and motioned us through. "Not the O'Bannions!" he repeated as he slammed the door shut behind us. We were on a rickety landing and a long steep cellar staircase stretched down into the darkness before us. A very feeble light flickered at the bottom of the stairs. While I was pleased we had gotten past the first barrier, I was surprised at what we found.

"Ah," said Tom, "not as welcoming as I expected."

"I was thinking the same thing. It lacks a certain ambience," I agreed as we picked our way cautiously down the stairs. The walls were cold and even slightly damp to the touch, but the railing was far sturdier than one would expect from its decrepit appearance.

"Remind me, who are the O'Bannions?" said Tom.

"Tell you all about them later," I said as we reached the bottom. One small lantern sat in a niche. It cast a pale light in what appeared to be a storeroom. A few dusty cases were stacked against the far wall.

"Uh, shouldn't there be more?" Tom asked, surveying the small space.

"I think there is," Wini said, pointing at the floor.

I looked where she pointed and laughed. "I'd never dare use such an obvious clue in one of my movies."

Three distinct footprints crossed the floor, the owner of the shoes probably having tracked through something wet and sticky. Two were clearly visible, but the third footprint was only half visible, the rest disappearing under the storeroom's east wall.

I examined the wall and guessed that the card was only the first step in accessing Nova's hideaway. Real guests were probably given instructions on what to do at this stage. But I wasn't about to march back up those stairs and ask.

"It cannot be too hard to figure out," I said. "It's set up to discourage the cops and possible gatecrashers, not drive away real customers."

The wall appeared to be ordinary wood, but as the other three walls were brick, I took that to be a sign that this section was more than it appeared to be. "There should be a latch," I said, running my hands along the sides and bottom. Tom joined me and stretched his long arms to the top edge.

"Here it is," he said as something clicked. The wall slid away and revealed another flight of stairs, much better lit than the ones we had just navigated. A faint tick-tick sound drifted up the stairs as well as the clink of glasses and murmur of voices.

"Perhaps I should have brought the Mauser," Wini said.

"It would never have fit under the dress," I replied, pretty pleased with myself for figuring out how to get us this far. I couldn't wait to see what came next. "Besides, if that's not a roulette wheel, I'll eat my best hat."

We descended the second flight of stairs to emerge into a simply gigantic cave. There was indeed a roulette wheel with eager gamblers gathered around it. At the far end of the room, an enormous, polished bar sported two bartenders, mixing, stirring, and shaking cocktails for a thirsty throng. Elsewhere, small café tables and chairs allowed for intimate conversation over the beverages. The rugs underfoot and the silk coverings stretched across the ceiling and the walls gave the entire place the feeling of the sultan's palace straight from Universal's *Thief of Baghdad*.

Beneath my feet, I could feel, rather than hear, the boom of ocean waves crashing against the cliff.

"Welcome to the Smuggler's Cave," said Nova Malone as she advanced upon us. If her sparklers had been splendid in the daytime, her jewelry at night was worthy of a pirate queen. She glanced at the purple-and-white card still clutched in my hand. "I see you've found one of my lost cards. Would you care to explain?"

"It began with a book," I said. "A grimoire. But I expect you know all about it." No doubt about it, the woman was intimidating. Even in my highest heels, she towered over me. But I refused to be intimidated. "I've even heard it called Miss Nova's glittering book."

Nova Malone looked amused. "I expect I do know something. But where are my manners? Please take a seat. Champagne? Brandy? Or something stronger?"

"Champagne is always nice when you've been dancing," I replied. "Excellent band, by the way."

"I think so," said Nova as she lowered herself with regal grace into the nearest chair and waved the rest of us to seats at the table. "Did you know we broadcast our dance music on Saturday evenings? Radio is a remarkable invention. Nearly as remarkable as airplanes. I expect both to change the world, much as the change from sail to steam revolutionized shipping in the last century."

A waiter came to the table. After some whispered instructions from Nova, he left and then returned with a bucket of champagne as well as the necessary glasses. The bottle was popped with a finesse that would have impressed Irving, and the bubbly poured out.

"Now, why are you here?" Nova said as she calmly sipped her champagne. The lights in the room sparkled off the diamonds in her hair, around her neck, and encrusting each finger. Only the purple cat brooch pinned to her breast was not completely covered in the glittering stones.

"Do you have the grimoire?" Tom asked with more bluntness than I had come to expect from him.

"If I have the Deadly Grimoire," replied Nova, "I paid for it."

"I have no argument there," Tom said, "but I would appreciate being allowed to give the university a refund and to return to Boston unmolested by your man Albie."

Nova sighed and shrugged. "Albie is an excitable sort. I've often told him it creates more trouble than it is worth, waving guns around and shooting at people," she said. "I blame the movies."

"Why Hollywood?" I retorted because a bootlegger blaming the movies for moral corruption – well, that was as bad as the congressmen who made such speeches annually. And as hypocritical.

"Those cowboy films. All those shoot-outs, and stickups, and so on," said Nova. "It creates an unreal impression for most people."

"It's entertainment," I said, quite stung by her criticism and, at the same time, aware that we were in far more trouble than I'd anticipated. There was no way out of this fantastical hideaway other than the door by which we entered. Given the number of large men dressed as waiters and bartenders swarming around the room, it seemed unlikely we could simply walk out without Nova Malone's express permission. I doubted the other patrons would give us a hand, especially since all the entertainment being held here was illegal upstairs.

For once, it seemed I had rushed into a place I could not rush out of. I didn't enjoy the feeling.

"I like your films," said Nova Malone to my surprise. "For all their silliness."

"My movies are not silly," I responded automatically, still trying to figure a way out of our current situation. "Wait, how do you know I'm an actress?"

"My dear," said Nova quite calmly. "I recognized you the first time you visited the Purple Cat. Your movies are quite popular. And your picture is in the *Arkham Advertiser* on a regular basis. I even recommended your films to my nieces. You solve your mysteries with brains, not relying upon some man to rescue you. Or to shoot your way out of trouble. Even if you do brandish your silver pistol in the earlier scenes. You are much too wise to think a gun with only six shots can save the day."

So much for the pistol in my purse, I thought, and shooting our way out. "I never want to disappoint my fans," I said. "They love a clever solution."

"Such an inspiration to other young women," replied Nova with approval. "I fought for many years to secure the vote. And to change the world. To shake it loose from the chains of the past. There are children going hungry in the winter, and farms going fallow in the spring. All because no bank will lend to Innsmouth fishers and farmers. But I will. I'll build this town back up brick by brick myself if I have to. I was born here, I will die here, and I will not let Innsmouth die with me."

I believed her. Her passionate declaration resonated with sincerity. I could see how her vision would appeal to the people of poverty-stricken Innsmouth. I was sure when Nova Malone's shipments came through the Innsmouth docks or down the back roads, people were happy to look away.

"I find all the world's recent changes encouraging," Nova continued. "The technology of today does not rely on strength alone to operate. Electricity, airplanes, and radio. I predict a much brighter future for us all."

"Madam, I hope you are right," said Tom. "If the last war taught us nothing else, technology can be used for good or evil. As can the grimoire."

"I have never feared anything," said Nova. "Not the inventions of this decade or the spells of the past. However, the grimoire has been something of a disappointment."

This last statement obviously surprised Tom. "Our grimoire has never been called disappointing," he said.

"First, I would say that it is my grimoire," Nova declared. "In fact, it could be called my family's grimoire, for we've held it almost as many years as yours. And, of course, Ezra Hughes claims it belongs to him based on his family's history. Although how being a cheat or being cheated gives one a claim, I am not sure."

"There was absolutely no cheating in our transaction," said Tom, sounding as aggrieved and peevish as I had when Nova Malone called my movies silly. She was clever to find all our sore spots. I wondered how she would needle Wini, for it was becoming clear Nova Malone was playing some game with us. I felt increasingly nervous about her ploys.

"Perhaps there was no deception intended this time,"

Nova said to Tom. "Simply poor bookkeeping by your uncle. But creating the False Grimoire for Bulkington Hughes? A not so innocent ruse by a Sweets."

"Oh, the family truly regrets the creation of the False Fish," said Tom.

"I am sure they did," said Nova Malone. "As much as your friend Betsy regrets what happened to Max, Jim, and, what was his name? Paul?"

At the recital of my lost friends' names, I was startled into an exclamation. "How did you know about Max? About Jim and Paul?" I said. All three had disappeared from the Fitzmaurice house during our filming there, but the newspapers rarely mentioned anyone by name. It was ancient history to most people. And almost nobody remembered Paul anymore. He'd disappeared slightly before Jim and Max, and his exact fate was never known.

"Three years of phone calls to the Arkham police, three years of calls from a studio in Hollywood," said Nova. "It's helpful when there's an Innsmouth woman working on the switchboard. When the same studio pays for the transfer of a man named Jim from the hospital to Bluff Mansion, that's intriguing, too. There are Innsmouth women working there as nurses as well as cleaning the floors and cooking for the patients. It's hard to hide anything from me. If I want to find out, I will."

The battle lines were drawn, and the match had begun in earnest now, I thought. "So you know what I am doing here."

"I might help your Max," said Nova, "if you help me. I'm a far better bet than Hughes for all his fascination with old window glass. He can only show you a glimpse of what is beyond."

"Do you know where Max is?" I said as bluntly as possible. I was tired of games.

"I know more than Minerva," Nova returned. At my look of consternation, she smiled, and it was a very cold smile indeed. "Cortland apples. I buy barrels from Minerva and her husband every year. They have a granddaughter working at the Purple Cat."

I didn't glance at Tom. I didn't look at Wini. I kept my eyes fixed on Nova. When a deadly predator crosses your path, one hunter told me, never look away. "I have no desire to end up in a hospital bed, dreaming my life away," I said. "Wherever Jim has been, it nearly broke him."

"He can be healed," said Nova. "So can my pilots. In fact, as odd as his explanations are, Ezra's ideas are not altogether wrong. I've had good reports of success at Bluff Mansion, good enough to trust my own people there."

Wini, never the most patient of souls, butted into the conversation. "It seems as if you have the book you want. Now, if you promise to stop shooting at my friends, we can all go our ways without any more trouble."

"Oh, no," said Nova Malone. "I need more from you. I want to charter a flight, a charting of a route if you will. It seems the Woman Without Fear would be the perfect pilot for me."

CHAPTER TWENTY-THREE

Wini quickly shook her head when Nova Malone asked for her help. "I have more than enough flights booked for the next few months," she said. "After we finish up our tour of New England, I am preparing for a race, an air derby. I cannot take any other business."

It was politely said. Also Wini didn't address Nova Malone's actual business or the legality or illegality of it. As for the lady herself, she gave no appearance of displeasure. But the room felt cold for all its luxurious hangings. Far below my feet, I was too aware of the restless boom of the surf against the cliffs. More acutely, I remembered Darrell's warning to avoid crossing Nova Malone.

"If you fly my route," said Nova, after a long silence where none of us moved, "you will win every race you enter. No one will ever find a faster way to traverse the country or even navigate around the globe. Imagine if you were to become the first woman to fly around the world."

"I have imagined it," said Wini. "I watched those eight men take off from Santa Monica on their flight around the world and wished I was part of that. Last year, I visited the *Chicago* in the Smithsonian just so I could see their plane. But I don't have three hundred or more hours for a flight. Or all the resources of the United States government. The round-the-world flight took more than half a year and plenty of supplies along the way."

"My route might only take a day. Perhaps less," Nova said. "I had a new seaplane delivered today."

Wini didn't quite snort, but she sounded firm when she replied, "There isn't any plane built today that could fly so fast. It cannot be done. That's a fantasy."

"Are you sure?" said Nova. "Even up and over the poles?"

"Circumnavigate via the poles?" said Wini. "Still not possible. I mean, you could fly over..." She paused and fiddled with her champagne glass. If she had had her silver cigarette case, I am sure Wini would have spun it on the tabletop. "Great-circle navigation, that's what you're talking about?"

Tom and I must have looked puzzled because Wini said, "It's about plotting a course around a globe, a circle that allows you to navigate the shortest distance between two points. Except such navigation doesn't allow for weather, air currents, refueling points, and all the rest."

"But what if you didn't need fuel or rest as you flew?" said Nova.

"Air resistance, winds," started Wini.

"What if you were in a space outside of all that?" said Nova. "What about a space that you could travel without gravity dragging you down?"

I finally understood her. "You're talking about Gulliver Malone's route? The one that let him win races," I said. "The one that took him on strange currents outside the world." It was exactly what Minerva warned against when we had talked to her. The cosmos where people could be lost forever without the right pattern to guide them home. The place where Max and Jim tumbled when they fell through a mirror.

Nova Malone smiled at that. "You are a clever woman," she said.

Tom shook his head. "There are no navigational charts in the grimoire. Nothing about great circles either."

"Have you've read it?" said Nova. "I thought the Sweets kept the book locked up and never let the grimoire sully their eyes. Just their bank account."

"It was the only thing I had to read on the train when I came to Arkham," Tom admitted. "I cannot say it made much sense. But I would remember navigation charts or maps. I always remember what I read."

"Do you?" said Nova. "What an interesting thing to know."

All in all, I disliked the whole tone and direction of this conversation. Especially the contemplative look Nova gave Tom after his last statement. Catching her attention was not in his interest. I believed that most strongly. In this subterranean room, with the roulette wheel ticking away like some mad clock, I knew our time was running out. Perhaps it was Nova Malone's almost unnatural calm or the way everyone else in the room ignored our table as if being with Nova Malone set us outside the circle of normal human curiosity.

No matter how thick the rugs beneath my feet, the stone was cold underneath, and the chill was creeping up my legs, the bone-cold freeze of the ocean. I remembered the stunt I'd discussed with Tom, the jump from ship to ship landing me in the Pacific. Even on a sunny day, the cold nearly shocked the breath out of me. The same cold enveloped me now.

I wanted to shake Nova Malone out of her calm, at least enough to create room for us to maneuver a way back up the stairs and out of the Purple Cat.

"You have the charts," I said to her. "The maps and navigation guides. You've been trying for months to use Gulliver's route for your own smuggling. To beat the O'Bannions and stay ahead of the feds."

At the mention of the O'Bannions, Nova's eyes narrowed the slightest bit. "The O'Bannions have their routes. I have mine. We don't interfere in each other's business."

"Not if you want to keep Naomi O'Bannion out of your hair," said Wini. "There's a woman I wouldn't want to upset."

"I am not afraid of the O'Bannions," said Nova.

"But you do have a problem with losing your planes," I said. "Everyone who has flown for you has come home. But what about the planes and cargo? How many have disappeared?"

"That's right," said Wini. "All those missing planes!"

"And ships and trucks, according to Darrell," I said. "All suffered the same fate as what happened to the original *Gulliver*. They all disappeared."

"A truck is easy to replace," said Nova without any concern. "But several thousand dollars' worth of Canadian whiskey. That's more difficult. Buyers grow impatient. Investors begin to ask questions."

The bartenders called for last orders and the customers began slipping away through the door leading upstairs. A glance at my watch showed it was well past midnight. The more the crowd thinned, the larger and more menacing Nova

Malone's employees looked. As people left, nobody spared us a glance.

"But your seaplane came through," Wini said to Nova. "They towed it back into the harbor."

"With the wings broken and the pilots wandering the cliff road," I said.

"A better result than our earlier flights without the grimoire," said Nova with a shrug. "Unfortunately, they missed the rendezvous and failed to pick up the cargo. That's still to be done."

"A ship to plane transfer, seaplane smuggling, and you're using Gulliver's routes to avoid the G-men," I said, ticking off my guesses or deductions with my fingers, remembering the newspaper stories over the past few months about bootleggers. "A ship is waiting for you to pick up their cargo, which would be diverted from Canada or Europe."

"You are clever," Nova said again. "A ship is docked at a small island north of here, which can only be reached by a seaplane or boat. We tried boats, but on Gulliver's route, it led to disappearances in the harbor. But, in the air, with the grimoire, I think we could transport our cargo safely. We nearly made it on this last run. Hughes claims his formula will let the pilots fly the entire route, so I'm prepared to make a deal with him. And with you." She stared straight at Wini.

Wini shook her head again. "No," she said firmly. "I'm not flying the grimoire's route or any other for you."

"Unfortunate," said Nova. "Then, for now, I think you should stay here. At least until I've made all my arrangements. Perhaps you'll reconsider your plans."

"We have a show tomorrow," said Wini.

"Yes, you do," said Nova implacably. "I wonder how well your other pilot will perform your tricks and how the newspapers will review the performance when it lacks the death-defying Winifred Habbamock. You may need another source of income sooner than you think. And you," she said, looking directly at me, "you missed the largest clue of all."

"What do you mean?" I said.

"All your running around the countryside," said Nova as she rose from her seat. "Talking to Minerva, visiting Captain Leo, all your snooping, looking for Max. And you could have found all your answers at Bluff Mansion this morning. I spotted it immediately when I signed my pilots into Hughes's care."

"What do you mean?" I cried again as Nova walked away.

She glanced back over her shoulder. "You should look at Ezra's register next time you visit his sanitarium."

The waiters completely surrounded our table. One poked me in the back. I recognized the feel of a pistol against my spine. I had played such a scene in enough movies to know what was what. I hissed at Nova Malone. "I thought you didn't believe in guns."

"I don't believe in shooting indiscriminately," she said to me. "But I'm perfectly happy to let my men use a pistol as an incentive for good behavior. Now, behave and follow their instructions."

The instructions boiled down to "Walk this way, sister" , and a slight shove through yet another storeroom door when we reached our destination. Tom and Winifred settled on packing crates. I tried to pace, but the room was barely wide enough for me to take even a few steps in either direction.

Everything had gone very wrong and, worst of all, I'd landed my friends in hot water with me.

"Now what?" asked Tom, who had the temerity or the foresight to snatch the champagne bottle and glasses from the table as we were being hustled away. He sat sipping a glass and looking as if booksellers spent all their evenings locked in storerooms.

"Why are you so calm?" I said to him.

"Would having hysterics help?" he said. "I'd be happy to oblige. I am seriously considering a career change. If gangsters are going to be part of the grimoire trade, I need a new job."

"Bill can handle the basic stuff, and there's always the plane rides," Wini muttered to herself. "But it's still a dirty trick to push us in here."

"And why are you worrying about the show?" I said to her. "We are locked in a room by a woman who thinks she can smuggle goods through… well, I don't know what I would call it, but given the glimpses I've seen, it's not a good idea at all." The world on the other side of the mirrors, the world I saw through the shard of glass Hughes carried should never be allowed to leak into our world. Of that I was certain. Storms and stinking weeds that tried to grab people and three-eyed fish. I was sure those things came from whatever Nova Malone was trying to do.

"I am worrying about my show to prevent myself from being upset," said Wini. "And I know that makes no sense."

"I understand," I said. And I did. I was doing the same thing, focusing on the small things to stop thinking about the larger implications.

"I don't," muttered Tom, but we both ignored him.

"We need to escape. The place should be empty of customers by now," I said, glancing at my watch.

"Nova didn't post a guard," Wini said to me. "At least, I didn't hear her give instructions for one."

"If you're right, now would be the time to escape," I said. "Would they just clean up and leave?"

"Perhaps," said Wini. "If Nova thought we would sit here quietly and wait for her to return."

"Obviously the lady doesn't know you two if she thinks you'll sit quietly anywhere," said Tom.

I stalked to the door and put my ear to the wood. "I don't hear anyone. Do you think they've finally gone home to bed?"

"The only way to find out is to get out," said Wini.

"Are we going to break down the door?" Tom asked.

"Like they do in the movies?" Wini said, looking at me.

"In the movies, those doors are paper," I said. I eyed the packing crates. There wasn't much we could use for tools. Certainly nothing to open the door.

"If I still had my purse, we could shoot the lock out," I said. Of course, my purse and, more importantly, my pistol was the first thing Nova Malone's goons had grabbed from me at the table. Nova had even smirked and said, "I'll have this returned to your hotel. We cannot have the Flapper Detective lose her silver pistol."

"I should have brought the Mauser," Wini grumbled.

"I still don't know where you expected to hide that. In your hair?" I said.

"In my hair? In my hair!" said Wini, springing off her crate.

"What are you doing?" I said as she knelt by the door.

"Picking the lock," she replied as she drew two hairpins out of the arrangement I had made. "It's not as good as my knife or my real lockpicks, but you were right, Betsy Baxter. These hairpins are useful."

CHAPTER TWENTY-FOUR

Wini took less than ten minutes to click the lock open. Once outside our prison, we found only a few flickering electric lights had been left on. The dimly lit corridor was empty of guards and there was no sound of footsteps. I checked my watch. It was nearly three in the morning. Hopefully too early for anyone working in the Purple Cat upstairs. I wondered when they opened for breakfast.

We explored the short corridor. Several unlocked doors revealed other storerooms, many so full of actual stores that all three of us would not have fit inside. The corridor itself ended in a blank wall of stone. If there were any hidden latches or other ways out, we failed to find them.

At the other end of the corridor, there was a door that led back into the Smuggler's Cave. It was the only locked door we had encountered since breaking out, so of course, we decided to pick that lock, too. Wini extracted more hairpins. The first two bent, but the next pair proved effective as she opened the door.

Lit by only one small night lamp, the Smuggler's Cave

itself seemed a vast space to cross in the shadowy gloom. We dodged our way around the tables with the chairs stacked for the morning cleaners.

"Doesn't this seem a little too easy?" asked Tom as we approached the door to the stairs.

"Escaping?" I said. "Did you want to stay?"

"Oh, no," he said. "But in the books, there's usually ropes to be cut by bits of broken glass while water rises around the tied-up hero or heroine."

"That's only in the pulps!" I said. "And some pictures. Well, my movies always."

"I cannot believe you're arguing about escaping," Wini said as we left the main room. On the Smuggler's Cave side, a now closed door had a simple and obvious latch to slide it open. With only a feeble light behind us, the stairs were hard to see.

"This is when we could use a match and a candle," I said. "Have you ever noticed how easily those things come to hand in the movies?"

"Or adventure novels?" said Tom. "Well, we know where the stairs are and there is a railing."

We inched our way up the first few steps like intrepid turtles. The long flight seemed even longer this time, ending in the false wall we had unlatched coming down. Once again, we groped along the top of the wall to find the lever. "I have it!" said Tom. The door swung open, and it was pitch black. What light filtered up the stairs from the open door at the bottom did not reach this far.

Walking into total darkness was more than a little intimidating. I knew in my head that there was a floor in front of us and somewhere quite close another flight of stairs that ended in the door to the Purple Cat. But to step into that darkness felt like plunging off a cliff. There was a terrible feeling of the unknown ahead of me.

"All right," I said, grabbing for Tom and Wini, "it's only a room. A small room with a staircase on one side. A staircase going up and not down, so no chance of falling. We are going to find those stairs together."

And my brave, reckless friends stepped into the darkness with me.

"Found it," yelped Tom when he was the first to stumble upon the stairs with his foot. We couldn't see him, and we couldn't see the stairs, but the elation of knowing we had a way out bubbled through my veins.

Wini and I groped our way forward. I felt for the first step and had it under my feet. "Upward," I said.

"I hope the next door isn't locked," said Wini. "I'm not sure I could pick locks in complete darkness."

We went up the stairs, gripping the banister and going slowly, feeling our way. Something about being without any light at all made every sound and smell more intense and even threatening. The clack of our shoes on the stairs was loud, the beating of my heart banged in my ears, and beneath that there was another sound – the booming I had felt more than heard while we were in the Smuggler's Cave. Finally, I said, "What is that? It sounds like waves."

"It probably is waves. The tide coming in," said Tom. "High tide is just before dawn."

"How can you know that?" I said as Wini yelped when she came to a landing and fell against me in the dark.

"High tide?" Tom sounded surprised behind me. "There's a tide chart in the airfield office. I suppose it's common enough around here, being so close to the ocean."

Tom made up the last in our line, the theory being if Wini or I fell, we probably wouldn't knock him off the stairs. If he fell on us, or at least on me, that might well start a chain reaction back to the bottom.

"But how can we hear the ocean inside?" I said.

"Sound carries, and there must be ventilation shafts," said Tom. "The air is fresh."

"And smells like seaweed," said Wini in front of us. "The horrible smell it gives off when it is rotting on the beach."

She was right. There was a strong smell reminiscent of a beach at the end of a hot day. Earlier, I had been too excited to take stock of such things, too eager to search out Nova's hideaway, but now the reek seemed to grow stronger with every stumbling step in the dark.

"I wish they hadn't taken my purse," I said. "I had a perfectly good book of matches in it."

"Oh," said Tom. "I forgot." There was a striking sound, and a match flared up, illuminating two annoyed women looking down at him.

"You forgot you had matches?" I said.

He shrugged and then yelped as the match burned down to his fingertips. The spark of the dropped match fell below us, winking out finally on the stone floor below.

"I don't smoke," said Tom. "I'm not sure why I have matches in this pocket. Oh, right, I wore this jacket to the Bibliophile Club's dinner. Somebody always wants a smoke, and nobody can ever find matches. Cigars, after dinner."

"Keep moving," Wini scolded us both. "We need to get back to the airfield!"

"Yes, yes," I said and proceeded up the rest of the stairs.

The final door, thankfully, was not locked, and we emerged into the Purple Cat. A single ghost light burned on the tiny stage where the band had been playing only a few hours ago. The light seemed almost unbearably bright when we emerged from the stairs. We stopped and blinked, all of us uneasily aware of how vulnerable we were to discovery.

Like the Smuggler's Cave below, the place was full of tables with upended chairs stacked across their tops. It, too, was empty. Everyone had gone home.

The booming sounded louder in the Purple Cat, almost like the giant heartbeat of a primordial beast.

"Are you sure that is the surf?" I whispered to Tom.

"It's night, so you notice it more?" he whispered back.

"Shh," said Wini as she circled her way around the tables toward the outer door.

"There's nobody to hear us," I said with a bravado that was more hope than certainty.

Still, I tiptoed as we crossed the room to leave. Every footstep seemed like a prelude to discovery and another confrontation with Nova. This time, I doubted we would simply be locked in a storeroom.

Reaching the door, Wini snarled to find it locked when she tried to pull it open. "Not again," she muttered, groping in her falling hair for a remaining hairpin.

"It's a bolt," I said, reaching around her to slide the bolt into the open position. The door swung open with a merry little jangle of its bell that caused us all to leap like scalded cats.

"My heart cannot stand much more of this," said Tom.

"Perhaps we should have gone out the kitchen door," I said. But nobody came running.

Outside, the grass was cold and damp as we walked through it, but the sky was still clear, and the moon waxed bright. Oddly, once we were outside, the booming noise disappeared. In fact, the silence seemed utter and oppressive.

Then I heard a long mournful hoot. It was followed by another and another.

"That's a foghorn," said Wini. "Why would anyone be sounding off a foghorn? It's perfectly clear."

I went around the Purple Cat toward the sound.

"Careful," said Tom, following me. "The cliff is close."

Once I'd gone around the building, the cliff fell away only a few yards behind the back door of the Purple Cat. A sea wind hit my face, carrying a clean salt scent. The wretched stink we'd experienced inside couldn't be detected.

The long mournful wail of the foghorn sounded again. I saw a flash of light.

"I know what that is," said Wini. "That's the Falcon Point Lighthouse. I didn't realize we were so close. A warning for ships and a beacon for night flyers. But I have never heard the foghorn wail like that."

A softer toot sounded, further out to sea. A light flashed three times, twice red and once green.

"There's a ship out there," I said, trying to make out something more. The moonlight gilded the waves and made each rolling breaker appear like the cresting back of some gigantic beast swimming beneath the water, but the ship was lost in the blue-black gloom of the horizon.

"Very far out," said Tom. "It's almost like they are signaling back to the lighthouse."

Wini looked troubled. "I thought the same," she said. "And I don't like it. Let's leave."

The others turned away, but I lingered. The light and the wail of the lighthouse's horn kept me rooted there. Then I saw a flash of light along the edge of one curling breaker, very faint, perhaps a phosphorescent flash, and suddenly, that feeling washed over me, that feeling of slipping out of one world into the next, the tipping upside down of all our reality I had experienced for a moment on Minerva's porch. Then the lighthouse's beacon turned toward me, and the light stung my eyes. I was simply Betsy again, standing on the edge of a cliff, and my friends were shouting at me to hurry.

"My roadster better be there," I said, concentrating on that worry rather than what had just happened. I didn't want to think about what had happened to me on the cliff's edge. I wanted to get off Nova Malone's troubled property. The wind shifted again and carried the stink of rotting seaweed.

Luckily, the car was still parked on the grass where we had left it.

"What about your key?" said Wini. "Did you lose it with your purse?"

"Of course not," I said. I hiked up my skirt and pulled the key from the pocket sewn onto my garter. Being a pleasant night, we'd left the top down and the doors unlocked.

"Another piece of Henry's advice?" said Tom as we climbed into the car.

"Of course. Never let yourself be stranded. Don't leave

your key in your purse. It could be stolen." I started up the engine. The roar sounded far too loud in the predawn stillness, but I drove away from the Purple Cat without any shouts or disturbance.

"I still think it is all too simple," said Tom

"Getting away?" asked Wini.

Tom nodded.

I had to agree with him. "Nova could have locked us up better. Or taken us someplace worse."

"There are all kinds of caves along this coast," Wini agreed. "Many at the base of this cliff. Be glad Nova didn't dump us in any of those. Some flood at high tide."

"I don't think she wanted to hurt us," I said. "I think Nova wanted to delay us or even blackmail us. But I don't think she hurts people unnecessarily."

"She seems to send them off someplace that's not terribly good for their health," Tom said.

"Yes, but she makes sure they find their way home again," I said. I remembered all the people we met that seemed to think Nova Malone was a good woman, or at least a generous one. "But I am worried about Jim being at Bluff Mansion."

"And he is?" asked Tom.

"A friend," I said. "A friend who needs time to heal. But I think he would be better back in California than here." I might want to believe Nova wouldn't be violent, but I couldn't leave Jim unprotected at the sanitarium, I decided. Nova might snatch him to blackmail me and, in turn, Wini. Or Hughes could use Jim as part of his seaweed experiment, which was making me increasingly uneasy. "I think I should get Jim out today," I decided. As for Nova's statement that I should look at the sanitarium's register, I had seen it just the day before. Nothing could be learned there, I almost convinced myself.

"But we're flying today," said Wini as we sped toward the airfield.

"Which might actually be a good time to go," said Tom.

"What do you mean?" I asked.

"Didn't you give free tickets away at the Purple Cat?" he said.

"And we sent some to Bluff Mansion," said Wini. "I posted them yesterday."

"We gave away tickets in the nearby towns," I said. "And more free tickets in Innsmouth," I added, remembering our conversation with Captain Leo.

"Then most folks will be at the show," Tom said.

"And not at the sanitarium," I said. "We could remove Jim while everyone is at the show. To make it truly safe, we could send a special invitation to Hughes. Maybe tell him Wini is interested in his theories. That should draw him out."

"Who is going to remove your friend from Bluff Mansion?" Wini asked. "We're performing."

"We're performing in an airplane," I pointed out. "Couldn't we just fly there, remove Jim, and fly back into the show. You said there was a field in Innsmouth."

"There is," said Wini. "It's not too far from Bluff Mansion."

"But how will you get Jim away? You cannot stash him in the plane, can you?" said Tom. "Wouldn't you need a car and driver?"

"And you don't drive," I said with a sigh. I obviously should have brought Farnsworth to Arkham. He could have organized a rescue or two. But I needed to work with what I had. "Lonnie?"

"No, she needs to stay with the show in case of problems with the planes," said Wini. "But how about a friend with a truck?"

"Who do you know with a truck?" I asked.

"Stella! She can help us," said Wini. "How about removing your friend via the US Mail?"

CHAPTER TWENTY-FIVE

I couldn't hear the crowd over the rumble of the motorcycle's engine and the even louder roar of the plane overhead. Lonnie leaned over the handlebars as if she could push an extra ounce of speed into the bike by sheer will alone. I placed my hands on her leather-clad shoulders and boosted myself off the seat into a standing position like the stance I learned from a bareback rider. The rope ladder trailed back from the plane flying in front of us. Wini had positioned the plane perfectly with the end of the ladder almost hitting the top of Lonnie's head. I went up and off the seat in a single jump, grasping the ladder's rung firmly in both hands.

The crowd roared!

Lonnie shot away. Wini pushed the plane toward the clouds as I pulled myself up the ladder, bringing up one leg and then the other, to anchor myself firmly on the rungs. When I was halfway up the ladder, Wini turned the plane so we would fly back over the field of spectators. The momentum spun me slightly, but it was no worse than dangling from a trapeze. I relaxed into the ladder and let it settle into position.

The great sense of the noise – the airplane's engine and the wind's roar – seemed to fall away. The wind against my face felt splendid. Watching the crowd below thrilled my heart like nothing else. All my earlier fears and worries were gone in the rush of the moment.

Down on the ground, the people of Innsmouth and Arkham raised their faces to look up at us, the daring women of the sky. I unhooked one hand to wave at the crowd. Was Nova Malone below? We'd already spotted Ezra Hughes in the crowd. Tom had pointed him out earlier.

But I forgot all those worries in the thrill of the stunt. I was tired of hunting through the shadows and running after rumors. Let everyone below squint into the sun for once, trying to see us. I was going to rescue Jim. And, I vowed, I would find Max!

We passed the end of the field. Wini held the plane level and steady as I continued to climb the ladder and onto the wing. As we discussed during our drive back from the Purple Cat, I stepped onto the lower wing and hooked my arm around the strut reinforced by Lonnie for a similar trick normally done by Charlie. Wini banked again and flew back over the crowd. I waved one more time from the wing as we passed.

We continued to fly out over the fields. Now the only eyes that turned up to see us were sheep. I popped into the cockpit as we had practiced early that morning. The whole stunt was based on the training I had received earlier in Los Angeles with a few adaptations of my own. Lonnie's clever engineering helped me as the small winch allowed me to draw up the ladder and secure it on the wing. I gave a thumbs-up to Wini in the rear cockpit and saw her signal in return.

If Wini breathed a sigh of relief, I couldn't hear it over the rush of the wind. As for myself, once I had practiced earlier this morning, I'd known that this would work. And it had!

The countryside rolled past us, the late dusty green of summer trees and ripening fields giving way to the silver ribbon of the Miskatonic River. Wini followed the river to the coast, angling away only a few miles from the sea. Soon, we saw the tiny Innsmouth airfield used by the Aerial Mail Service. No other planes were in sight as Wini took us in for a landing.

We hit the ground with the thump and the bounce and the second thump that now felt routine to me. As we rolled to a stop, I spotted Stella's mail truck driving toward us.

As soon as the plane was still, I came out of my seat and onto the wing, dropping to the ground with the ease of an experienced flyer. Wini jumped down after me.

She clapped me on the back. "Well done!" Wini said. "We must teach you how to fly. Next time, I want to try that trick of climbing up the ladder, but I need a pilot I can trust."

I laughed, still so exhilarated by the stunt that I could barely speak. "It was wonderful," I exclaimed. "We'll have to do it again for the film cameras. Can you imagine the audience's reaction?"

Wini's answering grin told me she understood the value of that stunt. "It would be something," she said. "But have you thought of a reason why the Flapper Detective would have to go up in a plane that way? Don't your stunts need to fit into the story?"

With a chuckle, I shook my head. "If it looks good on the poster," I said, "it will work for the audience."

Stella came strolling toward us. We'd called her as soon as

we reached the airfield. Once Stella heard our plans, she'd immediately agreed to help.

"Right on time," Stella said. "Even though the Innsmouth Post Office seems to be recovering, they were so happy I volunteered to take the route again today. They wanted to go to the air show."

Climbing up into the back of her mail van, I found a spare uniform neatly folded on one of the shelves next to the packages. A bit bigger than my usual size, the jacket pulled easily over my blouse. I stripped off my pants and pulled on the skirt. A couple of tugs to adjust the hemline, and I was set as a junior postmistress.

Outside, Wini said, "Right, so our next stop is Hughes's sanitarium?"

"Yes," said Stella. "I have some airmail for Bluff Mansion."

"Wealthy patients," I said, climbing out of the back of the van, "if they are getting airmail."

"Hughes only takes those who can pay," said Stella with some disapproval. "No charity cases for him, according to what I've heard. But there's plenty of wealthy folk with bad nerves. And families willing to pay to steady them."

"Are you sure his patients all go home to their families?" said Wini. I had been wondering the same thing. Jim had gone to the sanitarium just a few months ago, but I wondered where he would have ended up if I wasn't fetching him now.

"Where else would they go?" asked Stella as we settled into the front seat of her truck. Stella drove, Wini took the window seat, and I squashed into the middle, trying to keep my legs from interfering with Stella's shifting. From the airfield to Bluff Mansion, it was a short drive.

"They must have to repaint that every spring," said Wini, eyeing the imposing facade from the driveway after we drove through the gates. "New England winters are never kind to exteriors like that." She slid out of her seat and looked at me.

"Jim's room was on the second floor just off the back stair," I said, gesturing toward the rear of the house.

Wini nodded. "Should be easy. I'll bring him down that way if there's no staff around."

Along with the tricks, we'd also discussed who would do what in this little escapade. I decided Wini should fetch Jim. I would look for whatever Nova wanted me to see in the register. "Be quick," I said.

Wini checked her watch. "Bill will be flying loops now," she said. "Then there's the mock battle with Bill and some local flyers. If Tom talks that up enough, we should have at least thirty minutes."

"You saw how excited Tom was to be handed a megaphone," I said. "He'll still be speaking when we get back."

Stella climbed down from the driver's seat and went around to the back of the truck to fetch her mail bag. Wini took off for the rear of the house.

"Let's look at Hughes's register," I said to Stella. We'd talked on the phone about that and how to best go unnoticed into the sanitarium. "Dress as a mailwoman," said Stella, "because they will always look at the uniform and not the face."

"I don't want to run into anyone I met earlier," I told her. "I'm sure the uniform is a great disguise but not if it is Hughes or the same receptionist. She cannot be that blind."

"You'd be surprised, but when were you there?" said Stella.

"A couple of days ago," I said. So much had happened, I was surprised to realize my visit was such a short time before.

Stella shouldered her mail bag and nodded. "Let's hope they have a different person on the front desk on Saturday. It seems likely."

"So, a big staff?" I said, wondering how many were spies for Nova.

"The place employs a fair number from Innsmouth and even Arkham," said Stella. "From maintaining the grounds to supplying the kitchens. I asked around at the Innsmouth Post Office when I was picking up this mail. Lately, they've seen a lot of invoices from the local businesses."

"And are there always as many checks being mailed out as invoices received?" I asked.

"That's a good question," said Stella as we mounted the steps. "I heard the shops need to send their bills twice before payment goes out."

"Interesting," I said as we walked into the lobby. It made more sense that Ezra had approached Nova about treating her pilots with his seaweed cure. It sounded like he needed the bootlegger's money.

As I'd noticed before, the entry would have been a grand entrance hall for a family home. Now, without Hughes talking into my ear and other distractions, I noticed the shabbiness hidden by turning this hall into a receiving area for paying guests. The woman behind the main desk gave us both a slight nod. I didn't recognize her, so Stella had guessed correctly about different staff on Saturday.

"Good morning," said Stella. With a gesture toward me,

she said, "This is Betsy. She's traveling the mail route with me today."

Thus Stella neatly sidestepped actual untruths or revealing my true purpose, leaving the slightly disapproving woman with the impression that I was a new recruit to the mail service.

"It's so inconvenient," said the woman at the desk, "when you lot keep changing. And the last postman even lost a few letters."

"Sorry, ma'am, you should see the regular carrier next week," said Stella truthfully.

"It's so interesting," I gushed, taking over the conversation. "Why, this house is wonderful. I'm new to the region, but I've never seen anything finer."

The receptionist puffed up like a pigeon, obviously glad for a little praise. "Isn't it fine?" she said to me.

"Yes, it is," I said. The large visitor's register sat at her elbow. I wanted to see whatever Nova noticed yesterday. I gave a slight nod at Stella. She deliberately turned her back on me and began to unload mail on the desk.

"This one is so blurred," Stella said to the woman. "Can you tell if it is James or John?"

The receptionist leaned forward to check the address. I slid the register book toward me and flipped to the last page. The whole thing really was like a hotel register with patients' names shown as arriving on a certain date and leaving on a later date. Perhaps the families leaving them here pretended this was simply a vacation in the countryside.

There in a bold slash of a signature was Nova Malone's name and next to it were two men's names as arriving patients, probably her two pilots. Then I stared at the name of another patient recorded as arriving the same day. The name was Max Taelsman, the name of my Max. And, more puzzling, he was shown as checked out this morning.

"I think you're right," said Stella. "That's definitely a James."

I barely heard her. I couldn't form a coherent thought. Max's name knocked me for a loop just as if we were going upside down in Wini's plane. Where had Max been? How had he gotten to Bluff Mansion? Why was he gone now?

The receptionist started to turn. Hastily shoving the book away, I smiled brightly at her when she looked at me. The smile was automatic, a cover for the stunned expression that would have been plastered all over my face if I wasn't accustomed to acting one emotion while experiencing another.

"This sure is a swell place," I repeated as a million questions tumbled through my mind. It couldn't be Max? Could it?

Obviously approving of my praise, she returned my smile with her own. "It's one of the finest sanitariums in New England," the receptionist declared. "We're all so proud of the doctor's work."

"Come along," said Stella, "we have a number of stops still to do."

Nodding meekly, I followed her out the front entrance. When we got to the van, Wini was sitting inside, spinning her cigarette case on the dashboard. "Seven," she muttered. "Always seven near Innsmouth."

I decided to keep what I learned to myself. I needed to think it through. I needed to talk to Tom about the Deadly Grimoire. Had Nova's use of the book caused Max to fall back out of a mirror? Or had Hughes seen him through his odd piece of glass? It all seemed too ridiculous and too strange, but I was ready to believe in the power of the grimoire.

When I opened the passenger side door, Wini said to me, "Your friend is in the back."

I nodded and went around to the rear of the van, still thinking hard about what I should do next. What could I do next?

Jim was huddled up against the mail sacks dressed in casual slacks and a shirt similar to the one he'd worn when I visited.

"Betsy," he said with a slow blink. "Am I being mailed somewhere?"

"Yes, Jim," I said as I snagged my clothing. "We're sending you to a hotel tonight. Then home to California." Stella promised to drop Jim off at the hotel after she left us at the plane and delivered the rest of the mail. I owed Stella a lot more than a simple thanks.

As for Jim, I'd arranged for Irving to take him up to a room and for a traveling nurse to pick Jim up from there. The nurse would ride with him on the train back to California. It had taken a very expensive phone call to Farnsworth, but he had everything well in hand with all possible comforts for Jim.

"That's nice," Jim muttered, settling back into the mail sacks. "Oranges would be nice. I miss fresh orange juice." He was almost asleep again, much as he had behaved in the sanitarium. Although he'd always been a champion napper on movie sets as well.

I pulled on my flight pants and folded up Stella's spare uniform jacket and skirt.

Jim stirred in his corner when we bumped over the field

back to the airplane. I heard Wini and Stella chatting in the cab. It all seemed so normal, but my world was now officially upside down.

"Betsy," Jim murmured.

"Yes, Jim," I said as I fixed my goggles and helmet for the return flight. What I was going to do about Max, I hadn't decided. I supposed I could return to the Purple Cat to confront Nova. But this time I would keep a pistol in my hand, not in my purse, which meant finding a pistol to carry. I wondered if Wini would lend me her Mauser.

Jim made a distressed sound, the sort of muffled yell that a dreaming man makes.

"Jim?" I said. "Are you all right?"

Jim blinked his eyes open. "Who is Tom?" he said to me in a worried tone. "Why is Tom yelling in the mirror now?"

CHAPTER TWENTY-SIX

We flew back over the crowd with a slow barrel roll. If I had had a parachute, I would have jumped out of the plane. I was that desperate to be back on the ground.

Even when I'd told Wini what Jim had said, she'd reassured me. "We left Tom less than an hour ago," she said. "He was announcing Bill's act and the plane rides to the crowd. What could have happened to him?"

"I don't know, but I don't trust Nova Malone an inch," I said. "And we invited Ezra Hughes to the show, too." I had phoned the doctor earlier in the morning, telling him how much we admired his theories and that we had news of the grimoire. As I hoped, he'd immediately agreed to come to the show.

We circled the crowd with Wini waggling the wings in a salute to the spectators below, then circled again as I nearly wept with frustration. I needed to know what had happened to Tom. But eventually we landed.

Then we were nearly mobbed by the cheering crowd. Wini's crew had to wave them back, mostly to keep them from serious injury from the still spinning propeller.

As soon as I could break away, I searched for Tom. Everyone I asked had seen him earlier, and several people sang his praises. A few more tried to stop me and tell me how much they loved the show, but I waved them off. Nobody, not even Lonnie or Bill, could tell me where Tom was.

I finally went into the hangar where he had been sleeping. Tom's cot was easy to find. There were piles of books around it. I recognized the ones he had purchased from Captain Leo. Nothing indicated Tom had returned to his luggage since we started the show earlier.

Wini came into the barn, stripping off her gloves and her helmet as she spotted me. "Any sign of him?" she said.

"No," I answered. "I've asked everywhere. Everyone remembers him announcing our tricks through the megaphone, but nobody remembers seeing him after Bill finished his performance."

"Yes," said Lonnie, following Wini into the hangar. "I was surprised to see you flying back over the field with no announcement from Tom. I expected him to talk up your return."

"Did anyone see Nova Malone in the crowd?" I asked.

Lonnie, who'd never met Nova, looked puzzled but I explained what she looked like. And described her elegant Rolls.

"I don't remember seeing a Rolls," said Lonnie. "I might not have noticed her, but I definitely would have noticed such a car."

Wini started to look worried. "Even if he wandered off, Tom would be back by now."

"And he wouldn't leave all his books behind," I said. I could have wept with anger and frustration. I was so tangled up. I had found Max, or almost found Max, and I'd definitely lost Tom. If that was my fault because I defied Nova and teased Hughes, I'd never forgive myself.

"Miss Baxter, Miss Habbamock," a voice called outside the hangar.

"Darrell," I said to Wini. I looked through the hangar door to see the *Arkham Advertiser* reporter waving at us.

"A few photos?" he called, holding up his camera.

I went outside to question Darrell. "I'm looking for Tom," I told him. "Have you seen him since the show ended?"

Darrell started to shake his head, then stopped. "I did," he said slowly. "At least I think it was him. He was climbing into a car with Dr Hughes."

"When?" I asked, and I could have shaken Darrell when he paused to reflect.

"Just after you flew away and the other pilot started his aerobatics," Darrell said. "Yes, that's it. Tom announced those. Then a few minutes later, I saw him with Hughes."

"Do you remember what the car looked like?" I said.

"A Model T," said Darrell promptly. "And before you ask me, it was black. But it did have a dent on the front fender. I noticed it was splashed with mud and sand, like someone had been driving near the beach. There was even seaweed hanging off the back bumper."

"You wouldn't pick up seaweed along the cliff road," I said. Although the stuff seemed to be everywhere in Arkham and Innsmouth this summer.

"No," agreed Darrell. "But there's a lower road out of Innsmouth, heading toward Falcon Point, that runs right along the water's edge. It floods out whenever a storm blows in. There's always sand and mud that way. I've driven out there myself to take pictures."

"Anything else?" I said.

Darrell looked worried, never a good sign. "It's a bad area. As I said, it floods frequently. There are several caves, and that road is the only access to the beach. Last time I went, I was experimenting with low light photography in those caves."

"Caves?" I asked. "Like the ones where people were found earlier this summer?"

"Yes, a few of the missing pilots and that one boat crew was found in those caves," Darrell said. "So was Minerva Knowles, a farm wife who got lost on a fishing trip."

"I've met her," I told him.

Darrell looked a little surprised but continued, "That's one of the reasons I went back recently. To take pictures of where people were found. But I wasn't happy with the photos, so we didn't print them. I think I'm going to switch to one of the new Leica cameras. Better control on the shutter speed, better results."

"I don't suppose those caves run under the Purple Cat and Bluff Mansion?" I asked, an idea slowly forming in my head through the haze of worry over Tom.

Darrell nodded. "Yes. But most are only accessible during low tide. The sea goes right into them during high tide."

"Wait here," I said. "I'm going to get a map. Then you show me exactly where those caves are."

By the time Wini finished signing autographs and the crowd had completely dispersed, I knew where I wanted to go. I told Wini what Darrell had seen and what the map showed of the road along the shore.

"Look how it curves here," I said, tracing the route Darrell suggested. "This would put us almost underneath the Purple Cat. What if the Smuggler's Cave had a back entrance and a staircase that led all the way down to the water?"

"You think that's how Nova is bringing in her liquor?" said Wini.

I studied the map. "She could land a seaplane or bring a small boat along the coast here and unload into the caves," I said. "Shipments going elsewhere could be loaded into trucks that take the beach road, then driven wherever needed."

"Makes sense," said Wini. "In which case, calling her speakeasy the Smuggler's Cave seems pretty daring."

"She said she didn't fear anything. I guess that includes investigations by the feds," I said. "Besides, everyone around here seems to avoid that bit of coast due to unusual currents," I finished, remembering Minerva's tale.

"Or Nova Malone's excitable men, like Albie, protecting her stash," Wini said. "Maybe that's why she locked us up. So we weren't out on the cliff road when a ship came in. Remember the noises we heard on our way out of the Purple Cat and the ship flashing its lights?"

"Perhaps," I said. Although those booming sounds seemed stranger than just a seaplane landing or a ship coming close to shore. I remembered the odd flash of light I'd seen, and I was certain that somewhere out at sea, Nova had opened Gulliver Malone's route. "If Hughes took Tom to one of Nova's hideaways, and it does seem like he is working with her men, then that's the most likely place for them to go."

"You're not driving out to those caves alone," Wini said.

Lonnie finished up her inspection of Wini's plane and wanted to know where I was going. When I told her, she moaned. "I just finished putting your car back together. You can't take it down a road covered in sand. You'll probably even try to drive it into one of those caves."

"I'm not sure what's out there," I said, "but it is probably more dangerous than anything we've done so far."

"Then you need me to ride shotgun," Wini declared. "I'll fetch the Mauser."

"There's the Beretta, too," said Lonnie. "I'll get it. There's not much ammo for that, but you can get off a shot or two."

"Did you raid an army depot?" I said when she returned with the rifle.

"Won the rifle off another pilot," said Wini. "He bet the Beretta that I wouldn't copy one of his stunts."

"She flew through an actual barn," said Lonnie, "and only a maniac tries that one."

"I was wonderful," said Wini with a wink.

"You're a reckless daredevil," said Lonnie to Wini. Then she turned to me. "And you better take me with you. Wini is an ace with that Mauser, but I'm better with the Beretta. Also, I'll be there with my tools in case you break something." She heaved her toolbox onto the backseat of the roadster and settled beside it. "Wini, fetch the lanterns and the ropes we use to tie the tarps down. We may need those, too."

"Good idea," said Wini, who ran into the hangar. She came out a minute later and passed those supplies back to Lonnie. "I have extra matches in my pocket, too," she said to me as she climbed into the front seat. "And this." She flashed her switchblade at me. "In case Tom's tied up this time. And if we need to pick a lock–" she held up a case of lockpicks "–these are stronger than your hairpins."

"That's everything but a picnic basket," said Lonnie. "Let's go."

"You're both good friends," I said. "Let's find Tom." I tried to sound cheerful, but the sudden partnership of Ezra Hughes and Nova Malone made me very nervous indeed. If I'd been honest, I would have said, "Let's find Tom before it is too late."

CHAPTER TWENTY-SEVEN

The road ran right onto the beach at the base of the cliff. At times, the road actually disappeared under the sand. We pulled the chains out of my trunk and affixed them to the wheels. It was slow going, and Lonnie winced and muttered about damaging a fine machine every time I went over a bump, but we eventually made it to the very end.

The road stopped at some large boulders, obviously meant to keep idiots like us from driving into the surf during high tides. Getting out, Lonnie eyed the line of dead seaweed marking the tide line. The smell of rotting vegetation was brimstone strong, the worst I'd ever encountered near the ocean. It reminded me of the stench we noticed on the lower stairs of the Purple Cat.

"It looks like the water doesn't come past these rocks," said Lonnie, "but let's back up the car and turn it around."

I was impatient to go along to the sea caves. I could see the dark entrances from where we were parked. "Why waste time?" I said.

"Because if we have to leave in a hurry, we want to be able

to leave in a hurry," said Lonnie, pulling two lanterns and the Beretta out of the back. She slung the Beretta over her shoulder. Then she handed one lantern to me and one to Wini.

"Aren't you going to carry one?" asked Wini.

Lonnie shook her head. "You can shoot one-handed with that Mauser, but I need both hands for the rifle." She shouldered a coil of rope and slipped a wrench into her pocket. "Besides, I have a flashlight." She waved the flashlight at us, then shoved it under her jacket.

Rather than stand and argue with Lonnie, who appeared to have a stubborn streak a mile wide, I turned the car around and even drove it up the road a few yards to make sure I parked well above the high tide line. The strong smells and steady moan of the wind playing through the rocks and caves convinced me we were on the right track to finding a secret entrance to the Smuggler's Cave and Purple Cat. I was sure this was what we had been hearing and smelling when we had escaped earlier.

But why had Hughes snatched only Tom? Nova had obviously notified him that we'd escaped her. Why not wait until Wini and I were back on the ground and take all three of us? Fear of the crowd noticing? Or was he using Tom as bait? Why would he want to lure us here?

I rejoined Lonnie and Wini, and we picked our way over the rocks to the closest cave mouth. A glance inside showed it was a shallow cave with seaweed piled against the back wall. By the waterline marked on the cave walls, this was one that filled up at high tide.

"Nobody would store anything here," Wini decided. "It would be carried out to sea too soon."

"It's too close to the road," I said. "If someone was looking for smuggled goods, it would be the first place they'd look."

A couple more caves proved to be similar – shallow and filled only with the detritus brought in by the waves.

We continued down the beach. Right at the base of the cliff, we walked on rocks and shingle, sliding and grinding under our feet. Sometimes it was dry and sometimes wet as the cliff curved away and then back toward the ocean. After clambering over a group of boulders, we found ourselves walking across damp sand.

"Tide comes all the way up to the cliff's base here," said Lonnie.

"Yes, but maybe not into that cave," I said. This cave's mouth was a little above the beach, and there was a clear path leading up to it. As we followed the path upward, we found marks, signs that something heavy had been dragged across the sand.

In the entrance of the cave, some broken boards were piled in a corner and partially burned.

"Ship's pallet," Lonnie pronounced after examining it. She pulled our road map out of her pocket and marked the location of the cave as well as where we had left the car.

I stood by the remains of the fire, looking back out to sea. "At night," I said, "you could see this."

Wini nodded. "You could, but only from the sea. Not from the beach road. Not the way the cliff curves. Nor from above if you were going along the cliff road."

"Yes," I said. "I think you could only see it from out there." I pointed at the waves rolling toward us.

"You might spot it from a plane," said Wini. "Even more likely from a ship."

I nodded and turned away. The floor sloped upward from the entrance. The back of the cave was lost in inky darkness. This looked like a much more promising spot to explore than the earlier caves. I set out without waiting for the others. If Tom was in there, I was going to find him.

Coming behind me, Lonnie pulled her flashlight out of her jacket and directed the beam onto the ceiling and walls. She stopped at one point and used the flashlight to reveal where the cave walls had been chiseled to form shelves and niches. We lit the lanterns as we ventured deeper into the cave.

"Anything stored in these would be above the water, even if a storm surge came into this cave," Lonnie decided.

Wini moved to the front with her Mauser in one hand and lantern in the other. "It goes up here," she called back. "There's some steps carved into the stone, but it's mostly natural passageways, I think."

"Keep going," I said. "Talk later." I hoisted my lantern higher, hoping I would see some sign of Tom. But there was nothing except damp rock, gleaming in our lamplight.

The cave twisted and turned. At points, the stone walls were so close that we had to shift sideways to proceed. At other places, Lonnie, Wini, and I were able to walk three abreast. The further we went, the higher we went, the path ever twisting upward. At various points, Lonnie pulled a compass out of her pocket and compared its readings to our map.

"The way we are heading," she said, "I think we'll be almost under Bluff Mansion soon."

I checked the map and saw how she traced our possible

route under the cliff against the road above. I remembered the hedge blocking the view of the ocean from the patients in the garden. But I had heard the surf when I had been at Bluff Mansion.

"I was sure this would lead us under the Purple Cat," I said to Lonnie and Wini.

"No," said Wini, studying the map. "The Purple Cat is here." She tapped a spot on the map at some distance from where Lonnie marked our location. "This passage cannot lead to the Smuggler's Cave."

"What would Ezra need with smugglers' routes?" I wondered out loud.

"Just because the tunnels are here, doesn't mean he built them," said Wini. "My guess is that his ancestors were as crooked as the Malones. Smuggling and piracy were always big on this coast."

"That would explain the mansion," I said.

We continued on. Other than the burned and broken pallet at the entrance of the cave, we saw no evidence of bootlegging or even of anyone using the passage. But the further we went, the more obvious it became that the passageway was no longer natural but rather a carefully carved extension of the existing caves.

"We're almost directly under Bluff Mansion now," Lonnie said as she checked the map. "This is odd."

"What?" I said.

Lonnie had ducked into a niche carved out of the rock, almost a small alcove off the main path. I followed her. As we played our lights around the room, I realized the walls were carved with patterns. Patterns that were eerily reminiscent of those knitted by Minerva and her husband. Similar to the pattern of shells left by the minister's mother on a table in the church's vestibule.

But these patterns were not exactly the same. The strange symbols were carved in sprawling lines across the walls and whirled into spirals that spread across the ceiling and floor of the room. Just looking at them made me feel like I was standing on a ship's deck, a ship tossed by very angry seas.

Lonnie pulled her flashlight away from scribbling across the wall and concentrated the beam at the niche at the end of the room. "Is that glass?" she said.

"I think so," I said, moving closer. The room felt like the interior of an icebox. Goosebumps sprang up across my arms. Somebody had troweled plaster across the back of the niche and carefully placed shard after shard of beach glass into the plaster. It formed the shape of a creature. I would have called it a man for the arms and legs, but the head was wildly misshapen, more reminiscent of a fish than any mammal's head. The jaws were open and pointing toward the sky. The thing had teeth, teeth made of glass, that glittered in the lamplight.

Lonnie took one look and then turned away, following Wini down the passage, but I lingered. This was not Minerva's pattern. This was not what the minister's mother created in the church. This was different, something much colder. I was absolutely convinced without knowing why that this was truly evil.

A jaw big enough to swallow the world, that's what the artist had created. The more I looked at the monstrosity, the more the little pieces of glass forming the horror seemed to melt into one single image, a fish-man shaped window that showed me a view of a world that appeared both familiar and dreadful. When I walked with Jim in the garden and peered into the murky pool, I had seen shapes like this, creatures and plants that swayed as if submerged underwater.

Once before, in a house on fire, I had looked through the smoke and into a mirror that wasn't a mirror, reflecting a world that didn't exist.

At the house, Max pushed me out a door and saved me from the fire. But now I remembered he also saved me from the mirror's fascination. That was the moment in Arkham that I had forgotten, the memory of what had happened that day that had teased my dreams but I had lost until now.

Now I knew why I needed to save Max. Because that day, he had paused, stared into the mirror, and fallen through it to save me.

"Here's a door!" Wini shouted from a little ahead of us in the passageway. I stumbled out of the niche and toward the comforting light of her lantern.

The door that confronted us was sturdy and in good condition, but the hardware of the hinges and handle had the look of the last century. Wini tried it, but the door was locked.

"Now aren't you glad I brought these?" she said, pulling out her lockpicks.

"You have to teach me how to do that," I said as Wini knelt by the lock and fiddled with it.

"It's easy," said Lonnie. "I could teach you."

"Don't forget that you learned from me," said Wini, standing up and twisting the knob. The door clicked open.

"Anything you can do," Lonnie said as we advanced.

"I can still do better," said Wini. "Should I lock this again?"

"Best not," I said. "We may want to exit in a hurry." But I didn't want to go back down the passageway and pass the strange tribute to a mythical creature created in a glass mosaic. I hoped this way out would lead us to daylight and fresh air.

We entered what was clearly Bluff Mansion's cellars. Wine barrels were stacked around all the walls.

"So Hughes is smuggling?" Wini asked, looking at the barrels and crates that filled most of the room. At the edge of our lamplight, I spotted stairs leading up to the mansion.

"I don't think so," I said. A fishy, briny scent filled the room. I went over to one of the barrels. Spotting a crowbar left beside one, I used it to lift off the top.

"Aargh," said Wini. "What is that smell?"

"Not alcohol," I said, peering into the barrel. "Seaweed." Something about the almost gelatinous mass of decaying seaweed caught my eye. "Turn off your lantern," I said as I turned down the flame in mine. Wini looked at me strangely but shuttered her lantern.

"Shine the flashlight away from the barrel," I told Lonnie. She did so. "There, do you see it?"

"See what?" said Wini. "It's dark now."

"No, it's not," I said. "Look at the top of the barrel."

From the opened barrel of seaweed shone a pulsing, purple light.

"That's not normal." Wini sounded surprised, and I was almost as stunned. The purple light created horrendous shadows across the wall, almost as if tentacles reached out of the barrel toward the upper floors of Bluff Mansion.

"Do you think that's what Hughes is feeding his patients?" said Wini.

"If it is," I said, "I'm glad we got Jim out of here." And I needed more urgently than ever to find Tom and keep him away from this horrible seaweed. Whatever experiments Hughes was doing with the stuff were as dangerous as any game Nova played with the Deadly Grimoire.

"Wini, Betsy, come here!" called Lonnie from further into the room. "There's somebody tied up behind these barrels."

"Tom!" I cried, relighting my lantern and rushing toward Lonnie. "Is it Tom?" I felt a rush of relief at finding him.

Lonnie's flashlight revealed a pair of hands tied with rope, just visible by looking between a stack of barrels against the far wall. At our approach, the prisoner's heels drummed against one of the wooden barrels in a staccato signal for help. Muffled shouts also sounded as if the prisoner was gagged.

"Help me move these," I said to Wini, setting down the lantern and pushing the barrels to one side. Wini grabbed another and pulled it out of the way.

"Betsy," said Wini as we rolled away a third barrel. "That's not Tom."

I met the angry eyes of the prisoner as she rolled over to face us. Her hands were tied behind her back. Her ankles were also tied. Somebody had gagged her as well. Her hair was in disarray and one shoulder of her dress was torn as she'd obviously struggled to free herself.

"No, that's not Tom," I said. "Hand me your knife."

And I knelt to cut the ropes imprisoning a furious Nova Malone.

CHAPTER TWENTY-EIGHT

"It was Hughes," said Nova as soon as she had pulled the gag from her mouth. "That no-good skunk of a man stole my grimoire. And my pilots. Who he will use to hijack my plane."

"Why?" I said as I cut through the ropes around her ankles. "Why would Hughes want to fly your secret route?"

"Hughes doesn't want to fly my route," said Nova, shaking the ropes off her ankles. "Hughes never cared about bootlegging, except that I could afford his fees when my drivers and pilots needed his treatments. Hughes wants to be an explorer!"

She spat the last sentence out like a curse.

"What?" I sputtered with surprise. I'd considered several labels for the doctor, but that one didn't fit. "He's a doctor, not Byrd or Amundsen."

"He's going to end up dead if he uses the grimoire," said Nova, climbing to her feet. "That idiot of a doctor believes he can wander along Gulliver's route, harvesting various vegetation and bringing it back here for new medicines and treatments. He's convinced he's found the cure for every phobia. A new and more powerful drug to eliminate fear itself."

"The glowing seaweed?" I said, pointing at the barrels we'd found.

"Every time we sailed Gulliver's route," said Nova, "the seaweed would appear. Not just along the beach but everywhere in Innsmouth."

"And Arkham," I said, remembering Humbert's battles with the weeds on French Hill.

"Probably," said Nova. "I found it around the caves and draped over everything that came back from Gulliver's route, including my pilots. But the more we used Gulliver's route, the more storms happened and the more of the purple seaweed appeared. Ezra started collecting it, telling people he'd pay for any viable pieces if they'd bring it here. It's not easy to preserve. Sunlight or even a dry day will destroy it. It needs to be pickled in brine almost immediately or it will start to rot."

"And what does it do?" I said.

"Apparently, in a tea, it eliminates nightmares," said Nova. "The Innsmouth women who work here let me know. Hughes did find a cure that worked for his patients. It just makes the patients who drink it very calm, very sleepy, and, well, a little bit like Minerva."

"Like Minerva?" I said. The seaweed inspired knitting? I was now completely confused, and my energy flagged. I had been so certain we had found Tom.

"Spirit writing. Receiving messages from beyond," Nova said to me. "The nurses and the orderlies knew. They'd collect up the messages from the rooms and give them to Hughes.

He locked everything up in his desk and continued dosing people with his tea. He has plans to manufacture a cure-all and market it over the radio."

"Ambitious," I said with a shudder. The thought of that glowing purple seaweed going down willing people's throats made me queasy. But patent cures were popular. People paid for all sorts of strange concoctions, and this one might very well make Hughes rich. I could understand his motives.

"Don't doubt me," Nova said as she shrugged off the last of the ropes and climbed to her feet. "I would love to find an industry to help Innsmouth prosper. We are going to rot and blow away if we keep waiting for the whaling to return. It's done, and I cannot regret that because it was a hard business. Too many drowned men and too many widows. But there's other fishing, other shipping, other work to be had if people are willing to clear the harbor, repair the seawall, and invest in new technology."

"Like seaplanes," said Wini.

Nova nodded. "This could become a pleasant place for holidays, especially if you could fly up from New York or Boston harbor."

Considering the condition of the town I had visited, I doubted Nova could make Innsmouth into a summer destination.

"Why not manufacture Hughes's medicine if it works?" I said. "Medicines are legal. Booze is not. And you endangered men, too, taking Gulliver's route."

Nova stared at me for a long time in the dim light of that basement with the rotten smell of the purple seaweed rising around us.

"Partner with Hughes and manufacture his cure-all," I urged her. "It's less dangerous than bootlegging."

"Father poured a broth made from the purple seaweed down me when I was a child," said Nova. "It made a sickly babe into a large, strong, healthy girl. But it put the sea in my blood, and I'll never be able to wander far from these shores." She shoved up the sleeve of her dress and angled her arm toward the light. A patch of purple scales ran from elbow to wrist on the back of her forearm. When she shifted her arm in the light, the scales sparkled.

On Nova's arm, the scales had a weird beauty, but such a side effect wasn't desirable. It seemed Hughes's cure-all could prove to be deadly indeed.

Nova rolled down her sleeve. "I stopped drinking Papa's broth when I was a toddler. In those days, the seaweed only appeared in the winter, maybe for a day or two. Many Innsmouth families would harvest it for medicinal tea, but nobody drank it all the time," she said. "I never drank it as an adult. From what I hear, the adults, mostly men, who take it as Hughes's patients don't develop scales, but if they drink too much or too often, they become complacent, sleepy, and unable to think for themselves. They'll do what they're told and little more."

"They become lotus-eaters," I said and quoted, "'Surely, surely, slumber is more sweet than toil...'"

When Wini raised an eyebrow at me, I shrugged. "I had to memorize Tennyson's poem for school," I said. "That line stuck with me."

"Far too many in Innsmouth have become lotus-eaters in various ways," said Nova. "Waiting for something else or somebody else to change things for them but not being willing to do anything more than chant and moan and hope the sea will spit out a solution."

I thought about the niche further down the passageway and the figure made out of beach glass. Had the Hughes family looked for other, darker solutions to their money problems?

"So where is Hughes?" I said. "And Tom? And Max? And the grimoire?"

"Ezra Hughes stole my grimoire," Nova said. "And if you want to see your Tom and Max again, you need to help me get it back."

"What happened?" asked Lonnie, nailing down the lid of the open barrel of glowing seaweed. We all felt a little better with that pulsing purple light and smell once more stifled.

"Ezra had a new patient, a man named Max, when I came to visit my pilots yesterday. Ezra was going on and on about how he saw this man through that shard of glass he carries in his pocket," Nova said.

I remembered the strange world I glimpsed through the same shard and shuddered. If that was where Max had been for the past three years, he must have suffered horribly.

"The man's completely addicted to Ezra's tea," Nova continued. "Yesterday Ezra kept having him demonstrate how he could do simple tasks, like signing his name in the register, while actually in a state like sleepwalking. Ezra seemed to think I wanted men like that working for me. He claimed they'd make the perfect smugglers, never able to remember where they had been or what they had done if questioned by the cops."

Sydney and Max once tried to sell the studio on a script that was supposed to make people who watched the movie susceptible to their suggestions. I'd read the proposal and it had made me shudder. It was also why I helped Jeany hide all the evidence of that last movie at the Fitzmaurice house.

"As if I would poison the men who had lived in Innsmouth all their lives. The husbands, brothers, and sons of women who are my friends!" Nova said. "Ezra tried again today, and I turned him down flat. Then the doctor ordered Max to restrain me. I fought, but he hit me over the head, tied me up, and carried me down here. He stashed me behind those barrels."

"Where did they go?" I asked.

"The seaplane," said Nova. "It's taking off from Falcon Point to complete the rendezvous with my ship. Or at least that's what was supposed to happen. I think Ezra intends it to be a test flight to fetch back more of the seaweed. Or to prove he can control the route to his investors, similar to what his ancestors tried to prove when they set the *Bolide* out on Gulliver's route. If he's poured enough tea down my pilots' throats, they can make the flight safely. They'll also do exactly what Ezra tells them to do."

"But what about Tom?" I asked. Max's fate was horrible, but I could understand why Hughes wanted someone who wouldn't remember any crimes he was told to commit. Did he intend to control Tom the same way? The thought of his funny bright mind ruined by purple seaweed was appalling.

"Your Tom," said Nova, "has memorized the grimoire. He can say the spells without needing the book on the flight. From Ezra's point of view, that's much better than risking the loss of the grimoire."

I remembered Nova's fascination last night upon learning Tom had read the grimoire. Then she had locked him up. "That was your idea!" I accused. "You told Hughes that Tom could help the pilots navigate and you wouldn't have to risk the book. I bet you were even willing to pour that horrible tea down Tom's throat!"

Nova shrugged. "He's not an Innsmouth man. Nor could I risk losing the Deadly Grimoire again. The last time it disappeared on a voyage, with my ancestor, it took nearly thirty years to reappear at the Sweets' bookstore. The spells are vital. Gulliver's charts and maps, which are on the plane, can only take them so far. The spells keep them together, as it were, so everyone can return safely with the cargo."

"We'll have to go back through the passage and around the cliff for your car, Betsy," said Wini. "We might be able to make it to Falcon Point before they take off. Or meet them when they return? Are they coming back to the same spot?"

"They are," said Nova, checking her gold watch. "They won't have left yet. The timing has to be exact on these flights to navigate Gulliver's route. They'll take off right before sunset."

"Then we better start back," I said. "The tide should still be low enough to make it to the car." We needed to get Tom away from the doctor before he swallowed any of that purple seaweed. I eyed Nova, willing to tie her up again for all the trouble she had caused. Nova must have guessed my thoughts because she offered me a bargain I couldn't refuse.

"I know the fastest way there," said Nova, heading toward the steps leading out of the cellar and into the house. "My Rolls is parked in the driveway. Let me make one call upstairs and we'll have a dozen Innsmouth friends at Falcon Point to help us."

"I like how you think," Wini said, "and I'll drive."

"Winifred Habbamock, you are not driving a Rolls," said Lonnie as we surged up the stairs. "If anyone drives the Phantom, it is going to be me."

CHAPTER TWENTY-NINE

The Phantom was a marvelous car, and as we sped toward Falcon Point I decided I would buy one when I returned to Hollywood. The engine had a splendid growl. Lonnie drove at top speed with a steady hand, despite Wini's commentary on how she should have been the driver. Wini rode in the front while Nova and I shared the backseat with the gear we carried through the caves, including the rifle.

Nova seemed amused by the pair but a little distant, too. One of the first things she did upon exiting Bluff Mansion and regaining her car was to hand me back my purse. "I'm no thief. I was going to drop it off at your hotel, but you may need this now," she said. Inside, my pistol was still holstered in its usual pocket.

"Why not partner with Hughes?" I asked her again because the woman was a mass of contradictions, and I couldn't quite figure her out.

"Because a Hughes will never count the costs of what they do. The *Bolide* vanished with all its crew because the captain tried to sail Gulliver's route despite being warned against it.

Bulkington Hughes had Sweets create the False Fish to cheat Gulliver by swapping the two books, but he was caught," Nova answered. "I gave Ezra every opportunity, including lending him money to start Bluff Mansion, but then he started using the purple seaweed. I don't sell bathtub gin or wood alcohol colored to look like whiskey. I keep people as safe as I can. Ezra is like all his ancestors, determined to bend Innsmouth's peculiarities to his own advantage."

"But you're the one who opened Gulliver's route," I said as we sped along the road under a stormy sky. Purple clouds were building on the horizon with flashes of thunderbolts, a sure sign Ezra was preparing to open Gulliver's route, according to Nova.

"I never claimed to be without flaws," Nova finally said to me. "Sometimes, lacking fear makes a person… careless, shall we call it? I was careless about Gulliver's route, certain I could outwit the O'Bannions and the feds. But it caused trouble from the day I began to run cargo that way. Then I thought the grimoire was the answer. Now, I wonder…"

But what she was thinking I never knew. We came into sight of the Falcon Point Lighthouse. The sun was very low in the west, and there was another light, a violet hue, that swirled and pulsed along the edge of the water.

"There," Wini shouted, "there they are!"

Lonnie stopped the car as close to the beach as she could. A group of people were there, both men and women, but many wore coats with hoods or cowls pulled up over their heads, so I couldn't clearly see their faces. This cluster of onlookers stood far down the beach, apparently just watching as Ezra Hughes directed Nova's pilots into a boat.

Nova was out of the Rolls as soon as we stopped, grabbing Lonnie's rifle from the backseat. She strode toward Hughes and the crowd. "Clear your people out of here!" I heard her shouting. "That's my plane, Ezra Hughes."

"Look, there's the seaplane," said Wini, pointing across the water. The seaplane was anchored offshore, bobbing up and down in the waves. There was a second boat on the beach, prow up on the sand, the back end floating as the tide came in.

I pointed at it and said to Wini, "Feel like a little piracy or hijacking?"

"I'm in," said Wini. She whipped out her Mauser and ran for the boat. I followed hard on her heels. Behind us I heard Nova shouting and Lonnie yelling something, too.

As we ran for the boat, one of Hughes's cowled watchers made a grab at me with a distinctly animal-like hiss. I had a brief glimpse of a distorted face under the hood, but I pulled my arm free and plunged after Wini.

She leaped into the boat and moved to the motor. Wini tugged on the starter cord, and like all boat motors, it gave an apologetic cough rather than starting. Wini cursed and pulled again. On the second tug, the motor roared to life as I jumped into the boat. Lonnie was right behind us and gave the prow a shove, pushing us out into the water.

There were more shouts from the watchers, and I heard the bang of a gun.

"That's Nova," said Lonnie, who scrambled into the boat and now faced the beach. "She just popped one over their heads. Hughes started running away across the sand."

"I thought she didn't like guns," I said.

Arkham Horror

"Guess she makes an exception for Hughes," said Lonnie. "Say, who's driving this thing?"

"I am," said Wini, swinging the tiller about so we picked up speed and headed straight for the seaplane. Through the windows of the cabin, I saw two men watching us. Now that we were out on the water and moving toward the plane, my fears fell away. This I could do. I could rescue Tom and Max.

I heard the roar of another engine. Looking around, I spotted a second motorboat speeding toward us, carrying Hughes and the two pilots. On the shore, Nova was holding off the rest of Hughes's followers with the rifle. The blare of a car horn sounded behind us. Twisting around, I saw a couple of trucks careening down the road. They screeched to a halt behind the Rolls, and a dozen people, men and women, jumped out of the trucks. Nova's troops had arrived.

As we approached the seaplane, it began to rock violently. A door in the side popped open. Two men tumbled out, grappling with each other.

"Betsy!" one shouted.

"Tom!" I yelled back, waving wildly and standing up in the boat. Lonnie yanked me down into my seat by the back of my jacket. The boat nearly tipped over.

"Careful," she said. "We are almost there. Then you can leap to the rescue."

Tom struggled to free himself. The seaplane was now rocking dangerously, and both men were almost in the water. Then the other man hooked an arm around Tom's chest and dragged him into the cabin of the plane.

"I can't take a shot," I said, pulling the pistol out of my purse anyway. I might be able to use it when we got to the seaplane if only to threaten them into letting Tom go. "I might hit Tom."

"Or a fuel tank," said Lonnie. "Try not to blow anyone up."

A pop-pop sounded from the boat behind us. Wini ducked and grinned. "Guess those boys have guns, too. Keep low, ladies, and let's outrun them." She banked the boat, taking a long curve that shot up spray and sent a wave of water toward our pursuers. Their boat hit the wave straight on and nearly flew into the air. There were more gunshots, but Wini's wild zigzagging approach to the seaplane made it impossible for them to target us.

I let off a shot at our pursuers with no hope of hitting anything, but the bullet kicked up spray near the prow of the boat following us. The pilot steering the boat jerked away, sending his own vessel crosswise into the next wave and nearly flipping over.

We came up to the seaplane, bumping hard against its pontoon. I scrambled up and over the edge of the boat and into the cabin of the plane. Tom was on the floor, and another man, dressed like one of Hughes's patients, was crouched over him. Tom gasped at seeing me. His attacker grabbed Tom around the throat and began to choke him.

"Stop!" I yelled. He pressed his attack, and Tom's face turned an awful shade of red. I reversed the pistol in my hand and whacked Tom's attacker on the back of his head.

The man rolled off Tom and fell face up in the cabin. It was Max. I had found him, and I had more important things to do. I climbed over Max to get to Tom. "Are you all right?" I said.

Tom sat up, choking and wheezing. "Better," he croaked after a minute.

I patted Tom's shoulder and turned to Max. "Oh, Max," I said, looking at the gaunt man unconscious on the cabin floor. His hair was wild and streaked with white. His once beautifully manicured hands were scored with tiny scars, and the nails were broken to the quick. He looked so much older and worn. "Oh, poor Max," I said. I could feel nothing but pity for the beautiful young man who was, I had come to realize, much like Ezra Hughes. Max never counted the cost when it came to getting what he wanted. But the punishment seemed far too harsh.

"I don't think he understands English," said Tom. "Or not much. Hughes kept ordering him around, and he did what he was told, but it was odd. Like he barely understood what was happening."

"Or he drank too much of that tea," said Wini, clambering into the cabin with Lonnie. She pointed at a flask lying on the cabin floor. The liquid leaking from it had a familiar scent and was a horrid purple color.

"Yeah," said Tom, "he kept swigging that every few minutes."

"What do we do with him?" said Lonnie.

"Tie him up for now," I said, "so he doesn't attack anyone else." Later, I would deal with the problem of Max. Jim, I reminded myself, was getting better. Surely, with kinder treatment, Max could also recover. Nova never said the effects of the seaweed were permanent.

"Hughes is almost here with his pilots, or Nova's pilots.

I'm not sure which they are," Wini reported, glancing out the door of the cabin. "Pistols at sunset?"

The light was almost gone, and the sun was a glowing red ball disappearing rapidly to the west. On the beach, I could see Nova and the other group were still in a standoff.

"Can you fly this thing?" I asked Wini.

"Happy to try," she said with glee, hurtling into the pilot's seat.

Lonnie sighed but closed and locked the cabin door. The rumble of the engines indicated Wini had at least figured out how to start the seaplane.

There was the ping of a bullet off one of the cabin walls, and we all ducked.

"Get us out of here!" Lonnie yelled.

"Going, going," Wini yelled back.

The seaplane began to gather speed, taxiing across the waves. Tom and I were practically flat on the floor, struggling to secure Max with belts and scarves.

"I'm going to start carrying rope with me wherever I go," muttered Tom as he knotted my scarf around Max's hands.

The plane tilted up as we left the water for the air. Tom slung an arm around me and braced himself against the wall of the cabin. "Hey, I don't like heights," he said with a gulp.

"Then don't look out the window," I suggested.

"Good advice," he muttered. "Besides, there's better things to look at." He was staring straight at me.

"What happened to you?" I said.

"Hughes and Albie came up to me at the airshow," he replied. "Hughes sputtered something about the grimoire, and Albie shoved a gun in my ribs. It seemed best to go along with them. They took me to the strange group on the beach. All hoods and no talk."

"I noticed them earlier," I said.

Tom tightened his hold on my shoulders as Wini straightened out the plane. He leaned close and whispered, "One moment on the beach, I felt the world slip. Like Minerva described."

"You felt it, too?" I wrapped one arm around his waist.

Tom nodded. "I may have screamed. But I remembered what Minerva said about holding your place in your head. And, don't laugh, I thought I heard you ask where I was. Then I was in a boat being transferred to this plane."

Bless Jim for telling me about Tom, I thought, certain Tom had heard us talking, although I didn't know how. "I'm glad you're here now," was all I said. Then I exclaimed, "You didn't drink any of Hughes's tea?" I pointed at the thermos now rolling around the floor of the cabin, leaving dribbles of purple behind it.

"Hughes kept handing his friends a sample," Tom said. "And saying the purple stuff would make everyone rich." He pointed at the violet glob now drying on the cabin's floor. "For once, I didn't want a drink. But your man there kept pouring it down his throat."

I looked over at the unconscious Max. "Poor Max," I said. "He always wanted to be in control. The seaweed tea turned him into a puppet for Hughes."

"The doctor ordered him to keep me on the plane," Tom said. "I guess he took those orders literally."

Wini turned the plane toward the shore. "Shall we try a bit of low-level flying?" she called to us.

"What are you doing?" I asked.

"Figure if I buzz the beach, it should scatter the mob around Nova," she said.

I glanced out of the windows. Nova and her companions were backed almost to the Rolls by Hughes's supporters. Further down the beach, a few fistfights seemed to be taking place, but at least there were no bodies on the ground yet.

"Go on," I said, and Wini whooped as she sent the plane into a dive at the crowd.

Lonnie muttered something about "No way to treat a lady," and I think she was talking about the plane.

We passed over the crowd, the pontoons still dripping ocean water and a bit of seaweed. When the plane roared over their heads, the group below scattered and ran. Nova and some of her friends dived into the Rolls. The rest ran for their trucks.

As Wini turned for a second pass at the beach, I saw that Hughes and his boat were heading out to sea, toward the strange purple light glowing near the base of the lighthouse.

"Chase him off," I said to her. "Maybe dump him in the ocean."

"Betsy Baxter, you are a wicked woman," said Wini with a laugh, "and I do like that about you."

She banked the plane and buzzed over the doctor's boat. As we roared overhead, it rocked wildly. Hughes shook his fist at us, but they must have run out of ammunition because no more shots were made. The boat curved away and around Falcon Point. I saw a flash of purple and heard something like the pop of a firework. We circled the lighthouse but the boat was gone.

"Nova's leaving," Lonnie reported as the Rolls roared away from the beach.

"Now where?" Wini said to me.

"Back to Innsmouth," I suggested. "We can land by the wharf and call the police from there."

"Probably best," Wini agreed, "the light's starting to go."

The sun was nearly down. The lighthouse's great beam came on as we flew around it one more time on our way to Innsmouth's harbor.

"But where's the grimoire?" I said to Tom.

"Here," he said, grabbing a knapsack in the cabin. Out of it he pulled a green book ornamented with semiprecious stones in a design that reminded me of Minerva's knitted patterns and the shells on the church's table.

"There are some maps and charts as well," he said. The papers looked old and charred along one edge. "That's another thing Hughes told his buddy to guard until he came back for it."

"Those must be Gulliver's maps," I said. "The ones Nova's pilots were using for navigation."

Tom nodded and stuffed them back into the bag. A second book, also bound in green leather, fell out.

"What's that?" I said.

"Oh," said Tom, looking embarrassed. "That's the False Grimoire."

"Where did it come from?" I exclaimed.

"Ah." Tom ducked his head and rubbed the back of his neck. "My luggage. I've had it with me the whole time. When Hughes grabbed me, I told him I had a grimoire for him, and he made me get it. He said something about both books rightfully belonging to him."

"Tom Sweets," I said. "What were you planning to do with that forgery?"

"Give it to one of the buyers," he said. "I would have told them what it was. Most of the text is exactly the same as the Deadly Grimoire. I thought the professor might like it as a replacement if we had to give the Deadly Grimoire to Nova. I would have refunded the university's money. Well, most of it. A good fake does have value. We've received several offers from various collectors for the False Fish."

"Tom Sweets," I said. "I think your obsession with making a profit is..."

"Disgraceful for a bookseller?" he said. "I have heard that."

"Admirable," I said, giving him a quick hug. "But you might do better in Hollywood. Set up a store there and sell fabulous books to the stars. They are all building mansions and mansions need libraries. Or work as an advance man for the pictures. My studio could use a charmer like you."

"So you think I'm a charmer," said Tom.

"Hey, there's Devil Reef," yelled Wini from the pilot's seat. "We're going down. Brace yourselves."

"I'll tell you my opinion of you later," I said. "We have a few loose ends to tie up."

Tom groaned and then chuckled. "I'll hold you to that, Betsy Baxter."

Wini brought the plane down in Innsmouth Harbor. We taxied across the water to the sturdiest looking dock. When the plane bumped against the wharf, Lonnie opened the cabin door and jumped out to the dock. "Throw me a line," she said.

We tossed the mooring lines to her and secured the

plane to the dock. As we climbed out of the cabin, Tom took the knapsack with the two grimoires and Gulliver's charts.

"Now what?" Wini said as we stood on the dock.

"Find a ride back to the airfield. Send Max to the hospital in Arkham. I can arrange to have him taken to California from there," I said. Glancing into the cabin, I could see Max was still sleeping peacefully. It would take time, but eventually, he and Jim might be cured. I would do what I could. At least I no longer had to worry about what had happened to them.

Of course, I'd have a lot to explain to Jeany and my friends back home. They'd always seen Max as my grand romance. Myself, I hadn't been sure, and Arkham had split us apart before I could make up my mind. But now I knew what I wanted. It was time to catch a new streetcar and head in a different direction. I didn't need a man who schemed to own a studio and, like Hughes, thought being in charge was more important than anything else. I did enjoy dancing with a man who liked to read.

I linked my arm with Tom's. "You'll love California," I promised. "It's much more peaceful than New England, and the weather is better."

"I'm beginning to see the appeal," he admitted.

As we started to walk off the dock, a Rolls came speeding down the street. There was only one Rolls in Innsmouth, so we knew who it was.

"There's Nova," said Wini.

"Good," said Tom, shaking the Deadly Grimoire out of the knapsack. "This is hers. She bought it first."

Nova climbed out of the Phantom and stalked toward us. Her hair was wild around her face, and the light from the setting sun winked off the eyes of the purple cat brooch pinned to her breast.

"I think that's mine," she said, nodding at the Deadly Grimoire.

"It is," said Tom, tucking it under his arm. "As are these." He started to pull Gulliver's charts out of the knapsack.

"No!" shouted a voice from a boat pulling up to the dock. "Those are mine!"

Hughes sprang out of the motorboat as soon as it reached the jetty. In one leap, he was out of the boat and running toward us, waving a pistol in one hand.

"Where did he come from?" Wini asked.

A purple light shone at the end of the dock. Looking directly at it made my stomach lurch as if the world was whirling too fast under my feet. As I watched, it expanded, covering more and more of the dock. Hughes, I realized, had gone from Falcon Point to Innsmouth using Gulliver's fabled route.

"Get away," I shouted at Hughes, pulling my friends toward solid land.

"The book is mine. It was always mine," said Hughes, lunging at Tom and snatching the Deadly Grimoire from his hands. "You cannot have it. It's mine."

"You idiot," cried Nova as she ran past us and grabbed for the grimoire. "What have you done? You cannot open the way and leave it open."

The two of them fought like children playing tug-of-war, lurching back and forth, with the Deadly Grimoire clasped in both their hands. As Hughes pulled and Nova pushed, they moved closer and closer to the purple light consuming the end of the dock.

"Look out!" I cried.

But they never heard my warning. With a horrible scream, Hughes pulled the book completely out of Nova's hands. She leaped upon him like a wild cat with an equally fierce cry. They tumbled backward into the whirling pool of violet and blue light.

It winked out.

We stood there, on the edge of the dock, stunned. Everything looked as it had before. The seaplane bobbed in the water with the other boat moored beside it. Two confused looking men climbed out of the boat onto the dock. But Nova Malone and Ezra Hughes were gone.

"Now what?" Wini said again.

The sun was down. I stood there, staring out into the darkness, listening to the waves breaking over Devil Reef. Far off, I heard the mournful wail of the Falcon Point Lighthouse's horn, warning people away from the dangerous coast.

I regretted Nova's disappearance. I liked the woman for all her criminal ways. However, I thought, if anyone could save herself, it would be Nova Malone. But whether or not she bothered to save Ezra Hughes, I could not predict. I remembered Max's emaciated form and witless stare, and I thought how Hughes wanted to create an army of men like Max for criminal purposes. Nova could save Hughes, or she could leave the doctor to find his own way home. I found I didn't care either way.

I turned around and said in answer to Wini's question, "Now, we go home."

CHAPTER THIRTY

Of course, it wasn't quite as simple as that. It took a few days to arrange for Max's transfer to a pleasant place in upstate New York that came highly recommended by doctors I trusted. It was far from the ocean, something Max requested when he was awake enough to make requests. Like Jim, he tended to nod off in the middle of conversations, and he couldn't stand to have mirrors anywhere in the room.

As to where he had been, Max couldn't say. He claimed he didn't remember. He also claimed not to remember the fire or anything that happened during the making of Sydney's terrifying film three years ago. But when he said he knew nothing about the studio's plans, his eyes shifted away for a moment. I wasn't sure I believed him, but he'd suffered enough, judging by the scars and other signs of trauma the doctors reported to us.

"Are you still acting?" Max asked me during one visit.

"Yes," I said. I didn't discuss the studio or all I had done over the past three years. Max didn't seem to care. I knew it was time for us to go our separate ways. When he looked at me, however much he denied it, he saw smoke, and flames, and a mirror that wasn't a mirror. He flinched whenever I walked into the room.

I only saw a man who had been a friend. A man I hoped healed enough to enjoy the sound of waves and not turn away from mirrors. There were no more regrets or questions to keep me awake at night.

Tom and I spent September touring New England with Wini's air circus. Tom combined being an advance man with book scouting. Eventually, Wini threatened to make him learn to drive so he could ferry all his books from place to place in something other than her van. We compromised. Tom took driving lessons, and I shipped the books back to his uncle in Boston, who inventoried their store with an eye to opening a branch in Hollywood. We gave the False Grimoire to Christine, who pronounced herself enchanted with this addition to the Miskatonic University's collection. As for the real Deadly Grimoire, it fell off the pier with Nova and Ezra. Tom and I both hoped it would stay lost for a generation or two.

My stunts progressed until I was a bona fide wing-walker. But Charlie returned to the show, and the telegrams from Farnsworth about urgent messages from the studio became more and more creative in their polite insults. Apparently, even when you're the boss, you cannot take a holiday forever. And I did like to work.

"Whenever madam deigns to return their calls…" was a telegram which must have cost a fortune but Farnsworth's words made me laugh and decide it truly was time to go home. I was ready to return to Hollywood, but I would miss my friends.

We gathered at the Arkham train station to watch them roll my beautiful blue roadster up the ramp and into the boxcar.

"Take care of that machine," said Lonnie with a hug. "And take care of yourself, Betsy Baxter."

I hugged her back. "Come to Hollywood. I bought a Phantom. You and Henry can give me lessons on how to drive it properly. And I still need a few more hours in the air for my pilot's license."

"We'll see you soon," said Wini, pounding me on the back with her usual enthusiasm. "You have to cheer us at the starting line and the finish!"

"I will, I will," I promised. The air derby Wini had hoped to compete in was canceled. The organizers claimed it was a lack of talent, but several editorials had railed about imperiling women's lives for publicity. It didn't matter. I was going to fund an air derby where both sexes competed equally. Wini was plotting routes with other pilots. We hoped to have more than a dozen women take off from Santa Monica to cross the country. I wouldn't fly in the race, but I planned to fly with them, to be there at the start and the finish.

The train whistle sounded. "Goodbye, goodbye," I called to all my friends as Tom and I boarded the train.

"Someday we'll just fly from coast to coast," I said to Tom. "It will be so much quicker."

"I hope not," Tom answered. "How could you read on a plane?"

As we settled into our seats, Tom pulled several books out of his bag and stacked the volumes beside him with a contented sigh. His visits back to Captain Leo's shop had filled another crate or two.

"What do you think happened to Nova Malone and Ezra Hughes?" Tom said to me.

We chatted about this in idle moments, and there hadn't been much idle time when traveling with Wini, but all we really knew was that neither had been seen since they vanished off the end of the dock in Innsmouth.

"Nova might be lying low," I said, convinced the woman would find her way home if she wasn't there yet. Minerva had implied as much during a second visit to her farm. Besides, I noticed nobody in Innsmouth spoke of Nova Malone in the past tense. Whenever they said anything about "Miss Nova" at the Purple Cat, it was very much in the present. "The feds were swarming around Innsmouth and Arkham earlier this month."

It turned out that Darrell's stories and some pictures he'd passed to an investigator inspired considerable interest in various government agencies and several raids of Arkham and Innsmouth warehouses. Not as many arrests were made as might have been expected. Both Nova Malone and the O'Bannions apparently had hidden their assets well.

What to do about Bluff Mansion had been more of a head scratcher. Finally, the nurses had organized a cooperative arrangement to run it until Hughes returned, if he ever returned. I helped where I could and made sure all the purple seaweed had been destroyed, and the passage from the beach to the cellar was boarded up. The rest of the treatments were perfectly safe, focused on rest, clean air, and wholesome food. Minerva visited often, teaching knitting to the patients. It seemed to work wonders for many of them.

"I think what happened to Ezra Hughes and Nova Malone

is a mystery for someone else to solve," I said to Tom. "It's time for the Flapper Detective to crack a case in Hollywood. I've got a humdinger of a script idea from Christine."

"You've been giggling over her story for the last few days," said Tom. "Let me read it."

I passed the pages to him as the train picked up speed. Arkham disappeared in the distance.

"Betsy Baxter!" exclaimed Tom as he read the opening scene. "You wouldn't dare to do this."

"Oh, yes, I would," I said. "I have it all planned out. Let me tell you how we are going to film that scene."

EPILOGUE
October 30, 1926

My Dear Niece,

It is so kind of you to write, but tell your mother not to worry. Nova Malone is not dead yet. Although it took me a while to find my way home, I am back at the Purple Cat and working on our next radio broadcast. I look forward to experimenting even more with this fascinating invention. The possibilities are truly endless.

While I suffered some setbacks this year, I remain confident that my business will continue to flourish. Certainly, if your sister wishes to attend college, I would be happy to help with her tuition. Your generation shall accomplish such important work, far more than I or your mother could ever have dreamed of.

Do not fret about your own career! There will be forever those who tell us we cannot do what we wish to do because we are women. Ignore them. This summer, I met two amazing young women who offered me great hope for the future.

One was an actress who inspires thousands through her performances and her actions. Some have dismissed her work as silly fictions of the silver screen, but I know the power her films contain. Her stories will cause other women to seek adventures, and they will dare to achieve greatness because of her. I believe the spirit of the Flapper Detective will ripple through the decades to come.

The other young woman races through the skies. Already her flights have carried her far. Her story will lift other women higher than they have ever imagined. Her reckless courage could even take us to the stars someday.

These two women are clever, they are brave, and darkness will never consume them. I believe there are so many more like them, so many more to come. It gives me hope for the future. It gives me hope that we will find a way to restore Innsmouth and remove the trouble from Arkham.

While I know you are discouraged, never give up. Come here, and I will find a place for you.

Your loving aunt,
Nova Malone

ACKNOWLEDGMENTS

The initial inspiration for this novel came from the readers who asked, "Could you go back to Arkham? But don't make Jeany go back. She deserves her happy ending." I agree, for now, and instead had great fun sending Jeany's intrepid friend Betsy to Arkham and Innsmouth. This adventure had many godmothers, including all the ladies of the Monday night card bouts. Thank you to Lynn, Merrily, Susan, Carrie, Sharon, Karyl, Betsy (double thanks since I unwittingly borrowed her first name), and Phoebe for all the kind words about *Mask* and other encouragement. A special thank you also to Aconyte's Lottie and Anjuli for cheering on these adventures, and to Nick and Dan for making both the books and their covers look so good.

Another inspiration for this book came from a pack of cards. The minute I saw the Winifred Habbamock deck, I wanted one. The picture of Wini in her flight gear has been propped up on my computer throughout the writing of this book. I'm very grateful to the designers at Fantasy Flight Games for lending her, and the marvelous Stella, to this particular adventure along with other investigators from the game.

I'm equally grateful to all the aviation historians who documented the many flying women of the 1920s. I like to think Wini's spiritual godmother was Bessie Coleman, of African American and Cherokee descent, who tragically died in 1926. Her early death cut short her efforts to open the skies for other people of color. Coleman's flying career, and her famous refusal to perform before segregated audiences, inspired many people in her time. Her legacy continues to inspire today. Dr Mae Jemison carried Coleman's photo with her when she became the first African American woman in space aboard the space shuttle *Endeavor*.

As Wini notes, women were barred from competing in the popular air derbies of the 1920s. They would finally race in the 1929 Women's Air Derby. The pilots who took off from Santa Monica, California, were Florence Lowe "Pancho" Barnes, Marvel Crosson, Amelia Earhart, Ruth Elder, Claire Mae Fahy, Edith Foltz, Mary Haizlip, Opal Kunz, Mary von Mach, Jessie Miller, Ruth Nichols, Blanche Noyes, Gladys O'Donnell, Phoebe Omlie, Neva Paris, Margaret Perry, Thea Rasche, Louise Thaden, Evelyn "Bobbi" Trout, and Vera Dawn Walker. Crosson was killed in a crash, others were forced down by a variety of problems, but fifteen finished in Cleveland, Ohio. A crowd of eighteen thousand cheered as the planes came in. Episodes from many of these pilots' adventures made it into this novel but fall far short of the full accomplishments of these women.

The wing-walkers and stunt women who performed in the aerial circuses are less well documented, but there are several archives and collections showing photos of their astounding exploits, including playing tennis midair on the top of a wing. One owner of an aerial circus, Mabel Cody, billed herself as a niece of Buffalo Bill Cody. Her regular stunts involved transferring from a moving car to a plane, including a ladder climb. Many brave performers of both sexes found their way to Hollywood. Such stunts appear in action movies to this day (with a lot more safety precautions!).

As for the female bootleggers of the period, they were just as daring and just as varied as their flying sisters. A favorite of mine was Mary Louise Cecilia "Texas" Guinan, whose career included being an action star of silent Westerns, starting her own motion picture studio, and running a number of speakeasies. Both Betsy and Nova owe a bit to Texas.

While women made incredible strides in the 1920s, not all prejudices or injustices were overcome. Nor was enfranchisement universal. Congress passed the Indian Citizenship Act on June 2, 1924, which granted citizenship to all Native Americans born in the United States. Despite this, as well as the Fifteenth Amendment and the Nineteenth Amendment, access to the polls continued to be regulated by state laws and would vary widely across the country during this period.

Finally, I don't think this story or any of the many female detective stories that thrill us today would have been quite the same without the books written by Mildred Augustine Wirt Benson right at the end of the 1920s and first published in 1930. Her mysteries inspired three women to become Supreme Court justices – what a legacy for any writer! The expectation that young women could achieve as much as the men permeates the adventures of her most famous female detective and her other stories. Follow the clues and you'll figure out who I am talking about.

Thank you, as always, for reading along with this adventure.

ABOUT THE AUTHOR

ROSEMARY JONES is an ardent collector of children's books, and a fan of talkies and silent movies. She is the author of bestselling novels in *Dungeons & Dragons' Forgotten Realms* setting, numerous novellas, short stories, and collaborations. She lives in Seattle, Washington.

rosemaryjones.com
twitter.com/rosemaryjones

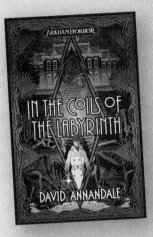

ARKHAM HORROR™

*Riveting pulp adventure as unknowable
horrors threaten to tear our reality apart.*

*Something monstrous has risen from the depths beneath
Arkham, Miskatonic University is plagued with missing
students and maddening litanies, and a charismatic
surrealist's art opens doorways to unspeakable places.*

*A web of terror lurks in the jungle, a director captures
unnameable horrors while making his masterpiece, and a
thief stumbles onto a necrophagic conspiracy.*

WORLD EXPANDING FICTION

Do you have them all?

ARKHAM HORROR
- ☐ *Wrath of N'kai* by Josh Reynolds
- ☐ *The Last Ritual* by S A Sidor
- ☐ *Mask of Silver* by Rosemary Jones
- ☐ *Litany of Dreams* by Ari Marmell
- ☐ *The Devourer Below* ed Charlotte Llewelyn-Wells
- ☐ *Dark Origins, The Collected Novellas Vol 1*
- ☐ *Cult of the Spider Queen* by S A Sidor
- ☑ *The Deadly Grimoire* by Rosemary Jones
- ☐ *Grim Investigations, The Collected Novellas Vol 2*
  (coming soon)
- ☐ *In the Coils of the Labyrinth* by David Annandale
  (coming soon)

DESCENT
- ☐ *The Doom of Fallowhearth* by Robbie MacNiven
- ☐ *The Shield of Daqan* by David Guymer
- ☐ *The Gates of Thelgrim* by Robbie MacNiven
- ☐ *Zachareth* by Robbie MacNiven *(coming soon)*

KEYFORGE
- ☐ *Tales from the Crucible* ed Charlotte Llewelyn-Wells
- ☐ *The Qubit Zirconium* by M Darusha Wehm

LEGEND OF THE FIVE RINGS
- ☐ *Curse of Honor* by David Annandale
- ☐ *Poison River* by Josh Reynolds
- ☐ *The Night Parade of 100 Demons* by Marie Brennan
- ☐ *Death's Kiss* by Josh Reynolds
- ☐ *The Great Clans of Rokugan, The Collected Novellas Vol 1*
- ☐ *To Chart the Clouds* by Evan Dicken *(coming soon)*

PANDEMIC
- ☐ *Patient Zero* by Amanda Bridgeman

TERRAFORMING MARS
- ☐ *In the Shadow of Deimos* by Jane Killick

TWILIGHT IMPERIUM
- ☐ *The Fractured Void* by Tim Pratt
- ☐ *The Necropolis Empire* by Tim Pratt

ZOMBICIDE
- ☐ *Last Resort* by Josh Reynolds
- ☐ *Planet Havoc* by Tim Waggoner *(coming soon)*